THE HIGH LORD

All heads turned to watch as Akkarin stepped into the room. Even without the outer part of his robes, he still looked imposing.

'My, what a lot of visitors,' he said. 'What brings you all to my residence so late at night?'

Balkan's eyebrows rose. He looked toward the stairway. Hurried footsteps could be heard, then Lorlen stepped into view. The Administrator turned to regard Akkarin, his expression unexpectedly composed.

'Lord Jolen and his household were murdered tonight.' Lorlen's voice was calm and controlled. 'Evidence has been found that has given us cause to suspect you are the murderer.'

'I see,' Akkarin said quietly. 'This is a serious matter. I did not kill Lord Jolen, but you will have to work that out for yourselves.' He paused. 'Will you explain to me how Jolen died?'

'With black magic,' Lorlen said. 'And since we have just found books on black magic in you house, including in Sonea's room, we have even more reason to suspect you.'

By Trudi Canavan

The Magician's Apprentice

The Black Magician Trilogy
The Magicians' Guild
The Novice
The High Lord

Age of the Five
Priestess of the White
Last of the Wilds
Voice of the Gods

The Traitor Spy Trilogy
The Ambassador's Mission
The Rogue
The Traitor Queen

Millennium's Rule
Thief's Magic

TRUDI CANAVAN

THE HIGH LORD

LORD

The Black Magician Trilogy: Book Three

www.orbitbooks.net

This book is dedicated to my friends, Yvonne and Paul.
Thank you for your help, honesty and patience, and for
reading this story over, and over, and over . . .

ORBIT

First published in Great Britain in 2004 by Orbit
This paperback edition published in 2010 by Orbit

11 13 15 14 12 10

A CIP catalogue record for this book is available from the British Library.

ISBN 978-1-84149-962-8

Typeset in Garamond 3 by Palimpsest Book Production Limited,
Grangemouth, Stirlingshire
Printed and bound in Great Britain by
Clays Ltd, St Ives plc

Papers used by Orbit are from well-managed forests
and other responsible sources.

MIX
Paper from
responsible sources
FSC
www.fsc.org FSC® C104740

Orbit
An imprint of
Little, Brown Book Group
100 Victoria Embankment
London EC4Y 0DY

An Hachette UK Company
www.hachette.co.uk

www.orbitbooks.net

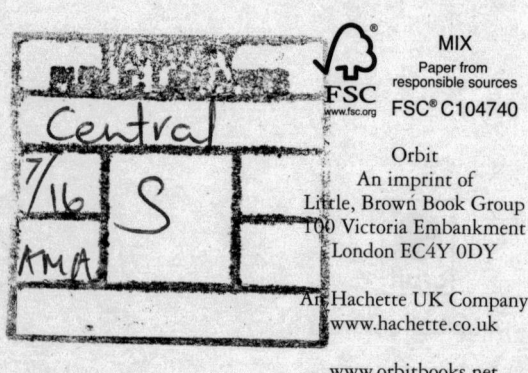

ACKNOWLEDGEMENTS

Many, many people have encouraged and assisted me in writing this trilogy. In addition to those people I acknowledged in *The Magicians' Guild* and *The Novice*, I'd like to give an additional nod to the people who helped me out during the writing of this book:

Once again, my proofreaders who give me such valuable advice: Mum and Dad, Paul Marshall, Paul Ewins, Jenny Powell, Sara Creasy and Anthony Mauricks.

Fran Bryson, my agent. Thank you for providing the perfect setting for my 'working holiday'.

Les Petersen, who patiently tolerated all my input and suggestions while producing the wonderful cover art for this series. Justin of Slow Glass Books, Sandy of Wormhole Books, and the booksellers who've taken on this trilogy with such enthusiasm. And all the publishers of the foreign language editions – especially the translators – who have helped take my stories to readers all over the world.

And thank you to all the people who have emailed me with praise for *The Magicians' Guild* and *The Novice*. Knowing you've enjoyed my stories helps keep the fires of inspiration burning high.

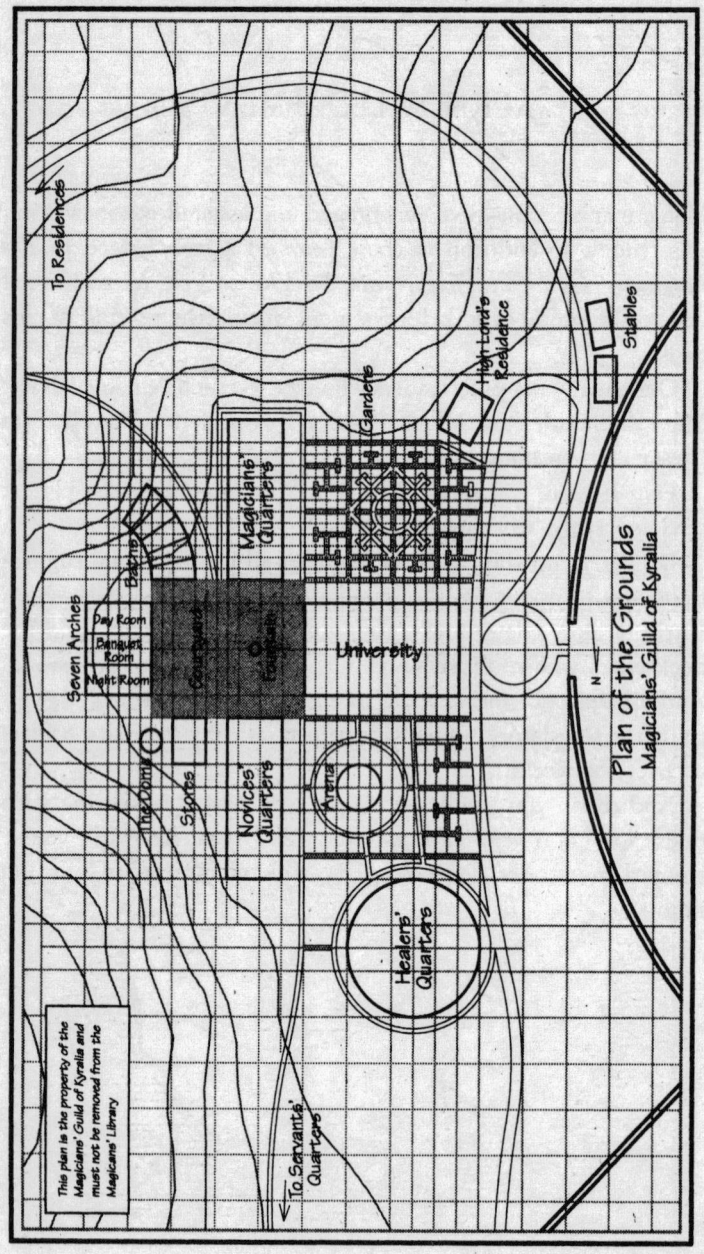

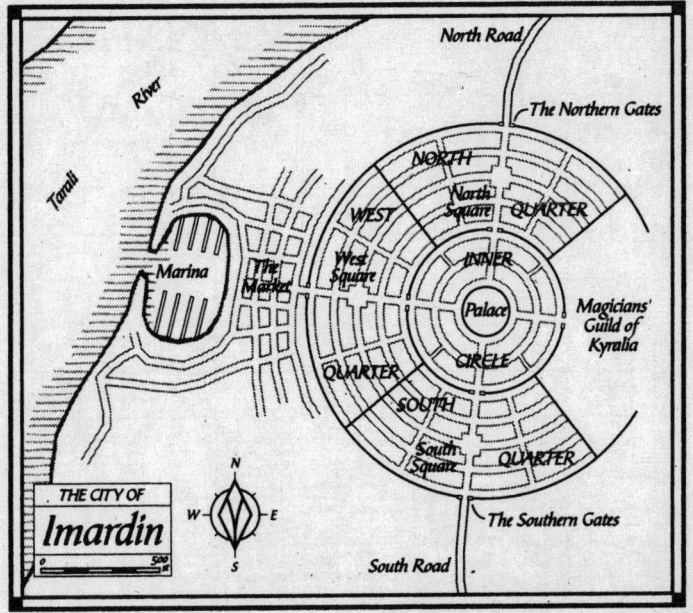

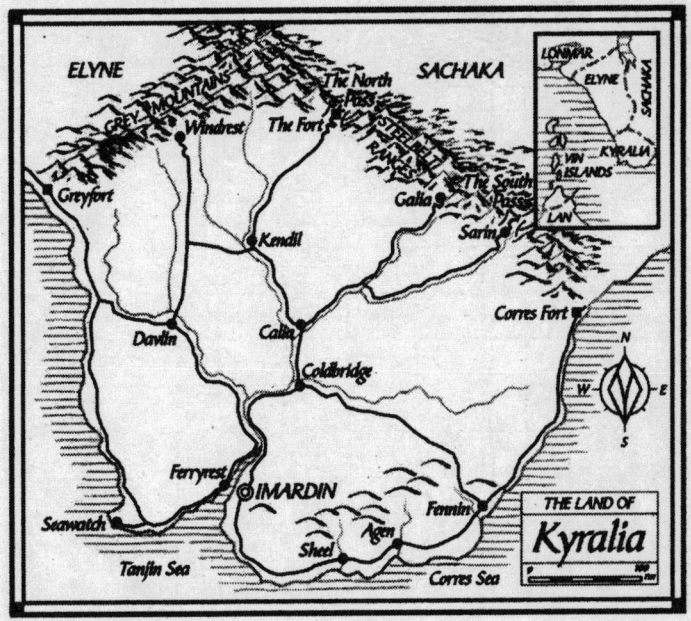

PART ONE

CHAPTER 1

THE MESSAGE

In ancient Kyralian poetry the moon is known as the Eye. When the Eye is wide open, its watchful presence deters evil – or encourages madness in those who do wrong under its gaze. Closed, with only a sliver of white to mark its sleeping presence, the Eye allows hidden deeds of both good or ill to remain unnoticed.

Looking up at the moon, Cery smiled wryly. This phase of the Eye, a narrow slit, was the one preferred by secret lovers, but he was not hurrying through the shadows of the city to such a rendezvous. His purpose was of a darker kind.

Whether his deeds were good or ill, however, was difficult for him to know. The men he hunted deserved their fate, but Cery suspected there was a deeper purpose to the work he'd been commissioned to do than just reducing the murders that had plagued the city for the last few years. He did not know everything about the whole nasty business – of that he was sure – but he probably knew more than anyone else in the city. As he walked, he considered what he did know. He had learned that these murders were not carried out by one man, but by a succession of them. He had also noted that these men were of the same race: Sachakan. Most importantly, however, he knew they were magicians.

As far as Cery knew, there were no Sachakans in the Guild.

If the Thieves were aware of any of this, they were keeping their knowledge well hidden. He thought back to a meeting of Thieves he had attended two years ago. The leaders of the loosely allied underworld groups had been amused by Cery's offer to find and stop the killer. Those who asked slyly why Cery hadn't succeeded after so long might be assuming there was only one murderer, or they might want him to *think* that was all they knew.

Each time Cery dealt with one of the murderers, another began his grisly work. Unfortunately, this made it appear to the Thieves that Cery was failing at his task. All he could do was shrug off their questions, and hope his success in other underworld activities made up for it.

From the dark square of a doorway the shape of a large man emerged. Distant lamplight revealed a grim, familiar face. Gol nodded once, then fell into step beside Cery.

Reaching an intersection of five roads, they approached a wedge-shaped building. As they stepped through the open doors, Cery savoured the heavy odour of sweat, bol and cooking. It was early evening and the bolhouse was full. He moved to a seat at the counter, where Gol ordered two mugs of bol and a dish of salted crots.

Gol munched his way through half of the beans before he spoke.

'At the back. Flash ring. What you say, son?'

Cery and Gol often pretended to be father and son when they did not want their true identities known – which was most of the time they spent in public these days. Cery was only a few years younger than Gol but, with his small stature and boyish face, he was often mistaken for a youth. He waited a few minutes, then let his gaze shift to the back of the bolhouse.

Though the room was crowded, it was easy to locate the man Gol had pointed out. His distinctive wide, brown Sachakan face stood out among the pale Kyralian ones and he was watching the crowd carefully. Glancing at the man's fingers, Cery noted a glint of red in the dull silver of a ring. He looked away.

'What you think?' Gol murmured.

Cery picked up his mug and pretended to gulp a mouthful of bol. 'Too much rub for us, da. Leave him for another.'

Grunting in answer, Gol drained his mug and set it down. Cery followed him outside. A few streets from the bolhouse, he reached into his coat, pulled out three copper coins and pressed them into Gol's large hand. The big man sighed and walked away.

Cery smiled wryly, then stooped and opened a grille set into a nearby wall. To any stranger, Gol appeared to be completely unperturbed by any situation. Yet Cery knew that sigh. Gol was scared – and he had good reason to be. Every man, woman and child in the slums was in danger while these murderers were about.

Cery slipped behind the grille into the passage below. The three coins he'd given Gol would pay three street urchins to deliver a message – three urchins in case the message was lost or delayed. The recipients were crafters of one kind or another, who would pass on the message via city guard or delivery boy or trained animal. Each man or woman along the path of the message knew nothing of the meaning behind the objects or passwords they were given. Only the man at the final destination would understand their significance.

When he did, the hunt would begin again.

Leaving the classroom, Sonea slowly made her way down the crowded, noisy main corridor of the University. She usually paid little attention to the antics of the other novices, but today was different.

A year today since the Challenge, she thought. *A whole year since I fought Regin in the Arena, and so much has changed.*

Most novices had gathered into groups of two or more and were walking toward the rear staircase and the Foodhall. A few girls lingered by a classroom door, talking in conspiratorial murmurs. At the far end of the corridor a teacher emerged from a classroom, followed by two novices carrying large boxes.

Sonea watched the faces of the few novices who noticed her. None glared or looked down their noses. Some of the first years stared at the incal on her sleeve – the symbol that declared her the favourite novice of the High Lord – then quickly looked away.

Reaching the end of the corridor, she started down the delicate, magically-fashioned staircase of the Entrance Hall. Her boots made a soft, bell-like sound on the treads. The hall echoed as more ringing steps joined hers. Looking up, she saw that three novices were ascending toward her, and she felt a chill run down her back.

The novice at the centre of the trio was Regin. His two closest friends, Kano and Alend, were by his side. Keeping her expression neutral, she continued her descent. As Regin noticed her, his smile vanished. His gaze met hers, then moved away again as they passed each other.

She glanced back and let out a small sigh of relief. Every encounter since the Challenge had been like this. Regin had adopted the demeanour of a gracious and dignified loser, and she let him. Rubbing in his defeat would have been satisfying, but she was sure he would come up with anonymous and subtle ways of getting his revenge if she did. Better they ignored each other.

Beating Regin in a public fight had done more than stop his harassment of her, though. It appeared to have won her the respect of other novices and most of the teachers. She wasn't just the slum girl now, whose powers had first manifested in an attack on the Guild during the yearly Purge of vagrants and miscreants from the city. Remembering that day, she smiled ruefully. *I was just as surprised that I had used magic as they were.*

Nor was she remembered for being the 'rogue' who had evaded capture by making a deal with the Thieves. *It seemed like a good idea at the time*, she thought. *I believed the Guild wanted to kill me. After all, they have never trained anyone outside the Houses before. It didn't do the Thieves any good, though. I was never able to control my powers well enough to be of use.*

Though some still resented it, she was no longer thought of as the outsider who brought about Lord Fergun's downfall, either. *Well, he shouldn't have locked Cery up and threatened to kill him to force me into co-operating with his schemes. He wanted to convince the Guild that lower class people couldn't be trusted with magic, but instead he proved that some magicians can't be.*

Thinking back to the novices in the corridor, Sonea smiled. From their wary curiosity she guessed the first thing they remembered about her was how easily she had won the Challenge. They wondered just how powerful she was going to become. She suspected that even some of the teachers were a little frightened of her.

At the bottom of the stairs Sonea crossed the Entrance Hall to the open University doors. Standing on the threshold, she looked at the grey, two-storey building at the edge of the garden and felt her smile fade.

A year since the Challenge, but some things haven't changed.

Despite winning the novices' respect, she still had no close friends. It wasn't that they were all intimidated by her – or her guardian. Several novices had made an effort to include her in their conversations since the Challenge. But while she was happy to talk to them during lessons or midbreak, she always refused invitations to join them outside class.

She sighed and started down the University steps. Every friend she made was another tool the High Lord could use against her. If she ever found the opportunity to reveal his crimes to the Guild, everyone she cared about would be in danger. There was no sense in giving Akkarin a larger selection of victims to choose from.

Sonea thought back to the night, now over two and a half years ago, when she had slipped into the Guild with her friend Cery. Though she had believed the Guild wanted her dead, the risk seemed worth taking. She had not been able to control her powers, making her useless to the Thieves, and Cery had hoped that she might learn how to do so by watching magicians.

Late that night, after seeing much that fascinated her, she had approached a grey building set apart from the rest. Peering through a ventilation grille into an underground room, she had witnessed a black-robed magician performing strange magic . . .

The magician took the glittering dagger and looked up at the servant.

'The fight has weakened me. I need your strength.'

The servant dropped to one knee and offered his arm. The magician ran the blade over the man's skin, then placed a hand over the wound . . .

. . . then she felt a strange sensation, like a fluttering of insects in her ears.

Sonea shivered as she remembered. She hadn't understood what she'd seen that night, and so much happened afterwards, she had tried to forget. Her powers had grown so dangerous that the Thieves had turned her over to the Guild and she discovered that the magicians did not want to kill her; they decided she could join them. Then Lord Fergun had captured Cery and blackmailed her into co-operating with him. The Warrior's plans had failed, however, when Cery was found imprisoned under the University, and Sonea consented to a truth-read by Administrator Lorlen to prove that Fergun had manipulated her. It was only during this mind-reading that her memory of the black-robed magician in that underground room had returned in full.

Lorlen had recognised the magician as his friend Akkarin, the High Lord of the Guild. He had also recognised the forbidden ritual of black magic.

From Lorlen's mind, Sonea had gleaned an understanding of what a black magician was capable of. By using the forbidden art, Akkarin would have gained strength beyond his natural limit. The High Lord was known to be unusually powerful as it was, but as a black magician he would be so powerful that Lorlen did not think even the combined strength of the Guild could defeat him.

Lorlen had therefore decided that a confrontation with the High Lord was out of the question. The crime must remain a secret until a way to deal with Akkarin safely was found. Only Rothen, the magician who was to be Sonea's guardian, was allowed to know the truth – in the course of teaching her he was likely to see her memory of Akkarin and learn the truth for himself anyway.

At the thought of Rothen she felt a pang of sadness, followed by a dull anger. Rothen had been more than a guardian and teacher; he had been like a father. She was not sure she could have endured Regin's harrassment without Rothen's support and help. For his trouble, he had endured the effects of the malicious rumours that Regin had started suggesting that Rothen's guardianship was gained in exchange for bedroom favours.

And then, just as it seemed the gossip and suspicion had passed, everything had changed. Akkarin had come to Rothen's room to tell them that he had discovered that they knew of his secret. He had read Lorlen's mind, and wanted to read theirs. Knowing that Akkarin was too powerful to fight, they dared not refuse. Afterwards, she remembered, Akkarin had paced the room.

'You would both expose me if you could,' he said. 'I will claim Sonea's guardianship. She will ensure your silence. You will never cause anyone to know that I practise black magic while she is mine.' His eyes shifted to Sonea's. 'And Rothen's wellbeing will be my guarantee that you will co-operate.'

Sonea set her feet on the path to the High Lord's Residence. That confrontation had taken place so long ago, it felt as if it had happened to someone else, or to a character in a story she had heard. She had been Akkarin's favourite for a year and a half now and it was not as bad as she'd feared. He hadn't used her as a source of extra power, or tried to involve her in his evil practices. Aside from the sumptuous dinners she attended with him every Firstday evening, she rarely saw him at all. When they did speak, it was only of her training in the University.

Except for that one night, she thought.

She slowed as she remembered. Many months ago, returning after classes, she had heard loud noises and shouting from below the residence. Descending the stairs to the underground room, she had witnessed Akkarin kill a man with black magic. He had claimed the man was a Sachakan assassin, sent to murder him.

'Why did you kill him?' she asked. 'Why not hand him over to the Guild?'

'Because, as you've no doubt guessed, he and his kind know things about me that I'd rather the Guild did not. You must be wondering who these people are, and why they want me dead. I can tell you only this: the Sachakans still hate the Guild, but they also fear us. From time to time they send one of these, to test me.'

Sonea knew as much about Kyralia's neighbour as any other third-year novice. All novices studied the war between the Sachakan Empire and the Kyralian magicians. They were taught that the Kyralians had won the war by forming the Guild and sharing magical knowledge. Seven centuries later, the Sachakan Empire was all but gone and much of Sachaka remained a wasteland.

When she thought about it, it was not hard to believe that the Sachakans still hated the Guild. This was probably the reason, too, why Sachaka was not a member of the Allied Lands. Unlike Kyralia, Elyne, Vin, Lonmar and Lan, Sachaka was not bound to the agreement that all

11

magicians must be taught and watched over by the Guild. It was possible magicians existed in Sachaka, though she doubted they were well trained.

If they *were* a threat, surely the Guild knew about it. Sonea frowned. Perhaps some magicians *did* know. Perhaps it was a secret only the Higher Magicians and the King were allowed to know. The King would not want ordinary people worrying about the existence of Sachakan magicians – unless the Sachakans became a serious threat, of course.

Were these assassins threat enough? She shook her head. The occasional assassin sent to kill the High Lord wasn't a serious matter if he could fend them off easily enough.

She checked her stride. Perhaps the only reason Akkarin *could* fend them off was because he strengthened himself with black magic. Her heart skipped a beat. That would mean the assassins were frighteningly strong. Akkarin had suggested that they knew he used black magic. They would not attack him without making sure they had a chance of killing him. Did this mean they, too, used black magic?

She shivered. *And each night I sleep in the same house as the man they're trying to kill.*

Perhaps this was why Lorlen hadn't come up with a way to get rid of Akkarin yet. Perhaps he knew Akkarin had a good reason for using black magic. Perhaps he didn't intend to oust Akkarin at all.

No, she thought. *If Akkarin's reasons were honourable, I would not be his hostage. If he'd been able to prove his motives were good, he would have tried to, rather than have two magicians and a novice constantly searching for a way to defeat him.*

And if he was at all concerned for my wellbeing, why keep me in the residence, where the assassins are likely to strike?

She was sure Lorlen was concerned for her wellbeing. He would tell her, if he knew Akkarin's motives were honourable. He wouldn't want her to believe she was in a worse situation than she really was.

Abruptly, she remembered the ring on Lorlen's finger. For more than a year, rumours had been circulating in the city about a killer who wore a silver ring with a red gemstone. Just like the one Lorlen wore.

But this *had* to be a coincidence. She knew a little of Lorlen's mind and she could not imagine Lorlen murdering *anyone*.

Reaching the door of the residence, Sonea stopped and took a deep breath. What if the man Akkarin had killed hadn't been an assassin? What if he had been a Sachakan diplomat who'd discovered Akkarin's crime, and Akkarin had lured him to the residence to kill him . . . and then discovered the man was a magician?

Stop! Enough!

She shook her head as if that would clear it of this fruitless speculation. For months she had considered these possibilities, going over and over what she had seen and been told. Every week she looked at Akkarin over the dinner table and wished she had the courage to ask him why he had learned black magic, but stayed silent. If she could not be sure that the answers were truthful, why bother asking the questions?

Reaching out, she brushed the handle of the door with her fingers. As always, it swung inward at the lightest touch. She stepped inside.

His tall, dark figure rose from one of the guestroom chairs. She felt a familiar twinge of fear and pushed it aside. A single globe light hovered above his head, casting his eyes into shadow. His lips curled upward at one side as if he was mildly amused.

'Good evening, Sonea.'

She bowed. 'High Lord.'

His pale hand gestured to the stairway entrance. Putting her case of books and notes down, Sonea entered the stairway and started climbing. Akkarin's globe light floated up the centre of the stairwell as he followed. Reaching the second level, she walked down the corridor and entered a room furnished with a large table and several chairs. A delicious smell filled the air and set her stomach rumbling quietly.

Akkarin's servant, Takan, bowed to her as she sat down, then left.

'What did you study today, Sonea?' Akkarin asked.

'Architecture,' she replied. 'Construction methods.'

One eyebrow rose slightly. 'Shaping stone with magic?'

'Yes.'

He looked thoughtful. Takan returned to the room carrying a large platter, from which he transferred several small bowls to the table, then strode away. Sonea waited until Akkarin began to select from the bowls, before loading her own plate with food.

'Did you find it difficult, or easy?'

Sonea hesitated. 'Difficult at first, then easier. It's . . . not unlike Healing.'

His gaze sharpened. 'Indeed. And how is it different?'

She considered. 'Stone does not have the natural barrier of resistance that the body has. It has no skin.'

'That's true, but something like a barrier can be created if . . .'

His voice trailed off. She looked up to find him frowning,

his gaze fixed on the wall behind her. His eyes shifted to hers, then he relaxed and looked down at the table.

'I have a meeting to attend tonight,' he said, pushing back his chair. 'Enjoy the rest of the meal, Sonea.'

Surprised, she watched him stride to the door, then looked at his half-eaten meal. Occasionally she arrived for the weekly dinner to find Takan waiting in the guestroom with the good news that the High Lord would not be attending. But only twice before had Akkarin left the meal early. She shrugged and continued eating.

As she finished the course, Takan reappeared. He stacked the bowls and plates onto the platter. Watching him, she noticed a tiny crease between his eyebrows.

He looks worried, she thought.

Remembering her earlier speculations, she felt a chill run up her spine. Was Takan afraid that another assassin might enter the residence looking for Akkarin?

Suddenly she wanted only to get back to the University. She stood up and looked at the servant. 'Don't worry about dessert, Takan.'

The man's face changed subtly. Reading disappointment, she could not help feeling a pang of guilt. He might be Akkarin's loyal servant, but he was also a gifted cook. Had he made a dish he was particularly proud of, and was dismayed that they were both leaving it uneaten?

'Was it something that will . . . keep a few hours?' she asked hesitantly.

He met her gaze briefly and, not for the first time, she caught a glimpse of a sharp intelligence there, not completely hidden behind his deferential manner.

'It will, my lady. Shall I bring it to your room when you return?'

'Yes,' she nodded. 'Thank you.'

Takan bowed.

Leaving the room, Sonea strode down the corridor and started down the stairs. She wondered again what part Takan played in Akkarin's secrets. She had witnessed Akkarin taking strength from Takan, yet Takan obviously hadn't been killed or harmed by it. And on the night of the assassination attempt, Akkarin had told her that Takan was from Sachaka. That brought up another question: if the Sachakans hated the Guild, why was one of them a servant of the High Lord?

And why did Takan sometimes call Akkarin 'master' instead of 'my lord'?

Lorlen was dictating an order for building materials when a messenger arrived. Taking the slip of paper from the man, Lorlen read it, then nodded.

'Tell the Stablemaster to prepare a carriage for me.'

'Yes, my lord.' The messenger bowed, then strode from the room.

'Visiting Captain Barran again?' Osen asked.

Lorlen smiled grimly at his assistant. 'I'm afraid so.' He looked at the pen Osen was holding, poised above a sheet of paper, and shook his head. 'I've lost the direction of my thoughts,' he added. 'We'll finish that tomorrow.'

Osen wiped the pen dry. 'I hope Barran has found the killer this time.' He followed Lorlen out of the office. 'Good night, Administrator.'

'Good night, Osen.'

As his assistant started down the University corridor toward the Magicians' Quarters, Lorlen considered the young magician. Osen had noted Lorlen's regular visits to the Guard House soon after they had begun. The young man was observant, and Lorlen knew better than to start making up complicated excuses. Sometimes giving the right amount of the truth was better than outright deceit.

He had explained to Osen that Akkarin had asked him to monitor the Guards' efforts to find the murderer.

'Why you?' Osen had asked.

Lorlen had been expecting that. 'Oh, I needed something to do in my spare time,' he had joked. 'Barran is a family friend. I was hearing about these murders from him anyway, so the communication between us has just become an official one. I could send someone else, but I don't want to be receiving the latest news thirdhand.'

'Can I ask if there's a particular reason for the Guild to take an interest?' Osen had probed.

'You can ask,' Lorlen had replied with a smile. 'I may not answer. Do you think there's a reason?'

'I had heard that some people in the city believe magic is involved.'

'Which is why the Guild must be seen to be keeping an eye on the situation. The people should feel we're not ignoring their troubles. We must take care not to show too much interest, however, or they'll think there is truth to the rumour.'

Osen had agreed to keep his knowledge of Lorlen's visits to the Guard to himself. If the rest of the Guild heard that Lorlen was following Captain Barran's progress they, too, would wonder if magic was involved.

Lorlen was still uncertain whether magic *was* involved. There had been one incident, over a year before, in which a dying witness had claimed the murderer had attacked him with magic. The burns on the witness had looked like

17

those from a heatstrike, but since then Barran had found no other evidence to confirm that the murderer — or murderers — used magic.

Barran had agreed to keep the possibility that the murderer might be a rogue magician to himself for now. If the news got out, Lorlen had explained, the King and the Houses would expect another hunt like the one that had been conducted for Sonea. They had learned from *that* experience that having magicians roaming all over the city would only send a rogue into hiding.

Lorlen strolled into the Entrance Hall. He watched as a carriage emerged from the stables and rolled down the road toward the University steps. As it pulled up, he descended to the vehicle, told the driver his destination and climbed aboard.

So what do we know? he asked himself.

For weeks, sometimes months, victims had been killed with the same, ritualised method — a method that occasionally resembled a black magic ritual. Then, for a few months, there were no deaths at all, until a new series of murders gained the Guard's attention. These, too, would be ritualised murders, but using a slightly different method than previously.

Barran had sorted the possible reasons for the change of method into two main categories. Either the murderer was acting alone and kept changing his habits, or each series of murders was carried out by a different man. A single man might change his habits to avoid detection, or to perfect the ritual; a succession of murderers might indicate some kind of gang or cult which required killing as an initiation or test.

Lorlen looked down at the ring on his hand. A few

witnesses lucky enough to see the murderer and survive had reported seeing a ring with a red gem on his hand. *A ring like this?* he wondered. Akkarin had created the gem out of glass and his own blood on the night he had discovered Lorlen, Sonea and Rothen knew he had learned and used black magic. It enabled him to see and hear everything Lorlen did, and to communicate by mind without other magicians hearing.

Whenever the murders resembled a black magic ritual, Lorlen was unable to avoid considering the possibility that Akkarin might be responsible. Akkarin did not wear a ring in public, yet he could be slipping one on when he left the Guild. Why would he, though? He didn't need to keep track of himself.

What if the ring allows someone else to see what the murderer is doing?

Lorlen frowned. Why would Akkarin want another person to see what he was doing? Unless he was acting on the orders of another. Now *that* was a frightening possibility . . .

Lorlen sighed. Sometimes he found himself hoping he would never learn the truth. He knew that, if Akkarin was the murderer, he would feel partly responsible for the deaths of his victims. He ought to have dealt with Akkarin long ago, when he had first discovered from Sonea that the High Lord used black magic. But he had feared that the Guild could not defeat Akkarin in a fight.

So Lorlen had kept the High Lord's crime a secret, persuading Sonea and Rothen to do the same. Then Akkarin had discovered that his crime was known, and had taken Sonea hostage to ensure Lorlen and Rothen remained silent. Now Lorlen could not move against Akkarin without risking *her* life.

But if I discovered that Akkarin was the murderer, and knew the Guild could defeat him, I would not hesitate. Not for our old friendship, or even Sonea's wellbeing, would I allow him to continue.

And Akkarin, through the ring, must know that.

Of course, Akkarin might *not* be the murderer. He had told Lorlen to investigate the murders, but that proved nothing. He might simply want to know how close the Guard was to discovering his crimes . . .

The carriage stopped. Lorlen glanced out of the window and blinked in surprise when he saw the front of the Guard House outside. He had been so lost in thought, he had barely noticed the journey. The carriage rocked a little as the driver climbed down to open the door. Lorlen stepped out and strode across the pavement to the Guard House entrance. Captain Barran greeted him in the narrow hall inside.

'Good evening, Administrator. Thank you for coming so quickly.'

Though Barran was still young, frown lines already marked his forehead. Those lines seemed deeper tonight.

'Good evening, Captain.'

'I have some interesting news, and something to show you. Come to my office.'

Lorlen followed the man down a corridor to a small room. The rest of the building was quiet, though a few guards were always present in the evenings. Barran ushered Lorlen to a seat, then closed the door.

'Do you remember me saying that the Thieves might be looking for the killer?'

'Yes.'

Barran smiled crookedly. 'I have had confirmation of

sorts. It was inevitable that, if the Guard and the Thieves were both investigating the murders, we'd cross paths. It turns out they have had spies here for months.'

'Spies? In the Guard?'

'Yes. Even an honourable man would be tempted to accept coin in exchange for information, when that information might lead to this murderer being found – particularly when the Guard aren't getting anywhere.' Barran shrugged. 'I don't know who all the spies are yet, but for now I'm happy to let them remain in place.'

Lorlen chuckled. 'If you want advice on negotiating with the Thieves I would send Lord Dannyl to you, but he is now a Guild Ambassador in Elyne.'

The Captain's eyebrows rose. 'That would have been interesting advice, even if I never had the opportunity to use it. I do not intend to negotiate for a co-operative effort with the Thieves, however. The Houses would never approve of it. I have made an arrangement with one of the spies that he pass on whatever he can safely divulge to me. None of his information has been useful yet, but it might lead to something that is.' The creases between his brows deepened again. 'Now, I have something to show you. You said you wanted to examine the next victim. One was discovered tonight, so I had the body brought here.'

A chill ran down Lorlen's spine, as if a cold draught had found its way under the collar of his robes. Barran gestured to the door.

'It's in the basement. Would you like to see it now?'

'Yes.'

He rose and followed Barran out into the corridor. The man remained silent as they descended a flight of stairs and continued down another corridor. The air grew distinctly colder. Stopping before a heavy wooden door, Barran unlocked and opened it.

A strong medicinal smell gusted into the corridor, not quite hiding a less pleasant odour. The room beyond was sparsely furnished. Bare stone walls surrounded three plain benches. On one was the naked corpse of a man. On another was a set of clothing, neatly folded.

Drawing closer, Lorlen studied the body reluctantly. As with all the recent killings, the victim had been stabbed through the heart, and a shallow cut ran down one side of the man's neck. Despite this the man's expression was unexpectedly peaceful.

As Barran began to describe the place where the victim was found, Lorlen considered a conversation he'd overheard during one of the regular Guild social gatherings in the Night Room. Lord Darlen, a young Healer, had been describing a patient to three of his friends.

'He was dead when he arrived,' Darlen had said, shaking his head, 'but the wife wanted a performance so she would know we'd done all we could. So I checked.'

'And found nothing?'

Darlen had grimaced. 'There's always plenty of life energy to detect afterwards, plenty of organisms that are active throughout decomposition, but his heart was still and his mind was silent. However, I detected another heartbeat. Small and slow, but definitely a heartbeat.'

'How can that be? He had two hearts?'

'No.' Darlen's voice was tortured. 'He'd . . . he'd choked on a sevli.'

At once the two Healers had burst into laughter. The third friend, an Alchemist, looked puzzled. 'What was he doing with a sevli in his throat? They're poisonous. Did someone murder him?'

'No.' Darlen had sighed. 'Their bite is poisonous, but their skin contains a substance that causes euphoria and visions. Some people like the effect. They suck on the reptiles.'

'*Suck* on reptiles?' The young Alchemist had been incredulous. 'So what did you do?'

Darlen's face had reddened. 'The sevli was suffocating, so I fished it out. Seems the wife didn't know about her husband's habit. She became hysterical. Wouldn't go home for fear her house was infested with them, and one crawled down her throat during the night.'

This had sent the two older Healers into new bouts of laughter. Lorlen almost smiled at the memory. Healers needed a sense of humour, though it was often a strange one. The conversation had given him an idea, however. A dead body was still full of life energy, but a body of someone who had been killed by black magic ought to have been drained of *all* energy. To confirm whether the murderer was using black magic, Lorlen only needed to examine a victim with his Healing senses.

As Barran finished his description of the scene, Lorlen stepped forward. Steeling himself, he placed a hand on the dead man's arm, closed his eyes and sent his senses out into the body.

He was startled at how easy it was, until he remembered that the natural barrier in living things that resisted magical interference dissipated at the moment of death. Sending his mind outward, he searched the body and found only the faintest traces of life energy. The process of decomposition had been interrupted – delayed – because of the lack of anything alive within the body to start it.

Opening his eyes, Lorlen lifted his hand from the man's arm. He stared at the shallow cut along the victim's neck, sure now that this was the wound that had killed the man. The stab wound to the heart had probably been made later, to provide a more plausible cause of death. Looking down, he regarded the ring on his finger.

So it's true, he thought. *The killer uses black magic. But is this Akkarin's victim, or do we have another black magician loose in the city?*

CHAPTER 2

THE HIGH LORD'S ORDERS

Picking up the steaming cup of sumi from the low dining table, Rothen walked over to one of the paper screens covering his guestroom windows. He slid it aside and looked out over the gardens.

Spring had come early this year. The hedges and trees bore small blossoms, and an enthusiastic new gardener had planted rows of brightly coloured flowers along the pathways. Though it was early morning, magicians and novices were walking through the garden.

Rothen lifted his cup and sipped. The sumi was fresh and bitter. He thought back to the previous evening and grimaced. Once a week he joined his elderly friend Lord Yaldin, and his wife Ezrille, for dinner. Yaldin had been a friend of Rothen's late mentor, Lord Margen, and still considered it his duty to keep an eye on Rothen – which was why, during the meal last night, Yaldin had felt he must tell Rothen to stop worrying about Sonea.

'I know you're still watching her,' the old magician had said.

Rothen shrugged. 'I'm interested in her wellbeing.'

Yaldin snorted softly. 'She's the High Lord's novice. She doesn't need you to monitor her wellbeing.'

'She does,' Rothen replied. 'Do you think the High Lord cares if she's happy or not? He's only concerned about her academic progress. Life isn't only about magic.'

Ezrille smiled sadly. 'Of course it isn't, but . . .' She hesitated, then sighed. 'Sonea has barely spoken a word to you since the High Lord claimed her guardianship. Don't you think she would have visited you by now? It's been over a year. No matter how busy she is with her studies, surely she would have found some time to see you.'

Rothen winced. He could not help himself. From their sympathetic expressions, he knew they had seen his reaction and thought he was merely hurt by Sonea's apparent abandonment of him.

'She *is* doing well,' Yaldin said gently. 'And that nonsense with the other novices ended long ago. Leave it be, Rothen.'

Rothen had pretended to agree. He couldn't tell them his true reasons for watching Sonea. To do so would place more than Sonea's life at risk. Even if Yaldin and Ezrille agreed to keep silent to protect Sonea, Akkarin had said no others were to know. Breaking that 'order' might be all the excuse Akkarin needed to . . . to what? Use black magic to take over the Guild? He was already the High Lord. What else could he possibly want?

More power, perhaps. To rule in place of the King. To rule all of the Allied Lands. To be free to strengthen himself with black magic until he was more powerful than any magician who had ever existed.

But if Akkarin had wanted to do any of that, surely he would have done it long ago. Rothen had to acknowledge, grudgingly, that Akkarin had done nothing to harm Sonea, as far as he could tell. The only time he had seen her in the company of her guardian had been the day of the Challenge.

Yaldin and Ezrille had let the subject drop eventually. 'Well, at least you've stopped taking nemmin,' Ezrille had murmured before asking after Dorrien, Rothen's son.

Rothen felt a small flash of annoyance at the memory. He looked at Tania, his servant. She was carefully wiping the dust off his bookshelf with a cloth.

He knew Tania had told Ezrille and Yaldin out of concern for his health, and would never reveal his use of a sleeping drug to anyone else, but he still could not help feeling a little resentful. But how could he complain when she willingly played the spy for him? Tania, through her friendship with Sonea's servant, Viola, kept him informed of Sonea's health, moods and occasional visits to her aunt and uncle in the slums. Clearly Tania hadn't told Yaldin and Ezrille of her own part in this, or they would have mentioned it as proof of his 'worrying'.

Dannyl would have been amused by all this 'spying'. Taking another sip of sumi, Rothen considered what he knew of his friend's activities in the last year. From letters, Rothen guessed that Dannyl had become close friends with his assistant, Tayend. The speculation regarding Tayend's sexual orientation had disappeared within weeks of it beginning. Everyone knew what self-indulgent gossips the Elynes were, and the only reason the assistant's rumoured tastes in lovers had drawn the attention of Guild magicians was because Dannyl had been accused of interest in other men in his youth. That accusation had never been proven to be true. When no further gossip about Dannyl or his assistant arose, most magicians had forgotten about the pair.

Rothen was more concerned about the research he had asked Dannyl to carry out. Wondering when Akkarin had found the opportunity to learn black magic had led Rothen to speculate on the journey Akkarin had made, years before, to study ancient magic. It seemed likely that Akkarin had discovered the forbidden arts during that time. The same sources of information might also reveal any weakness black magicians might have that could be exploited, so Rothen had asked Dannyl to do a little research on ancient magic for a 'book' he was writing.

Unfortunately, Dannyl had produced little that was useful. When he had returned to the Guild unannounced over a year before, to report to Akkarin, Rothen had been worried that he'd been found out. Dannyl had assurred Rothen afterwards that he'd told Akkarin the research had been for his own interest – and to Rothen's surprise Akkarin had encouraged Dannyl to continue. Dannyl still sent research notes every few months, but each bundle was smaller. Dannyl had expressed frustration at having exhausted all sources of knowledge in Elyne, yet, remembering how distant and evasive Dannyl had been during his visit to the Guild, Rothen could not help wondering occasionally if his friend was holding something back. Furthermore, Dannyl had mentioned discussing something confidential with the High Lord.

Rothen brought his empty cup back to the dining table. Dannyl was a Guild Ambassador and as such he would be trusted with all kinds of information he could not share with ordinary magicians. The confidential matter could have just been something political.

But he couldn't help worrying that Dannyl was unknowingly helping Akkarin in some dreadful, sinister plot.

He could do nothing about that, however. He could

only trust in Dannyl's good sense. His friend would not follow orders blindly, especially not if he was asked to do something questionable or wrong.

No matter how many times Dannyl visited the Great Library, the sight of it still filled him with wonder. Cut into a high cliff, the building's enormous door and windows were so large it was easy to imagine that a race of giant men had carved it out of the rock for their use. The corridors and rooms inside, however, were made to suit an ordinary man's proportions, so no race of giants had made *them*. As his carriage pulled up outside the massive door, a smaller door at the base of it opened and a striking young man stepped out.

Dannyl smiled and felt a glow of affection as he climbed out to greet his friend and lover. Tayend's bow was respectful, but was followed by a familiar grin.

'You took your time getting here, Ambassador,' he said.

'Don't blame me. You Elynes should have built your city closer to the library.'

'Now there's a good idea. I'll suggest it to the King next time I attend court.'

'You never attend court.'

'That's right.' Tayend smiled. 'Irand wants to speak to you.'

Dannyl paused. Did the librarian already know about the matters covered in the letter Dannyl had just received? Had he received a similar letter himself?

'What about?'

Tayend shrugged. 'I think he just wants to chat.'

They entered a corridor, then climbed a flight of stairs to a long narrow room. Mullioned windows dominated one side of the room, and groups of chairs were arranged informally along the length of the hall.

An elderly man sat in one of the closest chairs. As he began to push himself up out of it, Dannyl waved a hand.

'Don't trouble yourself, Librarian.' He dropped into a chair. 'How are you?'

Irand's shoulders lifted slightly. 'Well enough for an old man. Well enough. How are you, Ambassador?'

'Good. There isn't much work at the Guild House at the moment. A few testings, a few minor disputes, a few small parties. Nothing overly time-consuming.'

'And Errend?'

Dannyl smiled. 'The First Guild Ambassador is as cheerful as ever,' he replied. 'And most relieved to have me out of his way for the day.'

Irand chuckled. 'Tayend tells me your research is going nowhere.'

Dannyl sighed and glanced at Tayend. 'We could read every book in the library on the odd chance we might find something new, but we would need several lifetimes or a hundred assistants.'

While Dannyl had first started researching ancient magic at Lorlen's request, he had himself become intrigued by the subject. Akkarin had begun a similar search, long before he became High Lord, which had kept him roaming the lands for five years. He had returned empty-handed, however, and Dannyl had initially assumed Lorlen had asked him to retrace Akkarin's steps in order to gift his friend with some of the information he had lost.

But six months later, after Dannyl had travelled to Lonmar and Vin, Lorlen had abruptly informed Dannyl that he no longer needed the information. At the same time, Rothen had suddenly gained an interest in the same subject. This strange coincidence, and Dannyl's own growing fascination with the mysteries of ancient magic, had encouraged Dannyl and Tayend to continue.

Akkarin had eventually learned of Dannyl's project and ordered him home to report. To Dannyl's relief, the High Lord had been pleased with his work, though he had ordered Dannyl and Tayend to keep their strangest discovery, the Chamber of Ultimate Justice, a secret. The chamber, which they had found under the ruins of a city in the Elyne mountains, had contained a magically charged ceiling of stones that had attacked Dannyl, and nearly killed him.

How it worked was a mystery. After Dannyl had returned to reseal the entrance, he had searched the Great Library in vain for a reference to it. Clearly it used a form of magic unknown to the Guild.

'I suspect I'd find out more if I went to Sachaka,' Dannyl added, 'but the High Lord denied my request to journey there.'

Irand nodded. 'A wise decision. You can't be sure how well you'd be received. There's sure to be magicians there. Though they would not be as skilled as you and your colleagues, they would pose a danger to a lone Guild magician. After all, the Guild left much of their land wasted. There's bound to be some lingering resentment for that. So what will you do now?'

Dannyl drew a folded letter from his robes and gave it to Irand. 'I have a new task to perform.'

The librarian hesitated as he saw the remains of the High Lord's seal, then opened the letter and began to read.

'What is it?' Tayend asked.

'An investigation,' Dannyl replied. 'It seems some nobles in this land are trying to start their own rogue Guild.'

The scholar's eyes widened, then his expression became thoughtful. Irand drew in a breath and looked at Dannyl over the page.

'So he knows.'

Dannyl nodded. 'It appears so.'

'Knows what?' Tayend asked.

Irand handed the letter to Tayend. The scholar began to read aloud.

"'I have been watching for some years the efforts of a small group of Elyne courtiers to learn magic without the Guild's aid or knowledge. Only recently have they had some success. Now that at least one of them has managed to develop his powers, the Guild is entitled and obliged to deal with them. I have included information on this group with this letter. You will find your relationship with the scholar, Tayend of Tremmelin, helpful in persuading them that you can be trusted.'"

Tayend paused and stared at Dannyl. 'What does he mean by that?' he exclaimed.

Dannyl nodded at the letter. 'Read on.'

"'It is possible the rebels will try to use this personal information against you once you have arrested them. I will ensure that it is understood that I asked you to give them this information in order to achieve your goal.'"

Tayend stared at Dannyl. 'You said he didn't know about us. How *can* he know? Or has he just listened to the rumours and taken a chance that they might be true?'

'I doubt it,' Irand replied. 'A man like the High Lord does not take chances. Who else have you allowed to know of your relationship?'

Tayend shook his head. 'There is no-one else. Unless we have been overheard . . .' He glanced around.

'Before we start hunting for spies, there is one possibility we should consider,' Dannyl said. He grimaced and rubbed his temples. 'Akkarin has some unusual abilities. For the rest of us, there are limits to mind reading. We can't read an unwilling mind, and we must touch another person to be able to read them at all. Akkarin once searched the mind of a criminal to confirm his guilt. The man should have been able to block him, yet somehow Akkarin got past his mental barriers. Some magicians believe Akkarin can even read minds at a distance.'

'So you suspect he read your mind when you were in Kyralia?'

'Maybe. Or maybe he did when he ordered me to return to the Guild.'

Irand's eyebrows rose. 'While you were in the mountains? That he can read minds at such a distance is extraordinary.'

'I doubt he could have if I had not answered his call. Once contact is established, however, he might have been able to see more than I intended.' Dannyl nodded at the letter. 'Read on, Tayend. There is one more paragraph.'

Tayend looked down at the letter. '"*Your assistant has encountered these rebels before. He ought to be able to arrange an introduction.*" How could he possibly know *that*?'

'I hoped you could tell me.'

The scholar frowned down at the letter. 'Everyone in Elyne has a secret or two. Some you talk about, some are best kept to oneself.' He glanced at Dannyl and Irand. 'A few years ago I was invited to a secret party by a man named Royend of Marane. When I declined, he assured me it wasn't what I thought, that there'd be no, ah, indulgences of the flesh or the mind. He said it would be a scholarly gathering. But his manner was furtive, and I took that as a warning and didn't attend.'

'Did he give any hints that he was offering magical knowledge?' Irand asked.

'No, but what other scholarly pursuits would ever need to be kept hidden? It is no secret that I was once offered a place in the Guild, but declined. And my inclinations are well known.' He glanced at Dannyl. 'So he knows I had magical ability, and could guess at my reasons for not accepting the robes.'

Irand nodded. 'The High Lord probably knows this, too. It makes sense that these rebels approach all who decline or are refused entry into the Guild.' He paused and looked at Dannyl. 'And while Akkarin clearly knows the truth about you, he has not recalled or denounced you. Perhaps he is more tolerant than the average Kyralian.'

A chill ran down Dannyl's spine. 'Only because I am useful to him. He would have me risk much for the sake of finding these rebels.'

'A man in his position must be willing to use those that serve him,' Irand said sternly. 'You chose to be a Guild Ambassador, Dannyl. Your role is to act on behalf of the High Lord in matters that are the domain and responsibility of the Guild. Sometimes carrying out that role means taking risks. Let's hope this task risks only your reputation, and not your life.'

Dannyl sighed and bowed his head. 'You're right, of course.'

Tayend chuckled. 'Irand's always right, except when it comes to cataloguing meth—' He grinned as the librarian turned to glare at him. 'So I guess if the rebels thought Dannyl had reason to resent the Guild, they might consider him as a potential recruit, too.'

'And teacher,' Irand added.

Dannyl nodded. 'And they would believe that if I proved unco-operative, they could blackmail me into silence by threatening to reveal my relationship with Tayend.'

'Yes. You must plan this carefully, however,' Irand cautioned.

They began to discuss ways to approach the rebels. Not for the first time, Dannyl was glad to have the librarian's confidence. Tayend had insisted several months ago that they tell his mentor about their relationship, assuring Dannyl that he would trust Irand with his life. To Dannyl's consternation, the old man hadn't been at all surprised.

As far as Dannyl and Tayend could tell, the rest of the Elyne court still believed Dannyl was oblivious to, and certainly didn't share, Tayend's attraction to men. Rothen had told Dannyl that similar rumours had circulated in the Guild, but had been quickly forgotten. Despite this, Dannyl still feared that the truth about him would reach the Guild, and he would be stripped of his position and ordered home.

Which was why he had been shocked and angered by Akkarin's request that he allow the rebels to find out the truth. It was difficult enough keeping his relationship with Tayend a secret. Allowing the rebels to know was a risk he did not want to take.

It was late when the knock came. Looking up from her desk, Sonea regarded the door of her room. Was it her servant bringing a late cup of hot raka? She lifted a hand, then stopped. Lord Yikmo, the Warrior who had trained her in preparation for the Challenge, always said a magician should avoid the habit of gesturing when using magic – it gave away a magician's intent. Hands still, she now willed the door to open. Takan stood in the corridor beyond.

'My Lady,' he said. 'The High Lord requests your presence in the library.'

She stared at him and felt her blood slowly turn cold. What did Akkarin want with her at this time of night?

Takan gazed at Sonea and waited.

Pushing her chair back, she rose and approached the doorway. As Sonea entered the corridor, Takan started toward the library. When she reached the door, she peered through.

A large desk stood at one side. The walls were covered in bookcases. Two large chairs and a small table were arranged at the centre. Akkarin was sitting in one of the chairs. As she bowed, he gestured to the other, where a small book lay.

'This book is for you to read,' he said. 'It will help you with your studies on the construction of buildings with magic.'

Sonea entered the room and approached the chair. The book was small, bound in leather and very worn. She picked it up and opened it. The pages were filled with faded handwriting. She read the first few lines and drew in a quick breath. It was the diary of Lord Coren, the architect who had designed most of the Guild buildings, and who had discovered how to shape stone with magic.

'I don't think I need to tell you how valuable that book is,' Akkarin said quietly. 'It is rare and irreplaceable and,' his voice deepened, 'is not to leave this room.'

Sonea looked at him and nodded. His expression was serious, and his dark eyes bore into hers.

'You will not speak of it to anyone,' he added softly. 'Only a few people know it exists, and I would prefer it stayed that way.'

She took a step away as he pushed himself out of the chair and walked to the door. As he moved into the corridor she found that Takan was watching her with uncustomary directness, as if he was assessing her closely. She met his eyes. He nodded, as if to himself, then turned away. Two sets of footsteps faded into the distance. She looked down at the book in her hands.

Sitting down, she opened the cover and began to read:

I am Coren of Emarin, House Velan, and this is to be a record of my work and discoveries.

I am not one of those who writes an account of himself out of pride or habit or any need for others to know his life. There has been little in my past that I could not discuss with my friends or my sister. Today, however, I discovered a need to transcribe my thoughts to paper. I have encountered something that I must keep a solemn secret, yet at the same time I feel an urge to tell of it that cannot be denied.

Sonea looked to the top of the page and noted the date. She realised from her recent studies that at the time of writing this diary Lord Coren had been young, restless and in disfavour with his elders for drinking excessively and designing strange, impractical buildings.

I had the chest brought to my rooms today. It took some time to open it. I disengaged the magical locks easily enough, but the lid had rusted shut. I didn't want to risk damaging anything inside, so I took great care. When I finally had it open I was both disappointed and pleased. It was filled with boxes, so my first sight of the contents was very exciting. But as I opened each box I found only books inside. When I opened the last box I was greatly disappointed. I had found no buried treasure. Just books.

From what I have seen they are all records of some sort. I have been reading late into the night and much puzzles me. Tomorrow I will read some more.

Sonea smiled as she pictured the young magician locked away in his room reading. His following entries were haphazard, often skipping several days. Then came a short entry, underlined several times.

I know what I have found! These are the missing records!

He named some of the books, but Sonea did not recognise any of them. These missing volumes were 'full of forbidden knowledge' and Coren was reluctant to describe their contents. After a gap of several weeks there was a long entry describing an experiment, the conclusion of which read:

At last I have succeeded! It has taken so long. I feel both triumph and the fear I should have felt before. I'm not sure why this is. While I was failing to discover the ways to use this power I was still somehow uncorrupted. Now, I cannot truly deny that I have ever used black magic. I have broken my vow. I hadn't realised how ill that would feel.

Yet it did not deter him. Sonea found herself struggling to understand why this young man continued to do something that he clearly saw was wrong. He seemed unable to stop, driven forward to whatever end this discovery was leading him to, even if it be the discovery of his crime.

But it led to something else . . .

All who know me know my love of stone. It is the beautiful flesh of the earth. It has cracks and creases like skin, it has veins

38

and pores. It can be hard, soft, brittle or flexible. When the earth spills forth its molten core, it is as red as blood.

After learning of the black magics, I expected to be able to place my hands on stone and feel a tremendous store of life energy within, but I was disappointed. I felt nothing; less than the tingling of water. I wanted it to be full of life. That's when it happened. Like a healer trying to will a dying man back to health, I started to infuse energy into the stone. I willed it to live. Then a remarkable thing began to happen.

Sonea gripped the little book tightly, unable to take her eyes from the lines of text. This was the discovery that made Coren famous, and influenced Guild architecture for centuries to come. It was said to be the greatest development in magical knowledge for centuries. Though what he had done was not actually black magic, the forbidden arts had led to the discovery.

Sonea closed her eyes and shook her head. Lord Larkin, the architecture teacher, would give all his wealth for this diary, but he would be devastated if he learned the truth about his idol. She sighed, looked down at the pages and continued to read.

CHAPTER 3

OLD FRIENDS, NEW ALLIES

Cery signed the letter with a flourish, then regarded his work with satisfaction. His writing was neat and elegant. The paper was quality, and the ink dark and black. Despite the slang terms throughout – he had requested that Serin teach him to read and write, not make him sound like a member of one of the Houses – and the fact that it was a request for the execution of a man who had cheated him and fled to the Southside, it was a fine, well-written letter.

He smiled as he remembered asking Faren, the Thief who had hidden Sonea from the Guild, if he could 'borrow' Faren's scribe for a while. From Faren's mixed expression of reluctance and gratitude, Cery knew that the Thief would have refused if he hadn't desperately needed the boost to his position that the arrangement would bring.

Faren's hold on his status as Thief had been precarious for the first year after he had turned Sonea over to the Guild. A Thief's ability to do business relied on a network of people willing to work for him. While some worked for money, most preferred to 'help out' and be paid back in kind later. Favours were the second currency of the underworld.

Faren had used a lot of the favours owed to him while keeping Sonea out of the Guild's hands, but that should not have held him back for long. People knew he had made a deal with Sonea to hide her from the Guild in exchange for her using her magic for him – a deal he had broken. The other Thieves, worried by the Guild's warnings that her powers would grow dangerous if she wasn't trained to control them, had 'asked' him to turn her in. While he could hardly have refused the request of the other underworld leaders, a deal *had* been broken. Thieves needed people to believe they had at least *some* integrity, or only the desperate or the foolish would do business with them. Only the fact that Sonea had never used magic in any useful way, failing to uphold her side of the deal, had saved Faren from complete ruin.

Serin had remained loyal, however. He had given Cery little information about Faren's affairs during the reading and writing lessons – nothing Cery didn't already know, anyway. Cery had learned fast, though he attributed that partly to having watched some of Sonea's lessons with the scribe.

And by showing that he – Sonea's friend – was willing to deal with Faren – Sonea's 'betrayer' – Cery had assured people that the Thief was still trustworthy.

Taking a slim tube of dried reed out of his desk drawer, Cery rolled the letter and slipped it inside. He stoppered the tube and sealed it with wax. Picking up a yerim – a slim metal tool with a needle-like point – he scratched a name on the side.

Putting the tube aside, Cery balanced the yerim in his hand, then, with a flick of his wrist, threw it across the room. It landed point first in the wooden panelling of the opposite wall. He gave a small sigh of satisfaction. He'd had his own yerim made to be well balanced for throwing.

Looking down at the three remaining in the drawer, he reached out to take another, then stopped at a knock on the door.

Rising, Cery crossed the room to retrieve the yerim from the panelling before returning to his desk.

'Come in,' he called.

The door opened and Gol stepped inside. The man's expression was respectful. Cery looked closer. In Gol's eyes was a hint of . . . expectation, perhaps?

'A woman to see you, Ceryni.'

Cery smiled at Gol's use of his full name. This was an unusual woman, if Gol's manner was any indication. What would she be: spirited, beautiful, or important?

'Name?'

'Savara.'

No-one Cery knew of, unless the name was false. It was not a typical Kyralian name, however. It sounded more like a Lonmar name.

'Occupation?'

'She wouldn't say.'

Then perhaps her name is Savara, Cery mused. If she had lied about her name, why not make up an occupation as well?

'Why's she come?'

'Says she can help you with a problem, but wouldn't say what the problem was.'

Cery was thoughtful. *So she thinks I have a problem. Interesting.*

'Show her in, then.'

Gol nodded, then backed out of the room. Cery closed his desk drawer, then leaned back in his chair to wait. After a few minutes, the door opened again.

He and the newcomer regarded each other in surprise.

She had the strangest face he had ever seen. A broad forehead and high cheekbones angled down to a fine chin. Thick, black hair hung heavy and straight past her shoulders, but her most startling feature was her eyes. They were large and tilted upward at the outer corners, and the same light gold-brown as her skin. Strange, exotic eyes . . . and they were examining him with barely concealed amusement.

He was used to this reaction. Most customers hesitated when they first saw him, as they noted his stature, and his name, which was also the name of a little rodent common in the slums. Then they reminded themselves of his position and the likely consequences if they laughed out loud.

'Ceryni,' the woman said. 'You are Ceryni?' Her voice was rich and deep, and she had spoken with an accent he could not place. Definitely not Lonmar.

'Yes. And you're Savara.' He did not phrase it as a question. If she had lied about her name, he doubted she would offer the real one now just because he asked for it.

'I am.'

She took a step closer to the desk, her eyes shifting away to note features of the room, then back to him again.

'You say I've a problem you can fix,' he prompted.

A hint of a smile crossed her face and he caught his breath. *If she fully smiled, she may just turn out to be astonishingly beautiful.* No doubt this was the cause of Gol's suppressed excitement.

'I do.' She frowned. 'You do.' Her gaze slipped from his, moved over him as if considering something, then snapped back. 'The other Thieves say you are the one hunting the murderers.'

Murderers? Cery narrowed his eyes. *So she knows there is more than one.*

'How d'you plan to help me?'

She smiled and Cery's suspicion was confirmed – she *was* astonishingly beautiful. He hadn't anticipated the challenge and confidence that came with it, however. This one knew how to use her looks to get her way.

'I can help you find and kill them.'

Cery's heart began to race. If she knew who these murderers were, and believed she could kill them . . .

'And how're you going to do that?' he asked.

The smile vanished. She took another step closer. 'Find or kill?'

'Both.'

'I will say nothing of my methods of killing today. As for finding them,' a crease appeared between her brows, 'that will be harder, but easier for me than for you. I have ways of recognising them.'

'So do I,' Cery pointed out. 'Why's your way better?'

She smiled again. 'I know more about them. For now, I will tell you that the next one entered the city today. He will probably take a day or two to gather the courage, and then you'll hear of his first kill.'

He considered her reply carefully. If she didn't know anything, why offer this proof? Unless she planned to manufacture 'proof' by murdering someone herself. He looked at her closely and his heart went cold as he belatedly recognised the broad facial features and that particular shade of gold-brown skin. How had he not seen it earlier? But he had never seen a Sachakan *woman* before . . .

He had no doubt now that she was dangerous. Whether

she was dangerous to him, or to the murderers from her homeland, remained to be seen. The more he could get her to reveal of herself, the better.

'So you have watchers in your homeland,' he prompted, 'who tell you when a killer has entered Kyralia?'

She paused. 'Yes.'

Cery nodded. 'Or,' he said slowly, 'you'll wait a few days and kill someone yourself.'

Her gaze became steely. 'Then have your tags watch me. I will stay in my room and have food brought to me.'

'We both need to prove ourselves right-sided,' he told her. 'You came to me, so you do the proving first. I'll put a watcher on you now, and we'll have a chat once this man has done his deed. Happy with that?'

She nodded once. 'Yes.'

'Wait in the first room. I'll set things out, and have a friend take you back to your place.'

He watched, taking in as much detail as possible, as she walked to the door. Her clothes were plain, neither shabby nor expensive. The heavy shirt and trousers were typical of common Kyralians, but from the way she walked he doubted she had been ordered about much in her life. No, this one did the ordering.

Gol returned to the room promptly after she had left, his face tight with the effort of hiding his curiosity.

'Put four tags on her,' Cery told him. 'I want to know every move she makes. Keep an eye on whoever brings anything to her, food or otherwise. She knows she's going to be watched, so let her see two of the tags.'

Gol nodded. 'Want to see what she was carrying?'

He held out a bundle of cloth. Cery regarded it with mild surprise. *She* had *offered to kill the murderers*, he

45

reasoned. *I doubt she plans to do it with her bare hands*. He nodded.

Gol carefully unrolled the cloth on the desk. Cery chuckled as he saw the array of knives and daggers. He picked them up one by one, testing their weight. Some were etched with unusual designs and symbols, some with gems set into the metal. He sobered. Sachakan, most likely. He set the largest of the jewelled ones aside, then nodded to Gol.

'Give them back.'

Gol nodded, then rolled up the bundle and took it out of the room. When the door had closed, Cery leaned back in his chair and considered this strange woman. If everything she had said proved true, she could be as useful as she claimed.

If she was lying? He frowned. Was it possible a Thief had sent her? She had mentioned speaking to the 'other Thieves'. He could not think of a good reason for one to interfere, however. Time must be spent considering all the possibilities. He would be questioning his watchers closely.

And should I tell him? Cery thought. To communicate anything other than the arranged coded messages would require a meeting, and he was not about to arrange one unless it was absolutely necessary. Was this important enough?

A Sachakan woman who had contacts in her homeland. Of course it was.

But something made Cery pause. Perhaps he should wait and see if she proved herself useful first. And he had to admit, he didn't like consulting someone else every time he changed his tactics slightly. Even if he did owe that someone a great debt.

It was time he came up with a few strategies of his own.

* * *

As Sonea waited for Warrior class to begin she closed her eyes and rubbed them, then fought off the urge to yawn. She had finished Coren's diary late in the night, drawn on by the architect's recollections and half afraid that, if she left it there unfinished, she might return the next night to find it gone and never know how the story ended.

As the night turned to the earliest hours of morning, she had read the final entry:

I have decided. When the foundations of the University are complete I will secretly bury the chest, with all its contents, in the soil beneath it. Along with those terrible truths will go my own, in the physical form of this book. Perhaps, by carrying out this act of concealment, I will finally smother this nagging guilt at what I have learned and used. If I had the courage, I would destroy the chest and its contents, but I fear to judge differently from those who placed it in the ground in the first place. They were most definitely wiser men than I.

The chest must have been rediscovered, however, or she would not have had Coren's diary in her hands. What had happened to the rest of the books? Did Akkarin have them?

Or was the diary a fake, created by Akkarin to persuade the Guild that black magic was not as bad as it was thought to be? He might be testing it on her, to see if it would convince her.

If that were so, then he had made a mistake. Coren had believed that black magic was wrong. Reading the account, whether fictional or not, was not going to persuade anyone otherwise.

If it was real, why had Akkarin given it to her? Sonea frowned down at her notebook. He would not have allowed her to know of its existence on a whim. He must have a reason.

What had he revealed to her? That Coren had used black magic and that it had led him to discover how to manipulate stone. That another magician – a famous magician – had committed the same crime as he. Perhaps Akkarin wanted her to consider that he, too, might have learned it against his better judgment. Perhaps he wanted her sympathy and understanding.

Coren hadn't held a novice hostage to keep his crimes secret, however.

Would he have, if he had been faced with losing his powers, position, or even his life, as punishment? Sonea shook her head. Perhaps Akkarin simply wanted to destroy whatever illusions she might have of the famous figure that Coren was.

The sudden appearance of Lord Makin interrupted her thoughts. The teacher placed a large box on the front desk, then faced the class.

'Today I will be teaching you about illusion,' the Warrior told them. 'And how it is used in battle. The most important thing to remember with illusion is this: it is all about deception. An illusion cannot harm you, but it can lead you into danger. I'll demonstrate this with a story.'

Makin moved to his chair and sat down, folding his hands on the table. All sounds of boots scuffing the floor or novices shifting in their seats ceased. Lord Makin's stories were always interesting.

'Our histories tell us that, five centuries ago, two brothers lived in the Elyne mountains. Grind and Lond were both magicians skilled in battle. One day a caravan of travellers passed, led by a merchant named Kamaka. His daughter, a beautiful young woman, travelled with him. The two brothers saw the caravan and descended from their mountain home to buy goods. When they laid eyes on Kamaka's daughter they both fell instantly in love.'

Makin sighed and shook his head sadly, gaining smiles from the novices. 'An argument ensued between them over who would have the girl. The two brothers could not resolve their dispute with words, so they began to fight each other. It is said the battle continued for days (which is unlikely) and the brothers found themselves evenly matched in strength and skill. It was Grind who broke the stalemate. Seeing that his brother stood by a cliff on which was poised a large boulder, he contrived that this boulder should fall, but preceded it with another, illusory boulder.

'Lond saw his brother staring at something above his head. He looked up to see a boulder falling toward him, and instantly dismissed it as the illusion it was. Of course he did not see the second boulder, which was concealed behind the illusory one.

'Grind had expected his brother to detect the deception. When he realised he had killed his own brother, he became distracted with grief. The caravan was able to continue on its way, taking Kamaka's daughter with it. So you see,' Makin finished, 'while illusions cannot hurt you, allowing yourself to be deceived by them might.'

The Warrior rose. 'How do you make illusions? That is what I will be teaching you today. We will start by copying the objects I have brought with me. Seno, come to the front of the class.'

Sonea listened as the magician explained different ways of creating an image of something with magic, and watched as Seno followed the teacher's instructions. When the demonstration was finished, Seno passed Sonea's desk on the way to his own. He looked at Sonea and smiled. She let the corner of her mouth curl upward in response. He had been particularly friendly toward her since a Warrior practise session some weeks before, in which she had taught him a trick that weaker magicians could use against stronger ones.

As the lesson continued, she turned her mind to learning the illusion techniques. Just when she had managed to form an illusion of a pachi fruit something appeared in the air in front of her.

It was a flower, the petals made of bright orange autumn leaves. She reached out and her fingers passed through the strange blossom. It shattered into a thousand sparks of light that spun in a quick dance before vanishing.

'Well done!' Trassia exclaimed.

'It wasn't me.' Sonea turned to see Seno grinning at her, an orange leaf lying on the table in front of him.

At the front of the class, Lord Makin cleared his throat loudly. Sonea turned back to see the teacher regarding her sternly. She shrugged to protest her innocence. He looked pointedly at the fruit in front of her.

She concentrated until an illusory copy appeared beside it. It was a redder shade than it ought to be, and the texture of its skin was suspiciously like the veins of a leaf. She sighed. It would be easier if she didn't have a memory of autumn leaves so fresh in her mind. She pushed away her annoyance. Seno hadn't intended to distract her. He'd just been showing off.

But why flaunt his success to her and no-one else? Surely he wasn't trying to impress her.

Or was he?

She resisted the temptation to turn and see what he was

doing. Seno was a cheerful boy, talkative, and easy to like, and she was probably the only Kyralian girl who didn't tower over him . . .

What am I thinking? She scowled as she realised her illusion had changed into a shapeless glowing ball. *Even if I didn't have Akkarin to worry about, what of Dorrien?*

A memory flitted into her mind of Rothen's son standing by the spring in the forest behind the Guild. Of him leaning closer to kiss her. She pushed it away.

She hadn't seen Dorrien for over a year. Whenever she found herself thinking of him, she forced herself to concentrate on something else. There was nothing to be gained from regret – not when it would have been an impossible relationship anyway, with her stuck in the Guild until graduation, and him living – all but a few weeks each year – far away, in a village at the base of the mountains.

Sighing, she concentrated on the fruit, and began restoring her illusion.

As Lorlen reached the door of his office he heard a familiar voice call his name. Glancing behind, he smiled as he saw his assistant striding forward to meet him.

'Good evening, Lord Osen.'

The magical lock unwound under his will, and the door clicked open. Lorlen stepped aside and gestured for Osen to enter, but his assistant hesitated as he looked inside the room, his expression changing from surprise to a scowl. Following Osen's gaze, Lorlen saw the black-robed man who was relaxing in one of the room's comfortable chairs.

Akkarin had a way of turning up in locked rooms, or unexpected places, but this did not explain Osen's scowl. Lorlen looked at his assistant again. The young magician's expression was respectful now; no sign remained of the fleeting disapproval Lorlen had glimpsed.

I hadn't noticed his dislike of Akkarin before, Lorlen mused as he walked to his desk. *I wonder how long he has nursed it.*

'Good evening, High Lord,' Lorlen said.

'Administrator,' Akkarin replied. 'Lord Osen.'

'High Lord,' Osen replied, nodding.

Lorlen sat down at his desk and looked up at Osen. 'Was there something . . . ?'

'Yes,' Osen replied. 'I found a messenger waiting at the door about half an hour ago. Captain Barran says he has something interesting to show you if you are free.'

Another victim? Lorlen suppressed a shudder. 'Then I had better see what it is, unless the High Lord has reason to detain me.' He looked at Akkarin.

Deep creases had formed between Akkarin's eyebrows. *He looks genuinely concerned*, Lorlen thought. *Very concerned.*

'No,' Akkarin said. 'Captain Barran's request is more important than the issues I came to discuss.'

A short and awkward silence followed as Osen stayed by the desk and Akkarin remained in his chair. Lorlen glanced from one to the other, then rose.

'Thank you, Osen. Could you see to the ordering of a carriage for me?'

'Yes, Administrator.' The young magician nodded politely to Akkarin then strode out of the room. Lorlen looked at Akkarin closely, wondering if Osen's dislike had communicated itself.

What am I thinking? Of course Akkarin knows.

Akkarin had paid little attention to Osen's departure, however. He was still frowning as he rose and followed Lorlen to the door.

'You weren't expecting this?' Lorlen ventured as he stepped into the Entrance Hall. It was raining outside, so he stopped within the doors to wait for the carriage.

Akkarin's eyes narrowed. 'No.'

'You could come with me.'

'Better that you take care of it.'

He'll be watching, I'd wager. Lorlen looked down at the ring on his finger.

'Good night, then,' Lorlen ventured.

Akkarin's expression softened slightly. 'Good night. I'm looking forward to your views on this.' The corner of his mouth twitched upward, then he turned away and started down the stairs, the rain hissing as it met the invisible shield around him.

Lorlen shook his head at Akkarin's little joke. A carriage emerged from the stables and started along the road to the University. It pulled up at the bottom of the stairs and the driver jumped down to open the door. Lorlen hurried down and climbed aboard.

The journey through the city to the Guard House seemed longer than usual. The rain clouds blocked the starlight, but the wet road reflected lamplight up onto the buildings. Those few people roaming about hurried by in their cloaks, the hoods covering their heads. Only one delivery boy stopped to stare at the carriage as it passed.

The carriage finally pulled up outside the Guard House. Lorlen climbed out and strode to the door. He was greeted by Captain Barran.

'Sorry to call you out on such a miserable night, Administrator,' Barran said as he led Lorlen down the corridor to his office. 'I considered delaying my message until tomorrow, but that would have made what I have to show you even less pleasant.'

Barran did not stop at his office, but descended to the same basement room he had taken Lorlen to before. As they stepped through the door, a powerful smell of rot enveloped them. Lorlen saw with dismay that something human-shaped lay under a heavy cloth on one of the tables.

'Here.' The Captain moved quickly to a cupboard and took out a jar and two squares of cloth. He unstoppered the jar and tipped a few drops of yellow oil onto the cloths, then handed one to Lorlen. 'Hold this over your nose.'

As Lorlen did, a sharp and familiar medicinal smell overwhelmed the room's odour. Holding the other cloth to his own face, Barran moved over to the table.

'This man was found floating in the river today,' he said, his voice muffled. 'He's been dead a couple of days.' He lifted the cloth covering the body to reveal a pale face. The corpse's eyes were covered by small squares of material. As more of the body was revealed, Lorlen forced himself to ignore the signs of decay and what he guessed were the nibblings of fish. Instead, he noted the wound over the heart and the long slash down the man's neck.

'Another victim.'

'No.' Barran looked at Lorlen. 'He's been identified by two witnesses. This appears to be the murderer.'

Lorlen stared at Barran, then the corpse. 'But he's been killed in the same way.'

'Yes. In revenge, perhaps. See here.' The guard pointed to the left hand of the corpse. A finger was missing. 'He was wearing a ring. We had to cut it off.' Barran replaced the cloth, then moved to a covered dish on a nearby bench. The guard drew off the cover to reveal a dirty silver band.

'It had a stone, but it wasn't removed. Our investigator found shards of glass embedded in the skin, and the grips of the setting were bent in a way that suggests the ring was smashed. He believes the stone was glass.'

Lorlen resisted looking down at his own ring. Akkarin's ring. *So my suspicion about the murderer's ring must be true. I wonder . . .*

He turned to regard the covered corpse.

'Are you sure this is the murderer?'

'The witnesses were very convincing.'

Lorlen moved to the corpse and uncovered an arm. Steeling himself, he placed two fingers on the skin and sent his senses out. At once he detected energy within it, and felt relief. Something was odd, however. He searched, then drew back as he realised what the strangeness was. The life within the body was concentrated around the stomach, lungs, skin and wounds. The rest was all but empty.

Of course, he thought. This man has probably been floating in the river for a few days. Time enough for small organisms to invade. Another day or two and the true cause of death would have been undetectable.

Lorlen drew away from the table.

'Seen enough?' Barran asked.

'Yes.' Lorlen paused to wipe his fingers on the cloth before giving it to Barran. He held his breath until they were back in the corridor and the door was shut firmly behind them.

'What now?' Lorlen wondered aloud.

Barran sighed. 'We wait. If the murders begin again, we'll know for sure that we have a gang of killers to look for.'

'I'd prefer it if the murders simply stopped now,' Lorlen replied.

'As would most Imardians,' Barran agreed, 'but I still have the murderer's killer to look for.'

The murderer's killer. Another black magician. Akkarin, perhaps? He glanced at the door they had just passed through. That corpse was proof that there were – or had been – black magicians in the city other than Akkarin. Was the city filled with them? Now *that* was not a comforting thought. Suddenly, all Lorlen wanted was to go back to the Guild, to the safety of his rooms, and try to sort out the implications.

But Barran obviously needed to discuss the discovery further. Smothering a sigh, Lorlen followed the guard back to his office.

CHAPTER 4

THE NEXT STEP

Rothen sat in his favourite chair to one side of the Night Room and watched his fellow magicians. Every week, Guild members came to this room to talk and exchange gossip. Some remained in pairs or small circles, bound together by friendship or familiarity with others of the same discipline. Others were drawn together by family and House ties; though magicians were supposed to put aside such loyalties when they joined the Guild, the inclination to trust and distrust according to tradition and politics remained strong.

At the other side of the room sat three magicians who appeared to be engaged in anything but idle chatter. Lord Balkan, wearing the red robes and black sash of the Head of Warriors, was the youngest of them. Lady Vinara, the green-robed Head of Healers, was a stern, middle-aged woman. White-haired Lord Sarrin, the Head of Alchemists, wore his purple robes.

Rothen wished he could hear their conversation. The three had been talking energetically for an hour. Whenever anything was debated among the Higher Magicians, these three were the most vocal and most influential speakers. Between Balkan's direct reasoning, Vinara's compassion and insight, and Sarrin's conservative opinions, they usually managed to cover most sides of an issue.

But Rothen knew he would never get near enough to the trio to listen without being observed. Instead, he turned his attention to closer magicians. At once his heart skipped as he recognised a familiar voice. Administrator Lorlen . . . somewhere behind his chair. He closed his eyes and concentrated on the voice.

'. . . I understand that many of the Alchemists have been involved in long-term projects they are reluctant to put aside,' Lorlen said. 'All will have an opportunity to object to their involvement in the construction of the new Lookout, but they must prove that their work will be irretrievably harmed by the delay.'

'But . . .'

'Yes?'

There was a sigh. 'I just cannot see why we are wasting Alchemists' time on such . . . such foolery. *Weather* monitoring, of all things! Can't Davin build himself a little hut on that hill? Why a tower?' The magician objecting to the project was Lord Peakin, the Head of Alchemic Studies. 'And I do not see the need for the Warriors' involvement. Is this structure going to be for alchemic or military use?'

'Both,' Lorlen told him. 'The High Lord decided it would be short-sighted to construct a building of this kind without considering its defensive potential. He also saw that it was unlikely that the building would be approved by the King if its use was solely for monitoring the weather.'

'Then who will design this structure?'

'That is yet to be decided.'

Rothen smiled. Lord Davin had been considered an eccentric for years, but recently his study of weather patterns and prediction had gained a little respect and interest. Lord Peakin, however, had always found Davin's gushing enthusiasm and peculiar obsession irritating.

The discussion about the tower ended as a new voice joined the others.

'Good evening, Administrator, Lord Peakin.'

'Director Jerrik,' Peakin said. 'I have heard that Sonea will not be attending evening classes now. Is this true?'

At Sonea's name, Rothen was instantly tense and alert. And Jerrik, as University Director, oversaw all matters involving the training of novices. From this conversation, Rothen might learn about her progress.

'It is,' Jerrik replied. 'The High Lord spoke to me yesterday. A few of her teachers had commented to me that she appeared to be tired and was easily distracted. Akkarin had made the same observation, and agreed to let her have the evenings free for the rest of the year.'

'What of those subjects she has already begun studying?'

'She'll have to begin them again next year, though she won't have to repeat any projects if she doesn't need to. Her teachers will take into account what she has covered already.'

The voices were growing fainter. Rothen resisted the urge to look around.

'Will she be favouring a discipline?' Peakin asked. 'This will make it even more necessary that she focus her efforts on one soon, or she will not be proficient in any by graduation.'

'Akkarin hasn't decided yet,' Lorlen replied.

'*Akkarin* hasn't decided?' Jerrik repeated. 'The choice is Sonea's.'

There was a pause. 'Of course,' Lorlen agreed. 'What I meant by that is Akkarin hasn't indicated to me which he'd prefer her to choose, so I'm assuming he hasn't decided what to recommend.'

'Maybe he doesn't want to influence her in any way,' Peakin said. 'Which is why he . . . a good grounding . . . before . . .'

The voices faded into the distance. Guessing that the magicians were moving away, Rothen sighed and drained his glass.

So Sonea had her evenings to herself. His mood darkened at the thought of her stuck in her room in the High Lord's Residence, close to Akkarin and his evil habits. Then he remembered that she had always spent her spare time in the Novices' Library. No doubt she would simply go there every evening now she was free of classes.

Feeling a little better, Rothen rose, gave his empty glass to a servant, then went in search of Yaldin.

Since Irand had allocated them a study room, Dannyl and Tayend had gradually added furnishings until it was as comfortable as any nobleman's guestroom. In addition to the large table that had once dominated the room, there were comfortable chairs and a couch, a well-stocked wine cabinet and oil lamps for reading. The lamps were also the only source of heat when Dannyl was not there. Today, however, he had set a globe of magic in an alcove in one wall, and the heat had quickly chased away the chill of the stone walls.

Tayend had been absent when Dannyl arrived at the library. After talking to Irand for an hour, Dannyl had continued on to their study room to wait for his friend. He was struggling through the records of a seaside estate in the vague hope of finding a reference to ancient magic when Tayend finally arrived.

The scholar stopped in the middle of the room and swayed, clearly a little drunk.

'Looks like you've been having a good time,' Dannyl observed.

Tayend sighed dramatically. 'Ah, yes. There was good wine. There was fine music. There were even a few rather good-looking acrobats to admire . . . But I dragged myself away, knowing that I could only escape for a few sweet hours from slaving in the library for my relentlessly demanding Guild Ambassador.'

Dannyl crossed his arms and smiled. 'Slaving, indeed. You've never done an honourable day's work in your life.'

'Plenty of dishonourable ones, though.' Tayend grinned. 'And besides, I did a little work for us at this party. Dem Marane was there – the man who might be a rebel.'

'Really?' Dannyl uncrossed his arms. 'That's a coincidence.'

'Not really.' Tayend shrugged. 'I see him occasionally at parties, but I haven't had much conversation with him since he first introduced himself. Anyway, I decided to have a chat and give him a hint that we were interested in attending his parties.'

Dannyl felt a stab of alarm. 'What did you say?'

Tayend waved a hand dismissively. 'Nothing specific. I just commented that his invitations had stopped once I'd started assisting you, then I looked cautious, but interested.'

'You shouldn't have . . .' Dannyl frowned. 'How many times have you had these invitations?'

The scholar chuckled. 'You sound jealous, Dannyl. Only once or twice a year. Not invitations, really. He just hints that I'm still welcome to attend his parties.'

'And these hints stopped when you started assisting me?'

'Obviously he's terribly intimidated by you.'

Dannyl paced the room. 'You've just hinted that we've guessed what he and his friends are up to. If they are as involved as Akkarin says, they'll take even the slightest hint of danger seriously. *Very* seriously.'

Tayend's eyes widened. 'I just . . . sounded interested.'

'That is probably enough to send Marane into a panic. He's probably considering what to do about us right now.'

'What will he do?'

Dannyl sighed. 'I doubt he'll wait around to see if the Guild comes to arrest him. He's probably considering ways to silence us. Blackmail. Murder.'

'Murder! But . . . surely he'd know I wouldn't have approached him if I was going to turn him in? If I was going to turn him in I'd just . . . turn him in.'

'Because you only suspect he's a rebel,' Dannyl replied. 'He'll be expecting us to do exactly what we're planning to do – pretend to want to join them in order to confirm our suspicions. That's why Akkarin suggested we give him something to blackmail us with.'

Tayend sat down and rubbed his forehead. 'Do you really think he might try to kill me?' He cursed. 'I just saw an opportunity and, and . . .'

'No. If he has any sense, he won't risk trying to kill you.' Dannyl leaned against the table. 'He'll be finding out as much about us as possible, considering what is precious to us. What he could threaten to harm. Family. Wealth. Honour.'

'Us?'

Dannyl shook his head. 'Even if he has heard rumours, he would not rely on them. He wants something he's sure of. If we'd arranged for our little secret to come into his hands before this, we could rely on him aiming for that.'

'Do we still have time?'

Dannyl considered the scholar. 'I suppose if we act quickly . . .'

The bright excitement in the scholar's eyes was gone. Dannyl wasn't sure what he wanted to do more: give Tayend a reassuring hug or shake some sense into him. By seeking to learn magic on their own, the Elyne courtiers had broken one of the Allied Land's most important laws. Punishment for breaking it, depending on the circumstances, was imprisonment for life or even execution. The rebels would take any threat of discovery very seriously.

By the miserable look on Tayend's face, Dannyl knew that if the danger hadn't sunk in before, it had now. Sighing, he crossed the room and rested his hands on Tayend's shoulders.

'Don't worry, Tayend. You set things in motion a little early, that's all. Let's find Irand and tell him we need to act straightaway.'

Tayend nodded, then rose and followed him to the door.

It was late when Sonea heard the tapping at her bedroom door. She sighed with relief. Her servant, Viola, was late and Sonea was craving her nightly cup of raka.

'Come in.' Without looking up, she sent a thought at the door and willed it open. When the servant didn't move into the room, Sonea looked up and felt her blood freeze.

Akkarin stood in the doorway, all but his pale face hidden in the shadowy passage. He moved and she saw that he was carrying two large, heavy books. The cover of one was stained and tattered.

With her heart beating quickly, she stood and reluctantly approached the door, stopping a few strides away to bow.

'Have you finished the diary?' he asked.

She nodded. 'Yes, High Lord.'

'And what did you make of it?'

What should she say? 'It . . . it answers a lot of questions,' she said evasively.

'Such as?'

'How Lord Coren discovered how to manipulate stone.'

'Anything else?'

That he learned black magic. She didn't want to say it, but Akkarin obviously wanted some sort of acknowledgment of the fact. What would he do if she refused to talk about it? He would probably keep pressing her. She was too tired to think her way around a conversation like that.

'He used black magic. He saw it was wrong,' she said shortly. 'He stopped.'

The corner of his mouth curled up into a half-smile. 'Indeed. I do not think the Guild would like to discover that. The real Coren is not a figure they would want young novices to idolise, even if he redeemed himself in the end.' He held out the books. 'This is a far older record. I have brought an original as well as a copy. The original is deteriorating, so handle it only as much as you need to confirm the copy is true.'

'Why are you showing me these books?'

The question came out before she could stop it. She winced at the insolence and suspicion in her voice. Akkarin's eyes bored into her own and she looked away.

'You want to know the truth,' he said. It was not a question.

He was right. She did want to know. A part of her

wanted to ignore the books – to refuse to read them just because he wanted her to. Instead, she stepped forward and took them from him. She did not meet his eyes, though she knew he was watching her closely.

'As with the diary, you should not allow anyone to learn of these records,' he said quietly. 'Do not even allow your servant to see them.'

She backed away and looked down at the cover of the older book. *Record of the 235th Year*, the cover stated. The book was over five hundred years old! Impressed, she glanced up at Akkarin. He nodded once, knowingly, then turned away. His footsteps echoed down the corridor, then she heard the faint sound of his bedroom door closing.

The books were heavy. She pushed the door closed with a small pulse of magic, and moved to her desk. Pushing aside her notes, she laid the two books side by side.

Opening the original, she gently turned the first pages. The writing was faint and unreadable in places. Opening the copy, she felt a strange frisson as lines of elegant hand-writing appeared. Akkarin's handwriting.

After reading a few lines of the original, she checked them against the copy and confirmed that the two were identical. Akkarin had left notes where the text had faded, outlining what he thought the missing words might be. She turned more pages, checked again, then chose another page from the centre of the book and one from near the end. All seemed to match the copy perfectly. Later, she decided, she would check every page and every word.

Putting the original aside, she turned back to the first page of the copy and began to read.

It was a day-by-day record of a Guild much younger and smaller than the current one. After several pages, she had grown fond of the record-keeper, who clearly admired the people he was writing about. The Guild he knew was very different from the one she understood. Magicians took on apprentices in exchange for money or assistance. Then a comment by the author made it clear what that assistance entailed, and she stopped, aghast.

These early magicians strengthened themselves by drawing magic from their apprentices. They used black magic.

She read and reread the passage over and over, but its meaning was clear. They called it 'higher magic'.

She looked at the spine and saw that she was a quarter of the way through the book. Continuing, she found the records gradually focussed on the activities of a wayward apprentice, Tagin. It was discovered that the young man had taught himself higher magic against the wishes of his master. Abuses were uncovered. Tagin had taken strength from ordinary folk, which was never done except in times of great need. The record-keeper expressed disapproval and anger, then his tone abruptly changed to fear. Tagin had used higher magic to kill his master.

The situation grew steadily worse. As the magicians of the Guild sought to punish him, Tagin killed indiscriminately to gain the strength to resist them. Magicians reported the slaughter of men, women and children. Whole villages were all but destroyed, with only a few survivors to report the malicious nature of their attacker.

At a knock at her door, she jumped. She quickly closed the books, pushed them spine-first against the wall, and stacked several ordinary study books on top. Drawing her notes back in front of her, she arranged the desk as if she had been studying.

As she willed the door open Takan glided in with her raka. She thanked him, but felt too distracted to ask where Viola was. Once he had left, she gulped a few mouthfuls, then retrieved the records and began reading again:

It is difficult to believe that any man could be capable of such acts of needless violence. Yesterday's attempt to subdue him appears to have sent him into a passion. The last reports say he has slaughtered all in the villages of Tenker and Forei. He is beyond all controlling and I fear for the future of us all. I am amazed that he has not turned on us yet – but perhaps this is his preparation for that final strike.

Sonea sat back in her chair and shook her head in disbelief. She flicked back to the previous page and reread the last entry. Fifty-two magicians, strengthened by their apprentices and the livestock donated by frightened commoners, hadn't been able to defeat Tagin. The next few entries recorded Tagin's seemingly random path through Kyralia. Then came the words Sonea had been dreading:

My worst fears have come to life. Today Tagin killed Lord Gerin, Lord Dirron, Lord Winnel and Lady Ella. Will it end only when all magicians are dead, or will he not be satisfied until all life has been drained from the world? The view from my window is ghastly. Thousands of gorin, enka and reber rot in the fields, their strength given to the defence of Kyralia. Too many to eat . . .

From there the situation grew worse until over half the magicians in the Guild were dead. Another quarter had already taken their belongings and fled. The remainder were making a valiant effort to save stores of books and medicines.

What if this happened now? The Guild was larger but

each magician wielded only a tiny portion of the strength of their long-dead predecessors. If Akkarin did as Tagin had . . . she shivered and continued reading. The next entry caught her by surprise.

It is over. When Alyk told me the news I dared not believe it, but an hour ago I climbed the stairs of the Lookout and saw the truth with my own eyes. It is true. Tagin is dead. Only he could have created such destruction in his final moments.

Lord Eland called us together and read a letter sent from Indria, Tagin's sister. She told of her intention to poison him. We can only assume that she succeeded.

The record-keeper recounted a slow restoration. The magicians who had left returned. The stores and libraries were set in order again. Sonea mused over the long entries covering the common people's losses and recovery. It appeared the Guild had once been concerned for the well-being of ordinary people.

Truly the old Guild was destroyed with Tagin. I have heard some say that a new Guild was born today. The first of the changes occurred this morning when five young men joined us. They are our first 'novices', apprenticed to all and not one. They will not be taught the higher magics until they have proven them-selves trustworthy. If Lord Karron has his way they will never learn them at all.

Support for the ban of what Lord Karron had begun to call 'black' magic increased. Sonea turned a page and found one last entry, followed by blank pages.

I have not the gift of foresight, nor do I pretend to know enough of men and magic to guess the future, but after we made our deci-sion I was gripped by a fear that the Sachakans might rise against us again in the future, and the Guild would be found unpre-pared. I proposed a secret store of knowledge, to be opened only if the Guild faced certain destruction. The others of my company agreed, for many of my fellows held the same secret fear.

It was decided that the existence of a secret weapon would be known of by the Head of Warriors only. He would not know its nature, but would pass the location down to his successor. I now finish this record here. Tomorrow I will begin a new one. I sincerely hope that nobody will ever open this book and read these words.

Below this last entry was a note:

Seventy years later Lord Koril, Head of Warriors, died in a practise bout at the age of twenty-eight. It is likely that he did not have an opportunity to pass on the knowledge of the secret 'weapon'.

Sonea stared at Akkarin's postscript. Lord Coren had discovered a chest full of books. Was this the secret store of knowledge?

She sighed and closed the book. The more she learned, the more questions arose. She got to her feet and swayed, realising belatedly that she had been reading for hours. Yawning, she covered Akkarin's books with her notes, then changed into her bedclothes, slipped into bed and fell into a sleep filled with nightmarish scenes of power-crazed magicians stalking livestock and villagers.

CHAPTER 5

SPECULATION

Though he received news of a murder bearing all the indicators he'd been taught to look for, Cery had waited until a week passed since his meeting with Savara before he let her know she had been right. He wanted to see how long she would endure her self-imposed imprisonment in her hired room. When he heard that she had suggested some fighting practise with one of her 'guards', he knew her patience was running out. And curiosity got the better of him when the man admitted to losing every bout.

He paced his room as he waited for her to arrive. His investigations had revealed little. The owner of the room could only say Savara had started renting it a few days before her visit to Cery. Only two of the city's weapons sellers recognised her knife as Sachakan. The city's gutters all claimed, after bribes and other means of ensuring they told the truth, that they had never fenced a weapon like it before. He doubted he would find anyone in the city who could tell him more.

At a knock on the door he stopped pacing. He returned to his chair and cleared his throat.

'Come in.'

She smiled warmly as she entered the room. *Oh, she knows she's beautiful, and how to use it to get what she wants*, he thought. He kept his expression neutral.

'Ceryni,' she said.

'Savara. I hear my tag gave you some sport.'

A tiny crease appeared between her eyebrows. 'Yes, he was energetic, but needed the practise more than I.' She paused. 'The others might have proved more challenging.'

Cery resisted a smile. She had noticed more than one other watcher. Very observant.

'Too late to find out,' he said, shrugging. 'I have given them something else to do.'

The crease between her brows deepened. 'What of the slave? Did he not kill?'

'"Slave"?' Cery repeated.

'The man who replaced the last murderer.'

Interesting. Slaves owned by who?

'He killed, like you said,' Cery confirmed.

Her eyes flashed with triumph at the news. 'Then will you accept my help?'

'Can you lead us to him?'

'Yes,' she replied without hesitation.

'What do you want in return?'

She moved closer to his desk. 'That you say nothing of me to your master.'

A chill ran over his skin. 'My *master*?'

'The one who has ordered you to kill these men,' she said softly.

She should not know about *him*. She shouldn't even know that Cery was acting on the orders of another.

This changed everything. Cery crossed his arms and considered her carefully. Investigating her usefulness without consulting the one who arranged the hunt had seemed like a small risk. Now it appeared to have been greater than he had thought.

She knew too much. He ought to send his best knife to despatch her. Or kill her himself. Now.

Even as he thought it, he knew he wouldn't. *And it's not just because I find her interesting*, he told himself. *I need to know how she learned so much about the arrangement. I'll wait, have her watched, and see where this leads.*

'Have you told him about me?' she asked.

'Why don't you want him to know about you?'

Her expression darkened. 'Two reasons. These slaves know only one enemy hunts them. It will be easier for me to help you if they do not know I am here. And there are people in my country who would suffer if the slaves' masters learned I was here.'

'And you think that these slaves would find out about you if my "master", as you call him, knew?'

'Perhaps. Perhaps not. I'd rather not take the risk.'

'You are only asking this now. I might have told my customer about you already.'

'Did you?'

He shook his head. She smiled, clearly relieved. 'I didn't think you would. Not until you knew I could do what I said I could. So, do we have a deal, as you Thieves say?'

Cery opened the drawer of his desk and drew out her knife. He heard her indrawn breath. The jewels in the handle glittered in the lamplight. He slid it across the table.

'Tonight you'll tag this man for us. That's all. No killing. I want to be sure he is who you say he is before he's done in. In return, I keep my mug shut about you. For now.'

She smiled, her eyes bright with eagerness. 'I will go back to my room until then.'

Watching her saunter to the door, Cery felt his heartbeat quicken. *How many men have lost their wits over that walk – or that smile?* he wondered. *Ah, but I'd wager some of them lost more than their wits.*

Not me, he thought. *I'll be watching her very closely.*

Sonea closed the book she had been trying to read and looked around the library. It was too difficult to concentrate. Her mind kept returning to Akkarin and the records.

It had been a week since he'd given them to her, and he hadn't yet returned to collect them. The thought of what was lying on her desk in her room, hidden under a pile of notes, was like a itch no amount of scratching could ease. She wouldn't be able to relax until he took them back.

But she dreaded facing Akkarin again. She dreaded the conversation that would follow. Would he bring more books? What would they contain? So far, he had only shown her pieces of forgotten history. There had been no instructions on how to use black magic, yet the secret trunk that the record-keeper had buried – probably the same trunk that the architect Lord Coren had discovered and reburied – must contain enough information about the 'secret weapon' of black magic for a magician to learn it. What would she do if Akkarin gave her one of *those* books to read?

To learn about black magic was to break a Guild law. If she found herself reading instructions on its use, she would stop and refuse to read any more.

'Look, there's Lord Larkin!'

The voice was female and close by. Looking around, Sonea saw a movement at the end of a bookshelf. A girl was just visible, standing by one of the Novices' Library windows.

'The Building and Construction teacher?' another girlish voice replied. 'I never considered him before, but he is fairly good-looking, I suppose.'

'And still unmarried.'

'Not showing much interest in getting married, from what I hear.'

There was a giggle. Leaning out from her chair, Sonea recognised the first girl as one of the fifth-year novices.

'Oh, look! There's Lord Darlen. He's nice.'

The other girl made an appreciative noise. 'Pity he's married.'

'Mmm,' the first agreed. 'What do you think of Lord Vorel?'

'Vorel! You're kidding!'

'Not one for strong Warrior types, are you?'

Sonea guessed the girls were watching magicians heading toward the Night Room. She listened, amused, as they assessed the merits of many of the younger magicians.

'No . . . look there . . . now *that* I wouldn't turn down.'

'Oh, yes,' the other agreed in a hushed voice. 'Look, he's stopped to talk to Director Jerrik.'

'He's a bit . . . cold, though.'

'Oh, I'm sure he could be warmed up.'

The girls laughed slyly. When they had quietened again, one gave a sigh of longing. 'He's so handsome. Pity he's too old for us.'

'I don't know,' the other replied. 'He's not *that* old. My cousin was married off to a man much older. He might not look it, but the High Lord is no more than thirty-three or four.'

Sonea stiffened with surprise and disbelief. They were talking about *Akkarin*!

But, of course, they didn't know what he was like. They saw only an unmarried man who was mysterious, powerful and—

'The library is closing.'

Sonea jumped and turned to find Tya, the librarian, striding along the aisle between the bookshelves. Tya smiled at Sonea as she passed. The girls at the window gave one last sigh and left.

Rising, Sonea stacked up her books and notes. She lifted them in her arms then paused and looked back at the window. Was he still there?

She moved over to the glass and peered out. Sure enough, Akkarin was standing with Jerrik. Lines creased his forehead. Though his expression was attentive, it gave nothing of his thoughts away.

How could those girls find him attractive? she wondered. He was harsh and aloof. Not bright-eyed and warm like Dorrien, or even slickly handsome like Lord Fergun.

If the girls she had overheard hadn't joined the Guild, they would have been married off for the sake of family alliances. Perhaps they still looked for power and influence in men out of habit or long tradition. She smiled grimly.

If they knew the truth, she thought, *they would not find him very attractive at all.*

At midnight, three hours' carriage ride from the lights of Capia, the darkness was heavy and impenetrable. Only the small pools of light cast by the carriage lamps lit their passage down the road. Staring out into the blackness,

Dannyl wondered what the carriage looked like to the occupants of unseen country houses; probably a moving cluster of lights, visible for miles around.

The vehicle crested a rise and a point of brightness appeared beside the road ahead. As they drew rapidly closer, Dannyl saw that it was a lamp, the weak light illuminating the front of a building. The carriage began to slow.

'We're here,' Dannyl murmured.

He heard Tayend shift in his seat to look out the window. The scholar yawned as the carriage drew closer to the building and swayed to a stop. The sign on the resthouse read: 'River Rest: Beds, Meals & Drinks'.

The driver muttered to himself as he clambered down to open the door. Dannyl passed the man a coin.

'Wait for us inside,' he instructed. 'We'll be travelling on in an hour.'

The man bowed, then rapped on the door for them. There was a short pause and a hatch in the middle of the door opened. Dannyl could hear wheezing beyond.

'What can I do for you, my lord?' a muffled voice asked.

'A drink,' Dannyl replied. 'An hour's rest.'

There was no reply, but a metallic clang followed and the door swung inward. A small, wrinkled man bowed, then ushered them into a large room filled with tables and chairs. The heavy, sweet smell of bol hung in the air. Dannyl smiled wistfully as memories of his search for Sonea, so long ago now, returned. It had been a long time since he'd tasted bol.

'Urrend's my name. What you like to drink, then?' the man asked.

Dannyl sighed. 'Do you have any Porreni rumia?'

The man chuckled. 'You got good taste in wine. But

of course you have, two high-born men like yourselves. Got a nice guestroom for rich people upstairs. Follow me.'

The carriage driver had swaggered over to the bench where the bol was served. Dannyl wondered belatedly if he should have given the man the coin — he didn't want to find himself in an upturned carriage halfway to Tayend's sister's home.

They followed the resthouse owner up a narrow flight of stairs into a corridor. He stopped outside a door.

'This is my best room. I hope you find it comfortable.'

He gave a push, and the door opened. Dannyl stepped inside slowly, taking note of the well-worn furniture, the second door, and the man sitting near it.

'Good evening, Ambassador.' The man rose and bowed gracefully. 'I am Royend of Marane.'

'Honoured to meet you,' Dannyl replied. 'I believe you are already acquainted with Tayend of Tremmelin?'

The man nodded. 'Indeed I am. I have ordered some wine. Would you like some?'

'A little, thank you,' Dannyl replied. 'We will be travelling on in an hour.'

Dannyl and Tayend settled into two of the chairs. The Dem strolled around the room, inspecting the furniture and grimacing with distaste, then paused to look out of the windows. He was taller than the average Elyne, and his hair was black. Dannyl had learned from Errend that Dem Marane's grandmother had been Kyralian. He was middle-aged, married, father to two sons and very, very rich.

'So what do you think of Elyne, Ambassador?'

'I have grown to like it here,' Dannyl replied.

'You did not, at first?'

'It was not that I liked or disliked the country. It merely took some time to become used to the differences. Some of them were appealing, some were strange.'

The Dem's brows rose. 'What did you find strange about us?'

Dannyl chuckled. 'Elynes speak their mind, though not often plainly.'

A smile creased the man's face, but it disappeared again at a knock on the door. As he started toward it Dannyl waved a hand and exerted his will. The door swung open. The Dem halted and, as he realised that Dannyl had used magic, a look of hunger and frustrated desire crossed his face. It vanished a moment later as the resthouse owner stepped into the room with a bottle and three wine glasses.

No word was spoken as the bottle was unstoppered and the wine poured. When the resthouse owner left, the Dem picked up a glass and settled into a chair.

'So what do you find appealing about Elyne, then?'

'You have excellent wine.' Dannyl lifted his glass and smiled. 'And your minds are open and accepting. Much is tolerated here that would shock and scandalise Kyralians.'

Royend glanced at Tayend. 'You must be aware of those shocking and scandalous goings on, or you would not list them among the differences you find appealing in us.'

'Would I be a suitable Guild Ambassador if I was oblivious to such matters . . . as the Elyne court believe me to be?'

The Dem smiled, but his eyes remained hard. 'You have already proven yourself to be more well-informed than *I* believed you to be. It makes me wonder. Are you as open-minded and tolerant as we are? Or do you hold the same rigid opinions as other Kyralian magicians?'

Dannyl looked at Tayend. 'I am no typical Kyralian magician.' The scholar smiled crookedly and shook his head. 'Though I have grown adept at pretending I am,' Dannyl continued. 'I think, if my peers knew me better, they would not find me a suitable representative of the Guild at all.'

'Ah,' Tayend interjected quietly, 'but is it that you are unsuited to the Guild, or the Guild is unsuited to you?'

Royend chuckled at the comment. 'Yet they offered you a role as Ambassador.'

Dannyl shrugged. 'And it brought me here. I have often wished that the Guild had been formed in a less rigid culture. Differences in viewpoint stimulate debate, which improves understanding. Recently I have had more reason to wish this were so. Tayend has great potential. It is a great pity he cannot develop it simply because Kyralians do not tolerate men of his nature. There are some things I can teach him, without breaking Guild law, but not nearly enough to do his talents justice.'

The Dem's gaze sharpened. 'Have you?'

'No,' Dannyl shook his head, 'but I'm not averse to bending the Guild rules a little for his benefit. I killed a man once to save Tayend's life. Next time I might not be around to help him. I would like to teach him to Heal, but then a line would have been crossed, and I might place him in even greater danger.'

'From the Guild?'

'Yes.'

The Dem smiled. 'Only if they found out. It is a risk, but is it worth taking?'

Dannyl frowned. 'I would not take a risk like that without first planning for the worst. If it should ever be discovered that Tayend has learned magic, he must be able to evade the Guild. He has nobody to turn to but his family and his friends in the library – and I fear they could do little.'

'What about you?'

'There is nothing that frightens the Guild more than a fully trained magician turned rogue. If I disappeared, they would be much more determined to find us both. I would stay in Capia, and do what I could to help Tayend avoid capture.'

'It sounds as if you need others to protect him. People who know how to hide a fugitive.'

Dannyl nodded.

'And what would you be prepared to give in return?'

Narrowing his eyes, Dannyl regarded the man. 'Nothing that could be used to harm others. Not even the Guild. I know Tayend. I would be sure of the intentions of others before I trusted them as I trust him.'

The Dem nodded slowly. 'Of course.'

'So,' Dannyl continued, 'what do you think Tayend's protection would cost?'

Dem Marane picked up the bottle and refilled his glass. 'I can't say for sure. It is an interesting question. I would have to ask some colleagues of mine.'

'Of course,' Dannyl said smoothly. He stood and looked down at the man. 'I look forward to hearing their opinions. I'm afraid we must depart now. Tayend's family is expecting us.'

The Dem stood up and bowed. 'I have enjoyed our conversation, Ambassador Dannyl, Tayend of Tremmelin. I hope we have many more opportunities to further our acquaintance in the future.'

Dannyl inclined his head politely. He paused and passed a hand over the Dem's glass, warming the wine with a little magical heat. Smiling at the Dem's quick intake of breath, he turned away and walked to the door, Tayend following.

As they stepped into the corridor Dannyl looked back. The Dem was holding his glass cupped in both hands, his expression thoughtful.

CHAPTER 6

THE SPY

As always the door to the High Lord's Residence opened at the slightest touch. Stepping inside, Sonea was relieved and surprised to find only Takan waiting for her. He bowed.

'The High Lord wishes to speak to you, my lady.'

Anxiety replaced relief. Was he going to give her another book to read? Would this be the book she dreaded: the one containing information about black magic?

Sonea took a deep breath. 'Then you'd better take me to him.'

'This way,' he said. He turned and started toward the right-hand stairway.

Sonea felt her heart skip a beat. That stairway led down to the underground room where Akkarin performed his secret, forbidden magic. It also, like the left-hand stairway, led up to the top floor, where the library and banquet room lay.

She followed Takan to the door. The stairwell was dark, and she could not see which way he had chosen until she created a globe light.

He was descending to the underground room.

She stopped, her heart racing, and watched him continue down. At the door to the room below, he halted and looked up at her.

'He will not harm you, my lady,' he assured her. Opening the door, he gestured for her to enter.

She stared at him. Of all places in the Guild – in the whole city – this was the one she most feared. She glanced back at the guestroom. *I could run. It's not far to the guestroom door . . .*

'Come here, Sonea.'

The voice was Akkarin's. It was full of command, and a warning. She thought of Rothen, her aunt Jonna and uncle Ranel and her cousins; their safety depended on her cooperation. She forced herself to move.

Takan stepped aside as she reached the doorway. The underground room looked much as it had the previous times she had seen inside it. Two old, heavy tables had been placed against the left-hand wall. A lantern and a dark bundle of cloth lay on the closest table. Bookcases and cupboards stood against the other walls. Some showed signs of repair, reminding her of the damage the 'assassin' had done. In one corner was an old battered chest. Was this the chest that had contained the books on black magic?

'Good evening, Sonea.'

Akkarin was leaning back against a table, his arms crossed. She bowed. 'High L—'

She blinked in surprise as she realised he was wearing simple, roughly woven clothing. His trousers and coat were shabby, even threadbare in places.

'I have something to show you,' he told her. 'In the city.'

She took a step back, instantly wary. 'What?'

'If I told you, you wouldn't believe me. The only way for you to know the truth is for you to see it for yourself.'

She read a challenge in his eyes. Looking at his plain

clothes, she recalled him wearing similar ones, covered in blood.

'I'm not sure I want to see your truth.'

His mouth curled up at one corner. 'You've wondered why I do what I do since you first learned of it. Though I will not show you the *how*, I can show you the *why*. Someone should know, other than Takan and myself.'

'Why me?'

'That will become clear, in time.' He reached behind and picked up the dark bundle from the table. 'Put this on.'

I should refuse to go, she thought. *But will he let me?* She stared at the bundle in his hands. *And if I go, I might learn something that can be used against him later.*

And what if he shows me something forbidden? Something that will get me thrown out of the Guild?

If it comes to that, I'll tell them the truth. I took the risk in the hope of saving myself, and the Guild.

She forced herself to approach him and take the bundle. As he let go, it unrolled and she found herself holding a long, black cloak. Taking hold of the clasp, she swung the garment around her shoulders and fastened it.

'Keep your robes well covered,' he instructed. He picked up the lantern and strode toward a wall. A section slid aside, and the chill air of the underground tunnels spilled into the room.

Of course, she thought. She remembered the nights she had spent exploring the passages under the Guild, until Akkarin found her and ordered her out. She had followed one to this room. The shock of finding herself on the threshold of his secret domain had sent her hurrying away, and she had never returned to explore further along the passage.

It must lead to the city, if what Akkarin says is true.

Akkarin entered the passage, turned and beckoned to her. Sonea took a deep breath and let it out slowly. Walking to the opening, she followed him into darkness.

The lantern wick spluttered and a flame appeared. She wondered briefly why he bothered with an ordinary light source, then realised that, if he wasn't wearing robes, he intended to remain disguised as a non-magician. No non-magician would be following a globe light.

If it's important that nobody recognises him, then I have something I can use against him tonight, if I need to.

As she expected, he led off in the opposite direction to the University. He continued for over two hundred strides, then slowed to a stop. She sensed the vibration of a barrier blocking the way. A faint ripple of light flashed across the passage as the barrier dissipated. He continued on without speaking a word.

He stopped three more times to dismantle barriers. After they had passed the fourth, Akkarin turned and recreated it behind them. Sonea looked back. If she had dared to continue past Akkarin's underground room during her previous exploration, she would have encountered these barriers.

The passage curved slightly to the right. Side passages appeared. Akkarin turned into one without hesitation, and their path twisted through several crumbling rooms. When he stopped again they faced a fall of rocks and earth where the roof had caved in. She looked at him questioningly.

His eyes glittered in the lamplight. He stared at the blockage intently. A dry scraping sound filled the passage as stones crumpled inward to form rough stairs. A hole appeared at the top. Akkarin set his foot on the first tread and began to climb.

Sonea followed. At the top was another passage. The lamplight revealed rough walls made from a patchy mixture of small low-quality bricks. The air smelt damp and familiar. This place reminded her strongly of . . . of . . .

The Thieves' Road.

They had entered the tunnels under the city used by the criminal underworld. Akkarin turned and gazed back down the stairs. The treads slid forward to block the stairwell. Once they were in place, he started down the passage.

Questions began crowding Sonea's thoughts. Did the Thieves know that the High Lord of the Magicians' Guild used their passages, and that there were tunnels under the Guild that connected with their own? She knew they guarded their domain carefully, so she doubted he had avoided their notice. Had he gained their permission to use the road, then? She considered his rough clothing. Perhaps he had gained it using a false identity.

Several hundred paces on, a thin man with bleary eyes stepped out from an alcove and nodded to Akkarin. He paused to stare at Sonea, obviously surprised at her presence, but said nothing. Turning away, he started down the passage before them.

Their silent guide set a rapid pace, taking them on a long journey through a twisting, complex labyrinth of passages. Slowly Sonea became aware of an odour she knew but could not put a name to. It changed as much as the walls, but something about the changeability of the smell was also familiar. It wasn't until Akkarin stopped and rapped on a door that Sonea realised what she was smelling.

It was the slums. The smell was a mix of human and animal waste, sweat, garbage, smoke and bol. Sonea swayed as memories rushed over her: of working with her aunt and uncle, of sneaking out to join Cery and the gang of street urchins they hung about with.

Then the door opened and she returned to the present.

A large man filled the doorway, his rough shirt stretched over a broad chest. He nodded respectfully at Akkarin, then, as he looked at her, he frowned as if he recognised her face but wasn't sure why. After a moment he shrugged and stepped aside.

'Come in.'

Sonea followed Akkarin into a tiny room, barely large enough to fit the three of them and a narrow cupboard. On the opposite side was a heavy door. Sonea detected a vibration about it and realised it was strengthened by a strong magical barrier. Her skin prickled. What, in the slums, could possibly need such a potent binding?

The man turned to regard Akkarin. From his hesitant and anxious manner, Sonea guessed he knew who his visitor was – or at least enough to know he was facing someone important and powerful.

'He's awake,' he rumbled, casting a fearful look at the door.

'Thank you for watching him, Morren,' Akkarin said smoothly.

'No rub.'

'Did you find a red gem on him?'

'No. Searched him good. Found nothing.'

Akkarin frowned. 'Very well. Stay here. This is Sonea. I will send her out in a while.'

Morren's eyes snapped to hers.

'*The* Sonea?'

'Yes, the living, breathing legend,' Akkarin replied dryly.

Morren smiled at her. 'Honoured to meet you, my lady.'

'Honoured to meet you, Morren,' she replied, bemusement overcoming her anxiety for a moment. Living, breathing *legend*?

Taking a key from his pocket, Morren inserted it in the door's lock and twisted. He stepped back, allowing Akkarin to approach. Sonea blinked as she sensed magic surround her. Akkarin had created a shield about them both. She peered around his shoulder, tense with curiosity. Slowly the door swung outward.

The room beyond was small. A stone bench was the only furniture. On the bench lay a man, his legs and arms manacled.

As the man saw Akkarin his eyes filled with terror. He began to struggle weakly. Sonea stared at him in dismay. He was young, probably not much older than her. His face was broad and his skin a sickly brown. His thin arms were covered in scars, and a fresh cut fringed in dried blood ran down one forearm. He did not look as if he could harm anything.

Akkarin moved to the man's side, then placed a hand on his forehead. The captive's eyes widened. Sonea shivered as she realised Akkarin was reading the man's mind.

His hand shifted abruptly and he grasped the captive's jaw. At once the man closed his mouth tightly and began to struggle. Akkarin prised open the man's mouth. Sonea caught a glimpse of gold, then Akkarin tossed something on the floor.

A gold tooth. Sonea took a step backward, appalled, then jumped as the man began to laugh.

'They have stheen your woman now,' he said in a thickly accented voice, hampered by the missing tooth. 'Kariko sthays sthee will be histh after he killsth you.'

Akkarin smiled and glanced at her. 'What a pity neither you or I will be alive to see him try that.'

He lifted a foot and stamped on the tooth. To Sonea's surprise, it crunched under his boot. When he stepped away, she was surprised to see that the gold had split, and tiny fragments of red littered the floor.

Sonea frowned at the twisted lump that had been the tooth, trying to make sense of the exchange. What had the man meant? *'They have seen your woman.'* Who were 'they'. How could they have seen her? Clearly it had something to do with the tooth. Why put a gem inside a tooth? And it obviously wasn't a gem. It looked as if it had been glass. As she considered the fragments, she remembered that Akkarin had asked if Morren had found a red gem. The famous murderer wore a ring with a red gem. And Lorlen.

She looked at the captive. He was completely limp now. He stared at Akkarin fearfully.

'Sonea.'

She looked at Akkarin. His eyes were cold and steady.

'I have brought you here to answer some of your questions,' he told her. 'I know you will not believe me unless you see the truth for yourself, so I have decided to teach you something that I never intended to teach anyone. It is a skill that can too easily be abused, but if you—'

'No!' She straightened her back. 'I will not learn—'

'I do not mean black magic.' Akkarin's eyes flashed. 'I would not teach you that, even if you were willing. I wish to teach you how to read minds.'

'But . . .' She drew in a quick breath as she realised what he meant. He, of all the magicians in the Guild, was able to read another person's mind whether they were willing or not. She had experienced his mind-reading skills herself, when he had first discovered that she, Lorlen and Rothen knew that he practised black magic.

And now he wanted to teach her how to do it.

'Why?' she blurted out.

'As I said, I want you to know the truth for yourself. You would not believe me if I told you.' His eyes narrowed. 'I would not trust you with this secret if I did not know you have a strong sense of honour and morality. Even so, you must vow never to use this method of mind-reading on an unwilling recipient unless Kyralia is in great danger, and there is no other course of action.'

Sonea swallowed hard and kept her gaze steady. 'You expect me to restrict my use of it as you say, when you have not yourself?'

His eyes darkened, but his mouth widened into a humourless smile. 'Yes. Will you make the vow, or shall we return to the Guild now?'

She looked at the captive. Obviously Akkarin intended for her to read this man's mind. He would not have her do it if what she saw would endanger him. But would she see anything that would endanger herself?

It was impossible for the mind to lie. Conceal the truth, perhaps, but that was difficult – and impossible with Akkarin's mind-reading method. If he had arranged for this man to believe certain lies were truth, however, she could still be deceived.

But if she kept that in mind and carefully considered all she learned . . .

Knowing how to read minds could be a useful skill. Even if she did make this vow, it would not stop her using it in the fight against him. Kyralia was already in great danger just by having a black magician at the heart of the Magicians' Guild.

The captive stared back at her.

'You would have me vow never to read a mind unless Kyralia was in danger,' she said. 'Yet you want me to read his. Surely he is not a threat to Kyralia.'

Akkarin smiled. He seemed pleased by her question. 'He isn't now. But he was. And his claims that his master will enslave you after he kills me should prove there is a possible future threat. How can you know whether his master is capable of it, if you do not read his mind?'

'With that reasoning, you could justify reading the mind of anyone who made a threat.'

His smile broadened. 'Which is why I require you to make that vow. You will not use this skill unless there is no other choice.' His expression became serious. 'There is no other way I can show you the truth – not without putting your life at risk. Will you make the vow?'

She hesitated, then nodded. He crossed his arms and waited. She took a deep breath.

'I vow never to read the mind of an unwilling person unless Kyralia is in great danger and there is no other way of avoiding that danger.'

He nodded. 'Good. If I ever discover that you have broken that vow, I will ensure you regret it.' He turned to regard the captive. The man had been watching them closely.

'Will you let me go now?' the man said, his voice pleading. 'You know I had to do what I did. They made me. Now the sthtone is gone, they can't find me. I won't—'

'Silence.'

The man cringed at the command, then whimpered as Akkarin crouched beside him.

'Put your hand on his forehead.'

Sonea pushed aside her reluctance and squatted beside the captive. She rested a hand on his forehead. Her heart skipped as Akkarin pressed his hand over hers. His touch was cool at first, but quickly warmed.

—*I will show you how to read him, but once you have the skill of it, I will let you explore as you wish.*

She felt his presence at the edge of her thoughts. Closing her eyes, she visualised her mind as a room, as Rothen had taught her. She took a step toward the doors, intending to open them to greet him, then jumped back in surprise as Akkarin appeared within the room. He waved a hand at the walls.

—Forget this. Forget everything you have been taught. Visualisation slows and restricts your mind. Using it, you will only understand what you can translate into images.

The room disintegrated around her. So did the image of him. But the sense of his presence remained. Before, when he had read her mind, she had sensed little presence at all. Now she detected a hint of personality and a power that was stronger than anything she had encountered before.

—*Follow me . . .*

His presence moved away. Pursuing it, she sensed herself drawing close to a third mind. Fear emanated from this mind, and she encountered resistance.

—*He can stop you only if he can sense you. To prevent him sensing you, put aside all will and intent except for the single purpose of easing into his mind without disturbing it. Like this . . .*

To her amazement, Akkarin's presence *changed*. Instead of exerting his will on the man's mind, he seemed to give up. Only the faintest presence remained, a vague desire to drift into another's thoughts. Then his presence strengthened again.

—*Now you.*

She had a lingering sense of what he had done. It had seemed easy, yet every time she tried to emulate him she bumped up against the captive's mind. Then she felt Akkarin's mind drift into hers. Before she could feel any alarm, he sent something – a concept – into hers. Instead of trying to separate and lose all the intentions but one, she should concentrate only on the one needed.

Suddenly she knew exactly how to slip past the captive's resistance. In less than a heartbeat she had drifted into his mind.

—*Good. Now keep that light touch. Watch his thoughts. When you see a memory you wish to explore, exert your will on his mind. This is more difficult. Watch me.*

The man was thinking about the tooth, wondering if his master had been watching when the girl had appeared.

—*Who are you?* Akkarin asked.

—*Tavaka.*

Abruptly, Sonea became aware that he had been a slave, until recently.

—*Who is your master?*

—*Harikava. A powerful Ichani.* A face, distinctly Sachakan, flashed through his mind. It was a cruel face, hard and clever.

—*What are the Ichani?*

—*Powerful magicians.*

—*Why do they keep slaves?*

—For magic.

A multi-layered memory flashed through Sonea's mind. She had the impression of countless memories of the same incident: the slight pain of a shallow cut, the drawing of power . . .

The Ichani, she understood suddenly, used black magic to draw power from their slaves, constantly strengthening themselves.

—No more! I am a slave no longer. Harikava freed me.

—Show me.

The memory flashed through Tavaka's mind. Harikava sat in a tent. He spoke, saying that he would free Tavaka if he undertook a dangerous mission. Sonea sensed Akkarin take control of the memory. The mission was to enter Kyralia and find out if Kariko's words were true. Was the Guild weak? Had it spurned the use of greater magic? Many slaves had failed. If he succeeded, he would be accepted among the Ichani. If he did not, they would hunt him down.

Harikava opened a wooden box trimmed in gold and gems. Taking out a sliver of something clear and hard, he tossed it in the air. It floated there, slowly melting before Tavaka's gaze. Harikava reached to his belt and drew an elaborate curved dagger with a jewelled handle. Sonea recognised the shape. It was similar to the one she had seen Akkarin use on Takan, so long ago.

Cutting his hand, Harikava dripped blood over the molten globule. It turned red and solidified. Taking off a thin band of gold from many that ringed his fingers, he moulded it around the gem so that a tiny red glint was all that could be seen. She understood what this gem would do. Every sight, every sound, and every thought he had would be sensed by his master.

The man's eyes rose to meet Tavaka's. She felt an echo of the slave's fear and hope. The master beckoned and, with his bleeding hand, reached for his knife again.

The memory ended abruptly.

—*Now you try, Sonea.*

For a moment she considered what image to prompt the man with. On impulse, she sent a memory of Akkarin in black robes.

She was not prepared for the hatred and fear that filled the man's mind. Glimpses of a recent magical battle followed. Akkarin had found him before he could strengthen himself enough. Harikava would be disappointed and angry. Kariko would be too. An image of several men and woman sitting in a circle around a fire appeared: a memory Tavaka did not want her to see. He forced it away with the skill of someone well practised in hiding memories from searching minds. She realised she had forgotten to grasp for control of it.

—*Try again. You must catch the memory and protect it.*

She sent Tavaka an image of the circle of strangers as she remembered it. The faces were wrong, he thought. The face of Harikava appeared in his mind. Exerting her will, she 'caught' the memory and blocked his efforts to stop it.

—*That's right. Now explore as you wish.*

She examined the faces carefully.

—*Who are these Ichani?*

Names and faces followed, but one stood out.

—*Kariko. The man who wants to kill Akkarin.*

—*Why?*

—*Akkarin killed his brother. Any slave that turns on his master must be hunted down and punished.*

She almost lost control of his memory at that. Akkarin had been a *slave*! Tavaka must have sensed her surprise. She sensed a wave of savage glee.

—*Because of Akkarin, because Kariko's brother captured Akkarin and read his mind, we know the Guild is weak. Kariko says the Guild does not use the greater magics. He says we will invade Kyralia and defeat the Guild easily. It will be a fine revenge for what the Guild did to us after the war.*

Sonea's blood turned cold. This group of immensely strong black magicians intended to invade Kyralia!

—*When will this invasion be?* Akkarin asked suddenly.

Doubts entered the man's mind.

—*Don't know. Others are afraid of the Guild. No slaves return. Neither will I . . . I don't want to die!*

Abruptly a small white house appeared, accompanied by a terrible guilt. A plump woman – Tavaka's mother. A wiry father with leathery skin. A pretty girl with large eyes – his sister. His sister's body after Harikava came and—

It took all Sonea's control to resist fleeing the man's mind. She had heard and seen the aftermath of some cruel attacks by thugs while she had lived in the slums. Tavaka's family had died because of him. His parents might produce more gifted offspring. The sister might develop powers, too. The Ichani master did not want to cart the entire group around with him just in case, and he would not leave any potential sources of power around for his enemies to find and use.

Pity and fear warred within her. Tavaka had lived a dreadful life. Yet she also sensed his ambition. Given the opportunity, he would return to his homeland to become one of these monstrous Ichani.

—What have you done since entering Imardin? Akkarin asked.

Memories of a shabby bedroom in a bolhouse followed, then the crowded drinking room. Sitting in a place where he might briefly touch others, and search for magical potential. No sense in wasting time stalking a victim, unless he or she had strong latent magic. If he was careful, he would grow strong enough to defeat Akkarin. Then he would return to Sachaka, help Kariko gather the Ichani, and they would invade Kyralia.

A man was chosen and followed. A knife, a gift from Harikava, drawn and—

—Time to leave, Sonea.

She felt Akkarin's hand tighten over hers. As he pulled it away from Tavaka's forehead, the man's mind slipped immediately from her own. She frowned at Akkarin as suspicions rose.

'Why did I do that?' He smiled grimly. 'You were about to learn what you don't wish to learn.' He rose and looked down at Tavaka. The man was breathing quickly.

'Leave us, Sonea.'

She stared at Akkarin. It was not hard to guess what he intended to do. She wanted to protest, and yet she knew that she would not stop him even if she could. To release Tavaka would be to set loose a killer. He would continue preying on Kyralians. With black magic.

She forced herself to turn away, open the door and step out of the room. The door swung shut behind her. Morren looked up, and his expression softened. He held out a mug.

Recognising the sweet smell of bol, she accepted the mug and took several gulps. A warmth began to spread through her. When she had finished the drink, she handed the mug back to Morren.

'Better?'

She nodded.

The door clicked open behind her. She turned to face Akkarin. They regarded each other in silence. She thought of what he had revealed to her. The Ichani. Their plans to invade Kyralia. That he had been a slave . . . too elaborate to be a deception. Akkarin could not have arranged this.

'You have much to think about,' he said softly. 'Come. We will return to the Guild.' He stepped past her. 'Thank you, Morren. Dispose of him in the usual way.'

'Yes, my lord. Did you find out anything useful?'

'Perhaps.' Akkarin glanced back at Sonea. 'We shall see.'

'They're coming more often now, aren't they?' Morren asked.

Sonea caught the slightest hesitation in Akkarin's reply.

'Yes, but your employer is also locating them faster. Pass on my thanks, will you?'

The man nodded and handed Akkarin his lantern. 'I will.'

Akkarin opened the door and stepped through. As he started down the passage, Sonea followed, her mind still reeling from all that she had learned.

CHAPTER 7

AKKARIN'S STORY

The sound of metal striking metal echoed down the passage, followed by a gasp of pain. Cery stopped and looked at Gol in alarm. The big man frowned.

Cery jerked his head at the doorway ahead. Taking a long, wicked-looking knife from his belt, Gol hurried forward. He reached the door and peered into the room. His frown disappeared.

He glanced at Cery and grinned. Relieved, and now more curious than concerned, Cery strode forward and looked inside.

Two figures were frozen in position, one crouched awkwardly with a knife held at his throat. Cery recognised the loser as Krinn, the assassin and skilled fighter he usually hired for more important assignments. Krinn's eyes flickered toward Cery. His expression changed from surprise to embarrassment.

'Yield?' Savara asked.

'Yes,' Krinn replied in a strained voice.

Savara withdrew the knife and stepped away in one fluid movement. Krinn rose and looked down at her warily. He was at least a head taller than her, Cery noted with amusement.

'Practising on my men again, Savara?'

She smiled slyly. 'Only on invitation, Ceryni.'

He considered her carefully. What if he . . . ? There would be some risk, but there always was. He glanced at Krinn, who was edging toward the door.

'Go on, Krinn. Close the door behind you.' The assassin hurried away. When the door had shut, Cery stepped toward Savara. 'I invite you to try me out.'

He heard Gol's indrawn breath.

Her smile broadened. 'I accept.'

Cery drew a pair of daggers out of his coat. Leather loops had been attached to the handles to prevent them slipping out of his grasp, and to allow him to grab and pull. Her eyebrows rose as he slipped his palms through the loops.

'Two are hardly ever better than one,' she commented.

'I know,' Cery replied as he approached her.

'But you do *look* like you know what you are doing,' she mused. 'I expect that would intimidate the average lout.'

'Yes, it does.'

She took a few steps to the left, drawing a little closer. 'I'm not the average lout, Ceryni.'

'No. I can see that.'

He smiled. If her reason for offering to help him was to gain his trust long enough to get a chance to kill him, he was probably handing her the perfect opportunity. She would die for it, however. Gol would ensure that.

She darted toward him. He dodged out of reach, then stepped in and aimed for her shoulder. She spun away.

They continued like this for a few minutes, each testing the reflexes and reach of the other. Then she came closer and he blocked and returned several quick attacks. Neither quite managed to get past the other's guard. They stepped away from each other, both breathing heavily.

'What have you done about the slave?' she asked.

'He's dead.'

He watched her face closely. She did not look surprised, only a little annoyed. '*He* did it?'

'Of course.'

'I could have done it for you.'

He frowned. She sounded so confident. Too confident.

She darted forward, blade flashing in the lamplight. Cery slapped her arm away with his forearm. A fast and frantic struggle followed, and he grinned with triumph as he managed to lock her right arm out of the way, and slip his knife into her left armpit.

She froze, also grinning.

'Yield?' she asked.

A sharp point pressed into his stomach. Looking down, he saw a different knife in her left hand. The other still held her original knife. He smiled, then pressed his knife a little harder into her armpit.

'There's a vein here that goes straight to the heart. If cut, it would bleed so fast you wouldn't live long enough to decide how to curse me.'

He was gratified to see her eyes widen in surprise and her grin disappear. 'Stalemate, then?'

They were very close. She smelt wonderful, a mixture of fresh sweat and something spicy. Her eyes sparkled with amusement, but her mouth was a tightly held thin line.

'Stalemate,' he agreed. He stepped back and to one side so that her blade left his stomach before he removed his from her armpit. His heart was beating quickly. It was not an unpleasant sensation.

'You know these slaves are magicians?' he asked.

'Yes.'

'How do you plan to kill them?'

'I have my own ways.'

Cery smiled grimly. 'If I tell my customer that I don't need him to do in the murderers, he's going to ask some rough questions. Like, who's doing it instead?'

'If he did not know you found a slave, he would not need to know who did the killing.'

'But he knows when they're about. He's got the guard telling him about the victims. If they stop finding victims, without him killing the murderer, he's got to wonder why.'

She shrugged. 'That will not matter. They are not sending slaves one by one now. I can kill some of them, and he will not notice.'

This was news. Bad news. 'Who are "they"?'

Her eyebrows rose. 'He has not told you?'

Cery smiled, while silently cursing himself for revealing his ignorance. 'Perhaps he has, perhaps he hasn't,' he replied. 'I want to hear what you say.'

Her expression darkened. 'They are the Ichani. Outcasts. The Sachakan King sends those who have earned his disfavour out into the wastes.'

'Why are they sending their slaves here?'

'They seek to regain power and status by defeating Sachaka's old enemy, the Guild.'

This was also news. He slipped the loops of his knives from his palms. *Probably nothing to worry about*, he thought. *We're killing off these 'slaves' easily enough.*

'Will you let me kill some of these slaves?' she asked.

'Why do you need to ask? If you can find and kill them, you don't need to work with me.'

'Ah, but if I did not, you might mistake me for one of them.'

He chuckled. 'That could be unfort—'

A knock interrupted him. He looked at Gol expectantly. The big man moved to the door. An even larger man entered, his eyes flitting nervously from Gol to Cery to Savara.

'Morren.' Cery frowned. The man had sent the usual one-word message late last night to confirm that he had disposed of the murderer's body. He was not supposed to visit Cery personally unless he had something important to report.

'Ceryni,' Morren replied. He glanced at Savara again, his expression wary.

Cery turned to the Sachakan woman. 'Thanks for the practise,' he said.

She nodded. 'Thank *you*, Ceryni. I will let you know when I find the next one. It should not be long.'

Cery watched her walk out of the room. When the door closed behind her, he turned to Morren.

'What is it?'

The big man grimaced. 'It may be nothing, but I thought you might want to know. He didn't kill the murderer straightaway. He tied him up, then left. When he came back, he brought someone with him.'

'Who?'

'The girl from the slums who joined the Guild.'

Cery stared at the man. 'Sonea?'

'Yeah.'

An unexpected feeling of guilt stole over Cery. He thought of the way Savara had sent his heart racing. How could he let himself admire some strange woman, and one who probably couldn't be trusted, when he still loved Sonea? But Sonea was beyond his reach. And she had never loved him anyway. Not in the way he had loved her. Why shouldn't he consider another?

Then the implications of what Morren was saying sank in, and he began pacing the room. Sonea had been taken to see the murderer. She had been brought into the presence of a dangerous man. Though he knew she had probably been safe enough with Akkarin, he still felt a protective anger. He did not want her involved in this.

But had she been aware, all along, of the secret battle taking place in the darkest parts of Imardin? Was she being readied to join the fight?

He had to know. Turning on his heel, he strode toward the door.

'Gol. Send the High Lord a message. We need to talk.'

Lorlen stepped into the Entrance Hall of the University and stopped as he saw Akkarin pass between the enormous doors.

'Lorlen,' Akkarin said, 'are you busy?'

'I'm always busy,' Lorlen replied.

Akkarin's mouth curled into a wry smile. 'This should take only a few minutes.'

'Very well.'

Akkarin gestured toward Lorlen's office. *Something private, then*, Lorlen mused. He moved out of the Hall back into the corridor, but was only a few steps away from his office when a voice called out.

'High Lord.'

An Alchemist stood just outside the door of a classroom further down the corridor.

Akkarin stopped. 'Yes, Lord Halvin?'

The teacher hurried forward. 'Sonea has not appeared for class this morning. Is she unwell?'

Lorlen saw a look of concern cross Akkarin's face, but he could not tell if it was for Sonea's wellbeing, or that she was not where she was supposed to be.

'Her servant has not informed me of any sickness,' Akkarin replied.

'I'm sure there is a good reason. I just thought it unusual. She is normally so punctual.' Halvin glanced back at the classroom he had left. 'I'd best get back, before they turn into wild animals.'

'Thank you for informing me,' Akkarin said. Halvin nodded again, then hurried away. Akkarin turned to regard Lorlen. 'This other issue will have to wait. I had best find out what my novice is up to.'

Watching him stalk away, Lorlen struggled to hold back a growing feeling of foreboding. Surely if she was sick her servant would have informed Akkarin. Why would she deliberately neglect to attend classes? His blood turned cold. Had she and Rothen decided to move against Akkarin? Surely, if they had, they would have told him first.

Wouldn't they?

Returning to the Entrance Hall, he looked up the stairs. If they had planned something together, they would both be missing. He had only to check Rothen's classroom.

Moving to the stairs, he hurried upwards.

The noon sun streaked through the forest, touching the bright green of new leaves. Its warmth still radiated from the large rock shelf Sonea was sitting on, and lingered in the boulder she had set her back against.

In the distance a gong sounded. Novices would be hurrying out to enjoy the early autumn weather. She should go back, and pretend her absence was due to a sudden headache or other minor illness.

But she couldn't get herself to move.

She had climbed up to the spring in the early morning, hoping that the walk would clear her head. It hadn't, though. All that she had learned kept turning through her mind in a jumbled mess. Perhaps this was because she hadn't slept at all. She was too weary to make sense of everything – and too tired to face returning to classes and behaving as if nothing had changed.

But everything has changed. I have to take time to think about what I have learned, she told herself. *I have to sort out what it means before I face Akkarin again.*

She closed her eyes and drew on a little Healing power to chase away the weariness.

What have I learned?

The Guild, and all of Kyralia, were in danger of being invaded by Sachakan black magicians.

Why hadn't Akkarin told anyone? If the Guild knew it faced a possible invasion, it could prepare for it. It couldn't defend itself if it didn't know of the threat.

Yet, if Akkarin told them, he would have to admit to learning black magic. Was the reason for his silence as simple and selfish as that? Maybe there was another reason.

She still didn't know how he had learned to use black magic. Tavaka had believed that only Ichani possessed that knowledge. He had only been taught it so that he could kill Akkarin.

And Akkarin had been a slave.

It was impossible to imagine the aloof, dignified, powerful High Lord living as, of all things, a *slave*.

But he had been one, of that she was sure. He had

escaped somehow and returned to Kyralia. He had become High Lord. Now he was secretly and single-handedly keeping these Ichani at bay by killing off their spies.

He was not the person she had thought he was.

He might even be a good person.

She frowned. *Let's not go that far. He learned black magic somehow, and I'm still a hostage.*

Without black magic, however, how could he defeat these spies? And if there was a good reason for keeping all this a secret, he'd had no choice but to ensure she, Rothen and Lorlen remained silent.

'Sonea.'

She jumped, then turned toward the voice. Akkarin stood in the shadow of a large tree, his arms crossed. She rose hastily and bowed.

'High Lord.'

He stood regarding her for a moment, then he uncrossed his arms and started toward her. As he stepped up onto the rock shelf, his gaze shifted to the boulder she had been resting against. He dropped into a crouch and examined its surface carefully. She heard the scrape of stone against stone and blinked in surprise as a section slid outward, revealing an irregularly shaped hole.

'Ah, it's still here,' he said quietly. Putting down the slab of rock that he had removed, he reached inside the hole and drew out a small, battered wooden box. Several holes had been drilled into the lid in grid pattern. The lid sprang open. He tilted the box so Sonea could see the contents clearly.

Inside lay a set of game pieces, each with a small peg to fit into the holes in the lid.

'Lorlen and I used to come here to escape Lord Margen's

lessons.' He plucked out one of the pieces and examined it.

Sonea blinked in surprise. 'Lord Margen? Rothen's mentor?'

'Yes. He was a strict teacher. We called him "the monster". Rothen took over his classes the year after I graduated.'

It was as hard to picture Akkarin as a young novice as it was to imagine him as a slave. She knew he was only a few years older than Dannyl, yet Dannyl seemed much younger. It was not that Akkarin *looked* older, she mused, it was simply his manner and position that added an impression of greater maturity.

Replacing the game pieces, Akkarin closed the box and returned it to its hiding place. He sat down, bracing his back against the boulder. Sonea felt a strange discomfort. Gone was the dignified, threatening High Lord who had taken her guardianship from Rothen to ensure his crimes remained undiscovered. She wasn't sure how to react to this casualness. Sitting down a few steps away, she watched him looking around the spring as if checking that it was still the same as he remembered.

'I was not much older than you when I left the Guild,' he said. 'I was twenty, and I'd chosen the Warrior Skills discipline out of a hunger for challenge and excitement. But there was no adventure to be found here in the Guild. I had to escape it for a while. So I decided to write a book on ancient magic as an excuse to travel and see the world.'

She stared at him in surprise. His gaze had become distant, as if he were seeing an old memory rather than the trees around the spring. It seemed he intended to tell her his story.

'During my research I found some strange references to

old magic that intrigued me. Those references led me into Sachaka.' He shook his head. 'If I'd kept to the main road, I might have been safe. The occasional Kyralian trader enters Sachaka in search of exotic goods. The King sends diplomats there every few years, in the company of magicians. But Sachaka is a big country, and a secretive one. The Guild knows there are magicians there, but understands little about them.

'I entered from Elyne, however. Straight into the wastes. I was there for a month before I encountered one of the Ichani. I saw tents and animals and thought to introduce myself to this wealthy and important traveller. He welcomed me warmly enough, and introduced himself as Dakova. I sensed that he was a magician and was intrigued. He pointed at my robes and asked if I was of the Guild. I said I was.'

Akkarin paused. 'I thought that, being one of the strongest magicians of the Guild, I would be able to defend myself against anything. The Sachakans I'd encountered were poor farmers, frightened by visitors. I should have taken that as a warning. When Dakova attacked me I was surprised. I asked if I had offended him, but he didn't reply. His strikes were incredibly powerful and I barely had time to realise I was going to lose before I neared the end of my strength. I told him that stronger magicians would come looking for me if I did not return to the Guild. That must have worried him. He stopped. I was so exhausted, I could barely stand and I thought that was the reason he managed to read my mind so effectively. For a few days, I thought I'd betrayed the Guild. But later, when I spoke to Dakova's slaves, I learned that the Ichani were able to get past the mind's barriers at any time.'

As he paused, Sonea held her breath. Would he relate to her what it had been like to be a slave? She felt a mingled dread and anticipation.

Akkarin looked down at the pool below them. 'Dakova learned from my mind that the Guild had banned black magic, and was much weaker than the Sachakans believed. He was so amused by what he saw in my mind, he decided that other Ichani had to see it. I was too exhausted to resist. Slaves took my robes and gave me old rags to wear. At first I couldn't grasp that these people were slaves and that I was now one as well. Then, when I understood, I would not accept it. I tried to escape, but Dakova found me easily. He seemed to enjoy the hunt – and the punishment he dealt out afterwards.'

Akkarin's eyes narrowed. He turned his head a little toward her and she dropped her eyes, afraid to meet them.

'I was appalled by my situation,' he continued quietly. 'Dakova called me his "pet Guild magician". I was a trophy, kept to entertain his guests. Keeping me was a risk, though. Unlike his other slaves, I was a trained magician. So every night he read my mind and, to keep me from becoming dangerous, took from me the strength I had regained that day.'

Akkarin pulled up a sleeve. Hundreds of thin, shiny lines covered his arm. Scars. Sonea felt a chill run down her spine. This evidence of his past had been in front of her so many times, hidden by a mere layer of cloth.

'The rest of his slaves were made up of those he had taken from Ichani he had fought and defeated, and young men and women with latent magical potential that he had found among the Sachakan farmers and miners in the region. Every day he would take magical strength from them. He was powerful, but also strangely isolated. I eventually understood that Dakova, and the other Ichani that live in the wastes, were outcasts. For one reason or another – failed involvement in plots, inability to pay bribes or taxes or committing crimes – they had fallen out of favour with the Sachakan King. He had ordered them confined to the wastes, and forbidden others to contact them.

'You might think they would band together in this situation, but they nursed too much resentment and ambition for that. They constantly plotted against each other, hoping to increase their wealth and strength or take revenge for past insults, or simply steal supplies of food. An outcast Ichani can only feed so many slaves. The wastes yield little food, and terrorising and killing farmers certainly doesn't help increase productivity.'

He paused then to take a deep breath. 'The woman who explained everything to me at the beginning was a strong potential magician. She might have been a powerful Healer if she had been born Kyralian. Instead, Dakova kept her as a bed slave.' Akkarin grimaced.

'Dakova attacked another Ichani one day, and found himself losing. In desperation, he took all the strength of each of his slaves, killing them. He left the strongest of us to last, and managed to overcome his adversary before killing us all. Only myself and Takan survived.'

Sonea blinked. *Takan? Akkarin's servant?*

'Dakova was vulnerable for several weeks while he recovered the strength he'd lost,' Akkarin continued. 'He was less worried that another would take advantage of this than he might have been, however. All Ichani knew he had a brother, Kariko. The pair had made it known that if one should be killed, the other would avenge his death. No

Ichani in the wastes could defeat one of the brothers and regain their strength in time to survive an attack by the other. Soon after Dakova's near defeat, Kariko arrived and gave Dakova several slaves to help him regain his strength.

'Most of the slaves I encountered dreamed that Dakova or one of his enemies would release their powers and teach them how to use black magic, so they could be free. They would look at me with envy; I had only to learn black magic to be able to escape. They didn't know that the Guild forbade black magic.

'But as I witnessed what Dakova was capable of, I cared less about what the Guild did and didn't allow. He did not need black magic to perform evil. I saw him do things with his bare hands that I will never forget.'

Akkarin's gaze was haunted. He closed his eyes, and when he opened them again they were hard and cold.

'For five years I was trapped in Sachaka. Then one day, not long after receiving his brother's gift of new slaves, Dakova heard that an Ichani he despised was hiding in a mine after exhausting himself in a fight. He decided that he would find and kill this man.

'When Dakova arrived, the mine appeared to be deserted. He, myself and the other slaves entered the tunnels in search of his enemy. After several hundred paces the floor collapsed under me. I felt myself caught by magic and set down on a hard surface.'

Akkarin smiled grimly. 'I had been saved by another Ichani. I thought he would kill me or take me as his own. Instead, he took me through the tunnels to a small hidden room. There, he made me an offer. He would teach me black magic if I would return to Dakova and kill him.

'I saw that it was an arrangement that would probably

end in my death. I would fail and die, or succeed and be hunted down by Kariko. By then I cared little for my life, or for the Guild's ban on black magic, so I agreed.

'Dakova had been gathering strength over many weeks. I might know the secret of black magic, but I had no time to grow strong. The man understood this and told me what I must do.

'I did as the Ichani instructed. Returning to Dakova I told him I had been knocked unconscious in the fall, but had found a storeroom full of food and treasures on my way out. Though annoyed that his enemy had evaded him, Dakova was pleased at this find. He left me and the other slaves to cart the bounty out of the mines to his tent. I was relieved. If Dakova sensed even the slightest surface thought of betrayal, he would read my mind and discover the plot. I sent a slave out with a box of Elyne wine. The dust coating the bottles reassured Dakova that they hadn't been tampered with, and he began drinking. They were laced with myk, a drug that confuses the mind and distorts the senses. When I left the mine, he was lying in a dream-like state.'

Akkarin fell silent. He stared out into the trees, his gaze fixed on some distant place. As the silence lengthened, Sonea began to worry that he would not go on. *Tell me*, she thought. *You can't stop now!*

Akkarin drew in a deep breath and sighed. He looked down at the stony ground, his expression bleak. 'I did a terrible thing, then. I killed all Dakova's new slaves. I needed their strength. I could not bear to kill Takan. Not because we had been friends, but because he had been there since the beginning and we had got into the habit of helping each other out.

'Dakova was too addled by the drug and the wine to notice much. He woke as I cut him, but once the draining of power begins, it is almost impossible to use your powers.'

Akkarin's voice was low and quiet. 'Though I was now stronger than I had ever imagined I could be, I knew Kariko was not far away. He would try to contact Dakova soon, and then come looking for an explanation for his brother's silence. All I could think of was leaving Sachaka. I didn't even think to take food. I didn't expect to live. After a day I realised Takan was following me. He had packed a bag full of supplies. I told him to leave me, or Kariko would kill him too, but he insisted on staying – and on treating me like an Ichani master. We walked for weeks, though sometimes in the mountains it seemed like we had spent more time climbing than walking. Finally, we found ourselves in the foothills of the Steelbelt Ranges. I realised I had evaded Kariko and made it home.'

For the first time, Akkarin looked up to meet her eyes. 'All I could think of was returning to the safety of the Guild. I wanted to forget everything, and vowed never to use black magic again. Takan wouldn't leave me, but by making him my servant I felt as if I had freed him as best I could.' He looked toward the Guild buildings hidden behind the trees. 'I was greeted warmly and welcomed back. When asked where I had disappeared to, I related my experiences in the allied countries, then made up a story of retreating to the mountains to study in solitude.

'Then, soon after my return, the High Lord died. Custom dictated that the strongest magician take the position. I never considered I might be a candidate. I was only twenty-five, after all. But I had accidentally allowed Lord Balkan to sense my strength. I was surprised when he proposed that I be considered, and amazed at how much support the idea had. It is interesting what people will overlook when they desperately want to avoid electing a man they don't like.'

Intrigued, Sonea opened her mouth to ask who, but Akkarin continued.

'Balkan said that my travels had matured me, and I had experience in dealing with other cultures.' Akkarin snorted softly. 'If he had known the truth, he might not have been so insistent. While the idea seemed absurd, I began to see possibilities in it. I needed to distract myself from the memories of the previous five years. And I had begun to worry about the Ichani. Dakova and his brother had talked many times of how easy it would be to invade Kyralia. Though Kariko was alone now, and would probably never get the other Ichani to join him, an invasion was not impossible. What if he regained the favour of the King and convinced him to invade? I decided I needed to keep an eye on the Sachakans, and it would be easier to do that if I had the resources of a High Lord. And it was not difficult to convince the Guild to elect me, once I let them test my strength.

'After a few years I heard about murders in the city that sounded suspiciously like black magic. I investigated and found the first spy. From him I learned that Kariko had been stirring up the other Ichani with ideas of plundering Imardin, taking revenge for the Sachakan War, and forcing the Sachakan King to accept them again. He first had to convince them that the Guild does not use black magic. I have been convincing them otherwise ever since.' He smiled, then turned to face her. 'You are a good listener, Sonea. You did not interrupt me once. You must have some questions, now.'

She nodded slowly. Where to start? She considered the questions that crowded her mind.

'Why didn't you tell the Guild about the Ichani?'

Akkarin's brows rose. 'Do you think they would have believed me?'

'Lorlen might.'

He looked away. 'I am not sure of that.'

She thought of Lorlen's outrage when he had seen her memory of Akkarin performing black magic. When Akkarin had read *her* mind, he would have seen that outrage. She felt a pang of sympathy. It must have hurt to have their friendship spoiled by a secret he dare not tell.

'I think Lorlen would believe you,' she said. 'If he didn't, you could let him perform a truth-read.' She winced as she said it. After all that mind-reading from Dakova, Akkarin probably never wanted another person probing his memories again.

He shook his head. 'I can't risk that. Anyone reading my mind could easily learn the secret of black magic. That is why I stopped your mind-read of Tavaka last night.'

'Then . . . the Guild could send several magicians to Sachaka to confirm your story.'

'If they entered in large numbers and started asking dangerous questions, they would be considered a threat. It might start the very conflict we fear. Remember, too, that I knew there was no immediate threat from Sachaka when I first arrived here. I was so relieved to be home, and there seemed no sense in revealing that I'd broken the magicians' vow unless I had to.'

'But now there *is* a threat.'

His gaze flickered. 'Not until Kariko convinces the other Ichani to join him.'

'But the sooner the Guild knows, the better prepared it would be.'

Akkarin's expression hardened. 'I am the only one capable of confronting these spies. Do you think the Guild will allow me to continue as High Lord if it knows I have learned black magic? If I told them now, they would lose all of the trust they have in me. Their fear would blind them to the real threat. Until I have found a way for them to fight these Ichani without black magic, it is better they know nothing.'

She nodded, though she could not believe the Guild would punish him once they heard what he had just told her.

'*Is* there another way?'

'I have not found one yet.'

'So what will you do?'

'Continue hunting spies. My allies in the Thieves are proving more effective than those I previously hired to locate them.'

'The Thieves.' Sonea smiled. 'I thought so. How long have you been working with them?'

'About two years.'

'How much do they know?'

'Only that they are hunting rogue magicians with a nasty habit of killing people, and that these rogues all happen to come from Sachaka. They locate them, inform me, and get rid of the bodies.'

A memory flashed through her mind of Tavaka, pleading for his life. Promising to be good, while intending to kill as many Kyralians as he could so he might return to Sachaka and join the Ichani. If it weren't for Akkarin, Tavaka would be doing just that right now.

She frowned. So much depended on Akkarin. What if he died? Who would stop the spies then? Only Takan and she would know what was really going on, but neither of them knew black magic. Neither could do anything to stop the Ichani.

She froze as the implication of that rushed over her like icy water.

'Why did you tell me this?'

He smiled grimly. 'Somebody else needs to know.'

'But why me?'

'You knew much already.'

She paused. 'Then . . . can we tell Rothen? I know he'd keep quiet if he understood the threat.'

He frowned. 'No. Not unless we must reveal everything to the Guild.'

'But he still believes that I . . . What if he tries to do something? About me.'

'Oh, I'm watching Rothen closely.'

In the distance a gong rang. Akkarin pushed himself to his feet. The hem of his black robes brushed across her hand. Sonea looked up at him and felt a strange mixture of fear and respect. He had killed many times. He had learned and used the darkest magic. Yet he had done it to escape slavery, and to keep the Guild safe. And nobody but she and Takan knew.

Akkarin crossed his arms and smiled. 'Go back to your lessons now, Sonea. My favourite does not skip classes.'

Sonea dropped her eyes and nodded.

'Yes, High Lord.'

CHAPTER 8

CONTEMPLATING A CRIME

The corridor of the University echoed with the voices of the novices. The two who followed Rothen, carrying boxes of the chemistry tools and substances used in the previous class, were having a fascinating conversation in low voices. They had observed a girl watching them at the horse races last Freeday, and they couldn't decide which one she might be interested in.

Rothen was having a hard time keeping a straight face. But his mood darkened as a slight figure appeared at the top of the stairs. Sonea's expression was tight with annoyance. A large stack of heavy books filled her arms. She turned into the side passage that led to the Novices' Library.

The boys behind Rothen stopped talking and hummed with sympathy.

'Guess she asked for it,' one said. 'Got to admire her guts, though. I wouldn't dare skip classes if *he* was my guardian.'

Rothen glanced behind.

'Who skipped classes?'

The boy flushed as he realised he'd been overheard. 'Sonea,' he said.

'The High Lord punished her with a week's work in the library,' the other boy added.

Rothen couldn't help smiling. 'She'd like that.'

'Oh, no. The *Magicians'* Library. Lord Jullen makes sure punishment really is punishment.'

So Sonea *had* skipped a class, as Tania had said. He wondered why and where she had gone instead. She had no friends to slip away with, and no other hobbies or interests that might tempt her away from lessons. She knew that he and Lorlen would quickly become suspicious if she went missing. If she had risked alarming them, she must have had a better reason for skipping the class than a rebellious whim.

The more he thought about it, the more worried he became. He listened as they boys resumed the conversation, hoping to glean more information.

'She'll turn you down. She turned Seno down.'

'Maybe she turned Seno down because she doesn't like him.'

'Maybe. It doesn't matter, anyway. The punishment was for a week. That probably includes Freeday. She won't be able to come with us.'

Rothen resisted the urge to turn and stare at them in surprise. They were still talking about Sonea. Which meant that they, and another boy named Seno, had considered inviting her out to the races. He felt his mood lighten a little. He had hoped the other novices would eventually accept her. Now it looked as if some might even be interested in more than just friendship.

Then Rothen sighed. She had turned down this boy called Seno, and he knew she would probably turn down any other offers, too. It was a cruel irony that now the novices had started to accept her, she dared not befriend any for fear of complicating the situation with Akkarin.

* * *

As the carriage pulled up outside the mansion, Dannyl and Tayend regarded each other doubtfully.

'Nervous?' Tayend asked.

'No,' Dannyl assured him.

Tayend snorted. 'Liar.'

The door of the carriage opened, and the driver bowed as they stepped out. Like many Elyne mansions, the front of Dem Marane's house was open to the air. Arched openings allowed access to a tiled room decorated with sculptures and plants.

Dannyl and Tayend stepped through an archway and crossed the room. A large wooden door barred entry into the enclosed part of the house. Tayend tugged a rope hanging beside the door. A distant ringing sounded somewhere above.

They heard muffled footsteps inside the house, then the door opened and Dem Marane greeted them with a bow.

'Ambassador Dannyl. Tayend of Tremmelin. You are most welcome in my home.'

'We were honoured by your invitation, Dem Marane,' Dannyl replied.

The Dem ushered them into a luxuriously furnished room. He continued through two more, until they arrived at another open room. Archways allowed views of the sea and the carefully tended garden falling in tiers to the beach below. On the opposite wall, benches lined with cushions supplied seating for six other men. A woman sat demurely on a small couch in the centre of the room.

The strangers stared at Dannyl. They looked tense, and fearful. He knew the combination of his height and robes made him an imposing figure.

'May I introduce the Second Guild Ambassador to

Elyne, Lord Dannyl,' Royend announced. 'And some of you already know his companion, Tayend of Tremmelin.'

One of the men stood and bowed, and the others hesitantly followed suit. Dannyl nodded politely in return. Was this all there was of the group? He doubted it. Some would not reveal themselves until they were sure he could be trusted.

The Dem introduced them one by one. Royend was the oldest, Dannyl guessed. All were Elyne aristocrats of one wealthy family or another. The woman was the Dem's wife, Kaslie. When he was finished, she invited them all to sit while she fetched some refreshments. Dannyl chose an empty bench, and Tayend sat close beside him. Dannyl could not help feeling a twinge of anxiety as he saw the others taking note of this.

Idle talk followed. Dannyl was asked the usual questions: what he thought of Elyne, if he had met certain famous and important people yet. Some demonstrated that they had gathered information about him by asking about his journey to Lonmar and Vin.

Kaslie returned with servants carrying wine and plates of food. After all had been given a drink, the Dem sent the servants away and surveyed the room.

'It is time to talk of the business that has brought us here. We have come together because of a common loss. The loss of opportunity.' The Dem looked at Tayend. 'Some of us were offered this opportunity and were forced by circumstances to turn it down. Others were never offered that choice, or were given it, then had it taken away. Still more wish for an opportunity that does not require being shackled to an institution whose principles they do not agree with, based in a country they do not belong to.' The

Dem paused to look around the room. 'We all know the opportunity I speak of. The opportunity to learn magic.'

He looked at Dannyl. 'For the last two centuries the only legal way a man or woman could learn magic was to join the Guild. For us to learn to use magic outside of the Guild's influence, we must break a law. Ambassador Dannyl has complied with this law. But he, too, laments the loss of opportunity. His companion, Tayend of Tremmelin, has magical talent. Ambassador Dannyl wishes to teach him how to protect or Heal himself. A reasonable – no, an honourable wish.'

The Dem looked at the others, who were nodding. 'But should the Guild ever discover this, Tayend will need people who can hide and protect him. We have the right connections and arrangements. We can help him.'

He turned back to regard Dannyl. 'So, Ambassador, what will you give us in exchange for protecting your friend?'

The room fell silent. Dannyl smiled and glanced around at the faces.

'I can offer you the opportunity you have lost. I can teach you a little magic.'

'A little?'

'Yes. There are some things I will not teach you, and some things I cannot teach you.'

'Such as?'

'I would not teach the offensive Warrior Skills to anyone I did not trust. They are dangerous in the wrong hands. And I am an Alchemist, so my knowledge of Healing is limited to the basics.'

'That makes sense.'

'And I must be sure that you are able to protect Tayend, before I teach you anything.'

The Dem smiled. 'And we, of course, don't wish to give away any secrets until we are sure you will uphold your side of the bargain. For now I can only swear on my honour that we can protect your friend. I will not show you how it can be done yet. Not until you have demonstrated to us that you can be trusted.'

'How do I know *you* can be trusted?' Dannyl asked, gesturing around the room.

'You don't,' the Dem said simply. 'But I think you have the advantage over us tonight. A magician considering teaching a friend is not taking as great a risk as a group of non-magicians gathering for the purpose of learning magic. We have committed ourselves to the purpose, you have only dallied with an idea. It is unlikely the Guild will execute you for that, whereas we might face that penalty just for meeting like this.'

Dannyl nodded slowly. 'If you have evaded the Guild's notice for so long, perhaps you *can* keep Tayend from them. And you would not invite me here if you did not have a plan to escape should I prove to be a Guild spy.'

The Dem's eyes flashed. 'Exactly.'

'So what must *I* do to gain *your* trust?' Dannyl asked.

'Help us.'

Kaslie had spoken. Dannyl looked at her in surprise. Her voice had betrayed urgency and concern. She stared at Dannyl, her eyes filled with a desperate hope.

A suspicion slowly stole over Dannyl. He remembered Akkarin's letter. *Only recently have they had some success. Now that at least one of them has managed to develop his powers, the Guild is entitled and obliged to deal with them.*

Developed his powers, but not learned to control them. Thinking back quickly, Dannyl counted the weeks since he had received the letter, and added two for it to reach him. He looked up at the Dem.

'Help you with what?'

The man's expression was sober. 'I will show you.'

As Dannyl rose, Tayend followed suit. Royend shook his head. 'Stay, young Tremmelin. For your safety, it is best only the Ambassador come.'

Dannyl hesitated, then nodded at Tayend. The scholar dropped back onto the seat, frowning.

The Dem gestured for Dannyl to follow him. They left the room and started down a corridor. At the end was a stairway which descended to another corridor. They stopped before a heavy wooden door. The faint smell of smoke tainted the air.

'He's expecting you, but I have no idea what he'll do when he sees you,' the Dem warned.

Dannyl nodded. The Dem knocked on the door. After a long pause, he lifted a hand to knock again, but paused as the handle turned and the door swung inward.

A young man peered out. His eyes slid to Dannyl and widened.

A crash came from inside the room. The young man glanced inside and cursed. When he turned to look at Dannyl again, his expression was anxious.

'This is Ambassador Dannyl,' the Dem told the young man, then looked at Dannyl. 'This is my wife's brother, Farand of Darellas.'

'Honoured to meet you,' Dannyl told the man. Farand mumbled a reply.

'Are you going to invite us in?' the Dem said patiently.

'Oh. Yes,' the young man replied. 'Come in.' He pulled the door fully open and sketched an awkward bow.

Dannyl entered a large room with stone walls. It might have once been a cellar, but now it held a bed and other furniture, all looking battered and scorched. A pile of wood on one side of the room looked suspiciously like the remains of more furniture. On the floor were pieces of a large urn, surrounded by a rapidly spreading pool of water. Dannyl guessed this was what he had heard shatter.

A magician with no control tended to let loose magic when he or she reacted to strong emotions. For Farand, fear was his main enemy: fear of the magic he wielded, and fear of the Guild. Dannyl needed to reassure the man, before he did anything else.

He allowed himself a small smile. A situation like this came along so rarely, and yet he now encountered it for the second time in a handful of years. Rothen had managed to teach Sonea control, despite her deep distrust of the Guild. Teaching Farand could only be easier. And it would help if Farand knew that another had survived the same situation.

'From what I can see, your powers have surfaced, but you have no control of them,' Dannyl said. 'This is very rare, but we found another like you only a few years ago. She learned Control within a few weeks and is a novice now. Tell me, were you trying to bring them out, or did it just happen?'

The man lowered his gaze. 'I think I made it happen.'

Dannyl sat down in one of the chairs. The less intimidating he looked, the better. 'May I ask how?'

Farand swallowed and looked away. 'I've always been able to hear the thought conversations magicians have. I used to listen every day in the hope of discovering how to use magic. A few months ago I overheard a conversation about releasing magical potential. I tried what they said several times, but I didn't think it had worked. Then I started doing things without meaning to.'

Dannyl nodded. 'You have released your power, but you do not know how to control it. The Guild teaches the two together. I don't have to tell you how dangerous it is to have magic, but no control over it. You are fortunate that Royend has found a magician willing to teach you.'

'You'll teach me?' Farand whispered.

Dannyl smiled. 'Yes.'

Farand sagged against the bed with relief. 'I was so afraid they would have to send me to the Guild, and everyone would be found out because of me.' He straightened and squared his shoulders. 'When can we begin?'

'I don't see why we can't make a start now,' Dannyl said, shrugging.

A little fear crept back into the man's eyes. He swallowed, then nodded. 'Tell me what to do.'

Dannyl rose and looked around. He gestured at the chair. 'Sit down.'

Farand blinked at the chair, then hesitantly walked to it and sat down. Dannyl crossed his arms and regarded him thoughtfully. He was aware of the effect this change of position – from Farand standing over him, to him standing over Farand – would have. Now that he had agreed to cooperate, Farand needed to feel that Dannyl was in command, and knew what he was doing.

'Close your eyes,' Dannyl instructed. 'Concentrate on your breathing.' He talked Farand through the standard breathing exercises, keeping his voice low and steady. When he judged that the man had gained a measure of calm, he stepped behind the chair and lightly touched the man's temples. But before he could send his mind forth, the man jerked away.

'You're going to read my mind!' he exclaimed.

'No,' Dannyl assured him. 'It is not possible to read a mind that is unwilling. But I must direct you to that place in your mind where you access your power. The only way I can do that is if you allow me in to show you the way.'

'Is that the only way?' the Dem asked. Dannyl looked at Royend.

'Yes.'

'Is it at all possible that you might see things,' Farand asked, 'things I must keep secret?'

Dannyl regarded him soberly. He could not deny it. Once he was in Farand's mind the secrets would probably leap out at him. Secrets had a habit of doing that.

'It is possible,' Dannyl told him. 'To be honest, if you are worried about concealing something, then it will be foremost in your thoughts. That is why the Guild prefers to train novices as young as possible. The younger you are, the fewer secrets you have.'

Farand buried his face in his hands. 'Nooo,' he groaned. 'Nobody can teach me. I'm going to be like this forever.'

The covers of the bed began to smoke. The Dem drew in a sharp breath and stepped forward.

'Perhaps Lord Dannyl can swear that he would keep everything he sees to himself,' he suggested.

Farand laughed bitterly. 'How can I trust him to keep a promise when he's about to break a law?'

'How indeed?' Dannyl said dryly. 'You have my promise that I will not pass on any information I discover. If that is not acceptable, I suggest you put your affairs in order and leave here. Take yourself far from anyone and anything you don't wish to destroy, for when your powers break free completely they will not only consume you, but everything around you.'

The man paled. 'There really is no choice, is there?' he said in a small voice. 'I'll die if I don't do this. So it's death or . . .' His eyes flashed with sudden anger, then he drew in a deep breath and straightened. 'If that's the only choice, I'll just have to trust you won't tell anyone.'

Amused by this abrupt change, Dannyl talked Farand through the calming exercises once more. When he rested his fingers on the man's temples, Farand remained still. Dannyl closed his eyes and sent his mind forth.

Novices were usually taught Control by their teachers, and Dannyl had never been a teacher. He did not have Rothen's skill, but after several attempts he managed to get Farand to visualise a room and invite him into it. Tantalising hints of the man's secret appeared, but Dannyl concentrated on teaching Farand to hide them behind doors. They found the door to the man's power, but lost track of it as the secrets Farand was struggling to hide leaked out of the doors they had been stowed behind.

—*We both know I'm going to find out anyway. Show me, and we can get on with Control lessons*, Dannyl suggested.

Farand seemed relieved to be able to tell someone his secret. He showed Dannyl his memories of hearing mental conversations as he grew out of childhood. This was unusual, but not unheard of in those with magical potential. Farand was tested for ability and told he could apply to join the Guild when he was older. In the meantime the Elyne King learned of his ability to eavesdrop on magicians' mental conversations, and Farand was summoned to court where he kept the King informed of what he overheard.

One day, however, Farand accidentally witnessed the King making an agreement with one of the powerful Dems to have the Dem's political rival murdered, and upon realising this the King extracted an oath of silence from him. Later, when Farand had applied to join the Guild, he was refused. He did not discover until later that the King knew the secret agreement would be revealed during mind-reading lessons, and therefore had prevented him from becoming a magician.

It was an unfortunate situation, and one which had shattered Farand's dreams. Dannyl felt genuine sympathy for him. Now that the secret had been told, Farand was not as distracted. He found his source of power easily. After a few attempts to show Farand how to influence it, Dannyl left the man's mind room and opened his eyes.

'Is that it?' Farand asked. 'Have I got it?'

'No.' Dannyl chuckled and moved around the chair to face him. 'It takes a few sessions.'

'When will we try again?' There was an edge of panic to the man's voice.

Dannyl looked at Dem Marane. 'I will try to return tomorrow, if that is convenient.'

'It is,' the Dem confirmed.

Dannyl nodded at Farand. 'Do not drink wine or take any mind-affecting substance. Novices usually learn Control over a week or two. If you stay calm and avoid trying to use magic, you should be safe.'

Farand looked relieved, and there was a glint of excitement in Royend's eyes. The Dem moved to the door and pulled a chain that hung from a small hole in the roof.

'Shall we return to the others, Ambassador? They will be pleased to hear of our progress.'

'If you wish.'

The Dem did not take Dannyl back to the previous room, but to another section of the mansion. They entered a small library, where Tayend and the other members of the group were sitting in comfortable chairs. Royend nodded at Kaslie, and the woman closed her eyes and sighed with relief.

Tayend was reading a large and very worn book. He looked up at Dannyl, his eyes bright with eagerness.

'Look,' he said, waving at one of the bookcases. 'Books on magic. We might find something here to help us with our research.'

Dannyl could not help smiling. 'It went well. Thanks for asking.'

'What?' Tayend looked up from the book. 'Oh, that. I know you can take care of yourself. What did he show you?' Before Dannyl could reply, Tayend looked up at the Dem. 'Can I borrow this some time?'

Royend smiled. 'You can take it home with you tonight, if you wish. The Ambassador will be returning tomorrow. You are welcome to come as well.'

'Thank you.' Tayend turned to the Dem's wife, who was sitting beside him. 'Have you ever heard of the Chakan King?'

Dannyl did not hear her murmured reply. He looked around the room at the excited faces of the Dem and his friends. They would not trust him yet. Not until Farand was able to demonstrate an improvement in his control of magic. Once Farand had, however, he would be a dangerous man. He would be able to release magical ability in others, and teach them to control it. The group would not need Dannyl any more. They might decide it was safer to disappear than continue associating with a Guild magician.

He could stretch out the lessons over a few weeks, but no more. The moment Farand achieved Control, Dannyl ought to arrest him and the others. But he might not catch all of the group. The longer he remained with them, the more identities he might discover. He would have liked to consult with the High Lord. But Farand's ability to overhear mind communication prevented that and Dannyl did not have time to contact Akkarin by letter.

Dannyl accepted a fresh glass of wine. As the Dem began grilling him on what he was willing to teach them, Dannyl pushed all thought of arresting these people to the back of his mind and concentrated on his role as the rebellious Guild magician.

Sonea stood at her bedroom window and watched as grey wisps of cloud drifted across the night sky. The stars blinked in and out of sight and the moon was surrounded by a pale mist. The grounds were empty and silent.

She was bone tired. Despite a sleepless night, and carting books around for Lord Jullen for several hours after classes, she couldn't sleep. She still had many questions, but by listing them in her mind ready for her next encounter with Akkarin, she found she could push them out of her thoughts. One, however, refused to go away.

Why did he tell me?

He had said that someone else needed to know. A reasonable answer, but something still nagged at her. He could have written down his story and left it for Lorlen to find if he should ever be killed. So why tell her, a mere novice in no position to make decisions or act in his place?

There had to be another reason. The only reason she could think of was one that sent chills down her spine.

He wanted her to take over the fight if he died. He wanted her to learn black magic.

Leaving the window, she began pacing her room. He had said several times that he would not teach it to her. Had he said that just to reassure her? Was he waiting for her to grow older, perhaps until after she had graduated, when it would be clear to anyone else that she had made such a decision for herself?

She bit her lip gently. It would be a terrible thing to ask of someone. To learn something that most magicians believed was evil. To break a Guild law.

And to break this law was no small matter that would earn her some menial task or the withdrawal of luxuries or favour. No, the punishment for this was likely to be much, much worse. Expulsion perhaps, with her powers bound, or possibly imprisonment.

Only if the crime was discovered.

Akkarin had managed to hide his secret for years. But he was the High Lord. That gave him a lot of room to be mysterious and secretive. Which meant it would not be difficult for her to join him.

But what would happen if he died? She frowned. Lorlen and Rothen would reveal Akkarin's crime, and that her guardianship had been only a way to gain their silence. If she did not consent to a truth-read, there was no reason why anyone would discover that she had learned black magic. She could play the unhappy victim and attract no suspicion.

After that she would be dismissed and ignored. No longer the High Lord's favourite, she could hide in her ordinariness. She would slip away into the hidden passages at night. Akkarin had already arranged for the Thieves' help. They would find the spies for her . . .

She stopped and sat down on the end of her bed.

I can't believe I'm considering this. There's a reason black magic is banned. It's evil.

Or was it? Years before, Rothen had pointed out to her that magic was neither good nor evil; it was what the wielder did with it that mattered.

Black magic involved taking power from another. It didn't have to involve killing. Even the Ichani did not kill their slaves unless they had to. When she had first seen Akkarin using it, he had been taking power from Takan. Power that was obviously willingly given.

She thought back to the records that Akkarin had shown her. Black magic had once been commonly used by the Guild. Apprentices would willingly give strength to their masters in exchange for knowledge. Once deemed ready, the apprentices were taught the secret of 'higher magic' and became masters themselves. It was an arrangement that had encouraged co-operation and peace. No-one was killed. No-one was enslaved.

It had only taken one man with an insane desire for power to change that. And the Ichani used black magic to maintain a culture of slavery. When she considered these things, she understood why the Guild had banned black magic. It could be abused so easily.

But Akkarin hadn't abused it. Or had he?

Akkarin has used it to kill. Isn't that the worst abuse of power?

Akkarin had used it to free himself, and only killed the spies to keep Kyralia safe. That was not an abuse of power. It was reasonable to kill to protect oneself, and others . . . wasn't it?

As a child surviving in the slums, she had decided that

she would not hesitate to kill to defend herself. If she could avoid harming another, she would, but she was not going to let herself become a victim either. That determination had paid off a few years later when she had fended off an attacker with her knife. She didn't know if he had lived, and she had not spared much time wondering.

The Warriors learned how to fight with magic. The Guild continued passing on that knowledge in case the Allied Lands should ever be attacked. She never heard Lord Balkan agonising over whether magic should be used to kill in defence.

She lay back on the bed. Perhaps Akkarin was wrong about the Guild. Perhaps, when faced with no choice, they would accept the use of black magic only in defence.

Would magicians respect that restriction? She shivered as she imagined what Lord Fergun might have done with the knowledge. Fergun *had* been punished, though. As a whole, the Guild could probably keep control of its magicians.

Then she remembered the Purge. If the King did not baulk at using the Guild to drive the poor from the city to keep the Houses happy, what might he do with black magicians at his bidding?

The Guild would always be cautious about how black magic was used. If laws were put in place, if only those deemed worthy were taught – determined by a truth-read to test a candidate's character and moral integrity . . .

Who am I to think I have the wisdom to reshape the Guild? I probably wouldn't even be considered as a candidate if this system was in place.

She was the slum girl. Naturally, she had no moral integrity. No-one would even consider her.

I am considering me.

Rising, she moved to the window.

The people I care about are in danger. I have to do something. Surely the Guild will not execute me if I break a law trying to protect it. They may expel me, but if I must lose this luxury called magic in exchange for the lives of those I love, so be it.

She shivered, chilled by and yet sure of the rightness of this revelation.

There, it is decided. I will learn black magic.

She turned to regard the door of her room. Akkarin was probably in bed. She could not wake him up just to tell him this. It could wait until tomorrow.

Sighing, she slipped under the covers of her bed. She closed her eyes, hoping she would finally be able to sleep now that she had made her decision.

Am I being deceived? Once I learn this, I can't unlearn it.

She considered the books Akkarin had given her to read. They looked genuine, but they could have been clever fakes. She did not know enough about forgery to be able to tell.

The spy could have been manipulated to believe certain things in order for her to be deceived, but she was sure Akkarin could not have invented it all. Tavaka's mind had held a lifetime's worth of memories of the Ichani and slavery that could not have been arranged by the High Lord.

And Akkarin's story?

If he wanted to trick her into learning black magic so he could blackmail and control her, then he had only needed to convince her that the Guild was in great danger. Why admit to having been a slave?

She yawned. She must get some sleep. She needed a clear head.

Tomorrow she was going to break one of the Guild's strictest laws.

CHAPTER 9

AKKARIN'S HELPER

The room was too small for pacing. A single lamp hung from the roof, casting yellow light on the rough brick walls. Cery crossed his arms and silently cursed himself. Akkarin had told him they must avoid meeting unless they had to discuss something of great concern that could only be settled face to face.

Sonea's welfare is *of great concern,* Cery reasoned. *And this can only be settled face to face.*

But it was unlikely the High Lord would agree. Cery felt another twinge of anxiety. So far, he hadn't regretted any of the work he had done in return for being rescued from Lord Fergun, and for the assistance he'd received from Akkarin in establishing his place among the Thieves. Tracking the murderers was easy enough. Once you knew what to look for, they stood out like a guard in a smuggler's den. Getting rid of the bodies afterwards was standard work, though dumping them in the river was out of the question now the Guard were keeping an eye on it.

But bringing Sonea into it? No, that was too much. Not that Cery could make the decision for her. But, at the very least, he wanted to make sure Akkarin knew he disapproved.

The High Lord needed him. He was sure of that. Perhaps today he would discover how much.

Cery drummed his fingers against his sleeve. *If the High*

Lord ever arrives. There were few men in the city who would dare to be late to a meeting with a Thief. None but . . . the King, most in the Houses, the entire Guild . . .

He sighed, then considered once again the only other piece of information he had for the Guild leader: that another Sachakan had been seen entering the city. Perhaps this little tidbit would mollify Akkarin when he discovered Cery's real reason for requesting a meeting. Not for the first time, Cery wondered what Akkarin's reaction would be if he knew the source of the information. He chuckled as he pictured Savara. That smile. The way she walked. She was definitely not a safe person to be around.

But, then, neither was he these days.

A tap brought him back to the present. He peered through a spy hole in the door. A tall figure stood beside Gol's heavier frame, his face concealed in the hood of his cloak. Gol made the signal to confirm the visitor was the High Lord.

Cery drew in a deep breath, then opened the door. Akkarin stalked inside. The cloak parted slightly to reveal black robes beneath. A shiver ran down Cery's spine. Akkarin usually wore plain clothing when he was on the Thieves' Road. Was this a deliberate move to remind Cery just who he was dealing with?

'Ceryni,' Akkarin said, smoothly tugging the hood from his head.

'High Lord.'

'I do not have much time to spare. What is it you need to speak to me about?'

Cery hesitated. 'I think we've got another . . . murderer, in the city.' He had been about to say 'slave', but caught himself in time. Using that term would no doubt reveal that he'd been in contact with someone from Sachaka.

Akkarin frowned, his eyes almost disappearing in the shadows of his brows. 'You *think*?'

'Yes.' Cery smiled. 'There's been no murder yet, but the last killer arrived so soon after the one before, I have been paying some ear to talk I don't usually. Word is, she stands out. Should be easy to catch.'

'She?' Akkarin repeated. 'A woman. So . . . if the Thieves hear this they'll know there is more than one murderer. Will this be a problem for you?'

Cery shrugged. 'It won't change anything. They might even give a little more respect. Better we catch her quick, though, so they don't find out at all.'

Akkarin nodded. 'Is that all?'

Cery hesitated. He drew in a deep breath and pushed aside his doubts.

'You brought Sonea.'

Akkarin straightened. The lamplight reached his eyes. He looked amused.

'Yes.'

'Why?'

'I had my reasons.'

'Good ones, I hope,' Cery said, forcing himself to meet and hold Akkarin's gaze.

The High Lord's stare didn't waver. 'Yes. She was in no great danger.'

'Are you going to get her into any of this?'

'A little. Not in the way you fear, however. I need someone in the Guild to be aware of what I am doing.'

Cery forced out the next question. Just thinking about asking it brought difficult, contrary feelings. 'Will you bring her again?'

'No, I do not intend to.'

He breathed a short sigh of relief. 'Does she . . . does she know about me?'

'No.'

Cery felt a wistful disappointment. He wouldn't have minded showing off his success a little. He'd come a long way in the last few years. Though he knew she did not think too highly of Thieves . . .

'Is that all?' Akkarin asked. There was a hint of respect in his voice – or was it simply tolerance?

Cery nodded. 'Yes. Thank you.'

He watched the High Lord turn to the door and open it. *Take care of her*, he thought. Akkarin glanced back, nodded once, then strode away down the passage, his cloak flaring around his ankles.

Well, that went better than I expected, Cery mused.

Dannyl's rooms in the Guild House of Capia were large and luxurious. He had a bedroom, office and guestroom to himself, and he had only to ring one of many little bells around the place to attract a servant.

One had just brought a steaming cup of sumi when another entered the office to tell him he had a visitor.

'Tayend of Tremmelin is here to see you,' the servant informed him.

Dannyl put down his cup, surprised. Tayend rarely visited him here. They preferred the privacy of the Great Library, where they didn't have to worry about servants noticing anything in their behaviour toward each other.

'Send him in.'

Tayend was dressed appropriately for a meeting with an important personage. Though Dannyl was growing used to the flamboyant court dress of Elyne, he still found it amusing. However, the tightly fitting clothes, which looked so ridiculous on older courtiers, were flattering on Tayend.

'Ambassador Dannyl,' Tayend said, bowing gracefully. 'I have been reading Dem Marane's book and it contains some very interesting information.'

Dannyl gestured to one of the chairs set before his desk. 'Please sit down. Just . . . give me a moment.' Tayend had reminded him of something. He took a fresh piece of paper and began composing a short letter.

'What are you writing?' Tayend asked.

'A letter to Dem Marane expressing my deepest regrets that I cannot attend his dinner party tonight, due to some unexpected work that I must attend to without delay.'

'What about Farand?'

'He will survive. I do have work to sort out, but I also want to make them wait a little. Once I finish teaching Farand Control, they will no longer need me, and we might find our new friends have taken an unexpected journey abroad.'

'They'd be fools, then. Do they think all those years of training you went through are for nothing?'

'They can't appreciate the value of what they don't understand.'

'So you'll be arresting them as soon as Farand's ready?'

'I don't know. I haven't decided yet. It might be worth taking the risk that they'd disappear on us. I'm sure we haven't met everyone involved. If I wait, I might be introduced to more of the group.'

'Are you sure you don't need me to come with you to Kyralia once you've arrested them? The Guild might need another witness.'

'They don't need any more proof than Farand.' Dannyl looked up and shook a finger at the scholar. 'You just want to see the Guild for yourself. But when our new friends retaliate by spreading rumours about us, it won't help if we're seen together.'

'But we wouldn't be together all the time. I don't have to stay in the Guild. I have distant relatives in Imardin. And you said Akkarin would tell everyone it was all just a trick.'

Dannyl sighed. He didn't want to leave Tayend. Not even for a few weeks. If he was sure he could get away with returning to the Guild with the scholar in tow, he would make arrangements to take him. It might even help to disprove the rumours once and for all if they were seen to behave 'normally'. But he knew that it would take only a small hint of the truth to put ideas in suspicious minds – and he already knew there were plenty of those in the Guild.

'I'll be returning by sea,' he reminded Tayend. 'I would have thought you'd want to avoid that.'

Tayend's face clouded, but only for a moment. 'I'd put up with a little seasickness, if it came with good company.'

'Not this time,' Dannyl said firmly. 'One day we'll travel by carriage to Imardin. Then *you'll* be good company as well.' He smiled at Tayend's indignant glare, then signed the letter and put it aside. 'Now, what have you found?'

'Do you remember how the writing on the woman's tomb in the Tombs of White Tears said she performed "high magic"?'

Dannyl nodded. The visit to Vin in search of evidence of ancient magic seemed so long ago now.

'The words "high magic" were represented by a glyph

containing a crescent moon and a hand,' Tayend opened the Dem's book and slid it across the desk toward Dannyl. 'This is a copy of a book written two centuries ago, when the Alliance was made and the law was laid down that all magicians must be taught and controlled by the Guild. Most magicians outside Kyralia were members of the Guild, but some weren't. This belonged to one who wasn't.'

Drawing the book to him, Dannyl saw that the top of the page bore the same glyph they had been puzzling over for a year. He began to read the text below it:

The term 'higher magic' encompasses several skills that were once in common use throughout the lands. Minor skills include the ability to create 'blood stones' or 'blood gems' which enhance the maker's ability to mindspeak with another person at a distance, and 'store stones' or 'store gems' which can hold and release magic in specific ways.

The main form of higher magic is acquisitive. If a magician has the knowledge, he may draw power from living things to increase his store of strength.

Dannyl caught his breath and stared at the page in horror. This was describing something similar to . . . A chill slowly spread down Dannyl's spine. His eyes continued to follow the words, drawn on as if by another's will.

To do this, the natural barrier which protects the creature or plant must be broken or lowered. This is done most simply by cutting the skin deep enough to draw blood or sap. Other means involve voluntary or involuntary lowering of the barrier. With practise, the natural barrier can be voluntarily withdrawn. During the height of sexual pleasure, the barrier tends to 'waver', allowing a momentary opportunity for the drawing of power.

Dannyl had turned completely cold. In preparation for

his position, he had been given information that was kept from ordinary magicians. Some of it was political; some of it magical. Included among the magical warning signs he was taught to recognise were those for black magic.

And here he was, holding a book containing *instructions* on its use. Just by reading it, he was breaking a law.

'Dannyl? Are you all right?'

He looked up at Tayend, but couldn't speak. Tayend stared back, frowning with concern.

'You've gone completely white. I thought . . . well . . . if this book is right, we've discovered what high magic is.'

Dannyl opened his mouth, then closed it again and looked down at the book. He stared at the glyph of the crescent moon and hand. Not a crescent moon, he realised. A blade. Higher magic was black magic.

Akkarin had been researching black magic.

No. He wouldn't have known. He didn't get this far, Dannyl reminded himself. *He probably still doesn't know. Otherwise he wouldn't have encouraged me to continue my research*. He drew in a deep breath and let it out slowly.

'Tayend, I think it's time to tell Errend about the rebels. I may be taking that trip earlier than I thought.'

Sonea's heart beat faster as she approached the High Lord's Residence. All day she had been waiting for this moment. It had been difficult to concentrate during classes, even more difficult to endure Jullen's attempts to make her punishment in the library as tedious as possible.

The grey stone building loomed over her in the darkness. She stopped to take one long deep breath and gather her courage, then she walked up to the door and brushed the handle with her fingers. It clicked open and swung inward.

As always, Akkarin was sitting in one of the guestroom chairs. His long fingers were curled around a glass filled with dark red wine.

'Good evening, Sonea. How were your lessons today?'

Her mouth was dry. She swallowed, drew another deep breath, stepped inside, and heard the door close behind her.

'I want to help,' she told him.

His eyebrows lowered, and he stared intently at her. She struggled to hold his gaze, but soon found herself looking at the floor. Silence stretched between them, then in one movement he stood and set the glass aside.

'Very well. Come with me.'

He walked to the door of the stairway leading to the underground room. Opening it, he gestured for her to enter. Her legs were unsteady, but she forced them to move.

As she reached him there was a knock at the main door, and they both froze.

'Go on,' he murmured to her. 'It is Lorlen. I will have Takan deal with him.'

For a moment, she wondered how he knew it was Lorlen. Then understanding came in a flash. The ring Lorlen wore *did* contain a gem like the one in the spy's tooth.

As she descended the stairs she heard a new set of footsteps in the guestroom above. Akkarin gently closed the stairway door and followed her down. She stopped outside the door to the underground room, then stepped aside as Akkarin reached her. The door opened at a touch of his hand.

The room beyond was dark, but it brightened as two

globe lights appeared. She looked at the two tables, the battered old chest, and the bookcases and cupboards. Really, there was nothing threatening in there at all.

Akkarin appeared to be waiting for her to enter. She took a few steps inside, then turned to face him. He looked up at the ceiling and grimaced.

'He's gone. I have something to tell him, but it can wait.'

'Do you . . . should we do this later?' she ventured, half hoping he would agree.

The look he gave her was so direct, and *predatory*, she took a step backward.

'No,' he said. 'This is more important.' He crossed his arms, and the corner of his mouth lifted into a half-smile. 'Well then. How do you intend to help me?'

'I . . . you . . .' She was suddenly short of breath. 'By learning black magic,' she finally managed.

His smile vanished.

'No.' He uncrossed his arms. 'I cannot teach you that, Sonea.'

She stared at him, astonished. 'Then . . . then why did you show me the truth? Why did you tell me about the Ichani if you didn't mean for me to join you?'

'I never intended to teach you black magic,' he said firmly. 'I would not have you endanger your future in the Guild. Even if that did not concern me, I would not pass this knowledge on to anyone.'

'Then . . . how can I help you?'

'I intended . . .' He hesitated, then sighed and looked away. 'I intended you to be a willing source of power, as Takan is.'

A chill swept through her, but it quickly faded. *Of course*, she thought. *That's what all this was leading to.*

'The Ichani may never invade,' he said. 'If you learn black magic you will have risked your future for nothing.'

'It is a risk I'm willing to take,' she replied, her voice small in the large room.

Looking up, he fixed her with a disapproving stare. 'You would so easily break your vow?'

She held his gaze. 'If it was the only way I could protect Kyralia.'

His stare lost its fierceness. She could not name the expression that he wore now.

'Teach her, master.'

They both turned at this new voice. Takan was standing in the doorway of the room, regarding Akkarin intently.

'Teach her,' he repeated. 'You need an ally.'

'No,' Akkarin replied. 'What use is Sonea to me if I do? If I take her strength she is of no use as a black magician. If she is a black magician, who is she going to gather strength from? You? No. You already bear too much of that burden.'

Takan's gaze did not waver. 'Someone needs to know that secret other than you, master. Sonea does not need to use it, only be there to take your place if you die.'

Akkarin returned the servant's stare. For a long time they regarded each other in silence.

'No,' Akkarin said eventually. 'But . . . I will reconsider if they attack Kyralia.'

'By then it will be too late,' Takan replied quietly. 'They will not attack until they have removed you.'

'He's right,' Sonea interjected, her voice trembling. 'Teach me and use me as a source. I will not use black magic unless I have no other choice.'

He stared at her coldly. 'Do you know what the punishment is for learning and using black magic?'

She hesitated, then shook her head.

'Execution. No other crime earns such a punishment. Just seeking to learn about black magic will have you expelled from the Guild.'

A chill ran over her skin. His mouth twisted into a grim smile.

'But you can make yourself useful to me without committing a crime. There is no law against giving power to another magician. Indeed, you have already been taught to in Warrior Skills classes. The only difference is that I can store the power you give.'

She blinked in surprise. No knife? No cutting of the skin. But, of course, there was no need.

'A night's sleep was all you needed to recover most of your strength after facing Regin and his followers,' he continued. 'We should take care that you do not give too much power if you must tackle Warrior Skills classes the next day, however. And if you do intend to be capable of fighting these spies in my place, then I should take a hand in your training.'

Sonea felt a wave of dizziness sweep over her. *Warrior Skills lessons? With Akkarin?*

'Are you sure you want to do this?' he asked.

She took yet another deep breath. 'Yes.'

He frowned and considered her a moment. 'I will take a little of your strength tonight. Tomorrow we will see if you still wish to help.'

He beckoned. 'Give me your hands.'

She walked forward and offered her hands. She shivered as his long fingers linked with hers.

'Send out your power, as you have learned to when channelling power to another in Warrior Skills class.'

Drawing power, she sent it flowing out of her hands. His expression changed slightly as he became conscious of the energy and drew it into himself. She wondered how he stored it. Even though she had been taught how to receive power from other novices, she had always channelled it into strikes or added it to her shield.

'Leave yourself some energy for classes,' he murmured.

She shrugged. 'I barely use any. Not even in Warrior Skills classes.'

'You will soon.' His grip loosened. 'That is enough.'

She stopped sending power. As he released her hands she took a step back. He glanced at Takan, then nodded at her.

'Thank you, Sonea. Now, get some rest. Give Takan a copy of your schedule in the morning so that we can work around your Warrior Skills classes. If you are still willing, we will continue with this tomorrow night.'

Sonea nodded. She took a step toward the door, then stopped and bowed.

'Good night, High Lord.'

His stare was unwavering. 'Good night, Sonea.'

Her heart was pounding again. As she climbed the stairs she realised it was not with fear any more. It was racing with a strange kind of excitement.

I might not be helping him in the way I expected, she thought, *but I am helping*.

Then she chuckled ruefully. *But I might not be so happy about that when he starts assisting in my Warrior Skills lessons!*

CHAPTER 10

AN UNEXPECTED ADVERSARY

As Rothen waited for the last of his pupils to arrive, he looked out of the window. Longer, warmer days were turning the gardens into a labyrinth of green. Even the grey High Lord's Residence looked welcoming in the bright morning light.

As he watched, the door to the residence opened. He felt his heart skip as Sonea stepped out. It was a late start for her, he realised. According to Tania, she still rose at dawn.

Then a taller figure emerged, and Rothen felt his entire body tense. The folds of Akkarin's black robes were almost grey in the bright sunlight. The High Lord turned to Sonea and spoke. Her lips curled up into a small smile. Then the pair straightened and started toward the University, their expressions sober again. Rothen watched them until they moved out of sight.

Turning away from the window, he shivered. A chill had caught hold of him, and wouldn't let go.

She had *smiled* at Akkarin.

It had not been a polite, forced smile. Nor an open, unguarded smile. It had been sly and secretive.

No, he told himself. *I'm just seeing that which I most fear because it's what I'm always watching for. She was probably smiling to deceive or mollify Akkarin. Or perhaps she had found some comment he made amusing, was enjoying a little joke at his expense . . .*

But what if she hadn't been? What if there's another reason?

'Lord Rothen?'

Turning, he saw that the rest of the class had arrived and were patiently waiting for him to begin. He managed a rueful smile, then moved toward the desk.

He could not charge out of the classroom and demand an explanation from Sonea. No, for now he must put her out of his mind and concentrate on teaching. But later he would consider carefully what he had seen.

And watch her more closely.

As the carriage pulled away, Dannyl strode up to the door of Dem Marane's house and pulled on the bell cord.

He yawned, then drew on a little magic to soothe away weariness. A week had passed since Tayend had shown him the book, and many secret meetings had been held with Ambassador Errend and other Elyne magicians in preparation for this night. Now they would know if their plans would be successful.

Footsteps drew close to the door, then it opened and the master of the house bowed gracefully.

'Ambassador Dannyl. A pleasure to see you again. Please come in.'

'Thank you.' Dannyl stepped inside.

'Where is young Tremmelin?' the Dem asked.

'With his father,' Dannyl replied. 'They had a family matter to discuss. He sends his regards and said to tell you the book is enlightening and he will finish reading it tonight. I know he would much prefer to be talking to you and your friends than dealing with family business.'

Royend nodded and smiled, but his eyes expressed wariness. 'I shall miss his company.'

'How is Farand? No unintended events?' Dannyl asked, letting a hint of anxiousness enter his tone.

'No.' The Dem hesitated. 'One intentional one, however. Being young and impatient, he could not resist trying to do something.'

Dannyl let alarm show in his face. 'What happened?'

'Just another little fire.' The Dem smiled crookedly. 'I had to buy his host another bed.'

'The same hosts as last time?'

'No. Once again, I have moved Farand. I felt it prudent, for all our sakes, to move him away from the city, in case his little accidents grew so dramatic they started to draw unwanted attention.'

Dannyl nodded. 'That was wise, though probably unnecessary. I hope he is not too far away. I can only stay a few hours.'

'No, not far,' the Dem assured him.

They had reached the doorway of the next room. Royend's wife, Kaslie, rose to greet Dannyl.

'Greetings, Ambassador. It is good to see you again. Do you think my brother will learn Control soon?'

'Yes,' Dannyl replied gravely. 'Either tonight, or the next time. It will not be long now.'

She nodded, obviously relieved. 'I can't thank you enough for your help.' She turned to Royend. 'Best be on your way, then, husband.'

There was a note of resentment in her voice. The Dem's mouth twitched into a crooked smile. 'Farand will be safe soon, my dear.'

Her frown only deepened. Dannyl kept his expression

politely neutral. Tayend had observed that Kaslie rarely looked happy and sometimes appeared to be annoyed at her husband. He had guessed that she blamed Royend for her brother's situation because he had encouraged the young man to develop his abilities.

The Dem ushered Dannyl out of the house to a waiting carriage. It began to move before they had even settled into their seats. The windows were covered.

'For the protection of Farand's hosts,' the Dem explained. 'I may be willing to allow you to know *my* identity and residence, but there are others in the group who are less trusting. They have allowed Farand to stay with them only if I take these precautions.' He paused. 'Do you think me a fool for trusting you?'

Dannyl blinked in surprise. He considered the question, then shrugged. 'I expected you to take smaller steps. Arrange a few tests of my honesty, perhaps. But you couldn't; Farand needed help. You took a risk, but I'm sure it was a calculated one.' He chuckled. 'You would have had a few escape routes in place, and probably still have.'

'And you have Tayend to protect.'

'Yes.' Dannyl smiled good-naturedly. 'What I am waiting to discover is whether I will find myself no longer welcome in your house once I have taught Farand Control?'

The Dem laughed quietly. 'You'll just have to wait and find out.'

'And I expect I don't have to remind you of all the wonderful things I could teach Farand, once he has learned Control.'

Royend's gaze brightened. 'Please do.'

For the next hour they discussed uses of magic. Dannyl

took care to describe only what was possible, not how it was done, and the Dem was obviously aware he was being deliberately evasive. Finally, the carriage slowed to a stop.

The Dem waited until the door opened, then gestured for Dannyl to exit. It was dark outside, and Dannyl automatically created a globe light. It illuminated a tunnel, the brick walls glistening with moisture.

'Put that out, please,' the Dem requested.

Dannyl extinguished the light. 'Sorry,' he said. 'It's a habit.'

After the brightness of the light, all was utterly dark. A hand touched his shoulder and pushed him forward. Extending his senses, he detected a break in the wall. They moved into it.

'Careful,' Royend murmured. 'There are stairs here.'

The toe of Dannyl's boot met a hard edge. He carefully climbed a steep staircase, then was guided along a passage with many twists, turns and side entrances. Then he sensed a large room and a familiar presence, and the hand slid from his shoulder.

A lamp spluttered into life, revealing several pieces of practical furniture in a room carved out of solid rock. Water trickled from a crack in one wall into a basin, then out through a hole in the floor. The air was cold, and Farand was dressed in a large fur-collared coat.

The young man bowed, his movements more confident now that he was drawing closer to escaping his predicament.

'Ambassador Dannyl,' he said, 'welcome to my latest hiding hole.'

'It's a little cold,' Dannyl remarked. He sent out a glow of magic to warm the air. Farand grinned and shrugged out of the coat. 'I used to dream of doing grand and dramatic things with magic. Now I think I'll be happy if all I can do is something like that.'

Dannyl glanced pointedly at Royend. The Dem smiled and shrugged. 'Not everyone's sentiments, I assure you. I'm sure Farand wants to learn more than the basics.'

He was standing beside a rope that hung from a hole in the ceiling. The other end was probably attached to a bell, Dannyl guessed. He wondered who was waiting by it.

'Well,' Dannyl said. 'We'd best get started, then. No sense keeping you in cold hiding holes for any longer than necessary.'

Farand moved to a chair and sat down. He took a deep breath, closed his eyes and began the calming exercise that he had been taught. When the man's face had relaxed, Dannyl approached.

'This may be your last lesson,' he said, keeping his voice low and soothing. 'It may not. Control must become a well-learned habit, to keep you safe both day and night. It is better to learn it at your own pace, than to hurry it along.' He touched Farand's temples lightly, then closed his eyes.

It was impossible to lie effectively during mental communication, but the truth could be hidden. So far Dannyl had kept his mission and ultimate plan to betray the rebels safely concealed. Each time Dannyl had guided Farand mentally, however, the man had grown more used to the method of communication. He was beginning to sense more from Dannyl.

And now that the time had come to arrest the rebels, Dannyl's could not conceal a feeling of tension and anticipation. Farand sensed it and grew curious.

—*What are you expecting will happen tonight?* he asked.

—*You will probably achieve Control*, Dannyl replied. This was true, and part of what Dannyl knew was coming. It was an important enough event that the young man would accept it as the reason for Dannyl's excitement. But Farand's awareness of the consequences of learning magic illegally made him more suspicious than usual.

—*There's more. You're hiding something from me.*

—*Of course*, Dannyl replied. *I will keep much from you, until I know your people are not going to disappear as soon as you have learned Control.*

—*The Dem is honourable. He promised to protect Tayend in exchange for your help. He won't break that promise.*

Dannyl felt a momentary sympathy for this naive young man. He pushed it away, reminding himself that Farand might be young, but he was no fool.

—*We'll see. Now, take me to that place where your power is.*

It took less time for Farand to understand the finest nuances of Control than Dannyl had expected. As Farand contemplated his achievement, Dannyl steeled himself for what must come next. He cut into Farand's jubilant thoughts with a question.

—*Where are we?*

An image of a tunnel appeared, then the room they were in. Farand had no more idea of their location than Dannyl did.

—*Who is your host?*

Again, Farand didn't know.

But then, Royend would have guessed that Dannyl might be able to read this information from the young man's mind, so he would have made sure Farand knew nothing. Hopefully, discovering their location would only involve finding his way out of the passages and seeing where the tunnel emerged.

Farand had caught enough of Dannyl's thoughts to grow alarmed.

—*What are you . . .?*

Dannyl removed his hand from Farand's temples and broke the connection. At the same time, he created a weak shield in case Farand attempted to use his magic. The young man was staring at him.

'It was a trick,' Farand gasped. 'It was all a trick.' He turned to Royend. 'He means to betray us.'

Royend turned to stare at Dannyl, his expression hardening. As the Dem reached for the bell rope, Dannyl exerted his will. The man snatched his hand back from the sting of a barrier.

Dannyl focussed his mind beyond the room.

—*Errend?*

Farand's eyes widened as he heard the communication.

—*Dannyl. Do you have the rogue?*

—*Yes.*

At once, the edges of Dannyl's senses buzzed with the communications of a dozen magicians. Farand's eyes roved across the walls as he listened to them.

'They're arresting the others,' he said. 'No! This is all because of me!'

'No, it isn't,' Dannyl told him. 'It is the result of your King misusing a potential magician's abilities, and your sister's husband taking advantage of the situation in the hopes of achieving his own aims. I suspect your sister knows this, though I don't believe she would have betrayed either of you.'

Farand looked at Royend, and Dannyl saw from the

accusing look in the young man's eyes that he was right.

'Don't try to turn us against each other, Ambassador,' Royend said. 'It will not work.'

—*Where are you?* Errend asked.

—*I don't know exactly. An hour's carriage ride from the city.* He sent an image of the tunnel. *Look familiar?*

—*No.*

Farand glanced at Dannyl, then back at Royend. 'He still doesn't know where we are,' he said hopefully.

'Finding out will not be difficult,' Dannyl assured him. 'And you should know already, Farand, that it is considered rude for a magician to listen in on others' conversations.'

'We don't follow your rules,' Royend snapped.

Dannyl turned to regard the Dem. 'I've noticed.'

The man's gaze wavered, then he straightened his shoulders. 'They will execute us for this. Can you live with that?'

Dannyl held the Dem's gaze. 'You knew what you risked, at every step. If all of what you have done and planned was motivated by the need to protect and save Farand, you might be pardoned. I don't believe your motives were that honourable, however.'

'No,' the Dem growled. 'It wasn't just Farand. It was the injustice of it all. Why should the Guild decide who can use and teach magic? There are so many whose potential is wasted, who—'

'The Guild does not decide who learns to use magic,' Dannyl corrected. 'In Kyralia it is left to each family to decide if their sons or daughters will attend. In Elyne, the King decides who will be taught. Each country has its own system for choosing candidates. We only refuse those whose minds are unstable, or who have committed crimes.'

Royend's eyes flashed with anger. 'But what if Farand, or any other man, does not want to learn from the Guild? Why can't he learn elsewhere?'

'Where? At your own Guild?'

'Yes.'

'And who would you be answerable to?'

The Dem opened his mouth, then closed it again without speaking. He looked at Farand, then sighed.

'I am no monster,' he said. 'I did encourage Farand, but I would not have if I had known how dangerous it was.' He looked at Dannyl. 'You do realise the King might kill him rather than let the Guild discover whatever it is that he knows.'

'Then he will have to kill me as well,' Dannyl replied. 'And I don't think he will dare to attempt that. It would only take a short mental call for all magicians in the lands to know his little secret. And now that Farand has learned Control, he is a magician, and the King would break the treaty of the Allied Lands if he tried to harm him. Farand is the Guild's concern now. Once there, he should be safe from assassins.'

'The Guild,' Farand said in a small voice. 'I'm going to see the Guild.'

Royend ignored him. 'And what then?'

Dannyl shook his head. 'I cannot say. I would not give you false hopes by guessing what the outcome of this will be.'

Royend scowled. 'Of course not.'

'So. Will you co-operate? Or shall I drag you both with me as I find the way out of here?'

A glint of rebellion entered the Dem's eyes. Dannyl

smiled at the man's expression, guessing at the thoughts behind it.

—*Errend?*

—*Dannyl.*

—*Have you arrested the others?*

—*Everyone. Can you tell us your location yet?*

—*No, but I will have it soon.*

Dannyl looked up at Royend. 'Delaying will not give your friends time to escape. Farand will tell you this is so.'

The young man looked away and nodded. 'He's right.' His gaze strayed to the bell rope. Dannyl looked up at the ceiling, wondering who was stationed above. Farand's host, no doubt, with some method in place for warning others in the group. Would there be an opportunity to arrest this rebel as well? Probably not. Errend had agreed that Dannyl's first priority should be to capture Farand and Dem Marane. If he identified or arrested anyone else, it should not be at the risk of losing the rogue.

Royend followed Dannyl's gaze, then straightened his shoulders. 'Very well. I will show you out.'

The day had been bright and warm, but darkness had brought a chill that Sonea could not banish, even by warming the air in her room with magic. She had slept well the last few nights, but this one was different and she couldn't work out why.

Perhaps it was because Akkarin hadn't been present all evening. Takan had met her at the door when she returned from classes to tell her that the High Lord had been called away. She had eaten dinner alone.

He was probably carrying out official duties at court. Yet her imagination kept placing him in darker parts of the city, tending to his secret arrangements with the Thieves or facing another spy.

Sonea stopped in front of her desk and stared down at her books. *If I can't sleep*, she told herself, *I may as well study. At least then I'd have something to occupy my mind.*

Then she heard a noise outside her room.

Gliding to the door, she opened it a crack. Slow footsteps echoed softly in the far stairwell, growing louder. She heard them stop in the corridor, and then heard the click of a door latch.

He's back.

Something loosened within her and she sighed with relief. Then she nearly laughed aloud. *Surely I'm not worrying about Akkarin.*

But was that so strange? He was all that stood between the Ichani and Kyralia. Worrying about him being alive and well was perfectly reasonable when considered in that light.

She was about to close her door when a new set of footsteps filled the corridor.

'Master?'

Takan sounded surprised and alarmed. Sonea felt a chill run across her skin.

'Takan,' Akkarin's voice was barely audible. 'Stay and I will give you this to dispose of.'

'What *happened*?'

The shock in the servant's voice was clear. Before she could think twice, Sonea pulled open her door and padded down the corridor. Takan was standing in the entrance of Akkarin's bedroom. He turned as she approached, his expression uncertain.

'Sonea.' Akkarin's voice was low and quiet.

A tiny, weak globe light illuminated his bedroom. He was sitting on the end of a large bed. In the dim light his robes seemed to retreat into the darkness, leaving only his face and hands visible . . . and one forearm.

Sonea drew in a breath. The right sleeve of his robe hung strangely, and she saw that it had been cut open. A red mark ran down his arm from elbow to wrist. His pale skin was stained with streaks and smudges of blood.

'What happened?' she breathed, then added, 'High Lord.'

Akkarin looked from her to Takan and snorted softly. 'I can see I'll have no rest until you have both heard everything. Come in and sit down.'

Takan stepped inside the room. Sonea hesitated, then followed. She had never seen inside his bedroom before. A week ago it would have terrified her to think of entering it. As she looked around, she felt a wry disappointment. The furniture was similar to hers. The paper screens that covered his windows were a dark blue, matching the border of a large carpet that covered most of the floor. The door to his cabinet was open. It contained only robes, a few cloaks and a longcoat.

As she turned to look at Akkarin again, she found he was watching her, a faint smile on his lips. He gestured to a chair.

Takan had taken a jug of water from a cabinet beside the bed. He produced a cloth from within his uniform, moistened it, and reached toward Akkarin's arm. The High Lord plucked the cloth out of his hand.

'We have another spy in the city,' he said, wiping the blood from his arm. 'But she is no ordinary spy, I think.'

'She?' Sonea interrupted.

'Yes. A woman.' Akkarin handed the cloth back to

162

Takan. 'That is not the only difference between her and the previous spies. She is unusually strong for a former slave. She has not been here long, and could not have grown so strong by killing Imardians. We would have heard, if she had killed people.'

'They prepared her?' Takan suggested. His hands gripped the stained cloth tightly. 'Let her take strength from their slaves before she left?'

'Perhaps. Whatever the reason, she was ready for the fight. She let me think she was exhausted, then when I came close she cut me. She wasn't quick enough to get a hold on my wound and draw power, however. After that, she tried to draw attention to our fighting.'

'So you let her escape,' Takan concluded.

'Yes. She must have thought I'd let her go rather than endanger the lives of others.'

'Or she knows you'd rather the Guild didn't hear of magical battles in the slums.' Takan's lips thinned. 'She will be killing to strengthen herself again.'

Akkarin smiled grimly. 'I don't doubt it.'

'And you are weaker now. You've had little time to strengthen yourself after the last one.'

'That will not be a problem.' He looked at Sonea. 'I have one of the Guild's strongest magicians to help me.'

Sonea looked away, and felt her face warming. Takan was shaking his head.

'This sounds wrong to me. She is too different. A woman. No Ichani would free a woman slave. And she is strong. Cunning. Not like a slave at all.'

Akkarin regarded his servant closely. 'You think she is an Ichani?'

'Possibly. You should prepare as if she was. You

should . . .' He glanced at Sonea. 'You should take an ally.'

Sonea blinked at the servant in surprise. Did he mean she should go with Akkarin when he faced this woman again?

'We have already discussed this,' Akkarin began.

'And you said you would reconsider it if they attack Kyralia,' Takan replied. 'If this woman *is* Ichani, they are already here. What if she is too strong for you? You can't risk losing your life, and leaving the Guild with no defence.'

Sonea felt her pulse quickening. 'And two pairs of eyes are better than one,' she said quickly. 'If I had come with you tonight—'

'You might have got in the way.'

That stung. Sonea felt a flare of anger. 'You think so, do you? I'm just a soft novice like the rest. Don't know my way around the slums, or how to hide from magicians.'

He stared at her, then his shoulders slumped and he began to laugh softly.

'What am I to do?' he asked. 'You are both determined to wear me down on this.'

He rubbed his arm absently. Sonea looked down and blinked in surprise. The red wounds were now only pink. He had been Healing himself even as they spoke.

'I will teach Sonea only if this woman is Ichani. Then we will know they have become a real threat.'

'If she is Ichani, you may end up dead,' Takan said bluntly. 'Be prepared, master.'

Akkarin looked up at Sonea. His eyes were shadowed, his expression distant and thoughtful.

'What do you think, Sonea? This is not something you

should agree to without much careful consideration.'

She drew in a deep breath. 'I have considered it. If there's no other way, then I'll take the risk and learn black magic. After all, what is the point of being a good, lawabiding novice if there is no Guild? If you die, the rest of us probably will, too.'

Slowly, Akkarin nodded.

'Very well. I do not like it. If there was another way, I would take it.' He sighed. 'But there isn't. We will begin tomorrow night.'

CHAPTER 11

FORBIDDEN KNOWLEDGE

Three yerim thumped spike first into the door of Cery's office. Rising from his desk, he pulled out the scribe tools and returned to his seat. He stared at the door, then tossed the yerim again, one after another.

They landed just where he intended, at the points of an imagined triangle. Standing up again, he strolled across the room to retrieve them. Thinking of the merchant who was waiting behind that door, Cery smiled. What did the man make of this regular thudding on the Thief's door?

Then he sighed. He really ought to see the merchant and get it over with, but he wasn't in a generous mood, and this man usually visited to beg for more time to pay back his debts. Cery wasn't yet sure whether or not the man was testing the newest, youngest Thief to see how far he could be pushed. A slowly repaid debt was better than one not paid at all, but a Thief with a reputation for endless patience was a Thief without respect.

Sometimes he needed to show he was willing to use a firm hand.

Cery looked at the yerim, their points embedded deep in the grain of the door. He had to admit it. The merchant wasn't the real reason for his brooding.

'*She got away*,' Morren had reported. '*He let her.*'

Pressed for details, Morren had described a fierce battle.

Clearly, this woman had been stronger than Akkarin expected. He had been unable to contain her magic. It had wrecked the room in the bolhouse she had been staying in. Several other patrons had witnessed more than they should have – though Cery had ensured that most were well and truly inebriated beforehand by sending a few men into the bol servery with considerable 'winnings' from the races to share. Those who had not been drunk, or had been outside the bolhouse, had been paid to stay quiet – though that rarely stopped gossip for long. Not when it involved a woman floating to the ground from a third-storey window.

It's not a disaster, Cery told himself for the hundredth time. *We'll find her again. Akkarin will make sure he is better prepared*. He walked back to his desk and sat down, then opened the drawer and dropped the yerim into it.

As he expected, a tentative knock on the door followed after a few minutes of silence.

'Come in, Gol,' Cery called. He looked down and straightened his clothes as the door opened and the big man stepped inside. 'Better send Hem in.' He looked up. 'Get it done . . . what's got you?'

Gol was wearing a wide grin. 'Savara's here.'

Cery felt his pulse quicken. How much did she know? How much should he tell her? He straightened his shoulders.

'Send her in.'

Gol retreated. When the door opened next, Savara stepped into the room. She strode over to the desk, looking smug.

'I hear your High Lord met his match last night.'

'How'd you get that?' Cery asked.

She shrugged. 'People tend to tell me things, if I ask nicely.' Though her tone was flippant, there was a crease between her eyebrows.

'I don't doubt it,' Cery replied. 'What else did you get?'

'She escaped. Which would not have happened if you had let me take care of her.'

He couldn't help smiling. 'Like you'd have done better.'

Her eyes flashed. 'Oh, I would have.'

'How?'

'I have my ways.' She crossed her arms. 'I would like to kill this woman, but now Akkarin knows about her, I cannot. I wish you had not told him.' She gave him a very direct look. 'When are you going to trust me?'

'Trust you?' He chuckled. 'Not ever. Let you kill one of these murderers?' He pursed his lips, as if considering. 'Next time.'

She stared at him intently. 'Do I have your word on that?'

He held her gaze and nodded. 'Yes, you have my word. Find this woman, and give me no reason to change my mind, and you kill the next slave.'

Savara frowned, but did not protest. 'You have a deal. When he does kill this woman, I will be there whether you approve or not. I wish to see her death, at least.'

'What's she do to you?'

'I helped that woman a long time ago, and she made me regret it.' She regarded him soberly. 'You think you are tough and ruthless, Thief. If you are cruel, it is to maintain order and respect. Murder and cruelty are a game for Ichani.'

Cery frowned. 'What did she do?'

Savara hesitated, then shook her head. 'I can tell you no more.'

'But there is more, isn't there?' Cery sighed. 'And you ask me to trust you?'

She smiled. 'As much as you want me to trust you. You don't tell me the details of your deal with the High Lord yet you expect me to trust that you are keeping my existence a secret.'

'So you must trust me if I say whether you do or don't kill one of the murderers – or murderesses.' Cery allowed himself a smile. 'But, if you're set on watching this fight, then I'll also be there. I hate that I always miss the show.'

She smiled and nodded. 'That is fair.' She paused, then took a step backward. 'I should start looking for the woman.'

'I guess you should.'

Turning away, she walked across the room to the door. After she had gone he felt a vague disappointment, and he began considering ways he could have kept her around a little longer. The door opened again, but it was Gol.

'Ready to see Hem now?'

Cery grimaced. 'Send him in.'

He pulled the drawer open, picked up one of the yerim and a sharpening stone. As the merchant minced into the room, Cery began honing the point of the scribing tool.

'So, Hem, tell me why I shouldn't see how many holes I need to make before you start leaking money?'

From the University roof it was just possible to see the stump of the old, half-dismantled Lookout. Somewhere behind the trees, new stone was being taken by gorin-drawn carts up the long winding road to the summit.

'Construction may have to wait until after the summer break,' Lord Sarrin said.

'Delay construction?' Lorlen turned to the magician at his side. 'I was hoping this project wouldn't drag out any longer than three months. I'm already tired of the complaints about delayed projects and lack of free time.'

'I'm sure many would agree with you,' Lord Sarrin replied. 'Nevertheless, we can't tell everyone involved that they won't be visiting their families this year. The trouble with magically strengthened buildings is that they're not structurally sound until the stone has been fused, and we don't do that until everything is in place. In the meantime, we hold everything together consciously. Delays are not appreciated.'

Unlike Lord Peakin, Lord Sarrin had offered little input during the debate over the new Lookout. Lorlen wasn't sure if this was because the old Head of Alchemists didn't have a strong opinion on the matter, or if he had seen which side would win and kept prudently silent. Perhaps this was a good time to ask.

'What do you really think about this project, Sarrin?'

The old magician shrugged. 'I agree that the Guild should do something grand and challenging now and then, but I wonder if, perhaps, we should be doing something other than constructing yet another building.'

'I hear Peakin wanted to use one of Lord Coren's unused designs.'

'Lord Coren!' Sarrin rolled his eyes. 'How tired I am of hearing that name! I like some of what the architect designed in his day, but we have magicians alive today who are just as capable of designing attractive and functional buildings as he was.'

'Yes,' Lorlen agreed. 'I hear Balkan nearly had a fit when he saw Coren's plans.'

'He called them "a nightmare of frivolity".'

Lorlen sighed. 'I don't think it will just be the summer break that will delay this project.'

Sarrin pursed his lips. 'A little external pressure might speed it along. Is the King in a hurry?'

'Is the King ever *not* in a hurry?'

Sarrin chuckled.

'I'll ask Akkarin to enquire for us,' Lorlen said. 'I'm sure—'

'Administrator?' a voice called.

Lorlen turned. Osen was hurrying across the roof toward him.

'Yes?'

'Captain Barran of the Guard is here to see you.'

Lorlen turned to Sarrin. 'I had best see to this.'

'Of course.' Sarrin nodded in farewell. As Lorlen started toward Osen, the young magician stopped and waited for him.

'Did the Captain say why he has come?' Lorlen asked.

'No,' Osen replied, falling into step beside Lorlen, 'but he seemed agitated.'

They stepped through the door to the roof and made their way through the University. As Lorlen stepped out of the Entrance Hall he saw Barran standing by his office door. The guard looked relieved when he saw Lorlen approaching.

'Good afternoon, Captain,' Lorlen said.

Barran bowed. 'Administrator.'

'Come into my office.' Lorlen held the door open for Barran and Osen, then ushered his guest to a seat. Settling down behind his desk, he regarded the Captain soberly.

'So what brings you to the Guild? Not another murder, I hope.'

'I'm afraid so. And not just one murder.' Barran's voice was strained. 'There has been what I can only call a massacre.'

Lorlen felt his blood turn cold. 'Go on.'

'Fourteen victims, all killed in the same manner, found in Northside last night. Most were found on the street, a few in houses.' Barran shook his head. 'It's as if some madman roamed the slums, killing anyone he saw.'

'Surely there'd be witnesses, in that case.'

Barran shook his head. 'Nothing useful. A few people said they thought they saw a woman, others said it was a man. None saw the killer's face. Too dark.'

'And the manner of death?' Lorlen forced himself to ask.

'Shallow cuts. None that ought to have been fatal. No sign of poison. Fingerprints on the wounds. That is why I came to you. It is the only similarity to the previous cases we've discussed.' He paused. 'There is one other thing.'

'Yes?'

'One of my investigators was told by the husband of a victim that stories were going around about a fight in a bolhouse last night. A fight between magicians.'

Lorlen managed to look sceptical. 'Magicians?'

'Yes. One apparently floated to the ground from a third-storey window. I thought it was probably a fancy invented in the dark, except that the murders all occurred in a line pointing directly to this bolhouse. Or away from it.'

'And did you investigate the bolhouse?'

'Yes. One of the rooms was smashed up quite badly, so something did happen there last night. Whether it was magic . . .' He shrugged. 'Who can tell?'

'We can tell,' Osen said.

Lorlen looked up at his assistant. Osen was right; someone from the Guild should examine the bolhouse. *Akkarin will want me to do it*, Lorlen thought.

'I would like to see this room.'

Barran nodded. 'I can take you there now. I have a Guard carriage waiting outside.'

'I could go instead,' Osen offered.

'No,' Lorlen replied. 'I will do it. I know more about these cases than you. Stay here and keep an eye on things.'

'Other magicians may hear about this,' Osen said. 'They'll be concerned. What should I tell them?'

'Just that there has been another disturbing set of murders and that the bolhouse story is probably an exaggeration. We don't want people jumping to conclusions or causing a panic.' He stood, and Barran followed suit.

'And if you do find evidence of magic?' Osen added.

'We'll deal with that if it happens.'

Osen remained standing by the desk as Lorlen and Barran moved to the door. Looking back, Lorlen saw that his assistant was frowning with concern.

'Don't worry,' Lorlen assured him. He managed a wry smile. 'This is probably only as sinister as all the other murder cases.'

Osen smiled thinly and nodded.

Closing the door to his office, Lorlen strode into the Entrance Hall, then out of the University doors.

—*You should interview Captain Barran alone, my friend.*

Lorlen glanced toward the High Lord's Residence.

—*Osen is a sensible man.*

—*Sensible men can become quite irrational when their suspicions get the better of them.*

—*Should he be suspicious? What happened last night?*

—A lot of drunk dwells witnessed the Thieves' failed attempt to catch a killer.

—Is that really what happened?

'Administrator?'

Lorlen blinked, then realised he was standing by the open door of the carriage. Barran was regarding him questioningly.

'Excuse me.' Lorlen smiled. 'Just consulting with a colleague.'

Barran's eyes widened slightly as he realised what Lorlen meant. 'Must be a handy skill, that.'

'It is,' Lorlen agreed. He stepped up into the carriage. 'But it does have its limitations.'

Or it ought to, he added silently.

Sonea's stomach fluttered as she entered the underground room; it had been doing this whenever she thought of the coming lesson in black magic – which had been every few minutes. Doubts had worked their way into her thoughts, and a few times she had almost decided to tell Akkarin she had changed her mind. But if she sat calmly and thought it through, her resolve remained strong. Learning it was a risk to herself, but the alternative was to put the Guild and Kyralia at greater risk.

As Akkarin turned to regard her, she bowed.

'Take a seat, Sonea.'

'Yes, High Lord.'

She sat down, then glanced at the table. It was covered in a strange collection of items: a bowl of water, a common plant in a small pot, a cage with a harrel nosing about within, small towels, books, and a polished and unadorned wooden box. Akkarin was reading one of the books.

'What is all this for?' she asked.

'Your training,' he said, closing the book. 'I have not taught another what I will teach you tonight. My own learning did not come with an explanation. I discovered more only when I found the old books that Lord Coren had reburied under the Guild.'

She nodded. 'How did you find them?'

'Coren knew that the magicians who originally buried the trunk had been right to preserve the knowledge of black magic in case the Guild faced a stronger enemy one day. But it was of no use to anyone if it could not be found again. He wrote a letter to the High Lord, to be delivered only after his death, explaining that he had buried a secret store of knowledge under the University that might save the Guild if it faced a terrible enemy.' Akkarin glanced up at the ceiling. 'I found the letter wedged in a record book when the library here was moved after the renovations I had done. Coren's instructions for finding this secret were so obscure none of my predecessors had had the patience to decipher them. Eventually the letter's existence was forgotten. I guessed what Coren's secret was, however.'

'And you worked out the instructions?'

'No.' Akkarin chuckled. 'I spent every night for five months exploring the underground passages until I found the chest.'

Sonea smiled. 'Too bad if the Guild *had* faced a terrible enemy.' She sobered. 'Well, now it does.'

Akkarin's expression became serious. He glanced down at the items on the table.

'Much of what I will tell you, you already know. You have been taught that all living things contain energy, and that each of us has a barrier at the skin protecting us from external magical influences. If we did not, a magician could kill you from a distance by, say, reaching into your body with his mind and crushing your heart. This barrier will allow certain kinds of magic to penetrate, such as Healing magic, but only via skin-to-skin contact.'

He pushed himself away from the table and took a step closer. 'If you break the skin, you break the barrier. Drawing energy through this gap can be slow. In Alchemy classes you will have learned that magic travels faster through water than air or stone. In Healing classes you have learned that the blood system reaches every part of the body. When you cut deep enough to draw blood, you can draw energy from all parts of the body quite rapidly.

'The skill of drawing is not a difficult one to learn,' Akkarin continued. 'I could explain it to you as it is described in these books, then leave you to experiment on animals, but it would take many days, even weeks, before you learned to draw with any control.' He smiled. 'And smuggling in all the animals could be more trouble than it's worth.'

He sobered again. 'But there is another reason. The night you observed me drawing power from Takan, you sensed something. I had read that, as with ordinary magic, the use of black magic can be sensed by other magicians, particularly those close by. As with ordinary magic, this effect can be hidden. I did not know I was detectable until I read your mind. Afterwards I experimented until I was sure I was undetectable. I will need to teach you this quickly, to reduce the risk of discovery.'

He looked up toward the ceiling. 'I will guide you mentally, and we will use Takan as our first source. When he arrives, take care what you speak of. He does not want to learn these things, for reasons too complicated and personal to explain.'

Muffled footsteps came from the stairwell, then the door opened and Takan stepped into the room. He bowed.

'You called, master?'

'It is time to teach Sonea black magic,' Akkarin said.

Takan nodded. He moved to the table and opened the box. Inside, nestled in a bed of fine black cloth, lay the knife Akkarin had used to kill the Sachakan spy. Takan took it carefully, handling it with reverence.

Then, in a smooth, practised movement, Takan placed the knife across his wrists and approached Sonea, his head bowed. Akkarin's eyes narrowed.

'Enough of that, Takan – and no kneeling.' Akkarin shook his head. 'We are a civilised people. We don't enslave others.'

A faint smile played at Takan's mouth. He looked at Akkarin, his eyes bright. Akkarin snorted softly, then nodded at Sonea.

'This is a Sachakan blade, worn only by magicians,' he said. 'Their knives are forged and sharpened with magic. It is many centuries old and was passed down from father to son. Its last owner was Dakova. I would have left it behind, but Takan salvaged it and brought it with him. Take the knife, Sonea.'

Sonea accepted the blade gingerly. How many people had been killed with this knife? Hundreds? Thousands? She shivered.

'Takan will be needing that chair, too.'

She rose. Takan took her place, then began rolling up his sleeve.

'Make a shallow cut. Press lightly. It is very sharp.'

She looked down at the servant and felt her mouth go dry. The servant smiled at her and lifted his arm. His skin was crisscrossed with scars. Like Akkarin's.

'See,' Takan said. 'Done this before.'

The blade shook a little as she pressed it against Takan's skin. Lifting it away, she saw beads of red form along the cut. She swallowed hard. *I'm really doing this.* She looked up and found Akkarin watching her closely.

'You don't have to learn this, Sonea,' he said, taking the blade from her.

She took a deep breath. 'Yes I do,' she replied. 'What next?'

'Place your hand over the wound.'

Takan was still smiling. She gently pressed her palm over the cut. Akkarin reached out and placed his hands on her temples.

—Focus as you once did when you learned Control. Visualisation will help, to begin with. Show me the room of your mind.

She closed her eyes and drew up an image of the room and placed herself in it. The walls were covered in paintings of familiar faces and scenes, but she ignored them.

—Open the door to your power.

At once a painting stretched into a door shape and grew a handle. She reached for the handle and twisted. It swung outward and disappeared. An abyss of darkness spread before her, and within it hung the sphere of light that was her power.

—Now, step inside, into your power.

Sonea stilled. Step into the abyss?

—No, step into your power. Step into its centre.

—But it's so far away! I can't reach that far.

—Of course you can. It's your power. It is as far away as you wish it to be, and you can step as far as you want to step.

—But what if it burns me?

—It won't. It's your power.

Sonea hovered at the edge of the doorway, then steeled herself and stepped through.

There was a feeling of stretching out, then the white sphere swelled and she felt a thrill rush through her as she entered it. Suddenly she was weightless, floating in a white mist of light. Energy rushed through her.

—See?

—I see. It's wonderful. Why didn't Rothen show me this?

—You will know why soon. I want you to expand yourself. Reach out and feel all of the power that is yours. Visualisation is a useful tool, but you need to go beyond it now. You need to know your power with all your senses.

Sonea felt herself obeying before he had finished speaking. It was easy, when surrounded by nothing but whiteness, to stretch her senses out.

As she grew more aware of her power, a sense of her body came with it. At first she worried that becoming conscious of the physical meant she was losing her concentration. Then the realisation came that her power *was* her body. It didn't exist in some abyss within her mind. It flowed through every limb and bone and vein within her.

—Yes. Now focus on your right hand, and what lies beyond.

She did not see it at first, then something caught her attention. It was a gap, a glimpse of something beyond herself. Focussing on it, she sensed that an otherness lay beyond.

—Concentrate on that otherness, then do this.

He sent her a thought too strange for words. It was as

if she stepped into Takan's body, except she was still within her own. She was conscious of both.

—Be aware of the energy within his body. Take some of it into your own.

Abruptly she realised that Takan held a great store of power. He was strong, she realised, almost as strong as she. Yet his mind did not seem to be connected to it, as if he was not conscious of the power within him.

But she was. And through the gap in his skin, she had a connection to it. It was easy to direct it out of his body and into hers. She felt herself grow a little stronger.

Understanding sprang into her mind. She was drawing power.

—Now stop.

She relaxed her will and felt the trickle of energy cease.

—Begin again.

She drew power through the gap again. Just a slow leaking of magic. She wondered what it would be like to add all of his power to her own, and double her strength. Exhilarating, perhaps.

But what would she do with it? She certainly didn't need to be twice as strong. She didn't even use up her own strength during lessons at the University.

—Stop.

She obeyed. As Akkarin's hands slipped from her temples, she opened her eyes again.

'Good,' he said. 'You can heal Takan now.'

Sonea looked down at Takan's arm, then concentrated. The cut healed quickly, and her awareness of his body and power faded away. The servant grimaced and her heart skipped.

'Are you all right?'

He smiled broadly. 'Yes, Lady Sonea. You are very gentle. It's just that the Healing itches.' He looked up at Akkarin and sobered. 'She will be a worthy ally, master.'

Akkarin didn't reply. Turning, Sonea saw that he had moved away to the cabinet of books and was standing with his arms crossed and a frown creasing his brow. Sensing her gaze, he turned to meet it. His expression was unreadable.

'Congratulations, Sonea,' he said softly. 'You are now a black magician.'

She blinked in surprise. 'That is all? It's *that* easy?'

He nodded. 'Yes. The knowledge of how to kill in a moment, taught in a moment. From this day, you must never allow another into your mind. It would only take one stray thought for you to reveal this secret to another magician.'

She looked down at the tiny bloodstain on her hand and felt a chill rush over her.

I have just used black magic, she thought. *There is no turning back. Not now. Not ever.*

Takan was regarding her closely. 'Any regrets, Lady Sonea?'

She drew in a deep breath, then let it out. 'Not as many as I would have if the Guild was destroyed and I could have prevented it. But I . . . I hope I will never have to use this.' She smiled crookedly and looked at Akkarin. 'That would mean the High Lord had died, and I only recently stopped wishing that that would happen.'

Akkarin's eyebrows rose. Then Takan let out a bark of laughter.

'I like this one, master,' he said. 'You chose well when you took on her guardianship.'

Akkarin snorted quietly and uncrossed his arms. 'You know very well I didn't choose anything, Takan.' He approached the table and regarded the items on it.

'Now, Sonea, I want you to examine each of these living things on the table and consider how the skill I have taught you may be applied to them. Then I have some more books for you to read.'

CHAPTER 12

THE PRICE OF KEEPING
DEADLY SECRETS

Rising from his bed, Rothen slid aside one of his window screens and sighed. A faint light brightened one side of the sky. Dawn was close, and he was wide awake already.

He looked at the High Lord's Residence lurking at the edge of the forest. Soon Sonea would rise and make her way to the Baths.

He had watched her closely over the last week. Though he hadn't seen her with Akkarin again, something in her manner had definitely changed.

There was a new confidence in the way she walked. At midbreak, she would sit in the garden and study, giving him an opportunity to watch her from the University windows. During the last week she had been easily distracted. She would often stop and look around at the Guild with a frown of concern or worry. Occasionally she would stare at nothing, her expression grim. At these times she looked so grown up he barely recognised her.

But it was when she gazed at the High Lord's Residence that she gave him the most reason to fear. There was such a thoughtful look on her face at these times, but it was what was lacking in her expression that scared him most. There was no dislike or fear in it.

He shivered. How could she regard Akkarin's house without showing at least some discomfort? She had before. Why not now?

Rothen drummed his fingers on the windowsill. For a year and a half he had obeyed Akkarin's order to stay away from Sonea. The only times he had spoken to her had been in situations where, because others were watching, it would have seemed strange if he didn't.

I've been co-operative for so long. Surely he won't harm her if I try to speak to her alone just once.

The sky was a little lighter now. The gardens were growing clearer. All he had to do was go down there and catch her on the way to the Baths.

He turned from the window and began to dress. Only when he reached his door did he pause and reconsider. *A few questions*, he thought. *That's all. He probably won't even notice us.*

The Magicians' Quarters corridor was empty and silent. Rothen's boots rapped out a quick rhythm as he hurried down the stairs to the exit. He entered the courtyard and turned toward the gardens.

He chose to wait in one of the little garden rooms next to the main path. It was well hidden from the High Lord's Residence. Most of the garden was visible from the top floor of the University, but it was too early for any magicians to be roaming about up there.

Half an hour later he heard light footsteps approaching. He glimpsed her through the trees and sighed in relief. She was late, but was still following her routine. Then his heart began to race. What if she refused to talk to him? He rose and reached the entrance of the garden room just as she passed the entrance.

'Sonea.'

She jumped, then turned to stare at him.

'Rothen!' she whispered. 'What are you doing out here this early in the morning?'

'Trying to catch you, of course.'

She almost smiled, then a familiar wariness returned to her expression and she glanced up at the University.

'Why?'

'I want to know how you're getting along.'

Her shoulders lifted. 'Well enough. It's been a long time. I've got used to it – and good at avoiding him.'

'You spend every evening there now.'

Her gaze wavered. 'Yes.' She hesitated, then smiled faintly. 'It's good to know you're keeping an eye on me, Rothen.'

'Not as closely as I'd like.' Rothen took a deep breath. 'I have to ask you something. Is he . . . has he made you do anything you don't want to, Sonea?'

She blinked, then frowned and looked down. 'No. Other than becoming his favourite and studying so hard.'

He waited until she looked up to meet his gaze again. There was something about the way her mouth was set that was familiar. It had been so long, but it reminded him how she . . .

. . . how she almost smiles when she's telling the truth, but knows it's not the full truth!

He quickly reconsidered his question. 'Has he asked you to do anything *I* would not want you to?'

Her mouth quirked up at one corner again. 'No, Rothen. He hasn't.'

Rothen nodded, though her answer hadn't reassured him. He could not keep reshaping his question over and over. *Perhaps Ezrille is right*, he thought. *Perhaps I am worring too much.*

Sonea smiled sadly. 'I keep waiting for something bad to happen, too,' she said, 'but every day I'm learning more. If it ever comes to a fight, I won't be that easy to defeat.' She glanced in the direction of the High Lord's Residence, then took a step away from him. 'But let's not give anyone reason to start one yet.'

'No,' he agreed. 'Be careful, Sonea.'

'I will.' She turned to walk away, then hesitated and looked over her shoulder. 'You take care of yourself too, Rothen. Don't worry about me. Well, don't worry *too* much anyway.'

He managed a smile. Watching her walk away, he shook his head and sighed. She asked the impossible.

Reaching the centre of the Arena, Sonea noted the low position of the sun. It had been a long day, but soon classes would be over. Just this last bout to go.

She waited as the novices Balkan had chosen took their places. A ring of twelve formed around her, like the points of a compass. She turned a full circle, meeting the eyes of each in turn. They returned her stare confidently, no doubt reassured by their numbers. She wished she was feeling as sure of herself. Her adversaries were all from Fourth and Fifth Year classes, and most of them favoured the Warrior Skills discipline.

'Begin,' Balkan called.

All twelve novices attacked at once. Sonea threw up a strong shield and sent out a spray of forcestrikes in return. The novices combined their shields into one.

This would not happen if they were Ichani. She frowned as she remembered Akkarin's lessons.

'*The Ichani don't fight well together. They have battled and distrusted each other for years. Few know how to channel power to another, to construct a barrier with the power of several magicians, or to fight co-operatively.*'

Hopefully, she would never have to fight any Ichani. She would only need to face their spies, and then only if Akkarin died. Unless this latest one – the woman – *was* an Ichani. But Akkarin would deal with her.

'*These spies have a deep fear of Guild magicians, despite what Kariko tells them. When they kill, it is carefully planned and carried out so that they do not attract the Guild's attention. They strengthen themselves slowly. If you face one, and you are prepared, you should be able to defeat him quickly and quietly.*'

The novices increased their attack, forcing Sonea to concentrate on the fight again. She fought back. Individually, they were no match for her. Together they could eventually defeat her. But she had only to strike the inner shield of one novice to win the bout.

There was far more at stake than her pride. She had to win, and quickly, in order to save her strength.

Every night for the last week she had been giving Akkarin most of her strength. Talk of the murders in the city increased as new victims were found every day. It was difficult to say how much strength the Sachakan woman had recovered in that time. Akkarin, however, had only Sonea and Takan to take energy from each night.

She must not exhaust herself in this fight.

That was not going to be easy, however. Her adversaries were obviously well practised at combining shields. She remembered the first attempts her own class had made at this sort of fighting. Until they all learned the proper responses to different kinds of attacks, and learned to act as one, it was easy to become confused.

So I should do something unexpected to confuse them. Something they've never encountered before.

Like what she had done the night Regin and his friends had attacked her in the forest, so long ago. She couldn't effectively dazzle these novices with a bright light during the day, however. But if she did something similar so they didn't know where she was, she could sneak behind someone and . . .

She smothered a smile. Her shield didn't *have* to be transparent.

It took only a shift in her will for her shield to become a globe of white light. The disadvantage of this, she realised belatedly, was that she couldn't see *them* either.

Now for the deception. Creating several more shields like her first, she sent them out in different directions. At the same time she began walking, taking one shield with her.

She felt the novices' attack falter, and had to cover her mouth to stop herself laughing as she imagined how the Arena must look, with several big white bubbles floating around it. She couldn't strike back, however, or they would know which shield she stood within.

As the shields drew close to her adversaries, she felt them encounter the novices' barrier. She stopped and let all but one of the shields fall back a little. The novices began to attack the one still advancing. She let one of the stationary shields waver and disappear: another distraction.

Reverting the shield around her to a transparent one, she found herself standing near three novices. Gathering her power, she blasted one with a fierce attack of forcestrikes.

He jumped, and his neighbours whirled around to face her, but the rest of the novices were still too distracted by her other shields to realise their allies needed help.

The combined shield wavered and broke before her.

'Halt!'

Sonea turned to face Balkan. She blinked in surprise when she saw that he was smiling.

'An interesting strategy, Sonea,' he said. 'Not one we'd probably use in real combat, but certainly effective in the Arena. You win the bout.'

Sonea bowed. She knew that next time she attended his lessons she would find her multiple shield idea completely ineffective. The University gong rang, signalling the end of the class, and Sonea heard a few sighs among the novices. She smiled, but more at having ended the bout without using too much strength than at their obvious relief.

'Lesson over,' Balkan announced. 'You may go.'

The novices bowed and filed out of the Arena. Sonea saw that two magicians were standing just outside the entrance. Her heart skipped when she recognised them: Akkarin and Lorlen.

She followed the other novices out of the Arena. They bowed to the Higher Magicians as they passed. Akkarin ignored them and beckoned to Sonea.

'High Lord.' She bowed. 'Administrator.'

'You did well, Sonea,' Akkarin said. 'You assessed their strengths, recognised their weaknesses, and came up with an original response.'

She blinked in surprise, then felt her face warm.

'Thank you.'

'I wouldn't take Balkan's comment too seriously,

however,' he added. 'In real combat, a magician uses any strategy that works.'

Lorlen gave Akkarin a penetrating look. He looked as if he desperately wanted to ask a question, but didn't dare. *Or perhaps a dozen questions*, Sonea mused. She felt a pang of sympathy for the Administrator, and then she remembered the ring he wore.

It enabled Akkarin to sense everything Lorlen saw, felt and thought. Was Lorlen aware of its power? If he was, he must feel utterly betrayed by his friend. She shivered. If only Akkarin could tell Lorlen the truth.

But then, if he did, would he also tell Lorlen she had willingly learned black magic? Thinking of that made her feel very uncomfortable.

Akkarin started walking toward the University. Sonea and Lorlen followed.

'The Guild will lose interest in the murderer once Ambassador Dannyl arrives with the rogue, Lorlen,' Akkarin said.

Sonea had heard about the rebels that Dannyl had caught. News about the rogue magician he was bringing to the Guild had spread among the novices faster than the winter cough.

'Perhaps,' Lorlen replied, 'but they won't forget. Nobody forgets a killing spree like this. I wouldn't be surprised if someone demands the Guild do something about it.'

Akkarin sighed. 'As if having magic makes it any easier for us to find one person in a city of many thousands.'

Lorlen opened his mouth to say something, then glanced at Sonea and seemed to think better of it. He remained silent until they reached the University steps, then he bid them good night and hurried away. Akkarin started toward the residence.

'So the Thieves haven't found the spy yet?' Sonea asked quietly.

Akkarin shook his head.

'Does it usually take this long?'

He glanced at her, one eyebrow raised. 'You're eager to see us fight, then?'

'Eager?' She shook her head. 'No, I'm not eager. I can't help thinking that the longer she's out there, the more people she will kill.' She paused. 'My family lives in Northside.'

His expression softened a little. 'Yes. There are many thousands in the slums, however. The odds of her taking one of your relatives is small, particularly if they stay indoors at night.'

'They do.' She sighed. 'I worry about Cery and my old friends, though.'

'I'm sure your thief friend can take care of himself.'

She nodded. 'You're probably right.' As they passed the gardens, she thought about her early morning encounter with Rothen. She felt another stab of guilt. She hadn't *lied* to him, as such. Akkarin had never *asked* her to learn black magic.

But she felt terrible when she considered how Rothen would feel if he learned the truth. He had done so much for her, and sometimes it seemed like all she'd ever brought him was trouble. Perhaps it was good that they had been separated.

And she had to admit, begrudgingly, Akkarin had done more than Rothen could have to ensure she had the best training. She would never have been much good at Warrior Skills if he hadn't pushed her. Now it looked like she would need to use those skills to fight the spies.

As they reached the residence and the door swung open, Akkarin paused and glanced upward. 'I believe Takan is waiting for us.' He moved inside and approached the wine cabinet. 'Go on up.'

As she climbed the stairs she thought back to his comment at the Arena. Had there been a hint of pride in his voice? Was he actually pleased with her as a novice? The idea was strangely appealing. Perhaps she really had earned the title: the High Lord's favourite.

Her. The slum girl.

She slowed her step. Thinking back, she could not remember him ever expressing disdain or distaste about her origins. He *had* been threatening, manipulative and cruel, but he had never once reminded her that she had come from the poorest part of the city.

But then, how could he look down on another person? she suddenly thought. *He was a slave once.*

The ship was from the Elyne King's fleet and was larger than the Vindo vessels Dannyl had travelled in before. Made solely to transport important personages rather than cargo, there was space inside for several small but luxurious rooms.

Though Dannyl had managed to sleep for most of the day, he found it difficult to stop yawning as he rose, washed and dressed. A servant brought him a plate of roast harrel and some elaborately prepared vegetables. He felt better after eating, and a cup of sumi helped wake him up completely.

Through the ship's small windows he could see the sails of the other vessels glowing orange in the light of the setting sun. He left his room, then made his way down a long corridor to Farand's cell.

It wasn't a cell, really. Though it was the smallest and

plainest room in the ship, it was comfortably furnished. Dannyl knocked on the door. A short magician with a round face greeted him.

'Your turn then, Ambassador,' Lord Barene said, obviously relieved that his shift was over. He stared at Dannyl, then shook his head, muttered something under his breath and left.

Farand was lying on the bed. He looked at Dannyl and smiled faintly. Two plates lay on a small table. From the harrel bones left on them, Dannyl guessed they'd had the same meal as he.

'How are you feeling, Farand?'

The young man yawned. 'Tired.'

Dannyl sat down in one of the cushioned chairs. He knew Farand wasn't sleeping too well. *Neither would I*, he thought, *if I thought I might face death in a week*.

He did not believe the Guild would execute Farand. A rogue magician hadn't been discovered for over a century, however, and he had to admit he had no idea what would happen. The hardest part was, he wanted to reassure Farand, but he couldn't. It would be cruel if he turned out to be wrong.

'What have you been doing?'

'Talking to Barene. Or he's been talking to me. About you.'

'Really?'

Farand sighed. 'Royend is telling everyone about you and your lover.'

Dannyl felt a chill. So it had started.

'I'm sorry,' Farand added.

Dannyl blinked in surprise. 'Don't be, Farand. It was part of the deception. A way to convince him to trust us.'

Farand frowned. 'I don't believe it.'

'No?' Dannyl forced himself to smile. 'When we get to Kyralia, the High Lord will confirm it. It was his idea to have us pretend to be lovers, so the rebels felt they had something to blackmail us with.'

'But what he's telling them is true,' Farand said softly. 'When I saw you two together, it was obvious. Don't worry. I haven't told anyone my views on the matter.' He yawned again. 'I won't. But I can't help thinking you must be wrong about the Guild.'

'How so?'

'You keep telling me the Guild is always fair and reasonable. But from the way the other magicians are reacting to this news about you, I'm beginning to think it's not. And it wasn't fair of your High Lord to make you reveal something like that if he knew this was how the other magicians would react.' His eyelids closed, then fluttered open again. 'I'm so tired. And I don't feel so good.'

'Get some rest then.'

The young man closed his eyes. His breathing immediately slowed and Dannyl guessed he had fallen asleep. *No conversation tonight*, he mused. *It's going to be a long one.*

He looked out of the window at the other ships. So Royend was taking his revenge. *It doesn't matter if Farand believes it's true*, he told himself. *When Akkarin confirms that it was all a deception, nobody will believe the Dem.*

Was Farand right, though? Was it unfair of Akkarin to have used him and Tayend in this way? Dannyl could no longer pretend that he didn't know Tayend was a lad. Would people expect him to avoid Tayend from now on? What would they say when he didn't?

He sighed. He hated living with this fear. He hated

pretending that Tayend meant nothing more to him than a useful assistant should. He had no delusions that he could boldly admit to the truth, however, and somehow change Kyralian attitudes. And he missed Tayend already, like a part of himself had been left behind in Elyne.

Think of something else, he told himself.

His thoughts strayed to the book that Tayend had 'borrowed' from the Dem, now stowed with Dannyl's belongings. He hadn't mentioned it to anyone, not even Errend. Though finding the book had helped him decide it was time to arrest the rebels, it hadn't been necessary to reveal its existence. And he didn't want to. By reading those passages, Dannyl had broken the law against learning about black magic. The words were still in his memory . . .

Minor skills include the ability to create 'blood stones' or 'blood gems' which enhance the maker's ability to mindspeak with another person at a distance . . .

He thought about the eccentric Dem he and Tayend had visited in the mountains over a year ago, during their second journey to search for information about ancient magic. In the Dem Ladeiri's impressive collection of books and artefacts had been a ring, the symbol for high magic carved into the red glass 'gem' in the setting. A ring that according to the Dem enabled the wearer to communicate with another magician without the conversation being overheard. Was the gem in the ring one of these blood gems?

Dannyl shivered. Had he handled an object of black magic? The thought made him feel cold. He had actually put the ring on.

. . . and 'store stones' or 'store gems' which can hold and release magic in specific ways.

He and Tayend had trekked up the mountains above Ladeiri's home to an ancient ruined city. They had found a hidden tunnel which led, according to Tayend's translation of the writing carved into it, to a 'Chamber of Ultimate Justice'. Dannyl had followed the tunnel to a large room with a domed ceiling covered in glittering stones. Those stones had attacked him with magical strikes, and he had barely escaped alive.

His skin prickled. Was the ceiling of the Chamber of Ultimate Justice made from these store stones? Was this what Akkarin had meant when he'd said there were political reasons for keeping the chamber's existence a secret? It was a room full of black magic gems.

Akkarin had said something about the chamber losing strength, too. Clearly, he understood what it was. Knowing how to recognise and deal with such magic would be the High Lord's responsibility. Which was all the more reason why the book must remain concealed for now. He would give it to Akkarin when he arrived.

Farand made a small noise of distress in his sleep. Looking up, Dannyl frowned. The young man was pale and sickly. The distress of capture had taken quite a toll. Then Dannyl looked closer. Farand's lips were darker. They were almost blue . . .

Dannyl moved to the bed. He grabbed Farand's shoulder and shook him. The man's eyes opened, but didn't focus.

Putting a hand to the man's forehead, Dannyl closed his eyes and sent his mind forth. He sucked in a breath as he sensed the chaos within the man's body.

Someone had poisoned him.

Drawing on his power, Dannyl sent Healing energy out, but it was hard to know where to start. He applied it to the most affected organs first. But the deterioration continued as the poison gradually spread through the body.

This is beyond me, Dannyl thought desperately. *I need a Healer.*

He thought about the other two magicians in the ship. Neither were Healers. Both were Elynes. He thought of Dem Marane's warning.

'*You do realise the King might kill him rather than let the Guild discover whatever it is that he knows.*'

Barene had been here when the meal had been served. Had he given Farand the poison? Best not to call him, just in case. The other magician, Lord Hemend, was close to the Elyne King. Dannyl didn't trust him either.

There was only one other choice. Dannyl closed his eyes.

—*Vinara!*

—*Dannyl?*

—*I need your help. Someone has poisoned the rogue.*

The other two magicians would hear this call, but Dannyl couldn't help that. He put a magical binding on the door. Though it would not keep out a magician for long, it would prevent surprise intrusions or interruptions from non-magicians.

The sense of Lady Vinara's personality grew stronger, full of concern and urgency.

—*Describe the symptoms.*

Dannyl showed her an image of Farand, his skin now very white and his breathing laboured. Then he sent his mind back into the man's body and conveyed his impressions to her.

—*You must purge the poison, then attend to the damage.*

Following her instructions, Dannyl began a painfully complicated process. First he made Farand throw up. Then he took one of the knives used for the meal, cleaned and sharpened it with magic, and cut open a vein in the man's arm. Vinara explained how to keep the man's failing organs working, fight the effects of the poison, and encourage the body to make more blood as the contaminated fluid slowly drained away.

It took a great toll on Farand's body. Healing magic could not replace the nutrients needed to make blood and tissue. Reserves of fat and some muscle tissue were depleted. When he woke – if he woke – Farand would be barely strong enough to breathe.

When Dannyl had done all he could, he opened his eyes and, as he became aware of the room again, realised that someone was hammering on the door.

—*Do you know who did this?* Vinara asked.

—*No. But I have an idea why. I could investigate . . .*

—*Let the others investigate. You must stay and guard the patient.*

—*I don't trust them.* There. It had been said.

—*Nevertheless, Farand is your responsibility. You can't protect him and look for the poisoner at the same time. Be vigilant, Dannyl.*

She was right, of course. Rising from the bed, Dannyl straightened his shoulders and readied himself to face whoever was knocking at the door.

CHAPTER 13

THE MURDERESS

As Sonea entered the underground room, she noted the objects on the table. A dish contained some pieces of broken glass. Beside it was a broken silver fork, a bowl and a cloth. Next to these lay the wooden box that contained Akkarin's knife.

For two weeks she had been practising black magic. She had gained in skill and could now take a lot of power quickly, or a little power through the tiniest pinprick. She had drawn energy from small animals, plants and even water. The objects on the table were different tonight, and she paused to wonder what Akkarin intended to teach her next.

'Good evening, Sonea.'

She looked up. Akkarin was leaning over the chest. It was open, revealing several old books. He was examining one of them. She bowed.

'Good evening, High Lord.'

He closed the book, then walked across the room and set it beside the other objects on the table.

'Did you finish the records of the Sachakan war?'

'Nearly. It's hard to believe the Guild managed to lose so much of its history.'

'They didn't lose it,' he corrected. 'They purged it. Those history books not destroyed were rewritten so there was no mention of higher magic.'

Sonea shook her head. When she considered how much effort the Guild had once spent getting rid of all mention of black magic, she understood why Akkarin did not want to risk telling the present Guild the truth about his past. Yet still she could not imagine Lorlen and the Higher Magicians reacting so blindly to black magic if they knew the reason Akkarin had learned it, or if they understood the threat of the Ichani.

It's me they would condemn, she thought suddenly, *because I chose to learn it*.

'Tonight I am going to show you how to make blood gems,' Akkarin told her.

Blood gems? Her heart skipped as she realised what he was referring to. She would be making a gem like the one in the tooth of the spy, and in Lorlen's ring.

'A blood gem allows a magician to see and hear whatever the wearer sees and hears — and thinks,' Akkarin told her. 'If the wearer cannot see, neither can the maker. The gem also focusses mind communication on its maker, so that no other can hear conversations between maker and wearer.

'It has limitations, however,' he warned. 'The maker is constantly connected to the gem. A part of the maker's mind is always receiving images and thoughts from the wearer, and this can be quite a distraction. After a while you learn to block it out.

'Once made, the connection to the maker cannot be broken unless the gem is destroyed. So if a gem is lost by its wearer, and another finds and wears it, the maker will have to put up with the distraction of an unwanted mind connected to his own.' He smiled faintly. 'Takan told me a story once of an Ichani who had staked a slave out to be eaten alive by wild limek, and put a gem on the man so he could watch. One of the animals ate the gem, and the Ichani spent several days driven to distraction by its thoughts.'

His smile faded then, and his gaze became distant. 'But the Ichani are skilled at turning magic to cruel uses. Dakova once made a gem out of a man's blood, then made the man watch as his brother was tortured.' He grimaced. 'Fortunately, glass blood gems are easy to destroy. The brother managed to smash the gem.'

He rubbed his forehead and frowned. 'Because this connection to another mind can be distracting, it is not a good idea to make too many blood gems. I have three, at the moment. Do you know who carries them?'

Sonea nodded. 'Lorlen.'

'Yes.'

'And . . . Takan?' She frowned. 'He doesn't wear a ring, though.'

'No, he doesn't. Takan's gem is hidden.'

'Who has the third?'

'A friend in a useful place.'

She shrugged. 'I don't think I could ever guess. Why Lorlen?'

Akkarin's eyebrows rose at the question. 'I needed to keep an eye on him. Rothen would never have done anything to cause you harm. Lorlen, however, would sacrifice you if it meant saving the Guild.'

Sacrifice me? But of course he would. She shivered. *I probably would too, if I were in his position.* Knowing this, she wished even more that Akkarin could tell Lorlen the truth.

'He has proven very useful, however,' Akkarin added. 'He is in contact with the Captain in the Guard who is investigating the murders. I have been able to estimate how strong each of the spies is based on the number of bodies that are found.'

'Does he know what the gem is?'

'He knows what it does.'

Poor Lorlen, she thought. *He believes his friend has turned to evil magic, and knows that Akkarin can read his every thought.* She frowned. *But how hard is it for Akkarin to be always conscious of how his friend fears and disapproves of him?*

Akkarin turned to face the table. 'Come here.'

As she moved to the other side of the table, Akkarin flipped open the lid of the box. He lifted out the knife and handed it to her.

'When I first saw Dakova make a blood gem, I thought there must be something magical in blood. It wasn't until years later that I discovered this wasn't true. The blood merely imprints the maker's identity on the glass.'

'You learned to make them from the books?'

'No. A great part of the magic I learned by studying an ancient example I had come across during the first year of my research. I didn't know what it was at the time, but later I borrowed it for a while to study. Though its maker was long dead, and it no longer worked, enough magic was still imprinted in the glass for me to gain a sense of how it functioned.'

'Do you still have it?'

'No, I returned it to its owner. Unfortunately, he died soon after, and I don't know what happened to his collection of ancient jewellery.'

She nodded and looked down at the items on the table.

'Any living part of yourself can be used,' Akkarin told her. 'Hair works, but not well because most of it is dead.

There is a Sachakan folk tale in which tears were used, but I suspect that is just a romantic fancy. You could cut out a piece of your flesh, but that wouldn't be pleasant or convenient. Blood is the easiest.' He tapped the bowl. 'You'll only need a few drops.'

Sonea looked at the bowl and then the blade. Akkarin watched her silently. She considered her left arm. Where should she cut? Turning over her hand she noticed an old, faint scar on her palm from when she had cut herself on a drainpipe as a child. She brought the tip of the knife over to touch her palm. To her surprise, she felt no pain as the blade sliced open her skin.

Then blood welled from the cut and a sharp ache began to nag at her senses. She let the blood drip into the bowl.

'Heal yourself,' Akkarin instructed. 'Always heal yourself without delay. Even half-healed cuts are a break in your barrier.'

She concentrated on the wound. The blood stopped flowing, then the edges of the cut slowly sealed together. Akkarin handed her the cloth, and she wiped the blood off her hand.

Akkarin handed her a piece of glass. 'Hold this in the air and melt it. It will keep its shape easier if you set it spinning.'

Sonea focussed her will on the fragment of glass and lifted it up. She sent heat around it and willed it to spin. It began to glow around the edges, then slowly shrank into a globule.

'At last!' Akkarin hissed.

Startled, she lost her hold on the globule. It dropped to the table, where it made a small scorch mark.

'Oops.'

Akkarin hadn't noticed, however. His eyes were focussed far beyond the room. As she watched, his gaze sharpened. He smiled grimly, then picked up the knife.

'Takan has just received a message. The Thieves have found the spy.'

Sonea's heart skipped.

'Your lesson will have to wait until we return.' Moving to a cupboard, Akkarin took out the leather belt with the knife sheath she had seen him wearing the night she had spied upon him, so long ago. He wiped the blade of his knife on the cloth, and slipped it into the sheath. Sonea blinked in surprise as he then untied the sash of his robes and removed the outer garment. Beneath it he wore a black vest.

He strapped the belt about his waist, then moved to another cupboard and took out a long, worn-looking coat for himself, a cloak for Sonea, and a lantern.

'Keep your robes well covered,' he said as she donned the cloak. It had many small buttons down the front, and two side openings for her hands.

He paused to regard her, and frowned.

'I would not take you with me if I could avoid it, but if I am to prepare you to face these spies, I must show you how it may be done. You must do *exactly* as I instruct.'

She nodded. 'Yes, High Lord.'

Akkarin moved to the wall and the hidden door to the passages opened. Sonea followed him through. The lantern spluttered alight.

'We must not let this woman see you,' he told her as he started down the passage. 'Tavaka's master probably saw you through his gem before I destroyed it. If any of the Ichani see you with me again, they will guess I am training you. They will try to kill you while you are too weak and unskilled to defend yourself.'

He fell silent as they reached the first barrier, and did not speak again until they had navigated the maze of passages and reached the blocked tunnel. Akkarin gestured at the rubble.

'Have a good look with your mind, then shift the stairs into place.'

Extending her senses, Sonea examined the arrangement of rocks. At first it appeared to be a random jumble, then she began to see a pattern in them. It was like a large version of the wooden puzzles sold in the markets. Push on one particular spot, and the puzzle pieces slid against each other to form a new shape – or fell apart. She drew a little magic and began shifting the rocks. The passage filled with the sound of stone sliding against stone as the stairs moved into place.

'Well done,' Akkarin murmured. He strode forward, taking the stairs two at a time. Sonea followed him up. At the top, she turned and willed the rock slabs back into their former positions.

The light of the lantern illuminated the familiar brick walls of the Thieves' Road. Akkarin started forward. After several hundred paces they reached the place where the guide had met them before. A smaller shadow stepped out to greet them.

The boy was about twelve, Sonea guessed. His eyes were hard and wary, however – the eyes of a much older person. He stared at them both, then looked down at Akkarin's boots and nodded. Without a word, he indicated that they should follow him and started down the passages.

Though their path wound about from time to time, it

took them in one general direction. Their guide finally stopped beside a ladder and pointed up to a trapdoor. Akkarin shuttered the lamp and the passage filled with darkness. Sonea heard him set a boot on the rungs of the ladder and begin to climb. Faint light filled the passage as he lifted the trapdoor cautiously and peered out. He beckoned to her and, as she started up the ladder, opened the trapdoor fully and climbed out.

Following, Sonea found herself in an alley. The houses around her were roughly made from all kinds of scavenged materials. Some looked as if they might fall down at any moment. The smell of garbage and sewage was powerful. She felt a long-forgotten sympathy and wariness. This was the outer edge of the slums, where the poorest dwells scratched an existence. It was a sad and dangerous place.

A heavily built man stepped out of a nearby doorway and strolled toward them. Sonea let out a small sigh of relief as she recognised him as the man who had been guarding the previous spy. He stared at her, then turned to Akkarin.

'She just left,' the man said. 'We've been tagging her for two hours. The locals say she's been minding herself away down in there for two nights.' He pointed toward a nearby door.

'How do you know she'll come back tonight?' Akkarin asked.

'Had a look at the place after she left. She got some stuff down there. She'll be back.'

'The rest of the place is empty?'

'A few beggars and whores use it, but we told them to get busy for the night.'

Akkarin nodded. 'We'll have a look inside and see if it

is a suitable place for an ambush. Make sure no-one comes in.'

The man nodded. 'Hers is the last room on the right.'

Sonea followed Akkarin to the door. It squeaked in protest as he pulled it open. They descended crumbling steps of compacted dirt supported by rotting beams of wood, and started along a corridor.

It was dark inside, and the earth floor was uneven. Akkarin opened the shutter of his lamp just enough to light the way. The openings into the rooms had no doors. Some were covered with rough sacking material. The walls were lined with wood, but planks had fallen away here and there and the dirt behind them had formed mounds on the floor.

Most of the rooms were empty. The last entrance on the right was covered with sacking. Akkarin stared at the covering intently, then pushed it aside and opened the shutter of the lamp.

The room inside was surprisingly large. A few wooden crates and a warped plank formed a table. A shelf had been carved along one side of the room, and in one corner was a thin mattress and some blankets.

Akkarin began to walk around the room, examining everything closely. He looked through the bedding, then shook his head.

'Morren spoke of valuables. Surely he didn't mean this.'

Sonea smothered a smile. She walked over to the nearest wall and began to poke her finger between each of the boards. Akkarin watched as she made her way around the room. Near the bedding she felt a tell-tale sponginess.

The planks came away easily. The sacking that lay behind them was caked with dried mud, but here and there a thread showed. She carefully lifted a corner. Inside was an alcove large enough for a child to sit in, its roof supported by more rotting wooden planks. A small bundle of cloth lay at the centre.

Akkarin moved to her side and chuckled. 'Well, well. You *have* proven to be useful.'

Sonea shrugged. 'I lived in a place like this, once. Dwells call them Holes.'

He paused. 'For long?'

She looked up to find him regarding her appraisingly.

'For a winter. It was a long time ago, when I was very small.' She turned back to the alcove. 'I remember it was crowded, and cold.'

'But there are few people living here now. Why is that?'

'The Purge. It doesn't happen until the first snows of the year. This is where all those people the Guild drives out of the city go to. The ones the Houses say are dangerous thieves, when the truth is they just don't like ugly beggars and cripples making the city look shabby, and the real Thieves aren't inconvenienced by the Purge—'

From behind them came the faint, distant squeak of a door. Akkarin spun about.

'It's her.'

'How do you—'

'Morren would have stopped anyone else.' He snapped the shutter of the lamp mostly shut and looked quickly around the room. 'No other way out,' he muttered. He lifted the corner of the sacking covering the alcove. 'Can you fit in there?'

She didn't bother replying. Turning, she sat on the edge of the alcove and pushed herself backward. As she folded her legs into the small space, Akkarin let the sacking fall and pressed the boards back into place.

Complete darkness followed. The pounding of her heart was loud in the silence. Then Sonea suddenly found herself staring at lines of bright stars.

'You again,' a woman said in a strangely accented voice. 'I wondered when you would give me another chance to kill you.'

The stars brightened and Sonea felt the vibration of magic. Realising that the points of light were holes in the mud-soaked sacking, Sonea leaned forward, hoping to see into the room beyond.

'You came prepared,' the woman observed.

'Of course,' Akkarin said.

'I have, too,' she said. 'Your dirty city is a bit smaller now. And your Guild will soon be another man less.'

In one place, where the dried mud coating the sacking was thin and crumbling, Sonea could see moving shapes illuminated by flashes of light. She scratched at the sacking to unclog more of the cloth's rough weave.

'What will your Guild think when its ruler is found dead? Will they work out what killed him? I think not.'

Sonea could make out a figure now. A woman in a dull-coloured shirt and trousers stood on one side of the room. Sonea couldn't see Akkarin, however. She continued scratching at the mud coating of the sacking, trying to get a better view. How was she going to learn anything about fighting these spies, if she couldn't see the battle?

'They won't know what's hunting them,' the Sachakan continued. 'I was thinking of walking in and taking them all at once, but now I think it'll be more fun to lure them out and kill them one by one.'

'I recommend the latter,' Akkarin replied. 'You'll not get far, otherwise.'

The woman laughed. 'Won't I?' she sneered. 'But I know Kariko is right. Your Guild doesn't know higher magic. They are weak and stupid – so stupid that you must hide from them what you know or they would kill you.'

The room flared with light as strikes pounded at the woman's shield. The woman responded in kind. A creaking sound came from above. Sonea saw the woman glance up, then step sideways, toward the alcove.

'Just because we do not abuse our knowledge of magic, does not mean we are ignorant,' Akkarin said calmly. He moved into sight, maintaining a position opposite the woman.

'But I have seen the truth in the minds of your people,' the woman replied. 'I know this is why you chase me alone – why you cannot let anyone see us fighting. Let them see this, then.'

Suddenly the room filled with the deafening crack of splintering wood. A shower of wooden beams and roofing tiles fell down from the roof, filling the air with dust. The woman laughed and moved closer to the alcove and Sonea.

Then she stopped as another fall sent rubble down blocking her path. The Sachakan was suddenly thrown back against the side wall. Sonea felt the impact of Akkarin's forcestrike through the floor of the alcove, and a shower of dirt pattered onto her back.

The woman pushed herself away from the wall, snarled something, then strode toward the rubble . . . and through it. Sonea blinked in surprise as she realised it had been an illusion, then her heart skipped as she saw that the woman was walking straight toward her.

Akkarin attacked, forcing the woman to slow. As the woman stopped in front of her hidden store, Sonea found herself facing Akkarin's attack. Disturbed, she hastily put up a strong shield around herself.

The room vibrated as the two magicians struck at each other. More dirt trickled down Sonea's back. Reaching up, she felt the beams holding up the roof of the alcove beginning to split and sag. Alarmed, she expanded her shield to give them support.

A laugh brought her attention back to the room. Peering through the sacking, she saw that Akkarin was backing away. His strikes didn't seem to be as strong. He took a sideways step toward the door.

He's losing strength, she realised suddenly. Her stomach sank as he edged closer to the door.

'You're not getting away from me this time,' the woman said.

A barrier filled the doorway. Akkarin's expression darkened. The woman seemed to grow straighter and taller. Instead of advancing, she took a few steps backward and turned toward Sonea.

Watching Akkarin, Sonea saw his expression change to dismay and alarm. The woman reached out toward the alcove, then stopped as he threw a powerful strike at her.

He was faking, Sonea thought suddenly. *He was trying to draw her away from me.* But instead of following him, the woman had approached the alcove. *Why? Does she know I'm here? Or is it something else?*

Feeling around, Sonea found the bundle of cloth. Even in the dark she could tell that the material was of good quality.

She created a tiny, faint globe light. Unravelling the bundle, Sonea saw that it was a woman's shawl. As she lifted it, a small object fell out of the folds. A silver ring.

She picked it up. It was a man's ring, the kind that the elders of a House wore to indicate their status. A flat square on one side of it bore the incal of House Saril.

Then the alcove exploded into a storm of dirt and noise.

Sonea felt herself thrown backward. Curling into a ball, she concentrated on holding her shield around her. The weight pushing down on it increased, then became constant.

Then all was still. Opening her eyes, she created another tiny globe light. All about her was earth. Her shield was holding it back, forming a spherical hollow around her. She uncurled, rolled into a crouch and considered her situation.

She was buried. Though she could hold the shield for some time, the air within it would not last long. It would not be hard to push her way out. Once she did, however, she would no longer be hidden.

So I should stay here as long as possible, she decided. *I won't get to see any more of the fight, but that can't be helped.*

Thinking back on what she'd witnessed, she shook her head. The battle had been nothing like Akkarin had predicted. The woman was stronger than the usual spy. Her attitude was not like that of a slave, and she had referred to the Ichani as 'us' not 'my masters', as the previous spy had. She was skilled in fighting. The former slaves sent into Kyralia had no time to gain any fighting skills.

If this woman was no slave, then there was only one other thing she could be.

Ichani.

Sonea's stomach clenched at the realisation. Akkarin was fighting an Ichani. She concentrated and found she could feel the vibration of their magic somewhere near. The battle was still raging.

The pressure on her shield began to ease. Looking up, she saw a small hole appear where the soil was falling away from her shield. As she watched, it enlarged as more dirt slipped away.

A view of the room began to emerge. She straightened, and caught her breath in horror. The Sachakan woman was standing only a few steps away.

Alarmed, Sonea reduced the size of her shield, but this only sent the dirt cascading down faster. As it did, Akkarin came into view. His eyes flickered to hers once, but his expression did not change. He started to move forward.

Sonea crouched within her shield, helplessly watching the Sachakan woman's back as the dirt continued to fall away. She dared not move in case the woman heard something and turned around. The Sachakan took a step backward as Akkarin drew closer. Her body was stiff with concentration.

Sonea felt Akkarin's magic brush her shield as he encircled the woman with a barrier and tried to drag her forward. But the woman broke his hold and took another step back. As her shield drew closer, Sonea pulled her own inward to avoid contact. The woman's shield now buzzed within a hand's span of Sonea. Another step, and the woman would discover her.

If *she detects me*, Sonea thought. *If I stop shielding, her shield might slide over me without her noticing.*

The woman's shield was a globe, which was the easiest shape to hold. A globe-shaped shield protected a magician's feet by dipping under the ground a little, but for a shield to be strong enough to hold back a subterranean attack, it couldn't move through the ground. All novices learned to weaken the part of their shield that overlapped an obstacle or the ground as they moved, then strengthen it as soon as they were still again.

If this woman had the same habit, she might allow her shield to slide over Sonea – thinking Sonea was merely an obstacle – when she moved back again.

But she will *notice. She will sense my presence.*

Sonea caught her breath. *But I'll be* inside *her shield! For a moment, before she realises what has happened, she'll be defence-less. I just need something to . . .*

Sonea's eyes slid to the ground. A sliver of wood from the alcove lay half buried nearby. As she contemplated what she intended to do, her heart raced even faster. She drew in a deep, quiet breath and waited for the woman to step backward again. She did not have to wait long.

As the shield passed over her, Sonea grabbed the piece of wood, stood up and slashed it across the back of the woman's neck. The woman began to turn, but Sonea had anticipated that. She pressed her other hand against the wound and focussed all her will into drawing energy into herself as fast as she could.

The woman's eyes widened in horrified realisation. Her shield disappeared and her knees buckled. Sonea nearly lost her grip, and quickly wound her free arm around the woman's waist. The Sachakan was too heavy, however, and Sonea let the woman sink to the ground.

Power rushed into Sonea, then abruptly stopped. She drew her hand away and the woman fell onto her back. The Sachakan's eyes stared blankly at nothing.

Dead. A wave of relief washed over Sonea. *It worked*, she thought. *It actually worked.*

Then she looked at her hand. In the moonlight spilling

through the ruined roof the blood covering her palm looked black. A cold horror rushed over her. She staggered to her feet.

I have just killed someone with black magic.

Suddenly dizzy, she stumbled backward. She knew she was breathing too fast, but couldn't seem to stop herself. Hands gripped her shoulders and stopped her falling.

'Sonea,' a voice said, 'take a deep breath. Hold it. Let it out.'

Akkarin. She tried to do as he said. It took a few attempts. From somewhere he produced a cloth and wiped her hand.

'It's not pleasant, is it?'

She shook her head.

'It shouldn't be.'

She shook her head again. Her mind spun with contradictory thoughts.

She would have killed me, if I hadn't. She would have killed others. So why does it feel so horrible to know I've done this?

Perhaps because it makes me just that little bit more like them.

What if there are no spies to kill, and Takan isn't enough, and I have to look for other ways to strengthen myself to fight the Ichani? Will I start haunting the streets, killing the odd thug or mugger? Will I use the defence of Kyralia to justify preying on the innocent?

Sonea shook her head at the bewildering mixture of emotions she felt. She had never felt such doubt before.

'Look at me, Sonea.'

He turned her around. She reluctantly met his gaze. He reached out and she felt him gently tug something from her hair. A piece of the sacking fell from his hand to the ground.

'It is not an easy choice, the one you've made,' he said, 'but you will learn to trust yourself.' He looked up. Following his gaze, she saw that the full moon hung in the middle of the gap in the roof.

The Eye, Sonea thought. *It's open. Either it allowed me to do this because it was not evil, or I'm going to sink into madness.*

But I don't believe in silly superstitions, she reminded herself.

'We must get away from here quickly,' he said. 'The Thieves will take care of the body.'

Sonea nodded. As Akkarin moved away she reached up to smooth her hair. Her scalp tingled where he had touched her. Keeping her eyes averted from the body of the dead woman, she followed him out of the room.

CHAPTER 14

THE WITNESS

Something was pressing gently against Cery's back. Something warm. A hand.

Savara's hand, he realised.

Her touch brought him back to the present. He realised he had been in a daze. At the moment Sonea had killed the Sachakan woman, the world had tilted and spun around him. Since then he had been aware of nothing but the thought of what she had done.

Well, almost nothing. Savara had said something. He frowned. Something about Akkarin having an apprentice. He turned to look at the woman at his side.

She smiled crookedly. 'Aren't you going to thank me?'

He looked down. They were sitting on a section of the roof that was still intact. The top of the Hole had seemed a good place to watch the battle from. The roof was made of scraps of wood and the occasional patch of cracked tiles, leaving plenty of gaps. As long as they kept their weight on the beams, they were fairly safe.

Unfortunately, neither Cery nor Savara had considered the possibility that the combatants might knock their perch out from under them.

As the roof had collapsed, however, something had prevented Cery from falling. Before he could grasp how it was possible that he and Savara could be floating in the air, they had moved to the remaining area of roof, out of sight of the fighters below.

Everything about Savara now suddenly made sense: how she knew when a new murderer arrived, how she knew so much about the people the High Lord was fighting, and why she was so confident she could kill these murderers herself.

'So, when were you going to tell me?' he asked.

She shrugged. 'When you trusted me enough. I might have ended up like her if I had told you at the start.' She looked down at the corpse Gol and his assistants were dragging away.

'You still might,' he said. 'It *is* getting hard to tell the difference between you Sachakans.'

Her eyes flashed with anger, but her voice was calm as she replied.

'Not all magicians in my country are like the Ichani, Thief. Our society has many groups . . . factions . . .' She shook her head in frustration. 'You do not have a word that quite suits. The Ichani are outcasts, sent into the wasteland as punishment. They are the worst of my country. Do not judge us all by them.

'My own people have always feared the Ichani would band together one day, but we have no influence over the King, and cannot persuade him to stop this tradition of banishment to the wastes as punishment. We have watched them for many hundreds of years, and killed those most likely to control others. We have tried to prevent what is happening here, but we must be careful not to show our hand, as many in Sachaka need only a small excuse to attack us.'

'What *is* happening here?'

She hesitated. 'I'm not sure how much I may tell you.' To Cery's amusement, she began chewing her lip like a child questioned by its parent. At his chuckle, she looked at him and frowned. 'What?'

'You don't seem the sort to ask for anyone's say so.'

She returned his gaze steadily, then looked down. Following her gaze, Cery saw that Gol and the body were gone.

'You did not expect to see her, did you?' she said softly. 'Does it disturb you, to see your lost love kill another?'

He stared at her, suddenly uncomfortable. 'How did you know that?'

She smiled. 'It is in your face, when you see her or talk of her.'

He looked down at the room. An image of Sonea leaping at the woman flashed through his mind. Her face had been set with determination. She really had come a long way from the uncertain girl who had been so dismayed to discover she had magical abilities.

Then he remembered how the expression on her face had changed when Akkarin had brushed something out of her hair.

'It was a childhood crush,' he told Savara. 'I've known for a long time that she's not for me.'

'No, you have not,' she said, setting the roof creaking as she shifted her weight. 'You only learned that tonight.'

He turned back to face her. 'How can you—'

To his surprise, she had edged closer. As he turned to face her she put a hand behind his head, pulled him nearer and kissed him.

Her lips were warm and strong. He felt heat rush through his body. Reaching out, he tried to pull her closer, but the piece of wood he was sitting on slid sideways and he felt himself losing his balance. Their lips parted as he began to fall backward.

Something steadied him. He recognised the touch of magic. Savara smiled mischievously, leaned forward and grabbed his shirt. She dropped her shoulder to the roof and pulled him over her, and the supports creaked alarmingly as they rolled further away from the damaged area. When they stopped, she was lying on top of him. She smiled – the breathtakingly sensual smile that always set his pulse racing.

'Well,' he said. 'This is nice.'

She laughed quietly, then bent to kiss him again. He hesitated only a moment, as a feeling, like a premonition, touched the edge of his thoughts.

The day Sonea discovered her magic, she belonged somewhere else. Savara has magic, too. And she already belongs somewhere else . . .

But right now, he didn't care.

Lorlen frowned and blinked open his eyes. His bedroom was mostly dark. The light of the full moon set his window screens glowing faintly, making the gold Guild symbols appear as stark black shapes on the fine paper.

Then he realised why he was awake. Someone was hammering on his door.

What time is it? Sitting up, he massaged his eyes in an attempt to rub away sleepiness. The hammering continued. He sighed, rose and staggered out of his bedroom to the main door of his rooms.

Lord Osen stood outside, looking dishevelled and frantic.

'Administrator,' he whispered. 'Lord Jolen and his family have been murdered.'

Lorlen stared at his assistant. Lord Jolen. One of the Healers. A young man, recently married. *Murdered?*

'Lord Balkan has sent for the Higher Magicians,' Osen said urgently. 'You're to meet in the Day Room. Would you like me to go back, while you get dressed, and tell them you're on your way?'

Lorlen glanced down at his bed clothes. 'Of course.'

Osen nodded, then hurried away. Lorlen closed the door and walked back into his bedroom. He took down a set of blue robes from his cupboard and began to change.

Jolen was dead. So was his family. Murdered, according to Osen. Lorlen frowned as his mind began to fill with questions. *How* was this possible? Magicians were not easy to kill. The murderer was either knowledgeable and clever, or another magician. *Or worse*, he thought. A *black magician*.

He looked down at his ring as dreadful possibilities began to form in his mind.

No, he told himself. *Wait until you've heard the details*.

He tied the sash of his robe about his waist, then hurried out of his room. Once outside the Magicians' Quarters, he strode across the courtyard to the building called The Seven Arches. The leftmost room of this building was the Night Room, where the weekly social gathering of magicians was held. The room at the centre was the Banquet Room. On the right side of the building was the Day Room, a place created for receiving and entertaining important guests.

As Lorlen entered he blinked at the sudden brightness. The Night Room was all dark blue and silver but, in contrast, the Day Room was decorated in shades of white and gold, now lit by several globe lights. The effect was harsh.

Seven men stood in the centre of the room. Lord Balkan and Lord Sarrin nodded to Lorlen. Director Jerrik was talking to the two Heads of Studies, Peakin and Telano. Lord Osen was standing next to the only man not wearing robes.

As Lorlen recognised Captain Barran, his heart sank. A magician was dead, and the captain investigating the strange murders was here. Perhaps the situation was as bad as he feared.

Balkan stepped forward to greet him. 'Administrator.'

'Lord Balkan,' Lorlen replied. 'I guess you'll want me to hold my questions until Lady Vinara, Administrator Kito and the High Lord arrive.'

Balkan hesitated. 'Yes. But I have not summoned the High Lord. My reasons will be explained soon.'

Lorlen endeavoured to look surprised.

'Not Akkarin?'

'Not yet.'

They turned as the door opened. A Vindo magician entered. Kito's role as Expatriate Administrator kept him outside of the Guild and Kyralia most of the time. He had returned from Vin only a few days ago to deal with the rogue magician Dannyl was bringing for trial.

Lorlen remembered Akkarin's prediction: *The Guild will lose interest in the murderer once Ambassador Dannyl arrives with the rogue, Lorlen.*

If this is as bad as I fear, Lorlen thought, *I think the situation will be quite the opposite.*

As Balkan greeted Kito, Captain Barran approached Lorlen. The young guard managed a grim smile.

'Good evening, Administrator. This is the first time the

Guild has brought my attention to a murder, instead of the other way around.'

'Really?' Lorlen replied. 'Who informed you?'

'Lord Balkan. It seems Lord Jolen managed to communicate with him briefly before he died.'

Lorlen's heart skipped. Did Balkan know who the murderer was, then? As he turned to regard the Warrior, the door of the Day Room opened again and Lady Vinara stalked into the room.

She looked around at the faces, noting who was present, then nodded to herself. 'You're all here. Good. I think, perhaps, we should be seated. We have a serious and shocking situation to deal with.'

Chairs at the sides of the room floated to the centre. Captain Barran's expression was a mixture of fascination and awe as he watched the chairs arrange themselves into a circle. Once everyone was seated, Vinara looked at Balkan.

'I think Lord Balkan should begin,' she said, 'as he was the first to be alerted to the murders.'

Balkan nodded in agreement. He looked around the circle. 'Two hours ago my attention was caught by a mental call from Lord Jolen. It was very faint, but I heard my name and detected great fear. When I concentrated on it, however, all I caught was the identity of the caller, and the sense that he was being harmed by another – with magic – before the communication ended abruptly. I attempted to call Lord Jolen, but received no answer.

'I informed Lady Vinara of the communication, and she told me Lord Jolen was staying with his family in the city. She could not contact him either, so I decided to visit the family home. When I arrived, no servant came to open the door. I unlocked it, and found a terrible scene inside.'

Balkan's expression darkened. 'The entire household had been killed. I searched the house, discovering the bodies of Jolen's family and servants as I went. I investigated the victims, but could find nothing more than scratches and bruises. Then I found Jolen's body.'

He paused, then Lord Telano made a noise of confusion.

'His *body*? How can it still be whole? Did he exhaust himself?'

Vinara, Lorlen saw, was staring at the floor, shaking her head.

'I then called to Vinara, to ask her to come and examine the victims,' Balkan continued. 'After she arrived, I hurried to the Guard House to see if they had received any reports of strange activity in the area. Captain Barran was there, having just interviewed a witness.' Balkan paused. 'Captain, I think you should relate her tale to us.'

The young guard glanced around the circle, then cleared his throat.

'Yes, my lords – and lady.' He folded his hands together. 'With the increase in murders taking place, I have interviewed many witnesses lately, but few have seen anything useful. Some people come in the hope that something they have seen – say, a stranger walking about their street at night – might be relevant. This woman's story was much the same, but there was one striking element to it.

'She had been walking home late after delivering fruit and vegetables to one of the houses in the Inner Circle. Partway home, she heard screams inside a house – the residence of Lord Jolen's family. She decided to hurry on, but as she reached the next house, she heard a noise behind her. She was frightened and stepped into the shadows of a doorway. Looking back, she saw a man emerge from the servants' entrance of the house she had just passed.'

Barran paused and looked around the circle. 'She said this man wore magicians' robes. Black magicians' robes.'

The Higher Magicians frowned and exchanged glances. All except Balkan and Osen looked doubtful, Lorlen noted. Vinara did not look surprised.

'Was she sure they were black?' Sarrin asked. 'Any colour may look black in the darkness.'

Barran nodded. 'I asked her the same question. She was sure of it. He walked past the doorway she was hiding in. She described black robes, with an incal on the sleeve.'

Expressions changed from scepticism to alarm. Lorlen stared at Barran. He could hardly breathe.

'Surely n—' Sarrin began, but fell silent as Balkan gestured for him to wait.

'Go on, Captain,' Balkan said quietly, 'tell them the rest.'

Barran nodded. 'She said his hands were covered in blood, and he was carrying a knife. She described it well. A curved blade, with gemstones set into the handle.'

A long pause followed, then Sarrin drew in a deep breath. 'How reliable is this witness? Can you bring her here?'

Barran shrugged. 'I took her name and noted the workplace on her token. To tell the truth, I did not begin to give her story any credit until I heard what Lord Balkan had discovered in the house. Now I wish I had asked her more questions, or kept her at the Guard House longer.'

Balkan nodded. 'She will be found again. Now,' he turned to Vinara, 'perhaps it is time to hear what Lady Vinara has discovered.'

The Healer straightened. 'Yes, I fear it is. Lord Jolen was living with his family so that he could tend to his sister, who was having a difficult pregnancy. I investigated his body first and I made two disturbing discoveries. The first . . .' she reached into her robe and pulled out a scrap of black cloth embroidered with gold thread, 'was this, clutched in his right hand.'

As she held it up Lorlen went completely cold. The embroidery formed part of a symbol that was all too familiar to him: the incal of the High Lord. Vinara's eyes flickered to his and she frowned with concern and sympathy.

'What was the second discovery?' Balkan asked, his voice low.

Vinara hesitated, then drew in a deep breath. 'The reason Lord Jolen's body still exists is because it was completely drained of energy. The only wound on his body was a shallow cut down one side of his neck. The other bodies bore the same indicators. I was taught to recognise these indicators by my predecessor.' She paused and looked around the circle. 'Lord Jolen, his family and their servants, were killed with black magic.'

Gasps and exclamations followed, then a long silence as the implications began to sink in. Lorlen could almost hear them thinking about Akkarin's strength, and weighing the chances of the Guild defeating him in battle. He saw fear and panic in their faces.

He felt strangely calm and . . . relieved. For over two years he had been burdened with the secret of Akkarin's crime. Now, for better or worse, the Guild had discovered that secret for itself. He looked around at the Higher Magicians. Should he admit to having known of Akkarin's crime? *Not unless I have to*, he thought.

Then what should he do? The Guild was no stronger, and Akkarin – if he was guilty of this crime – was certainly no weaker. He felt a familiar fear chase away his relief.

To protect the Guild, I should do anything I can to prevent a confrontation between it and Akkarin. But if Akkarin did this . . . No, he may not have. I know other black magicians have been killing Kyralians.

'What do we do?' Telano asked in a small voice.

All turned to regard Balkan. Lorlen felt the tiniest stirring of indignation at that. Wasn't he the Guild's leader, in lieu of Akkarin? Then Balkan looked at him expectantly, and he felt a wry regret as the familiar weight of his position settled over him.

'What do you suggest, Administrator? You know him best.'

Lorlen forced himself to sit a little straighter. He had rehearsed what he would tell them in this situation so many times.

'We must be cautious,' he warned. 'If Akkarin is the murderer, he will be even stronger now. I suggest we consider this very carefully before confronting him.'

'How strong is he?' Telano asked.

'He easily overcame twenty of our strongest magicians when we tested him for the position of High Lord,' Balkan replied. 'With black magic, there is no way to tell how strong a magician is.'

'How long has he been practising it, I wonder?' Vinara said darkly. She looked at Lorlen. 'Have you ever noticed anything odd about Akkarin, Administrator?'

Lorlen did not have to pretend to be amused by the question. 'Odd? Akkarin? He's always been mysterious and secretive, even to me.'

'He could have been practising for years,' Sarrin muttered. 'How strong does that make him?'

'What bothers me is how he came by the knowledge,' Kito added quietly. 'Did he learn it during his travels?'

Lorlen sighed as they began discussing all the possibilities he had considered since discovering the truth for himself. He gave them some time, then, just as he was considering interrupting, Balkan spoke up.

'For now, it does not matter how or where he learned black magic. What matters is whether we can defeat him in a confrontation.'

Lorlen nodded. 'I have doubts about our chances. I think, perhaps, we should keep this to ourselves—'

'Are you suggesting we ignore this?' Peakin exclaimed. 'Leave a black magician at the head of our Guild?'

'No.' Lorlen shook his head. 'But we need time to consider how we may remove him safely if, indeed, he is the murderer.'

'We're not getting any stronger,' Vinara pointed out. 'He is.'

'Lorlen is right. Careful planning is essential,' Balkan replied. 'I was taught by *my* predecessor the means by which a black magician may be fought. It is not easy, but neither is it impossible.'

Lorlen felt a stirring of interest and hope. If only he had been able to consult with the Warrior before Akkarin had discovered Lorlen knew his secret. Perhaps they had a chance of removing Akkarin after all.

He caught himself, then. Did he really want Akkarin dead? *But what if he did kill Jolen and his household? Doesn't he deserve to be punished for that?*

Yes, but we had better be sure it was him.

'We should also consider that he may not be the killer,' Lorlen said. He looked at Balkan. 'We have the account of a witness and a scrap of cloth. Could another magician have dressed as Akkarin? Could he have put that scrap of material in Jolen's hand?' Something occurred to Lorlen, then. 'Let me see it again.'

Vinara handed him the scrap. Lorlen nodded as he examined it. 'Look, it has been cut off, not torn. If Jolen had been able to do this, he must have had a blade of some sort. Why didn't he simply stab his attacker instead? And it is strange, don't you think, that the killer didn't notice his sleeve had been cut? A clever murderer would not leave behind such evidence — or wander out into the street carrying the weapon he used.'

'So you think it might have been another Guild magician, trying to convince us that Akkarin is guilty of his crimes?' Vinara asked, frowning. 'I suppose it is possible.'

'Or a magician not of the Guild,' Lorlen added. 'If Dannyl can find a rogue in Elyne, it is possible that others exist.'

'We've seen no other evidence of a rogue magician in Kyralia,' Sarrin protested. 'And rogues tend to be untrained and ignorant. 'How would a rogue learn black magic?'

Lorlen shrugged. 'How would any magician learn black magic? In secret, obviously. We might not like the idea, but whether the killer is Akkarin or someone else, he learned black magic somehow.'

The others paused to consider this.

'So perhaps Akkarin isn't the killer,' Sarrin said. 'If he isn't, he knows we must investigate in the usual fashion, and will co-operate with us.'

'But if he is, he may turn on us,' Peakin added.

'So what should we do?'.

Balkan rose and began pacing. 'Sarrin is right. If he is innocent, he will co-operate. If he is guilty, however, then I believe we should act now. The number of deaths that have occurred tonight, with no effort to hide the evidence, has the appearance of the preparations of a black magician who is planning for a fight. We must confront him now, or we may leave it too late.'

Lorlen's heart skipped. 'But you said you needed time to plan.'

Balkan smiled grimly. 'I said that careful planning makes all the difference. It is part of my duties as Head of Warriors to ensure we are always ready to face such a danger. The key to success, according to my predecessor, is to catch the enemy by surprise, when he is isolated from his allies. My servant has informed me that only three people remain within the High Lord's Residence at night. Akkarin, his servant, and Sonea.'

'Sonea!' Vinara exclaimed. 'What is her role in this?'

'She dislikes him,' Osen said. 'I would even say she hates him.'

Lorlen looked at his assistant in surprise.

'How so?' Vinara asked.

Osen shrugged. 'An observation I made when she became his favourite. Even now, she doesn't like to be in his company.'

Vinara looked thoughtful. 'I wonder if she knows anything. She could be a valuable witness.'

'And ally,' Balkan added. 'So long as he doesn't kill her for her strength.'

Vinara shuddered. 'So how are we going to separate them?'

Balkan smiled. 'I have a plan.'

* * *

Their guide for the return journey through the underground passages was the same hard-eyed boy. As they followed him, Sonea felt the turmoil of her thoughts settle into a reasonable calm. By the time the guide left them, she was full of new questions.

'She was Ichani, wasn't she?'

Akkarin glanced at her. 'Yes, a weaker one. I can't imagine how Kariko persuaded her to come here. A bribe, perhaps, or blackmail.'

'Will they send more like her?'

He considered. 'Perhaps. I wish I'd had the opportunity to read her mind.'

'Sorry about that.'

His mouth curled up at one side. 'Don't apologise. I prefer that you are alive.'

She smiled. During the journey back he had been distant and thoughtful. Now he seemed anxious to return. She followed him down the passage. They reached the alcove filled with rocks. As Akkarin regarded them, the rocks began to form stairs. Sonea waited until the scrape of stone against stone had ended before posing her next question.

'Why did she have a ring of House Saril and an expensive shawl in the alcove?'

Halfway down the stairs he stopped and turned back to stare at her.

'She did? I . . .'

His gaze shifted somewhere beyond her. The same thoughtful frown he had worn for the last hour returned. Then his expression darkened.

'What is it?' she asked.

He held up a hand to silence her. As Sonea watched,

he drew in a sharp breath and his eyes widened. Then he uttered a curse she had assumed only slum dwellers knew.

'What is it?' she repeated.

'The Higher Magicians are in my residence. In the underground room.'

Her breath caught in her throat. A coldness rushed through her body.

'Why?'

Akkarin's gaze was fixed somewhere beyond the walls of the passage.

'Lorlen . . .'

Sonea felt her stomach knot. Surely Lorlen hadn't decided to rally the Guild against Akkarin.

Something in Akkarin's expression kept all questions locked in her throat. He was thinking hard, she guessed. Making difficult choices. Finally, after a long silence, he took a deep breath and let it out slowly.

'Everything changes from here,' he said, looking up at her. 'You must do what I say, no matter how difficult you find it.'

His voice was quiet and strained. She nodded and tried to hold back a growing fear.

Akkarin climbed back up the stairs until they stood face to face. 'Lord Jolen was murdered tonight, with his family and household, probably by the woman you just killed. That is why she had a shawl and a ring of House Saril – trophies, I suspect. Vinara found a scrap of my robes in Jolen's hand – no doubt cut from my sleeve by the Ichani during our first confrontation – and she has recognised that the deaths were caused by black magic. A witness saw someone dressed as me leave the house carrying a knife.'

He looked away. 'I wonder where the Ichani got the robes from, and where she put them . . .'

Sonea stared at him. 'So the Guild thinks you're the killer.'

'They are considering the possibility, yes. Balkan had rightly decided that, if I am innocent I will co-operate, and if I am guilty I must be confronted without delay. I was considering how I would deal with this, and what you should do and say, when the situation changed just now.'

He paused and sighed heavily. 'Balkan wisely planned to isolate me from you and Takan. He sent a messenger with news of Jolen's death and a summons to meet with the Higher Magicians. When he heard I wasn't at the residence, he sent for you. He hadn't discussed with the others what he would do if you weren't there either, so I assumed he would do so next, and I'd hear of his intentions through Lorlen. But he must have already formed a plan.' Akkarin frowned. 'Of course he had.'

Sonea shook her head. 'This has been going on while we were on our way back, hasn't it?'

Akkarin nodded. 'I could not say anything, with our guide present.'

'So what did Balkan do?'

'He returned to the residence and searched it.'

Sonea went cold as she thought of the books and objects Balkan would find in the underground room. 'Oh.'

'Yes. Oh. They didn't break into the underground room at first. But once they found books on black magic in your room, they became more determined to search every corner.'

Sonea's blood turned to ice. Books on black magic. In her room.

They know.

The future she had envisioned flashed before her eyes. Two more years of training, graduation, choosing a discipline, perhaps persuading the Healers to help the poor, perhaps even convincing the King to stop the Purge.

None of it would happen. Ever.

The Guild knew she had sought knowledge of black magic. The punishment for that crime was expulsion. If they knew she had learned black magic, and used it to kill . . .

But she had done it, and risked her future, for a good reason. If the Ichani invaded, graduation or stopping the Purge would never happen anyway.

Rothen is going to be very, very upset.

She put that thought out of her mind with an effort. She needed to think. Now that the Guild knew, what should they do? How would she and Akkarin continue to fight the Ichani?

It was clear they couldn't return to the Guild. They would have to hide in the city. Avoiding discovery by the Guild would make everything harder, but not impossible. Akkarin knew the Thieves. She had a few useful connections, too. She looked at Akkarin.

'What do we do now?'

He looked down the staircase. 'We go back.'

She stared at him. 'To the Guild?'

'Yes. We tell them about the Ichani.'

Her heart skipped.

'You said you didn't think they'd believe you.'

'I don't. But I have to give them the opportunity.'

'But what if they don't believe you?'

Akkarin's gaze wavered. He looked down. 'I am sorry

I brought you into this, Sonea. I will protect you from the worst of it, if I can.'

She caught her breath, then silently cursed herself. 'Don't apologise,' she told him firmly. 'It was my decision. I knew the risks. Tell me what I must do, and I will do it.'

His eyes widened slightly. He opened his mouth, then his gaze grew distant again.

'They're taking Takan away. We must hurry.'

He disappeared down the stairs. Sonea hurried after. As he strode into the maze of passages she glanced back.

'The stairs?'

'Leave them.'

She broke into a run and caught up with him. Keeping pace with his long strides was difficult, and she bit back a comment about him having some consideration for people with shorter legs.

'Two people must be protected through all this,' he said. 'Takan and Lorlen. Mention nothing of Lorlen's ring, or of his prior knowledge of any of this. We may need him in the future.'

All too soon he slowed and stopped before the door to the underground room. He took off his coat, folded it and placed it beside the door. Then he unbuckled the belt of the knife sheath and set it on top. A globe light sparked into life above their heads. Akkarin shuttered the lamp and placed it beside the coat.

For a long time he stood regarding the door to the underground room, his bare arms crossed over his black vest. Sonea waited silently beside him.

It was difficult to believe that this had happened. Tomorrow she was supposed to be studying how to heal broken ribs. In a few weeks the mid-year tests would start. She felt a pull toward the door, a strange feeling that she had only to find her way to her bed, and she would wake up to find everything continuing as it always had.

But the room beyond was probably filled with magicians waiting for Akkarin's return. They knew that she had learned about black magic. They suspected Akkarin had killed Jolen. They would be ready for a fight.

Still Akkarin remained motionless. She was just beginning to wonder if he was going to change his mind when he turned to look at her.

'Stay here until I call you in.'

Then he narrowed his eyes at the door and it silently slid open.

The backs of two magicians blocked the way into the room. Beyond them, Sonea could see Lord Balkan pacing the room slowly. Lord Sarrin was sitting at the table, regarding the items on it with a puzzled frown.

They didn't notice the door open. Then one of the magicians standing in front of the doorway shivered and glanced over his shoulder. Seeing Akkarin, he sucked in a breath and backed away, dragging his companion with him.

All heads turned to watch as Akkarin stepped into the room. Even without the outer part of his robes, he still looked imposing.

'My, what a lot of visitors,' he said. 'What brings you all to my residence so late at night?'

Balkan's eyebrows rose. He looked toward the stairway. Hurried footsteps could be heard, then Lorlen stepped into view. The Administrator turned to regard Akkarin, his expression unexpectedly composed.

'Lord Jolen and his household were murdered tonight.'

Lorlen's voice was calm and controlled. 'Evidence has been found that has given us cause to suspect you are the murderer.'

'I see,' Akkarin said quietly. 'This is a serious matter. I did not kill Lord Jolen, but you will have to work that out for yourselves.' He paused. 'Will you explain to me how Jolen died?'

'With black magic,' Lorlen said. 'And since we have just found books on black magic in your house, including in Sonea's room, we have even more reason to suspect you.'

Akkarin nodded slowly. 'Indeed you have.' The corner of his mouth curled upward. 'And you must all be frightened out of your wits by the discovery. Well, now. No need to be. I will explain myself.'

'You will co-operate?' Lorlen asked.

'Of course.'

The relief on every face was clear to see.

'But I have one condition,' Akkarin added.

'What is that?' Lorlen replied warily. Balkan glanced at him.

'My servant,' Akkarin replied. 'I made him a promise once that he would never have his freedom taken from him again. Bring him here.'

'And if we don't?' Lorlen asked.

Akkarin took a step to one side. 'Sonea will go in his place.'

Sonea felt her skin prickle as the magicians noticed her standing in the passage. She shivered as she considered what they must be thinking. Had she learned black magic? Was she dangerous? Only Lorlen might hope she would rebel against Akkarin; the rest did not know the real reason she had become the High Lord's novice.

'Bring them both here, and he will have two allies at hand,' Sarrin warned.

'Takan is not a magician,' Balkan said quietly. 'So long as he remains out of Akkarin's reach, he is no threat to us.' He looked at the other Higher Magicians. 'The question is: would you prefer to have Sonea in custody, or the servant?'

'Sonea,' Vinara replied without hesitation. The others nodded.

'Very well,' Lorlen said. His gaze flickered to the distance, then back again. 'I have ordered him to be brought.'

A long, tense silence followed. Finally, footsteps were heard coming down the stairs. Takan appeared, his arms firmly held by a Warrior. He was pale and anxious.

'Forgive me, master,' he said. 'I couldn't stop them.'

'I know,' Akkarin told him. 'You should know better than to try, my friend.' He took several steps away from the passage entrance, stopping beside the table at one side of the room. 'The barriers are down and I have left the stairs open. You will find what you need just outside the door.'

Takan nodded. They stared at each other, then the servant nodded again. Akkarin turned toward the passage.

'Come in, Sonea. When Takan is released, go to Lorlen.'

Taking a deep breath, Sonea stepped into the room. She looked at the Warrior holding Takan, then at Lorlen. The Administrator nodded.

'Let him go.'

As Takan stepped away from his captor, Sonea started toward Lorlen. The servant stopped as he reached her, and bowed.

'Take care of my master, Lady Sonea.'

'I'll do what I can,' she promised.

Her throat was suddenly tight. As she reached Lorlen she turned to watch the servant leave. He bowed to Akkarin, then stepped into the passage. When he had disappeared into the darkness, the panel slid back into place.

Akkarin turned to face Lorlen, then looked down at the table and chairs beside him. The top part of his robes were still draped over the back of a chair. He picked up the black garment and shrugged into it.

'So, Administrator, how can Sonea and I help you in your investigations?'

CHAPTER 15

BAD NEWS

Rothen had just donned a fresh set of robes when he heard the door to his rooms open.

'Lord Rothen?' Tania called.

Hearing the urgency in his servant's voice, he hurried to the bedroom door. Tania was standing in the middle of the room, wringing her hands.

'What is it?' he asked.

She turned to regard him, her expression pained. 'The High Lord and Sonea were arrested last night.'

He drew in a breath, and felt hope and relief surge through him. Akkarin arrested at last! The Guild must have discovered his crime – and confronted him – and won!

But why would the Guild arrest Sonea, too?

Why indeed? Excitement withered away and was replaced by a familiar, nagging fear.

'What were they arrested for?' he forced himself to ask.

Tania hesitated. 'I only heard it fourth or fifth hand, Rothen. It could be wrong.'

'What for?' he repeated.

She grimaced. 'The High Lord was arrested for murdering Lord Jolen and his household, and for learning some kind of magic. Black magic, I think? What is that?'

'The evilest of all magics,' Rothen replied heavily. 'But what of Sonea? What was she arrested for?'

Tania spread her hands. 'I'm not sure. As his accomplice, perhaps.'

Rothen sat down in one of the guestroom chairs. He took a long, deep breath. The Guild would have to consider the possibility that Sonea was involved. That didn't mean she was guilty of the charges.

'I didn't bring any food,' Tania said apologetically. 'I knew you'd want to know as soon as possible.'

'Never mind,' he said. 'It doesn't look like I'll have time to eat this morning, anyway.' He rose and took a step toward the door. 'I think I had better have a little chat with Sonea.'

Tania's smile was strained. 'I thought you might. Let me know what she says.'

The young man sitting opposite Dannyl in the carriage was painfully thin. Though Farand had recovered well enough to walk in the week since his poisoning, it would still be some time before he regained his full strength. But he was alive, and very grateful for it.

Dannyl had watched over the young man night and day throughout the voyage. It had been easy enough to hold back sleep and weariness with his Healing powers, but doing so always took a toll. After a week, he felt almost as bad as Farand looked.

The carriage turned into the Guild gates. Farand drew in a quick breath as the University came into view.

'It's beautiful,' he breathed.

'Yes.' Dannyl smiled and looked out of the window. Three magicians stood at the bottom of the stairs: Administrator Lorlen, Expatriate Administrator Kito and Lady Vinara.

Dannyl felt a little twinge of anxiety and disappointment. He had hoped the High Lord would meet him. *But he'll probably want to discuss everything in private.*

The carriage pulled up in front of the stairs, and Dannyl climbed out. As Farand followed, the three Higher Magicians regarded him with wary curiosity.

'Ambassador Dannyl,' Lorlen said. 'Welcome back.'

'Thank you, Administrator Lorlen. Administrator Kito, Lady Vinara,' Dannyl replied, inclining his head. 'This is Farand of Darellas.'

'Welcome, young Darellas,' Lorlen said. 'I'm afraid you will find us somewhat preoccupied with another matter in the next few days. We will make you as comfortable as possible, and deal with your unique situation as soon as this other matter is resolved.'

'Thank you, Administrator,' Farand replied uncertainly.

Lorlen nodded, then turned away and started up the University stairs. Dannyl frowned. There was something odd in Lorlen's manner. He seemed even more harassed than usual.

'Come with me, Farand,' Vinara said to the young man. She looked at Dannyl and her expression became grim. 'Get some sleep, Ambassador. You need to make up for what you've lost.'

'Yes, Lady Vinara,' Dannyl agreed. As she led Farand away, he looked at Kito questioningly.

'What is this other matter that Administrator Lorlen spoke of?'

Kito sighed heavily. 'Lord Jolen was murdered last night.'

'Murdered?' Dannyl stared at him. 'How?'

The magician grimaced. 'With black magic.'

Dannyl felt his face grow cold. He glanced at the carriage where the book lay deep within his travel trunk.

'Black magic? Who . . .?'

'The High Lord has been arrested,' Kito added.

'Akkarin!' Dannyl felt the chill spread through his body. 'Not him!'

'I'm afraid so. The evidence is damning. He has agreed to assist with our investigations. There will be a Hearing tomorrow.'

Dannyl barely heard him. Strange coincidences and occurrences were shifting into new places in his mind. He thought of the research Lorlen had asked him to begin, then cease. He thought of Rothen's sudden interest in the same information – just after Sonea had become Akkarin's favourite. He thought of what the Dem's book had revealed. Ancient magic – higher magic – was black magic.

He'd assumed Akkarin's search had ended without this discovery.

It seemed he was wrong.

Had Lorlen suspected this? Had Rothen? Was this the reason for the research?

And I was going to give that book to Akkarin!

'We will discuss the rogue after the Hearing,' Kito said.

Dannyl blinked, then nodded. 'Of course. Well, I had best obey Lady Vinara's orders.'

The Vindo magician smiled. 'Sleep well, then.'

Dannyl nodded, then started toward the Magicians' Quarters. Sleep? How could he sleep after learning this?

I continued this research with Akkarin's blessing, and I've got a book on black magic in my trunk. Will that be enough for me to appear guilty of the same crimes? I could hide the book. I'm certainly not going to be giving it to Akkarin . . . or discussing anything with him.

He drew in a quick breath as he realised what this meant for him personally. Who was going to believe Akkarin now, when he explained that Dannyl and Tayend's relationship was just a ruse to entrap the rebels?

The last time Sonea had been inside the Dome had been during her training for the Challenge. It was a huge, hollow stone sphere, once the practise room of Warriors. The Guild had abandoned it after the Arena had been built, but she had used it while preparing for the fight with Regin so that her lessons would not be observed by him or his supporters. Akkarin had strengthened the walls to ensure she did not damage them. Ironically, his magic was now helping to keep her imprisoned.

Not that she intended to make any escape attempts. She had told Akkarin she would do whatever he instructed. He had said only that they must protect Takan and Lorlen. Then he had exchanged her for Takan. So he had meant for her to be here.

Either that, or he was willing to sacrifice her for the sake of keeping the promise he had made to his servant.

No, she thought, *he needs me to back up his story*. Takan was too close to Akkarin. Nobody would believe him.

She paced the Dome interior. The plug-like door remained open to allow air into the room. A pair of magicians stood beyond it, watching her whenever she was alone.

But she hadn't been alone much. Vinara, Balkan and Sarrin had each questioned her about Akkarin's activities. She did not want to risk revealing anything before Akkarin was ready, so she had refused to answer. They had eventually given up.

Now that she was alone at last, she found she didn't like it. She kept wondering where Akkarin was, and if she was doing what he wanted by keeping silent. It was impossible to tell the time, but she guessed it was well past dawn now. She hadn't slept all night, but she doubted she would have even if there had been a soft bed instead of the sandy floor.

A movement beyond the door caught her eye. Looking up, she felt her heart twist painfully.

Rothen.

He stepped into the Dome, his face lined with worry. As she met his eyes, he tried to smile, and she felt her stomach sink with guilt.

'Sonea,' he said, 'how are you?'

She shook her head. 'That's a silly question, Rothen.'

He looked around the Dome and nodded. 'Yes. I suppose it is.' He sighed and looked at her again. 'They haven't decided what to do with you yet. Lorlen told me they found books on black magic in your room. Were they planted there by Akkarin or his servant?'

She sighed. 'No. I was reading them.'

'Why?'

'To understand my enemy.'

He frowned. 'You know that just reading about black magic is a crime.'

'Yes, I know.'

'Yet you read them?'

She met his eyes. 'Some risks are worth taking.'

'In the hope that we could use this information to defeat him?'

She looked down. 'Not exactly.'

He paused. 'Then why, Sonea?'

'I can't tell you. Not yet.'

Rothen took a step closer. 'Why not? What has he told you to make you an accomplice? We've found your aunt Jonna and uncle Ranel. They're safe and well as are their children. Dorrien is alive and well. Is there anyone else you're protecting?'

She sighed. *The whole of Kyralia*.

'I can't tell you, Rothen. Not yet. I don't know what Akkarin has told anyone, or what he wants me to reveal. It'll just have to wait until the Hearing.'

Rothen's eyes flashed with anger. 'Since when have you cared about what he wants?'

She held his gaze. 'Since I learned the reasons for what he does. But that is his story, not mine. You will understand why, when he tells it.'

He regarded her doubtfully. 'I find that hard to believe. But I will try. Is there anything I can do for you?'

She shook her head, then hesitated. Rothen knew that Lorlen had been aware of Akkarin's crime for more than two years. What would happen if he told the Guild this? She looked up at him.

'Yes,' she said quietly. 'Protect Lorlen.'

Savara ran a hand over the sheets and smiled.

'Nice.'

Cery chuckled. 'A Thief has to make his guests feel welcome.'

'You are not like other Thieves,' she remarked. 'He had a hand in all this, didn't he?'

'Who?'

'The High Lord.'

Cery humphed in indignation. 'Wasn't *all* him.'

'No?'

'Part of it was 'cause of Sonea. Faren agreed to hide her from the Guild, but the other Thieves made him turn her in. So some say Faren didn't honour his side of the deal.'

'So?'

'If I was willing to deal with Faren, other people would too. He helped me out with a few things.'

'So Akkarin had nothing to do with it?'

'Well, a little,' Cery admitted. 'Maybe I wouldn't have had the guts if he hadn't pushed me. Maybe if he hadn't given me all the right news about each of the Thieves, so they wouldn't try to stop me. It's hard to say no to someone who knows too many of your secrets.'

She looked thoughtful. 'Sounds like he had planned this for a long time.'

'That's what I thought.' Cery shrugged. 'When the murderer started to get the other Thieves riled, I offered to find him. They liked that. They didn't know I'd been onto it for months. They act like it's funny I haven't found him, though – but none of them have had any luck either.'

'But you *do* find them.'

'They think there's only one.'

'Ah.'

'At least I think they did,' he added.

'And now they know, because the last one was a woman.'

'Probably.'

He looked around the room at the furniture. Quality pieces, but not extravagant. He did not like to think it was *all* due to Akkarin's help.

'I've tried to make my place in other ways,' he said. 'If the market for finding murderers for magicians dries up, I want to stay alive and in business.'

She smiled slyly and ran a finger slowly down the middle of his chest.

'I definitely prefer you alive and in business.'

He caught her hand and pulled her closer. 'Do you? What sort of business are you into?'

'Making contact with potential allies,' she said, snaking her arm around him. 'Preferably very close contact with one in particular.'

Her kisses were firm and enticing. He felt his heart beginning to race again.

Then someone knocked on the door. He pulled away and grimaced apologetically. 'Got to get this.'

She pouted. 'Must you?'

He nodded. 'Gol wouldn't knock unless it was important.'

'Better be.'

He rose, pulled on his trousers and a shirt, and slipped out of the room. Gol was pacing Cery's guestroom, his expression very different from the foolish grin Cery was expecting.

'The High Lord's been arrested by the Guild,' Gol said. 'So's Sonea.'

Cery stared at his second. 'Why?'

'A Guild magician was killed last night. And a whole lot of people in his house. They think the High Lord did it.' He paused. 'The whole city knows about it.'

Moving to the nearest chair, Cery sat down. Akkarin *arrested?* For *murder?* And Sonea, too? He heard the door of his bedroom open. Savara peered out, now fully dressed. As she met his eyes, she frowned.

'Can you tell me?'

He smiled briefly, amused by her question. 'The High

Lord's been arrested. The Guild thinks he murdered a Guild magician last night.'

Her eyes widened. She moved into the room. 'When?'

Gol shrugged. 'Don't know. Everyone in this magician's house was killed too. With some kind of bad magic. Black magic. Yes, that was it.'

She drew in a quick breath. 'So it is true, then.'

'What is true?' Cery asked.

'Some of the Ichani claim the Guild do not know high magic and say it is evil. Akkarin uses it, so we thought this could not be true.' She paused. 'So that is why he works in secret. I had thought he did not want others to know that his past actions contributed to this situation.'

Cery blinked. 'What past actions?'

She looked at him and smiled. 'Oh, there is more to your High Lord than you know.'

'How so?'

'That is not for me to say,' she said. 'But I can tell you that—'

She stopped at a knock on the wall. Cery nodded to Gol. The big man approached the wall, checked its spy hole, then pulled aside a painting. One of the boys Cery employed for odd jobs peered in.

'There's a man wants to see you, Ceryni. He gave a big code word, and says he's got bad news about a friend of yours. Says it's urgent.'

Cery nodded, then turned to look at Savara. 'I better see what this is.'

She shrugged and returned to the bedroom. 'I will have a bath, then.'

Turning away, Cery found Gol grinning.

'Get that look off your face,' Cery warned.

'Yes, Ceryni,' the man replied humbly, but the grin remained as he preceded Cery into the passage.

Cery's office was a short distance away. There were several ways of getting in and out of it. Gol chose the standard route, giving Cery a moment to observe the visitor in the waiting room through a spy hole.

The man was Sachakan, Cery saw with dismay. Then he recognised the coat and his heart skipped.

Why was this man wearing the coat Akkarin had worn the night before?

As the man turned, the coat parted to reveal a Guild servants' uniform.

'I think I know who this is,' Cery breathed. He moved to the door of his office. 'Send him in as soon as I sit down.'

A few minutes later, Cery was seated at his desk. The door to his office opened and the man entered.

'So,' Cery said, 'you say you got bad news about a friend of mine.'

'Yes,' the man replied. 'I am Takan, servant to the High Lord. He has been arrested for the murder of a Guild magician. He has sent me to assist you.'

'Assist me? How?'

'I can communicate with him by mind,' Takan explained, touching his forehead.

'You're a magician?'

Takan shook his head. 'We have a link, made by him long ago.'

Cery nodded. 'Then tell me something only he and I know.'

Takan's gaze shifted to the distance. 'The last time you met, he said he would not bring Sonea with him again.'

'That's right.'

'He regrets that he could not hold to that.'

'So does Sonea, I'd guess. What's she been arrested for?'

Takan sighed. 'Learning about black magic. They found books in her room.'

'This black magic is . . .?'

'Forbidden,' Takan said. 'She faces expulsion from the Guild.'

'And the High Lord?'

Takan looked genuinely distressed. 'He has been charged with murder and using black magic. If they find him guilty of either, the punishment is execution.'

Cery nodded slowly. 'When will the Guild decide?'

'They will hold a Hearing tomorrow to examine the evidence and judge whether he is guilty or not.'

'Is he?'

Takan looked up, and his eyes flashed with anger. 'He did not murder Lord Jolen.'

'What of this charge of black magic?'

The servant nodded. 'Yes, he is guilty of that. If he had not used it, he would not have been able to defeat the murderers.'

'And Sonea. Is she guilty?'

Takan nodded again. 'The Guild has only charged her with learning about black magic. That is why she faces a lesser punishment. If they knew the truth, she would face the same charges as Akkarin.'

'She used black magic to kill the woman, didn't she?'

Takan looked surprised. 'Yes. How did you know that?'

'A lucky guess. Should I go to this Hearing as a witness?'

The man paused, and his gaze shifted to the distance. 'No. He says thank you for the offer. You should not reveal your involvement. If all goes well, he may need your help in the future. For now, he has only one favour to ask.'

'Yes?'

'That you ensure the Guard find the body of the murderess. And make sure she is wearing her knife.'

Cery smiled. 'I can do that.'

Looking out of his office window, Lorlen saw that Akkarin was still in the same position as before. He shook his head. Somehow Akkarin still managed to look dignified and self-assured, even when he was sitting on the Arena floor, with his back against one of the supports, and with twenty magicians standing around the Arena, watching him.

Turning away, Lorlen surveyed his office. Balkan paced in the middle. Lorlen had never seen the Warrior this agitated. He had heard Balkan mutter something about betrayal earlier. That was understandable. Lorlen knew the Warrior had held Akkarin in high esteem.

Sarrin sat on one of the chairs, leafing through one of the books from Akkarin's chest. They had decided one of them must be allowed to read them, even though doing so was a crime. Sarrin's expression was a mixture of horror and fascination. Occasionally he would mutter quietly to himself.

Vinara stood quietly by the shelves. Earlier, she had called Akkarin a monster. Balkan had reminded her that they could not be sure Akkarin had done anything more than read about black magic. She hadn't been convinced. When it came to the subject of Sonea, however, she looked distressed and uncertain.

Lorlen looked down at the objects on his desk: shards of broken glass, a partly melted silver fork, and a dish coated with dried blood. The others were still puzzled about the items. The little globe of glass they had found on the table had confirmed Lorlen's guess. Had Akkarin been creating another ring like Lorlen's, or had he been teaching Sonea how to make them?

Like Sonea, Akkarin had refused to answer any questions. He was determined to wait until the entire Guild had assembled for the Hearing before he explained himself. So much for co-operation.

That's unfair, Lorlen thought. He considered the ring in his pocket. Akkarin had told Lorlen to take it off and keep it at hand. If Sarrin continued reading the books, he would learn about such rings and recognise what Lorlen was wearing. Lorlen had considered discarding the ring altogether, but he could see advantages in keeping this link with Akkarin. His former friend still seemed inclined to confide in him. The only disadvantage was that Akkarin could eavesdrop on conversations when Lorlen was wearing it, but that was less of a problem now. Lorlen could stop Akkarin listening by simply taking off the ring.

Akkarin wanted to keep Lorlen's prior knowledge of his interest in black magic a secret.

—*The Guild needs a leader they trust*, Akkarin had sent. *Too much change and uncertainty will weaken it.*

Rothen and Sonea were the only other people who knew. Sonea had remained silent, and Rothen had agreed to keep Lorlen's involvement to himself so long as it brought no further harm. In return, Lorlen had allowed the magician to visit Sonea.

At a polite knock on the door, all looked up. Lorlen willed the door open and Captain Barran stepped inside, Lord Osen following. The guard bowed and addressed them formally, then turned to face Lorlen.

'I have visited the shop the witness works at,' he said. 'Her employers say she did not appear this morning. We checked her home address, and her family told us she did not return home last night.'

The Heads of Disciplines exchanged glances.

'Thank you, Captain,' Lorlen said. 'Is there anything else?'

The young man shook his head. 'No. I will return tomorrow morning, as you requested, unless further information comes my way.'

'Thank you. You may go.'

As the door closed, Vinara sighed. 'No doubt the guard will find her body in the next few days. He was certainly busy last night.'

Balkan shook his head. 'But it doesn't make sense. How did he know about her? If he'd detected her watching, he would have ensured she didn't reach the Guard House.'

Sarrin shrugged. 'Unless he was unable to catch up with her. Then, when she left the Guard House, he made sure she'd be unable to give any more evidence against him.'

Balkan sighed. 'It's not behaviour I would expect of a black magician. If he cared about hiding evidence, why be so careless earlier in the night? Why not disguise himself? Why—'

He stopped at another knock on the door. Lorlen sighed and willed it open. To his surprise, Dannyl stepped inside the office. Dark shadows lay under the Ambassador's eyes.

'Administrator,' Dannyl said. 'Might I have a word with you? In private?'

Lorlen frowned in annoyance. 'Is this about the rogue, Ambassador?'

'Partly.' Dannyl glanced at the others and appeared to

choose his words carefully. 'But not solely. I would not come to you if I did not feel I had urgent matters to discuss.'

Vinara rose. 'I am heartily sick of speculation, anyway,' she declared. She gave Sarrin and Balkan direct and meaningful looks. 'If you need us, Administrator, just call.'

Dannyl stepped aside and inclined his head politely as the three magicians left the room. When the door closed, Lorlen moved to his desk and sat down.

'What urgent matter do you speak of?'

Dannyl approached the desk. 'I'm not sure where to start, Administrator. I am in an awkward situation. Two awkward situations, if that is possible.' He paused. 'Though you said my help was no longer needed, I continued researching ancient magic out of my own interest. The High Lord, when he learned of this, encouraged me to continue, but by then there was little left to discover in Elyne. Or so I thought.'

Lorlen frowned. Akkarin had *encouraged* Dannyl to continue?

'Then, when my assistant and I were gaining the rebels' trust, we discovered a book in Dem Marane's possession.' Dannyl reached into his robes and drew out an old book. He placed it on Lorlen's desk. 'It answered many questions we had about ancient magic. It seems the form of ancient magic known as higher magic is actually black magic. This book contains instructions on its use.'

Lorlen stared at the book. Was this a coincidence, or had Akkarin known the rebels had the book? Or had he been working *with* the rebels? He drew in a quick breath. Was this how he learned black magic?

If so, then why turn them in?

'So you see,' Dannyl said. 'I am in an awkward position.

Some might consider that I have researched black magic with the High Lord's permission, and that Akkarin's orders to capture the rebels were an attempt to gather more knowledge.' He grimaced. 'In truth, I have read part of that book, which means I have broken the law against learning about black magic. But I didn't know what it contained until I began reading.'

Lorlen shook his head. No wonder Dannyl was worried. 'I understand your concern. You could not have known what the research would lead to. *I* didn't know what the research would lead to. If anyone thought to suspect you, they would have to suspect me as well.'

'Should I explain all this at the Hearing?'

'I'll discuss it with the Higher Magicians, but I don't think it will be necessary,' Lorlen replied.

Dannyl looked relieved. 'There is one other matter,' he added quietly.

More? Lorlen stifled a groan. 'Yes?'

Dannyl looked at the floor. 'When the High Lord requested that I find the rebels, he suggested that my assistant and I cause them to know something that could be used to blackmail us into co-operating. Akkarin said he would ensure the Guild knew that this information was merely a deception created to gain the rebels' trust.' Dannyl looked up. 'But obviously Akkarin is no longer in a position to do that.'

Abruptly, Lorlen remembered a conversation with Akkarin beside the Arena, while they were watching Sonea fighting.

The Guild will lose interest in the murderer once Ambassador Dannyl arrives with the rogue, Lorlen.

Had he been referring to more than the existence of the

rebels? What was this information that Dannyl had created to gain the rebels' trust?

He looked at Dannyl; the man glanced away, clearly embarrassed. Slowly Lorlen began to piece together scraps of gossip he'd heard, until he had guessed what Dannyl had let the rebels believe.

Interesting, he thought. *And a bold move, considering the troubles Dannyl faced as a novice.*

What should he do? Lorlen rubbed his temples. Akkarin had been so much better at this sort of thing.

'So you fear that nobody will believe what Akkarin says about you, because his integrity is in question.'

'Yes.'

'Is the integrity of these rebels any stronger?' Lorlen shook his head. 'I doubt it. If you are worried that nobody will believe Akkarin, then let people believe it was your own idea.'

Dannyl's eyes widened. He straightened and nodded. 'Of course. Thank you, Administrator.'

Lorlen shrugged, then looked at Dannyl a little closer. 'You look as if you haven't slept for a week.'

'I haven't. I didn't want someone to undo all the hard work I'd done in saving Farand's life.'

Lorlen frowned. 'Then you had best go back to your rooms and rest. We may need you tomorrow.'

The young magician managed a tired smile. He nodded at the book on Lorlen's desk. 'Now that I've got *that* off my hands, sleep shouldn't be a problem any more. Thank you again, Administrator.'

As he left, Lorlen sighed. *At least someone is going to get some sleep.*

CHAPTER 16

THE HEARING

Sonea's first thought as she began to wake was that Viola hadn't come to wake her, and she was going to be late for classes. She blinked away the fuzziness of sleep. Then she felt sand between her fingers and saw the faintly illuminated stone wall of the Dome around her, and she remembered.

That she had slept at all amazed her. The last she could recall of the previous night was lying in darkness, thoughts of the day to come running in circles through her mind. It had taken all her will to resist calling out to Akkarin mentally, to ask him if she should tell the Guild anything yet, or simply to know where he was, if he was being treated well . . . or if he was still alive.

In her worst moments of doubt, she could not shake the thought that the Guild might have passed judgment on him already, without telling her. The Guild of the past had been frighteningly thorough in its efforts to rid the Allied Lands of black magic. Those long-dead magicians would have executed Akkarin without delay.

And me, she thought, with a shiver.

She wished again that she could talk to him. He had said he would tell the Guild about the Ichani. Did he intend to admit to learning black magic, too? Did he mean for them to know she had as well?

Or was he going to deny using black magic? Or admit to it himself, but claim she had done nothing wrong?

But she *had*. An unwanted image of the dead Ichani woman flitted through her mind. With it came intense, but contradictory feelings.

You're a killer, a voice in her mind accused.

I had to, she thought in reply. *There was no choice. She would have killed me.*

But you would have done it anyway, her conscience replied, *even if there had been a choice.*

Yes. To protect the Guild. To protect Kyralia. Then she frowned. *Since when have I been so concerned about killing, anyway? I would have killed without hesitation, if I'd been attacked in the slums. In fact, I may have killed already. I don't know if that thug who dragged me off the street survived after I stabbed him.*

That's different. You didn't have magic then, her conscience pointed out.

She sighed. She could not help thinking that, with all the advantages that having magic abilities gave her, she ought to be able to avoid killing anyone. But the Ichani had wielded magic, too.

She had to be stopped. I happened to be in a position to stop her. I don't regret killing her, only that I had to in the first place.

Her conscience fell silent.

Keep bothering me, she told it. *I'd rather that, than kill and not feel bad about it.*

Still nothing.

Great. She shook her head. *Maybe that old superstition about the Eye is true. Not only am I having conversations with myself, but now I'm refusing to talk to me. This has got to be the first sign of madness.*

A sound outside drew her attention back to the room. Sitting up, she saw the Warrior guards step aside as Lord Osen stopped in the doorway. A globe light flared above his head, filling the spherical room with light.

'The Hearing is about to begin, Sonea. I'm here to escort you to the Guildhall.'

Suddenly her heart was racing. She stood up, brushed the sand off her robes, and walked to the door. Osen stepped back and allowed her to pass.

A short set of stairs led to another open door. She paused as she saw the circle of magicians waiting beyond. Her escort was a collection of Healers and Alchemists. The Warriors and the stronger magicians of the Guild would be guarding Akkarin, she guessed.

They watched her intently as she stepped out into the middle of the circle. Seeing the suspicion and disapproval in their expressions, she felt her face grow warm. She turned around to see that her two Warrior guards had completed the circle. Osen stepped through a momentary break in the barrier they held around her.

'Sonea,' he said. 'Your guardian is accused of murder and of practising black magic. As his novice, you will be questioned about your knowledge of these matters. Do you understand?'

She swallowed to wet her throat. 'Yes, my lord.'

He paused. 'Due to the discovery of books on black magic in your room, you will also be accused of learning about black magic.'

So she, too, was to be judged.

'I understand,' she replied.

Osen nodded. He turned to face the gardens beside the University. 'To the Guildhall, then.'

The escort kept pace as Osen led her to the path alongside the University. The grounds were empty and eerily quiet. Only their footsteps and the occasional chirrup of a bird broke the silence. She thought of the families of magicians, and the servants that populated the grounds. Had they been sent away, in case Akkarin sought to overtake the Guild?

When the escort had nearly reached the front of the University, Osen suddenly stopped. The magicians surrounding them exchanged worried looks. Realising they were listening to a mental communication, she focussed her senses.

— . . . *says he will not enter until Sonea is here*, Lorlen sent.

—*What shall we do?* Osen asked.

—*Wait. We will decide.*

Sonea felt her heart lighten a little. Akkarin was refusing to enter the Guildhall without her. He wanted her there. Osen and the escort were tense with anxiety, however, obviously fearing what Akkarin might do if Lorlen refused. They had no idea how strong Akkarin was.

She sobered. *Neither do I.*

As they waited, she tried to estimate his strength. He had taken energy from her and Takan for two weeks before the fight with the Ichani. Sonea had no idea how strong he had been before then, but the fight would have diminished his store of magic considerably. He might still be several times the strength of a Guild magician, but she doubted he was powerful enough to fight the entire Guild.

And me?

She was aware of a great increase in her strength since she had taken the Ichani woman's energy, but she could not guess how much more powerful it made her. Not as powerful as Akkarin, she guessed. He had been winning the fight with the Ichani before Sonea had stepped in so the Ichani would have been weaker. The power Sonea had taken from her couldn't have been as much as he had.

Unless the Ichani had been pretending to be weaker for some reason . . .

—*Bring her.*

Lorlen did not sound happy. Osen made a small noise of disgust, then began walking again. The escort followed. As they neared the front of the University, Sonea's heart began to race again, but this time in anticipation.

A crowd of magicians milled around the front of the building. They turned to watch as Sonea's escort appeared, then parted as it started up the stairs.

Akkarin stood in the centre of the Entrance Hall. She felt a thrill as she saw him. The corner of his mouth curled up in a familiar half-smile as he saw her. She almost smiled in reply, but schooled her expression as she saw the tense faces of the magicians surrounding him.

The Entrance Hall was crowded. Akkarin's escort was made up of over fifty magicians, most of them Warriors. Nearly all of the Higher Magicians were present, looking nervous and angry. Lord Balkan's expression was dark.

Lorlen stepped forward to regard Akkarin.

'You may enter together,' he said, his voice full of warning, 'but you must remain out of each other's reach.'

Akkarin nodded, then turned and beckoned to her. She blinked in surprise as her escort stepped back to allow her through.

Murmuring filled the Entrance Hall as she moved into the circle of magicians surrounding Akkarin. She stopped beside him, but far enough away that they could not have reached out to grasp hands. Akkarin looked at Lorlen and smiled.

'Now, Administrator, let's see if we can sort out this misunderstanding.'

He turned and started down the passage to the Guildhall.

Rothen had never felt so ill. The last day had been one of the longest in his life. He had been dreading the Hearing, yet was also impatient for it to begin. He needed to hear Akkarin's excuses, and to know what had drawn Sonea into breaking a law. He wanted to see Akkarin punished for what he had done to Sonea. Yet he also dreaded the moment Sonea's punishment would be announced.

Two long lines of magicians stood along the length of the Guildhall. Behind them were two lines of novices, ready to give their strength if it was needed. A low buzz of voices had filled the room as all waited for the Hearing to begin.

'Here they come,' Dannyl murmured.

Two figures entered the hall. One wore black robes, the other the brown of a novice. Akkarin walked as confidently as he always had. Sonea . . . Rothen felt a pang of sympathy as he saw how she was keeping her gaze on the floor, her expression fearful and self-conscious.

The Higher Magicians followed, their expressions wary and grim. When Akkarin and Sonea reached the end of the hall, they stopped. Rothen was pleased to see that Sonea was keeping her distance from the High Lord. The Higher Magicians stepped around the pair and formed a row before the tiered seats at the front of the hall. The remaining magicians escorting the pair formed a large circle around the two accused.

Rothen and Dannyl followed as all the other magicians and novices moved to the seats on either side. When everyone was settled, Lorlen struck a small gong.

'All kneel to King Merin, ruler of Kyralia,' he intoned.

Sonea looked up in surprise. She stared at the top row of tiered seats as the King appeared with two magicians. A dark, vibrant orange cloak of shimmering cloth surrounded his shoulders, with the royal mullook sewn in gold all over it. An enormous gold halfmoon hung across his chest: the royal pendant.

As the entire Guild dropped to one knee, Rothen watched Sonea carefully. She glanced at Akkarin and, as she saw he was going to kneel too, followed suit. Then she looked up at the King again.

He could guess what she was thinking. Here was the man who ordered the Purge each year, the man who, two and a half years before, had ordered her family and neighbours to be evicted from their homes.

The King surveyed the room, then stared down at Akkarin, his expression unreadable. His eyes slid to Sonea, and she looked down at the floor. Satisfied, he stepped back and sat down in his chair.

After a pause, the magicians began to rise again. The Higher Magicians climbed to their places among the tiered seats at the front. Akkarin continued to kneel until all grew quiet again, then stood.

Lorlen looked around the hall, then nodded. 'We have called this Hearing today to judge Akkarin of family Delvon, of House Velan, High Lord of the Magicians' Guild, and Sonea, his novice. Akkarin has been accused of murdering Lord Jolen of House Saril, and his family and servants, and of seeking knowledge of, learning, and practising black magic. Sonea has been accused of seeking knowledge of black magic.

'These crimes are of the most serious kind. The evidence to support them will be presented for us to judge. I call forth the first speaker, Lord Balkan, Head of Warrior Skills.'

Balkan rose from his seat and descended to the floor. He turned to face the King, and dropped to one knee.

'I swear that all I speak in this Hearing will be the truth.'

The King remained expressionless and made no gesture to acknowledge Balkan's words.

The Warrior straightened and faced the assembled magicians.

'Two night ago, I heard a faint call from Lord Jolen. It was clear that he was in some trouble. When I could not contact him again, I visited his family home.

'I found Lord Jolen, and his entire household, dead. Every man, woman and child, be they family or servant had perished. On closer investigation, I found evidence that the murderer had entered through the window in Lord Jolen's room, indicating, perhaps, that Lord Jolen had been the first victim.

'I did not search the bodies for the cause of death, leaving that task to Lady Vinara. When she arrived, I continued on to the Guard House. When I arrived I found that Captain Barran, the guard investigating the recent spate of murders in the city, had just interviewed a witness to the crime.'

Balkan paused and looked up at Lorlen. 'But before I summon Captain Barran, I recommend we hear what Lady Vinara found in her investigations.'

Lorlen nodded. 'I call forth Lady Vinara, Head of Healers.'

Lady Vinara rose and descended gracefully to the floor. She turned, knelt to the King and swore the oath of truth. Then she rose and regarded the audience gravely.

'When I arrived at Lord Jolen's family home I examined the bodies of twenty-nine victims. All bore a few scratches and bruises around their necks, and no other injury. They had not been strangled, suffocated or poisoned. Lord Jolen's body was still intact, which was the first sign that alerted me to the cause of death. On examination, I found that his body had been completely drained of energy, leaving me to conclude that Lord Jolen had either expelled all his strength as he died, or it had been taken from him. Examination of the other bodies confirmed the latter cause. All members of the household were drained of energy, and since none but Lord Jolen could have exhausted themselves deliberately, I was left with one remaining explanation.' She paused, her expression grim. 'Lord Jolen, his family and the servants were killed with black magic.'

The hall filled with low voices at this revelation. Rothen shuddered. It was too easy to picture Akkarin slipping into the house, stalking his victims and killing them. He looked down at the High Lord. Akkarin watched Vinara soberly.

'A closer examination of Lord Jolen's body revealed faint finger marks in blood on the neck,' the Healer continued. She glanced at Akkarin. 'It also revealed this, still clutched in one hand.'

Vinara looked to one side and beckoned. A magician approached, carrying a box. She opened it and lifted up a piece of black cloth.

Gold embroidery glittered in the light. Enough of the incal remained for it to be recognisable as the High Lord's. The creaking of wood and rustling of robes filled the hall as magicians shifted in their seats, and the buzz of voices grew louder.

Vinara draped the cloth over the top of the box, then gave both back to her assistant. He moved away to stand at the side of the hall. Vinara looked at Akkarin, who was now frowning, then glanced over her shoulder to nod to Lorlen.

'I call forth Captain Barran, investigator of the Guard,' Lorlen said.

The room quietened again as, from one side, a man in guard uniform entered, knelt to the King and spoke the vow. Rothen estimated the man was in his mid-twenties. The rank of captain was high for a man of his youth, but such positions were occasionally given to younger men of the Houses, if they proved to be talented or hard-working.

The Captain cleared his throat. 'Half an hour before Lord Balkan came to see me, a young woman entered the Guard House claiming to have seen the murderer that has been preying on this city these last weeks.

'She told me she was returning home from delivering fruit and vegetables to one of the houses in the Inner Circle. She was still carrying the empty basket and a token of admission to the area. While passing the family home of Lord Jolen, she heard screams from inside. The screams stopped and she hurried on, but as she reached the next house she heard a door open behind her. She hid in a doorway, from which she saw a man emerge from the servants' entrance of Lord Jolen's family home. This man wore black magicians' robes, with an incal on the sleeve. His hands were bloodied, and he carried a curved blade, with gemstones set into the handle.'

Exclamations echoed through the hall as the Guild

expressed its horror. Rothen nodded to himself as he remembered the knife Sonea had described Akkarin using when she had spied on him so long ago. Lorlen raised a hand and the noise gradually subsided.

'What did you do then?'

'I took her name and noted the workplace on her token. At your request, I sought her out the next day. Her employer told me that she had not returned to work that morning, and gave me her family's address. Her family were concerned, as she had not returned to her home that night either.

'I feared that she had been murdered,' Barran continued. 'Later that day we found her body. Like Lord Jolen, his household, and many of the other murders I have investigated these last few weeks, she bore no wounds except for a shallow cut.'

He paused, and his eyes strayed to Akkarin, who remained calm and outwardly unmoved.

'Though I was able to identify her as the witness, we called the family to the Guard House to verify. They told us this woman was not their daughter, but confirmed that she was wearing their daughter's clothing. They were distraught to find that another dead girl we had discovered, naked and apparently strangled, *was* their daughter. Another puzzling discovery was that the witness was found carrying a knife just like the one she had described the murderer carrying. Needless to say, all this casts some doubts on the integrity of the witness.'

The hall echoed with subdued voices. The Captain looked back at Lorlen. 'That is all I can tell you for now.'

The Administrator rose. 'We will take a break to discuss

and examine the evidence. Lady Vinara, Lord Balkan and Lord Sarrin will convey your views to me.'

At once the hall began to echo with raised voices as magicians gathered into groups to discuss and speculate. Yaldin turned to face Dannyl and Rothen.

'The knife could have been planted on the witness when she was killed.'

Dannyl shook his head. 'Perhaps, but why would she lie about who she was? Why was she wearing the other woman's clothes? Was she paid or bribed to take the other woman's place, without realising she would be killed? But that would mean it was all prearranged.'

'That doesn't make sense. Why would Akkarin arrange for a witness to identify him?' Yaldin asked.

Dannyl drew in a quick breath. 'In case there were other witnesses. If this one's story was disproved, any others would be cast into doubt.'

Yaldin chuckled. 'Either that or there's a black magician out there trying to have Akkarin blamed for his crimes. Akkarin could be innocent.'

Rothen shook his head.

'You don't agree?' Dannyl asked.

'Akkarin uses black magic,' Rothen told him.

'You don't know that. They found books on black magic in his rooms,' Dannyl pointed out. 'That doesn't prove that he actually *uses* it.'

Rothen frowned. *But I know he does. I have proof. I . . . I just can't tell anyone. Lorlen asked me to keep our involvement secret, and Sonea wants me to help Lorlen.*

At first Rothen had assumed the Administrator was trying to protect them both. He had realised later that Lorlen's position in the Guild would be weakened if he revealed that he had known about Akkarin's crime for years. If the Guild suspected Lorlen of conspiring with Akkarin, it would lose confidence in someone it needed to trust.

Unless . . . was Lorlen still hoping to avoid a confrontation with Akkarin by allowing him to be proven innocent? Rothen frowned and shook his head. One crime had been proven without a doubt: Akkarin and Sonea had both been in possession of forbidden books. That alone would have them expelled from the Guild. Lorlen could not prevent that.

Rothen's stomach sank. Every time he thought about Sonea being expelled, it hurt. After all she had gone through – believing the Guild wanted to kill her, nearly losing control of her powers, capture, being blackmailed by Fergun, enduring the harassment of the other novices, bearing the scorn of magicians, becoming Akkarin's hostage, giving up Dorrien's affection – she would lose everything she had worked so hard for.

He drew in a deep breath and brought his mind back to the question of Lorlen's intentions. Perhaps Lorlen hoped that Akkarin would accept expulsion and go. If Akkarin was faced with execution, however, he might not be so co-operative. And if the threat of execution pushed Akkarin into fighting the Guild, Sonea would probably help him. She might die in the battle. Perhaps it would be better if the Guild expelled them.

But if the Guild expelled Akkarin, it was required to block his powers first. Rothen doubted Akkarin would accept that either. Was there any way they could resolve this without it coming to a fight?

Rothen was vaguely aware that Dannyl had left to speak to Lord Sarrin. Yaldin seemed to have realised that Rothen was deep in thought, and had left him alone. After several minutes, Lorlen's voice echoed through the hall.

'Please return to your seats.'

Dannyl reappeared, looking smug. 'Have I told you how much I love being an Ambassador?'

Rothen nodded. 'Many times.'

'People *listen* to me now.'

As magicians took their seats, quiet returned to the hall. Lorlen looked down at the Head of Warriors.

'I call on Lord Balkan to continue.'

The Warrior straightened. 'Two nights ago, after learning of the murders, Vinara's conclusions, and examining the evidence and the witness' story, it was decided that the High Lord must be questioned. I soon learned that the residence was empty, but for the High Lord's servant, so I ordered it searched.'

He looked at Sonea. 'The first disturbing discovery we made was of three books on black magic in Sonea's room. One had small pieces of paper inserted between the pages, with notes written in her own hand.'

He paused, and a disapproving murmur followed. Rothen forced himself to look at Sonea. She was staring at the floor, her jaw set with determination. He thought of her excuse: '*To understand my enemy.*'

'Continuing our search, we found all doors unlocked but one. It was bound by powerful magic and appeared to lead to an underground room. The High Lord's servant claimed it was a storeroom and that he had no access to it. Lord Garrel ordered that the servant turn the handle, having guessed that the man was lying. When the servant refused, Lord Garrel took hold of the man's hand and placed it on the handle.

'The door opened and we entered a large room. In it we found a chest containing more books on black magic, many of them quite old. Some of these books had been copied by the High Lord. One contained his own records of his experiments and use of black magic. On the table . . .' Balkan stopped as the cries of outrage in the hall drowned his words.

Dannyl turned to Rothen, his eyes wide.

'*Use* of black magic,' he repeated. 'You know what that means.'

Rothen nodded. He could barely breathe. The Guild, by law, must execute Akkarin. Lorlen was not going to be able to prevent a confrontation now.

And I have nothing to lose by trying to prevent Sonea from being expelled.

From where he stood, Lorlen could see heads shaking and arms moving in rapid, expressive gestures. Some magicians were still and silent, obviously stunned by this revelation.

Akkarin stood calmly, watching it all.

Lorlen considered how the Hearing had gone so far. As he'd expected, Captain Barran's news had caused the magicians to question the evidence, and the possibility that Akkarin was the murderer. Some had asked why the High Lord would walk boldly out into the street after committing a crime. Others had proposed that Akkarin had deliberately arranged for a witness to come forward and then be discredited so that any other witnesses might be dismissed, too. This could not be proven, however. More than one magician had noted the cleanly cut edges of the scrap of cloth. Surely Akkarin would have noticed if Jolen had cut away part of his robes. He would not leave such a damning piece of evidence behind.

Lorlen was sure Akkarin would not have been found guilty of murder if the books on black magic had not been discovered. But now that the Guild knew of Akkarin's secret, it would believe him capable of anything. The murder charge was irrelevant. If the Guild followed its law, it would vote for his execution.

Lorlen drummed his fingers on the arm of his chair. There were tantalising references to a group of magicians who used black magic in Akkarin's notebooks. Lord Sarrin was worried about the possibility that such a group still existed. Akkarin had said there were good reasons for what he did.

Now, at last, Lorlen could finally ask what it was.

Standing up, he raised his hands for silence. The clamour died away surprisingly quickly. The magicians were eager to hear Akkarin questioned, Lorlen guessed.

'Does anyone have further evidence to offer this Hearing?'

A moment of silence followed, then somewhere to the right came a voice.

'I have, Administrator.'

Rothen's voice was calm and clear. All faces in the hall turned toward the Alchemist. Lorlen stared at him in dismay.

'Lord Rothen,' he forced himself to say. 'Please come down to the floor.'

Rothen descended to stand next to Balkan. He glanced at Akkarin, and the anger was clear in his face. Following his gaze, Lorlen saw that Akkarin was looking up at him. He slipped his hand in his pocket and felt the smoothness of the ring.

—I asked him to stay silent, Lorlen said.

—Perhaps you didn't ask nicely enough.

Rothen dropped to one knee and swore the oath of truth. Standing up again, he looked at the Higher Magicians.

'Sonea told me that the High Lord practised black magic over two years ago.'

The hall filled with whispers and murmuring.

'She had witnessed him taking power from his servant. Though she did not understand what she had seen, I did. I . . .' He looked down. 'I had heard much about the High Lord's strength and feared what he might do if challenged by the Guild. I hesitated to speak out. Before I could decide what to do, the High Lord learned that we had discovered his secret. He claimed Sonea's guardianship, and since then she has been his hostage, ensuring that I would not reveal his crime.'

As exclamations of anger and outrage filled the hall, Lorlen sighed with relief. Rothen had concealed Lorlen's part in it, and had risked nothing by mentioning his own. Then he saw why Rothen had spoken out. By revealing that Sonea had been Akkarin's victim, he might have given her a hope of reprieve.

Looking around the hall, Lorlen read shock and concern in the magicians' faces. He noted that Dannyl was staring at Rothen in open-mouthed amazement. He also noted that the novices now gazed at her in sympathy and even admiration. For a long time they had thought her unjustly favoured by the High Lord. Instead she had been his prisoner.

Is she now? Lorlen wondered.

—No.

Lorlen looked from Akkarin to Sonea. He recalled the

way she had obeyed Akkarin's every word when they were arrested in the underground room. He remembered her expression as she had joined Akkarin in the Entrance Hall. *Something* had changed her opinion of Akkarin. He felt a stab of impatience.

Lorlen raised his hand again. The magicians quietened reluctantly. He looked at Rothen.

'Do you have anything more to tell us, Lord Rothen?'

'No, Administrator.'

Lorlen looked up at the hall. 'Has anyone any further evidence to offer this Hearing?' When no answer came he looked down at Akkarin.

'Akkarin of House Velan, will you answer our questions truthfully?'

The corner of Akkarin's mouth twitched. 'I will.'

'Then swear it.'

Akkarin looked up above Lorlen's head, then dropped to one knee.

'I swear that all I speak in this Hearing will be the truth.'

The Guildhall was utterly silent. As Akkarin rose to his feet, Lorlen turned his attention to Sonea.

'Sonea, will you answer our questions truthfully?'

Her eyes widened. 'I will.'

She dropped to one knee and spoke the oath. When she had risen to her feet again, Lorlen considered all the questions he wanted to ask. *Begin with the accusations*, he decided.

'Akkarin,' he turned to face his former friend. 'Did you kill Lord Jolen?'

'No.'

'Have you studied and practised black magic?'

'Yes.'

A murmur rose in the hall and quickly subsided.

'How long have you been studying and practising black magic?'

The slightest frown passed over Akkarin's face.

'The first time . . . was eight years ago, before I returned to the Guild.'

A momentary silence followed that revelation, and then the hall filled with the buzz of speculation.

'Did you teach yourself, or did another teach you?'

'I learned from another magician.'

'Who was this magician?'

'I did not learn his name. I know only that he was Sachakan.'

'So he was not of the Guild.'

'No.'

Sachakan? Lorlen swallowed as foreboding began to grow in the pit of his stomach.

'Explain to us how you came to learn black magic from a Sachakan magician.'

Akkarin smiled. 'I was wondering if you would ever get around to asking.'

CHAPTER 17

THE TERRIBLE TRUTH

Sonea closed her eyes as Akkarin began his story. He spoke briefly of his quest to find ancient magical knowledge, and how what he had unearthed led him to enter Sachaka. There was a self-mocking tone to his voice, as if he thought that young man he had been was a fool.

Then he described his encounter with the Ichani, Dakova. Though she had heard him recount this before, she had been too caught up in what he was telling her to notice the slight hint of remembered dismay and horror in his voice. Then bitterness crept in as he related the years he had been a slave, and the cruel ways of the Ichani.

She realised he had probably never told anyone about that time in his life until the day he had related the story to her beside the spring. He had hidden that part of his life for years, and not just because it revealed that he had learned and used black magic. It pained and humiliated him to recount what he had seen and endured.

Opening her eyes, she almost expected to see some of that pain in his face, but though his expression was serious, no emotion showed.

To the magicians in the hall, he appeared to be calm and in control. They probably didn't notice the tension in his voice. Neither would she have a few months ago.

Somehow she had grown so familiar with his manner that she could see a little of what lay underneath.

She heard regret in his voice as he told of the Ichani who had offered to teach him black magic so he might murder his master. He explained that he did not expect to survive; that, even if he managed to kill Dakova, the Ichani's brother, Kariko, would hunt him down in revenge. He spoke of killing the other slaves, and then Dakova, with cold simplicity. Then he described his long journey home in a few short sentences.

His voice softened a little as he spoke of his relief at reaching the Guild, and how he had only wanted to forget Sachaka and black magic. He told how he had accepted the role of High Lord to keep himself busy, and so he could more easily keep an eye on the Ichani. He paused then, and the hall was utterly silent.

'Two years after my election I heard rumours of strange, ritual murders in the city,' he said. 'The Guard said the victims were marked in a certain way to indicate that they had been punished by the Thieves. I knew better.

'I followed the cases closely, and disguised myself so I could enter the slums, where the murders had taken place, to question and listen. When I found the murderer, he was exactly what I had suspected: a Sachakan black magician.

'Fortunately, he was weak and easily subdued. From his mind I read that he was a slave, freed and taught black magic in exchange for undertaking a dangerous mission. Kariko had sent him to gauge the strength of the Guild and, if the opportunity arose, assassinate me.

'Dakova had told Kariko much of what he had learned from me, including that the Guild had banned black magic and was much weaker than it had once been. But Kariko dared not attack the Guild alone. He needed to convince others to join him. If he could prove that the Guild was as weak as his brother had claimed, he would easily find allies among the Ichani.'

Akkarin looked up. Following his gaze, Sonea saw he was looking at the King. The monarch watched Akkarin intently. Sonea felt a spark of hope. Even if the King did not completely believe Akkarin's story, surely he would feel it prudent to check. He might allow Akkarin to live and stay at the Guild until . . .

The King's gaze suddenly shifted to hers. She found herself staring into a pair of unwavering green eyes. Swallowing hard, she forced herself to hold that gaze. *It is true*, she thought at him. *Believe him*.

'What did you do with this slave you found in the city?' Lorlen asked.

Sonea looked back down at the Administrator, then at Akkarin.

'I could not set him free to continue preying upon the people of Imardin,' Akkarin said. 'Nor could I bring him to the Guild. He would relay everything he saw, including our weaknesses, to Kariko. I had no choice but to kill him.'

Lorlen's eyebrows rose. Before he could ask further questions, Akkarin continued, his tone dark with warning.

'In the last five years I have tracked down and killed nine of these spies. Through them I have seen Kariko's attempts at uniting the Ichani fail twice. This time, I fear, he will succeed.' Akkarin's eyes narrowed. 'The last spy he sent was no slave. She was Ichani, and had no doubt read Lord Jolen's mind and learned all that I hoped to prevent the Sachakans from discovering. If she had made Jolen's death look natural, and left his family and servants alive, none of us would have thought to question it, I might not have realised the Ichani knew the truth about the Guild. Instead, by trying to make it look as though I killed him she has forced me to reveal the existence of the Ichani to you.' He shook his head. 'I only wish that was to your advantage.'

'So you believe this Ichani woman murdered Lord Jolen?'

'Yes.'

'And these spies are the reason why you started practising black magic again?'

'Yes.'

'Why didn't you tell us of this five years ago?'

'The threat was not great then. I hoped that, by killing off the spies, I might eventually convince the other Ichani that the Guild was not as weak as Kariko claimed. Or Kariko might eventually give up trying to gain their support. Or one of the Ichani might kill him; he did not have his brother's protection any more.'

'Yet you should have let us decide that.'

'It was too great a risk,' Akkarin replied. 'If I was publicly accused of using black magic, the Ichani would learn of it and know Kariko was right. If I managed to convince you of the truth, you might decide that learning black magic yourselves was the only way to protect Kyralia. I would not have that on my conscience.'

The Higher Magicians exchanged glances. Lorlen looked thoughtful.

'You have used black magic to strengthen yourself, so that you could fight these spies, and this Ichani woman,' he said slowly.

'Yes.' Akkarin nodded. 'But it was strength given willingly, by my servant and lately by Sonea.'

Sonea heard indrawn breaths. 'You used black magic on Sonea?' Lady Vinara gasped.

'No.' Akkarin smiled. 'There was no need. She is a magician, and can give her strength to another in more conventional ways.'

Lorlen frowned and glanced at Sonea. 'How much did Sonea know of all this before today?'

'All,' Akkarin replied. 'She had, as Lord Rothen pointed out, accidentally discovered more than she should have, and I had to take steps to ensure she and her former guardian remained silent. I recently decided to allow her to know the truth.'

'Why?'

'I realised that someone should know of the Ichani threat other than myself.'

Lorlen's eyes narrowed. 'So you chose a novice? Not a magician, or one of the Higher Magicians?'

'Yes. She is strong, and her knowledge of the slums has proved useful.'

'How did you convince her?'

'I took her to see one of the spies, then taught her to read his mind. She saw more than enough there to know that what I told her of my own experiences in Sachaka was true.'

Murmuring filled the hall as the implications of that sank in. The eyes of the Higher Magicians turned to Sonea. She felt her face warming and looked away.

'You told me that you couldn't teach another that skill,' Lorlen said quietly. 'You lied.'

'No, I didn't lie.' Akkarin smiled. 'I couldn't teach another, at the time, or you would have realised it had been taught to me, and asked where I had learned it.'

Lorlen frowned. 'What else have you taught Sonea?'

At the question, Sonea felt her blood turn to ice.

Akkarin hesitated. 'I have given her certain books to read, so that she might better understand our enemy.'

'The books from the chest? Where did you get them?'

'I found them in the passages under the University. They were placed there by the Guild after black magic was banned, in case such knowledge was needed again. I'm sure you have read enough of them to know this is true.'

Lorlen glanced back at Lord Sarrin.

The old Alchemist nodded. 'It is true, according to the records I found in the chest. I have studied them carefully and they do appear to be genuine. They relate how, before the Guild banned black magic five centuries ago, its use was common. Magicians kept apprentices, who gave them power in exchange for knowledge. One of these apprentices killed his master and massacred thousands in an attempt to rule the land for himself. After he died, the Guild banned black magic.'

The hall filled with murmuring voices that quickly rose into a clamour. Listening carefully, Sonea heard snatches of conversation.

'How are we to know if any of his story is true?'

'Why haven't we heard of these Ichani?'

Lorlen lifted both arms and called for quiet. The noise subsided.

'Do the Higher Magicians have any questions for Akkarin?'

'Yes,' Balkan rumbled. 'How many of these outcast magicians are there?'

'Somewhere between ten and twenty,' Akkarin replied. A scattering of laughter followed. 'Every day they take power from their slaves, who have strong magical potential equal to any of us. Imagine a black magician with ten slaves. If he took power from half of them every few days, he would be hundreds of times stronger than a Guild magician within weeks.'

Silence followed his words.

'Yet, that power diminishes as it is used,' Balkan said. 'After battle, a black magician is weaker.'

'Yes,' Akkarin answered.

Balkan looked thoughtful. 'A smart attacker would kill the slaves first.'

'Why haven't we heard of these Ichani before?' Administrator Kito's voice echoed through the hall. 'Merchants travel into Sachaka every year. They have occasionally reported meeting magicians in Arvice, but not black magicians.'

'The Ichani are outcasts. They live in the wastes and are not spoken of publicly in Arvice,' Akkarin replied. 'The court of Arvice is a dangerous political battlefield. Sachakan magicians do not allow others to know the limits of their skills and power. They are not going to allow Kyralian merchants and ambassadors to discover what they keep from their own countrymen.'

'Why do these Ichani want to invade Kyralia?' Balkan asked.

Akkarin shrugged. 'Many reasons. The main one, I suspect, is to escape the wastes and regain status and power in Arvice, but I know some desire to take revenge for the Sachakan War.'

Balkan frowned. 'An expedition to Arvice would confirm the truth of this.'

'Anyone recognisable as a Guild magician will be killed

if they approached the Ichani,' Akkarin warned. 'And I suspect few in Arvice would be aware of Kariko's ambitions.'

'How else will we confirm the truth?' Vinara said. 'Will you submit to a truth-read?'

'No.'

'That hardly inspires us to trust you.'

'The reader may learn the secret of black magic from my mind,' Akkarin added. 'I will not risk that.'

Vinara's eyes narrowed. She looked at Sonea. 'Perhaps Sonea then?'

'No.'

'She has learned black magic, too?'

'No,' he replied, 'but I have trusted her with information that should not be shared, unless in the greatest need.'

Sonea's heart was pounding. She looked at the floor. He had lied about her.

'Is Rothen's story true?' Vinara asked.

'It is.'

'You admit to claiming her guardianship merely to force Rothen and Sonea to remain silent?'

'No, I also claimed Sonea's guardianship because she has great potential. A potential which was being shamefully neglected. I've found her to be nothing less than honest, hard-working and exceptionally gifted.'

Sonea looked up at him in surprise. She felt a sudden mad urge to grin, but managed to control it.

Then she went cold as she suddenly understood what he was doing.

He was convincing them to keep her within the Guild by telling them she had skills and information that they might need. Even if they didn't believe him, they might take pity on her. She had been his hostage. She had been deceived into helping him. The Guild might even pardon her. She had, after all, only read a few books, and then only at the instigation of Akkarin.

She frowned. This made Akkarin look worse however. And he was encouraging them to see things that way. Since she had first learned of the Ichani, she had nursed the hope that the Guild, if it learned the truth, would pardon him. But now she wondered if Akkarin had ever considered that a possibility.

If he wasn't hoping to be pardoned, what was he planning? Surely he didn't mean to let them execute him?

No, if it came to that, he would fight his way out and escape. Would he make it?

She considered, again, how much of his power the fight with the Ichani woman must have used. Her heart began to race as she realised he could easily be too weak to escape the Guild.

Unless she gave him all her strength, including that which she had taken from the Ichani woman.

All she had to do was touch him and send him the power. The warriors surrounding them would try to stop her. She would have to fight them.

When they did, however, they would realise that she was using more power than she ought to possess.

And then they would not be at all inclined to pardon her.

So the only way she could save Akkarin was to reveal her own use of black magic.

'Sonea.'

She looked up to find Lorlen regarding her intently.

'Yes, Administrator.'

His eyes narrowed.

'Did Akkarin teach you how to read an unwilling mind?'

'Yes.'

'And you are sure what you saw in the spy's mind was true?'

'I am sure.'

'Where were you on the night Lord Jolen died?'

'I was with the High Lord.'

Lorlen frowned. 'What were you doing?'

Sonea hesitated. Now was the time to reveal herself. But Akkarin might have a reason for wanting her not to.

He wants someone who knows the truth to remain in the Guild.

What use will I be, though, with him dead? Better that we escape together. If the Guild needs our help, they can contact us through Lorlen's blood ring.

'Sonea?'

One thing I am sure of. I can't let them kill Akkarin.

Taking a deep breath, she lifted her eyes to meet Lorlen's.

'He was teaching me black magic.'

Gasps and exclamations filled the hall. In the edge of her vision she saw Akkarin turn to stare at her, but she kept her eyes on Lorlen. Her heart was pounding, and she felt sick, but she forced herself to continue. 'I asked him to teach me. He refused at first. It was only after he had been injured by the Ichani spy that I—'

'You learned black magic *willingly*?' Vinara exclaimed.

Sonea nodded. 'Yes, my lady. When the High Lord was injured, I realised there would be nobody with the ability to continue fighting if he died.'

Lorlen glanced at Akkarin. 'Now there won't be.'

His words sent a chill down her spine. Clearly Lorlen had understood what Akkarin had been trying to do.

Knowing that she had been right in her suspicions gave her only a bitter satisfaction.

Looking at Akkarin, she was shocked to see the anger in his face. She quickly looked away. *I said I would do as he instructed.* She felt doubts beginning to gather. *Was I wrong? Did I just ruin some plan I wasn't clever enough to see?*

But surely Akkarin had realised she would understand that he was sacrificing himself so that she could remain in the Guild. He must have considered that she might refuse to abandon him.

'Sonea.'

Heart still pounding, she forced herself to look at Lorlen.

'Did Akkarin kill Lord Jolen?'

'No.'

'Did he kill the witness?'

Her stomach fluttered at the question. 'I don't know. I haven't seen this witness, so I couldn't tell you. I can say that I have never seen him kill a woman.'

Lorlen nodded and looked up at the Higher Magicians. 'Any further questions?'

'Yes,' Balkan said. 'When we arrived at Akkarin's residence, neither you nor Akkarin were there. You arrived together later. Where did you go?'

'We went into the city.'

'Why?'

'To deal with another spy.'

'Did Akkarin kill this spy?'

'No.'

Balkan frowned at her but remained silent. Lorlen looked at the Higher Magicians, then turned to regard the rest of the hall.

'Does anyone have any more questions?'

Silence answered him. Sonea breathed a sigh of relief. Lorlen nodded.

'We will now discuss what we have—'

'Wait!'

Lorlen turned to the front. 'Yes, Lord Balkan.'

'One more question. For Sonea.'

She forced herself to meet Balkan's gaze.

'Did *you* kill this Ichani woman?'

Cold swept over her. She looked at Akkarin. He was staring at the floor, his expression hard and resigned.

What difference would it make to tell them? she thought. *Only to show that I believe what he says is the truth.* She lifted her chin and stared back at Balkan.

'Yes.'

The hall filled with exclamations. Balkan sighed and rubbed his temples.

'I told you not to let them stand together,' he muttered.

CHAPTER 18

THE GUILD'S JUDGMENT

As soon as Lorlen called for another break for discussion, Dannyl hurried to Rothen's side. He had seen his friend react to Sonea's admission as if he had been struck a physical blow. Now Rothen stood staring at the floor.

Dannyl reached his friend and put a hand on his shoulder.

'You two never stop surprising me,' Dannyl said gently. 'Why didn't you tell me the real reason you lost Sonea's guardianship?'

Rothen shook his head. 'I couldn't. He might have . . . well, I guess he has now.' He looked at Sonea, then sighed. 'This is my fault. I convinced her to join the Guild in the first place.'

'No, it isn't. You couldn't possibly know this would happen.'

'No, but I made her question her beliefs when she first came here. I taught her to look beyond them, so she would accept her place among us. She probably did the same for . . . for . . .'

'What if all this is true? Then she had good reasons for what she did.'

Rothen looked up, his expression bleak. 'Does it matter? She just ensured her own execution.'

Surveying the room, Dannyl noted the expressions of

the Higher Magicians, then the King. They looked wary and anxious. Then he looked at Sonea and Akkarin. Sonea stood straight and determined, though how much of that was forced he couldn't guess. The High Lord's expression was . . . controlled. Looking closer, Dannyl read anger in the set of Akkarin's jaw.

He hadn't intended for Sonea to reveal so much, Dannyl mused.

But, despite this, he and Sonea now stood closer together. A few steps, and they would be side by side. Dannyl nodded to himself.

'I don't know if she has, Rothen.'

Once the Higher Magicians had returned to their seats, they began to relate what the members of their disciplines had expressed. Lorlen listened closely.

'Many find his story hard to believe,' Vinara said, 'but some have pointed out that, if he was seeking to justify his actions with a fabricated story, surely he would come up with something more convincing than this.'

'My Warriors also find it disturbing,' Balkan added. 'They say we cannot ignore the possibility that he speaks the truth, and we face a threat of attack from Sachaka. We must investigate further.'

Sarrin nodded. 'Yes, my people agree. Many have asked if there is information in the books we might use to defend ourselves, should an attack come. I fear there is not. If Akkarin is telling the truth, we may need him.'

'I, too, would like to question Akkarin further,' Balkan said. 'I would normally ask that he be detained until his claim is proven.'

'We cannot imprison him effectively,' Vinara reminded him.

'No.' Balkan pursed his lips, then looked up at Lorlen. 'Do you think he would co-operate?'

Lorlen shrugged. 'He has up till now.'

'That doesn't mean he will continue to,' Vinara said. 'For all we know, we could be doing everything he intended us to do. He might become very unhelpful if we took a different path.'

Sarrin frowned. 'If he wanted to take control of us by force, he would have attempted it already.'

'That clearly isn't what he wants,' Balkan agreed. 'Though this whole story of Sachakan magicians might be meant to confuse and delay us.'

'Delay us for what?' Sarrin asked.

Balkan's shoulders lifted. 'I have no idea.'

'But we cannot let him go,' Vinara said firmly. 'Akkarin has freely admitted to practising black magic. Whether he committed the murders or not, we cannot show any tolerance for someone of his standing breaking one of our most serious laws. Akkarin must be seen to be punished.'

'The appropriate punishment is execution,' Sarrin reminded her. 'Would you continue co-operating if you knew that was to be your punishment?'

'No doubt he would object to us trying to bind his powers, too.' Vinara sighed. 'How strong is he, Balkan?'

The Warrior considered. 'That depends. Is he telling the truth? He said a black magician with ten slaves could grow to the strength of hundreds of Guild magicians in a matter of weeks. He has been back eight years, though he claims he did not begin using it again until five years ago. Five years is a long time to be strengthening oneself, even if it was only from one servant – until recently.'

'He has fought nine slaves during that time,' Sarrin added. 'That would weaken him, too.'

Balkan nodded. 'He might not be as strong as we fear. If he isn't telling the truth, however, the situation may be far worse. He may have been strengthening himself for longer. He may have been killing people in the city. And then there's Lord Jolen and his household.' Balkan sighed. 'Even if I could be sure of his honesty and strength, there is another factor that makes it impossible to predict what will happen if we tried to use force.'

'What is that?' Vinara asked.

Balkan turned to the left. 'Look at Sonea closely. Do you sense it?'

They turned to stare at the novice.

'Power,' Sarrin said.

'Yes,' Balkan said. 'A great deal of it. She hasn't yet learned to hide it as he does.' He paused. 'She said he was teaching her black magic two nights ago. I don't know how long this training ought to take, but he claims he learned the gist of it in one lesson. Sonea didn't have this aura of strength when she was practising in the Arena a week ago. I'm sure I would have sensed it if she had. I think this woman she admits to killing was the source of her sudden increase in strength. Sonea could not have become so powerful in one night by killing any ordinary woman.'

They turned to regard the novice in thoughtful silence.

'Why did Akkarin attempt to hide Sonea's involvement?' Sarrin wondered aloud.

'And why did she decide to reveal it?' Vinara added.

'Perhaps he wanted to ensure someone with the ability to fight the Sachakans remained alive,' Sarrin said. He frowned. 'That does suggest that the books, alone, are not enough.'

'Perhaps he just wanted to protect her,' Vinara said.

'Lord Balkan,' a new voice spoke.

The Warrior looked up in surprise. 'Yes, Your Majesty?'

All heads turned to face the King. He was leaning over the back of the empty High Lord's chair, his green eyes bright and piercing.

'Do you believe the Guild is capable of driving Akkarin out of the Allied Lands?'

Balkan hesitated. 'I honestly don't know, Your Majesty. Even if we managed it, it would exhaust most of our magicians. Should these Sachakan magicians exist, they may see it as the perfect opportunity to invade.'

The young King absorbed this.

'Administrator Lorlen, do you believe he will comply if he is commanded to leave the Allied Lands?'

Lorlen blinked in surprise. 'Do you mean . . . exile?'

'Yes.'

The Higher Magicians looked at each other thoughtfully.

'The nearest non-allied land is Sachaka,' Balkan pointed out. 'If his story is true . . .'

Lorlen frowned, then slipped his hands in his pockets. His fingers touched the ring.

—*Akkarin?*

—*Yes?*

—*Will you accept exile?*

—*Instead of fighting my way out of here?* Lorlen caught a faint amusement. *I was hoping for better.*

Silence followed.

—*Akkarin? You know where they'll send you.*

—*Yes.*

—Should I try to convince them to take you somewhere else?

—No. They would have to take me far from Kyralia. The Guild needs the magicians it would send as my escort to remain here and defend Kyralia if the Ichani invade.

He fell silent again. Lorlen glanced at the other magicians. They were watching him expectantly.

—Akkarin? The King is waiting for an answer.

—Very well. See if you can talk them into keeping Sonea here.

—I'll see what I can do.

'I guess we can only try to convince him to leave peacefully,' Lorlen said. 'The alternative, if you wish to avoid a confrontation, is to allow him to stay here as a prisoner.'

The King nodded. 'To imprison a man you cannot control is foolish, and he must be seen to be punished, as Lady Vinara said. This threat from Sachaka must be investigated and confirmed, however. If he is proven right, and trustworthy, we may find and consult with him.'

Balkan frowned. 'I would like to question Akkarin further.'

'You can do so on the way to the border.' The King's eyes were hard.

The others exchanged worried glances, but none protested.

'May I speak, Your Majesty?'

All turned to see Rothen standing at the base of the stairs.

'You may,' the King replied.

'Thank you.' Rothen bowed his head for a moment, then looked at each of the Higher Magicians.

'I ask that you consider Sonea's youth and impressionability when you judge her. She had been his prisoner for some time. I do not know how he persuaded her to join him. She is stubborn and good-hearted, but when I persuaded her to join the Guild, I encouraged her to question her distrust of magicians. Now, perhaps, that has led her to discard her distrust of Akkarin.' He smiled faintly. 'I think once she has realised she has been deceived she will punish herself better than any of us could.'

Lorlen looked up at the King. He was nodding.

'I will consider your words, Lord . . . ?'

'Rothen.'

'Thank you, Lord Rothen.'

Rothen dropped to one knee, then rose and moved away. The ruler watched him go, then drummed his fingers on the back of the High Lord's chair.

'How do you think the High Lord's novice will react when her guardian is exiled?'

Sonea stood in utter silence.

The Warriors surrounding her and Akkarin had enclosed them in a barrier that blocked all noise in the hall. She had watched as magicians had gathered to debate. After a long break, the Higher Magicians had returned to their seats and began an intense discussion.

Akkarin shifted a step closer, but didn't look at her.

'You chose an inopportune time for disobedience, Sonea.'

She winced at the anger in his voice. 'Did you really think I'd let them execute you?'

There was a long pause before he replied.

'I need you to remain here and continue the fight.'

'How can I do that with the Guild watching my every move?'

'Little opportunity is better than none. If nothing else,

they would have you to call on as a last resort.'

'If they had me, they would never have considered allowing you to live,' she retorted. 'I won't let them use me as an excuse to kill you.'

He began to turn toward her, then stopped as sound abruptly returned. Lorlen stood up and struck a gong.

'It is time to judge whether Akkarin of family Delvon, of House Velan, High Lord of the Magicians' Guild, and Sonea, his novice, are guilty of the crimes of which they have been accused.'

He held out a hand. A globe light appeared above it, then floated up to the ceiling. The other Higher Magicians followed suit, then hundreds more globe lights floated up from the rest of the magicians, and the Guildhall was filled with brightness.

'Do you judge that Akkarin of family Delvon, of House Velan, is undoubtedly guilty of the murder of Lord Jolen, his family and servants?'

Several of the globes slowly turned red, but most remained white. The Higher Magicians stared up for a long time, and Sonea realised they were counting the globes. When they looked down again at Lorlen each shook their head once.

'The majority choose the negative,' Lorlen declared. 'Do you judge that Akkarin of family Delvon, of House Velan, is guilty of seeking knowledge of, learning, practising and, in addition to earlier accusations, killing with black magic?'

At once all of the globes turned red. Lorlen did not wait for the Higher Magicians to count the globes.

'The majority choose the affirmative,' Lorlen called. 'Do you judge that Sonea, the High Lord's novice, is guilty of seeking knowledge of and, in addition to this earlier accusation, learning, practising and killing with black magic?'

The globe lights remained red. Lorlen nodded slowly.

'The majority choose the affirmative. The punishment for this crime as set down by law is execution. We, the Higher Magicians, have debated the appropriateness of this penalty in light of the reasons given for the crime, if they be true. We would prefer to delay judgment until the validity of these reasons is established, but due to the nature of the crime, feel immediate action must be taken.' He paused. 'We have chosen exile as Akkarin's punishment.'

The hall filled with muttering as this was considered. Sonea heard a few weak protests, but no magician raised his or her voice to argue.

'Akkarin of family Delvon, of House Velan, you are no longer welcome in the Allied Lands. You will be escorted to the nearest non-allied country. Do you accept this judgment?'

Akkarin looked up at the King, then dropped to one knee.

'If the King wills it.'

The ruler's eyebrows rose.

'I do,' he said.

'Then I will go.'

The hall was silent as Akkarin rose to his feet again. Lorlen's sigh of relief was audible. He turned to regard Sonea.

'Sonea. We, the Higher Magicians, have decided to offer you a second chance. You will remain here with us under these conditions: you must vow to never use black magic again, you will not be allowed to leave the Guild grounds from this day, and you will never be allowed to teach others. Do you accept this judgment?'

Sonea stared at Lorlen in disbelief. The Guild had exiled Akkarin yet forgiven her, even though they had both committed the same crime.

But it wasn't the same. Akkarin was their leader and his crime seemed worse because he was supposed to represent the Guild's values. She was just an impressionable young woman. The slum girl. Easily corrupted. They believed she had been led astray, and that Akkarin had embraced black magic willingly. In truth she had chosen to learn it, and *he* had been forced to.

So they would allow her to stay in the temporary safety and the comfort of the Guild, while Akkarin was sent out of the Allied Lands to the nearest non-allied country, which was . . . She caught her breath.

Sachaka.

Suddenly she could not breathe. They were going to send him into the hands of his enemies. They must know that if his story was true he would die.

But this way, they won't have to risk a battle they might lose.

'Sonea,' Lorlen repeated. 'Do you accept this judgment?'

'No.'

She was surprised by the anger in her voice. Lorlen stared at her in dismay, then looked at Akkarin.

'Stay.' Akkarin told her. 'There is no sense in us both going.'

Not if we're going to Sachaka, she thought. *But perhaps, together, we might survive*. She could help him strengthen himself. Alone, he would only grow weaker. She clung to this small hope and turned to face him.

'I made Takan a promise to take care of you. I intend to keep it.'

His eyes narrowed. 'Sonea—'

'Don't tell me I'll get in the way,' she said under her breath, conscious of the many witnesses. 'That didn't stop me before, and it won't now. I know where they're sending you. I'm coming with you, whether you like it or not.' Turning to the front, she raised her voice so all could hear.

'If you send High Lord Akkarin into exile, you must send me too. Then, when you come to your senses, he might still be alive and able to help you.'

The hall was silent. Lorlen stared at her, then looked up at the Higher Magicians. Sonea could see defeat and frustration in their faces.

'No, Sonea! Stay here.'

Sonea felt her stomach turn over at the voice. She forced herself to look across the room at Rothen.

'I'm sorry, Rothen,' she said, 'but I will not stay.'

Lorlen took a deep breath. 'Sonea, I can give you only one more chance. Do you accept this judgment?'

'No.'

'Then let it be known throughout the Allied Lands that Akkarin of family Delvon, House Velan, formerly High Lord of the Magicians' Guild, and Sonea, formerly the High Lord's novice, have been exiled for the crimes of learning, practising and killing with black magic.'

He turned to Lord Balkan and said something in a voice too quiet to hear. Then he descended from his seat, strode into the circle of Warriors and stopped a step away from Akkarin. Reaching out, he grasped the black robe in both hands. Sonea heard the material rip.

'I cast you out, Akkarin. Do not enter my lands again.'

Akkarin stared at Lorlen, but did not speak. The Administrator turned away and approached Sonea. He met her eyes for a moment, then looked down, took hold of her sleeve and ripped it.

'I cast you out, Sonea. Do not enter my lands again.'

Turning on his heel, he strode away. Sonea looked down at the rip in her sleeve. It was small, only a finger-length long. A small gesture, but so final.

The Higher Magicians rose to their feet and began to descend from the tiers of seats. Sonea's heart sank as Lord Balkan stepped into the circle and approached Akkarin. As he tore the black robes and spoke the ritual words, the rest of the Higher Magicians formed a line behind him, and she realised they were waiting their turn.

As Balkan approached she forced herself to watch as the Warrior tore her robe and spoke the ritual words. It took all her determination, but she managed to meet his gaze, and then those of each of the magicians who followed.

When the Higher Magicians had all performed the ritual, Sonea sighed with relief. The rest of the Guild rose from their seats. Instead of walking out of the Guildhall doors, they began to approach Akkarin one by one.

It looked as if she would have to endure this ceremony of rejection many, many more times.

The realisation unsettled her. It took all her will to face them. She kept still as magicians who had taught her stopped to tear her robes, their expressions disapproving or disappointed. Lady Tya's ritual words were barely audible, and she quickly hurried away. Lord Yikmo gazed at her searchingly, then shook his head sadly. At last there were only a few magicians left. She looked up as they entered the circle, and felt her stomach twist.

Rothen and Dannyl.

Her former guardian approached Akkarin slowly. He stared at Akkarin, his eyes burning with anger, then Akkarin's lips moved. She could not quite hear what he said, but the fire in Rothen's eyes died. Rothen murmured a reply and Akkarin nodded once. Frowning, Rothen reached forward to tear Akkarin's robe. He spoke the ritual words, then kept his eyes on the floor as he took the few short steps to her.

She felt her throat constrict. Rothen's face looked haggard and deeply lined. He looked up at her and his pale blue eyes shimmered as tears gathered in them.

'*Why*, Sonea?' he whispered hoarsely.

She felt moisture spring into her eyes. She closed them tightly and swallowed hard.

'They send him to his death.'

'And you?'

'Two may survive where one would fail. The Guild has to find out the truth for itself. When it does, we'll return.'

He drew in a deep breath, then stepped forward and embraced her.

'Take care, Sonea.'

'I will, Rothen.'

She choked on his name. He stepped away. As he retreated, she realised he hadn't torn her robes. She felt a trickle of moisture run down her cheek and quickly wiped it away as Dannyl stepped in front of her.

'Sonea.'

She forced herself to look up at him. Dannyl met her gaze levelly.

'Sachakans, eh?'

She nodded, not trusting her voice.

He pursed his lips. 'We'll have to look into it.' He patted her shoulder, then turned away. She watched him walk to Rothen's side.

Her attention was drawn away then as, one by one, the Warriors surrounding her and Akkarin stepped in to perform the ritual. When they were done, she looked around and discovered that the magicians had formed two lines leading to the Guildhall doors. Behind them stood the novices. She sighed with relief that they hadn't been included in the ritual. Facing Regin in that situation would have been . . . interesting.

The Higher Magicians formed a second circle around the Warrior guard, with Lorlen at the front. As the Administrator started walking toward the Guildhall doors, this double escort followed, and proceeded past the two lines of magicians out of the Guildhall to the University doors.

Outside the building was a circle of horses, held in position by grooms. Two horses waited in the centre. Akkarin approached the central pair, Sonea following. As he swung up into the saddle of one, she hesitated and looked at the remaining horse dubiously.

'Are you doubting your decision?'

Sonea turned to find Lord Osen standing beside her, holding the reins of his mount.

Sonea shook her head. 'No, it's just . . . I've never ridden before.'

He glanced back at the crowd of magicians pouring out of the doors behind her, then turned his horse so it blocked them from view.

'Put your hand on the front of the saddle, and then put the toe of your left boot in here.' He took hold of her horse's stirrup and held it still. Sonea did as he said and, following his further instructions, she managed somehow to get into the saddle.

'Don't worry too much about directing him,' he told her. 'He'll follow the others.'

'Thank you, Lord Osen.'

He looked up at her and nodded once, then turned away and swung up onto his own mount.

From her new vantage point, she could see the crowd of magicians gathered outside the Guild. The Higher Magicians stood in a line along the bottom step of the University, except for Lord Balkan who had joined the guard of Warriors on the horses. Sonea looked for the King, but he was nowhere in sight.

Lorlen stepped forward and slowly approached Akkarin. He looked up and then shook his head.

'You have a second chance of sorts, Akkarin. Use it well.'

Akkarin regarded him for a moment. 'And you, my friend, though I fear you will face worse troubles than I do. We will speak again.'

Lorlen smiled crookedly. 'I'm sure we will.'

He moved away and returned to his place among the Higher Magicians, then nodded at Balkan. The Warrior nudged his horse into motion and the rest of the escort followed suit.

As her horse began to move, Sonea gripped the pommel of her saddle. She looked at Akkarin, but his eyes were fixed on the Guild Gates. When she had passed through the entrance, she cautiously turned to take one last look at the University, standing tall and graceful among the other Guild buildings.

A pang of sadness and regret caught her by surprise.

I hadn't realised how much I considered this place home, she thought. *Will I survive and return to see it again?*

Or, a darker voice added, *will I come back only to find it a pile of rubble?*

PART TWO

CHAPTER 19

A REQUEST

Sonea shifted in her saddle and flexed her aching thigh muscles. Though she Healed away the soreness each night, it did not take much riding before her body was hurting again. Lord Osen had told her that she would grow used to the saddle if she didn't Heal herself, but she couldn't see the point in toughening up for riding when the horse would soon be taken from her.

She sighed and looked up at the mountains ahead. They had first appeared on the horizon the day before. The shadowy line had slowly grown larger and this morning the sun had revealed slopes of jagged rock and forest ascending to high peaks. The mountains looked savage and impassable, but now that the escort had reached the low hills at the base, Sonea could see a ribbon of white winding between the trees toward a dip between two of the peaks. Somewhere at the end of that road stood the Fort and the entrance to Sachaka.

The slowly changing landscape fascinated her. She had never roamed beyond the edge of the city of Imardin. Travelling was a new experience, and she might have enjoyed it, if not for the circumstances.

At first the road had run alongside fields striped with rows of different plants. The workers digging the soil, planting or harvesting the crops, were men and women, young and old. Both adults and children were seen herding domestic animals of all sizes along the road. Little houses stood alone in great stretches of land. Sonea wondered if their occupants were happy living such an isolated life.

From time to time the road had taken them through clusters of houses. At a few of these villages, Lord Balkan had sent one of his Warriors away to buy food. At midday on each of the previous two days, they had encountered a magician and several local men waiting with fresh horses. They changed mounts to allow the group to continue travelling through each night. The escort did not pause or stop to sleep, and she assumed they were Healing away their weariness. When she had asked Lord Osen why they didn't refresh the horses with Healing power, he told her that animals didn't endure the mental fatigue that came with a lack of rest as humans did.

So far, she felt she was coping with the lack of sleep fairly well. The first night had been clear, and their way had been lit by moonlight and starlight. Sonea had dozed as well as could be managed on horseback. Clouds had covered the sky the next night, and they had travelled under a cluster of globe lights.

Looking at the mountains looming so close, Sonea wondered if they would have a third night in Kyralia.

'Halt!'

The beating of hooves on the road changed to a shuffling as the escort slowed to a stop. Her horse moved forward to stand next to Akkarin's. Sonea felt a spark of hope as Akkarin turned to regard her. He hadn't spoken to her, or anyone, since leaving Imardin.

But he said nothing and turned away to watch Lord Balkan.

The Head of Warriors handed something to one of his magicians. Money to buy food at the next village, Sonea guessed. She looked around and realised that they were standing at a meeting of roads. One continued toward the mountains; the other, smaller track descended into a small, sparsely forested valley, where a group of houses huddled close together beside a narrow river.

'Lord Balkan,' Akkarin said.

All heads immediately turned to face him. Sonea resisted an urge to smile at the escorts' expressions of alarm and surprise. *So he's finally decided to speak.*

Balkan regarded Akkarin warily. 'Yes?'

'If we enter Sachaka in these robes we will be recognised. Will you allow us to change into ordinary clothing?'

Balkan's gaze shifted to Sonea, then back to Akkarin. He nodded and turned back to the waiting Warrior.

'Clothes as well, then. Nothing fancy or bright.'

The magician nodded, then gave Akkarin and Sonea a measuring look before riding away.

Sonea felt the knot in her stomach tighten. Did this mean they were close to the pass? Would they reach the border today? She looked up at the mountains and shivered.

She had hoped many times to hear a mental call from Lorlen, ordering them back, yet she did not believe it would come. The manner of their departure from Imardin had made it clear to all that she and Akkarin were not welcome in Kyralia any more.

She grimaced as she remembered. Balkan had chosen a winding route through the city that took them through every Quarter. At each major intersection of streets they had stopped, halting all activity as Balkan announced her and Akkarin's crimes, and the Guild's punishment. Akkarin's expression had darkened with anger. He had called the magicians fools, and had refused to speak since.

The procession had attracted large crowds, and by the time the escort had reached the North Gates an expectant throng of slum dwellers had gathered. As stones flew toward Sonea, she had hastily created a shield.

An awful feeling of betrayal had come over her as the dwells shouted and threw missiles at her and Akkarin, but it had quickly faded. The dwells probably saw two bad magicians from a Guild they despised anyway, and had taken advantage of the opportunity to throw stones and insults without reprisal.

Turning in her saddle, Sonea looked back down the road. The city was far beyond the horizon now. The Warriors behind her watched her closely.

Lord Osen was among them. His frown deepened as their eyes met. He had spoken to her several times during the journey, mostly to help her with the horses she had ridden. A few times he had hinted that the Guild might allow her to return to Imardin if she changed her mind. She had decided not to respond wherever he made any such suggestion.

But fear, discomfort and Akkarin's silence had worked against her resolve. Turning away from Osen, she considered Akkarin again. Her attempts to talk to him had been met with stony silence. He seemed determined to ignore her.

Yet, now and then, she had seen him watching her. If she gave no indication that she had noticed him, his gaze lingered for a long time, but if she looked in his direction his attention turned to something else.

This was both infuriating and intriguing. It was not his looking that bothered her; it was that he did not want her to see him looking. Sonea smiled wryly. Was she actually beginning to miss the penetrating, hard-to-meet stares that she had avoided for so long?

She sobered. No doubt he wanted her to feel unwelcome, so that she would turn tail and scamper back to the Guild. Or was it something simpler? Did he truly not want her around? She had wondered many times if he blamed her for the discovery of their secret. Would Balkan have forced his way into Akkarin's underground room if he hadn't found books on black magic in her bedroom? Akkarin had told her to keep them hidden. She had, but obviously not well enough.

Perhaps he simply thought he would be better off without her.

Then he is wrong, she told herself. Without a companion from whom he could draw strength, he would only grow weaker each time he used his powers. With her there, he might be able to defend himself against an Ichani attack. *It doesn't matter whether he likes having me around.*

Ah, but it would be so much better if he did.

Would he be friendlier once they had reached Sachaka, and there was no longer any point in trying to persuade her to leave him? Would he accept her choice, or would he continue to be angry with her for disobeying him? She frowned. Didn't he understand that she had given up everything to save him?

She shook her head. It didn't matter. She didn't want his gratitude. He could be as silent and sulky as he liked. She only wanted to be sure he survived, and not just because this meant he would be able to return and help save the Guild from the Ichani. If she truly hadn't cared about him, she would have stayed in Imardin, even if it meant becoming a prisoner of the Guild. No, she had come with him because she could not bear the thought of abandoning him after all he'd been through.

I've replaced Takan, she thought suddenly. The former slave had followed Akkarin out of Sachaka and become his faithful servant. Now she was following Akkarin *into* Sachaka. What was it about him that inspired such devotion?

Me, devoted to Akkarin? She almost laughed aloud. *So much has changed. I think I might even like him, now.*

Then her heart skipped a beat.

Or is it more than that?

She considered the question carefully. Surely, if there was more to it, she would have noticed before now. Abruptly, she remembered the night she had killed the Ichani. Afterwards, Akkarin had brushed something out of her hair. The touch had left her feeling so strange. Light. Elated.

But that was just an effect of the battle. Surviving such a close scrape with death was sure to generate feelings of elation. It didn't mean she was . . . she felt . . .

All I have to do is look at him, and I'll know.

Suddenly she was afraid to. What if it was true? What if he met her gaze and read something foolish in her expression? He'd be even more determined to make her stay in Kyralia.

A murmuring between the escorts saved her. She looked up and saw that the Warrior who had ridden into the village was returning. Across the man's knees lay a sack and a bundle. He handed the bundle to Balkan as he reached the group.

Balkan untied it, then lifted up a coarsely woven shirt and a pair of narrow-legged trousers and a long woollen shirt like those Sonea had seen village women wearing. He looked at Akkarin.

'Suitable?'

Akkarin nodded. 'They will do.'

Balkan rolled up the clothes again and tossed them to Akkarin. Sonea hesitated as Akkarin began to dismount, then forced her aching legs to move. As her feet touched the ground, Akkarin pressed the long shirt and a second pair of trousers into her hands.

'Look away,' Balkan ordered.

Sonea glanced around and saw that the rest of the magicians were turning their backs. She heard a silken rip as Akkarin pulled off the top part of his robe and let it drop to the ground. The material shimmered in the sunlight, the ribbons of torn cloth fluttering as the wind caught them. Akkarin paused to look at it, his expression unreadable, then straightened and reached for the waist of his trousers.

Sonea quickly turned away, her face suddenly hot. She looked down at her robes and swallowed hard.

Best get this over with.

Taking a deep breath, she undid her sash and quickly pulled off the top half of her robes. Her horse edged away nervously as Sonea dropped the garment onto the ground and hurriedly pulled the shirt over her head.

She was grateful for the generous length of the shirt, covering her almost to the knees, as she changed into the trousers. Turning around, she found Akkarin regarding the reins of his horse closely. He glanced at her once, then swung up onto his horse.

Balkan, she saw, had remained facing them. *Well, someone had to keep an eye on us*, she thought wryly. She stepped over to her horse, put her boot into the stirrup, and managed to haul herself up into the saddle.

Akkarin looked strange in the heavy clothing. His shirt hung awkwardly on his thin frame. His chin was shadowed where a dark stubble was beginning to grow. He looked nothing like the imposing High Lord who had intimidated most of the Guild for so long.

She looked down at herself and snorted softly. She was hardly the picture of elegance herself. The shirt was probably the cast-off of a farmer's wife. The rough weave felt harsh against her skin, but it was no worse than what she had worn before she had joined the Guild.

'Hungry?'

Sonea started as she realised Lord Osen had brought his horse alongside hers. He held out a chunk of grainy bread and a mug. She took them gratefully and began to eat, washing down the bread with gulps of watered wine. The wine was cheap and sour, but it numbed the ache in her muscles a little. She gave the mug back.

When the escort finished eating, they resumed their journey, and her horse returned to its jolting gait. She smothered a groan and resigned herself to many more hours of riding and sore muscles.

As Gol entered Cery's guestroom, his eyes strayed to Savara. He nodded politely, then turned to Cery.

'Takan says they're close to the border,' he reported. 'They'll reach the Fort tomorrow night.'

Cery nodded. He had given Takan a comfortable suite of underground rooms to stay in, but had been careful to hire servants who hadn't heard of the mysterious foreign woman Ceryni had taken a liking to. Savara had asked him to ensure Takan never learned anything of her. She had rightly guessed that Akkarin was able to communicate with his servant, and if Akkarin was captured by the Ichani, she explained, they might learn from him of her presence in Kyralia. 'There is much hatred between my people and the Ichani,' she had said. She did not say why, and Cery knew better than to press for more information.

Gol sat down and sighed. 'What are we going to do?'

'Nothing,' Cery replied.

Gol frowned. 'What if another murderer gets into the city?'

Cery looked at Savara and smiled. 'I think we can handle it. I did promise Savara the next one.'

To his surprise, she shook her head.

'I cannot help you now. Not with Akkarin gone. The Ichani will suspect others are involved if their slaves continue dying.'

Cery regarded her soberly. 'That would put them off sending them, wouldn't it?'

'Perhaps. But my orders are to draw no attention to my people.'

'So. It's up to us, now. How do you suggest we kill them?'

'I do not think you will have to. They have what they sent the slaves for.'

'So it was Akkarin they were after?' Gol asked.

'Yes and no,' she replied. 'They will kill him, if they can. But now that they know the Guild's weakness, it will be their target.'

Gol stared at her. 'They'll attack the Guild?'

'Yes.'

'When?'

'Soon. The Guild might have had some time to prepare if they had sent Akkarin away quietly. But they have told all the lands about him.'

Cery sighed and rubbed his temples. 'The procession.'

'No,' she replied. 'Though it was foolish of them to announce Akkarin's crime and punishment publicly, it would have taken days or even a week or two for the Ichani to hear about it.' She shook her head. 'The Guild magicians have been discussing Akkarin mind to mind for days. The Ichani will have heard everything.'

'Has the Guild got a chance?' Gol asked.

She looked sad. 'No.'

Gol's eyes widened. 'The *Guild* can't stop them?'

'Not without higher magic.'

Cery rose and began to pace the room. 'How many Ichani are there?'

'Twenty-eight, but the ones you need to be concerned with form a band of up to ten.'

'Hai! Only *ten*?'

'Each of them is many, many times stronger than a Guild magician. Together, they can defeat the Guild easily.'

'Oh.' Cery crossed the room a few more times. 'You said you'd have killed that Ichani woman on your own. So you've got to be stronger than a Guild magician.'

She smiled. 'Much stronger.'

Cery noticed that Gol had turned a little pale. 'What about the rest of your people?'

'Many are equal to, or stronger, than me.'

He chewed on his lip thoughtfully. 'What would your people want in return for helping Kyralia?'

She smiled. 'Your people would be no happier to accept my people's help than Ichani rule. We, too, use what the Guild calls black magic.'

Cery made a dismissive gesture. 'If the Ichani come, they might change their minds about that.'

'They might. But my people will not reveal themselves.'

'You said they didn't want the Ichani in Kyralia.'

'Yes, that is true. But they will not intervene if it puts themselves at risk. We are just another faction in Sachaka, and one many powerful people fear and would destroy. We can only do so much.'

'Will *you* help us?' Gol asked.

She sighed heavily. 'I wish I could. But my orders are to keep out of this conflict. My orders . . .' she looked at Cery, 'are to go home.'

Cery nodded slowly. So she was leaving. He had guessed she would that night on the rooftop. It was not going to be easy saying goodbye, but he, too, could not afford to let his heart rule his head.

'When?'

She looked down. 'Straightaway. It is a long journey. The Ichani will be watching the Kyralian border. I must go through Elyne. But . . .' She smiled slyly. 'I do not see why leaving tonight or tomorrow morning will make much difference.'

Gol covered his mouth with a hand and coughed.

'I don't know,' Cery replied. 'It might make plenty of difference. For the sake of Kyralia, I ought to give turning your mind around a good go. With a little roasted rasook and a bottle of Anuren dark . . .'

Her eyebrows rose. 'Anuren dark? You Thieves do better than I thought.'

'Actually, I've got a deal going with a few wine smugglers.'

She grinned. 'Of course you have.'

At a knock on the main door to his rooms, Rothen sighed and extended his will. He didn't bother turning to see who it was.

'Back again, Dannyl? You've spent more time in my rooms than your own since you arrived. Haven't you got any rebels or secret missions to keep you busy?'

Dannyl chuckled. 'Not for another week. In the meantime, I thought I'd catch up with my old friend before they send me away again.' He stepped into the half-circle of chairs in the guestroom and sat down opposite Rothen. 'I guessed you wouldn't be visiting the Night Room tonight.'

Rothen looked up to see understanding in Dannyl's eyes. 'No.'

Dannyl sighed. 'I really ought to go. Face the gossips, and all that. But . . .'

It isn't easy, Rothen finished. Dannyl had told him what Akkarin's plan to catch the rebels had involved. Dem Marane's claims about his captor had reached every corner of the Guild now. Though most magicians appeared willing to dismiss them, Rothen knew there were always some who believed any scandal that came their way.

Rothen had endured the same speculative and disapproving looks two years before when the Guild had questioned the appropriateness of Sonea staying in his rooms. Facing the gossips had been hard, but important – and having Yaldin and Ezrille to support him had also helped.

As I ought to support Dannyl now.

Rothen drew in a deep breath, then stood up. 'Well, we had better move along, then, if we're not going to miss the fun.'

Dannyl blinked in surprise. 'I thought you weren't . . . ?'

'Like it or not, I've got two former novices to look after.' Rothen shrugged. 'I'm not going to do either of you any favours moping away in my rooms.'

Dannyl rose. 'Are you sure?'

'Yes.'

'Thank you.'

Rothen smiled at the gratitude in Dannyl's voice. He had been relieved to find his friend was, in private, still the same man he had always been. Dannyl didn't appear to be conscious of it, but he adopted a different manner in public now. There was a new confidence and authority in his bearing that, when added to his height, gave him a formidable presence.

Amazing what a little responsibility can do, Rothen mused.

Dannyl followed Rothen out into the corridor, then down the stairs to the entrance of the Magicians' Quarters. The sun was setting and the courtyard outside was bathed in red-orange light. They crossed to the Night Room door.

Inside, it was warm and noisy. Rothen noted how many magicians turned to note their arrival and continued to watch them. It did not take long before the first few stepped forward and the questions began.

For over an hour, he and Dannyl were approached by magicians who wanted to know more about the rebels. Rothen read both respect and curiosity in their faces and very little suspicion. Dannyl was hesitant at first, then grew more confident. After one group of Healers left, having finished discussing Vinara's instructions on saving the rogue from poisoning, Dannyl turned to Rothen and smiled ruefully.

'I'm afraid I'm stealing all the attention from you, my friend.'

Rothen shrugged. 'What attention? I'm hardly fending off questions about Sonea.'

'No. Perhaps they've decided to leave you in peace, for once.'

'That's not likely. It's just that—'

'Ambassador Dannyl.'

They turned to find Lord Garrel approaching. Rothen frowned as the Warrior inclined his head politely. He had never liked Garrel, and still felt the magician could have tried harder to discourage his favourite, Regin, from taunting Sonea.

'Lord Garrel,' Dannyl replied.

'Welcome back,' the Warrior said. 'Is it good to be home?'

Dannyl shrugged. 'Yes, it is nice to see my friends again.'

Garrel glanced at Rothen. 'You've done us yet another great service. At great personal sacrifice, too, I hear.' He leaned a little closer. 'I admire your courage. I wouldn't have taken such a risk, myself. But then, I prefer direct action to subterfuge.'

'And you're so much better at it, from what I hear,' Dannyl replied.

Rothen blinked in surprise, then turned away to hide his smile. As the conversation continued, he found himself growing increasingly glad that he had come to the Night Room. Clearly, Elyne court had taught Dannyl more than how to look and sound authoritative.

'Lord Garrel,' a new voice said. A young Alchemist stepped around the Warrior's shoulder. Lord Larkin, the Building and Construction teacher.

'Yes?' Garrel replied.

'I thought you might like to know: Lord Harsin expressed a desire to talk to you about your novice's progress in Ailments.'

The Warrior frowned. 'I had better seek him out, then. Good night, Lord Rothen, Ambassador Dannyl.'

As Garrel walked away, Larkin grimaced. 'I thought you might want rescuing,' the young magician said. 'Not that you'd need it, Ambassador. It's just that several of us have noticed that those who Garrel engages in conversation tend to crave an interruption sooner or later. Generally sooner.'

'Thank you, Lord Larkin,' Dannyl said. He glanced at Rothen and smiled crookedly. 'I thought we were the only ones who'd noticed.'

'Oh, being that skilled at making people uncomfortable takes practise. I expected Garrel figured you'd be a good target, after this latest bit of fuss about nothing.'

Dannyl's eyebrows rose in surprise. 'Do you think so?'

'Well, it's hardly as bad as . . . as using black magic,' the young magician said. He looked at Rothen, then flushed. 'Not that I believe what the rebel says, of course, but . . .' He glanced around the room, then took a step back. 'Excuse me, Ambassador, Lord Rothen. Lord Sarrin just indicated that he wishes to speak to me.'

Larkin nodded to them both, then hurried away. Dannyl glanced around the room.

'How interesting. Sarrin's not even here.'

'Yes,' Rothen replied. 'It is interesting. Particularly the

bit about you needing rescuing. You clearly don't, Dannyl. In fact, I don't believe you even needed me to come along at all.' He gave an exaggerated sigh. 'It really is quite deflating.'

Dannyl grinned and patted Rothen on the shoulder. 'It must be such a disappointment, always seeing your novices going places.'

Rothen shrugged, then his smile turned into a grimace. 'Ah, if only that place wasn't Sachaka.'

CHAPTER 20

THE GUILD'S PUNISHMENT

As Dannyl reached the door to Administrator Lorlen's office, he paused to take a deep breath and straighten his shoulders. The request to meet with the Higher Magicians had come sooner than he expected, and he had a nagging feeling he ought to be more prepared. He looked down at the folder containing his report, then shrugged. Even if he did think of something, it was too late to make changes now.

He knocked on the door. It swung open and Dannyl stepped inside. He nodded to the magicians seated in the chairs. Lady Vinara and Lord Sarrin were present, as was Expatriate Administrator Kito. As usual, Lorlen was sitting behind his desk. The Administrator gestured to an empty chair.

'Please be seated, Ambassador Dannyl,' Lorlen said. He paused as Dannyl took the offered seat. 'I would have liked to have waited until Lord Balkan's return before asking you to relate the full details of your encounter with the rebels, but the need to investigate Akkarin's claims as soon as possible has convinced us it would be best not to delay, and your story may shed a little light on his activities. So, tell us what Akkarin's orders were.'

'I received a letter from him a little over six weeks ago.' Dannyl opened the folder and took out the letter. He sent it floating to Lorlen's desk.

The Administrator picked it up and read it aloud.

"'*I have been watching for some years the efforts of a small group of Elyne courtiers to learn magic without the Guild's aid or knowledge. Only recently have they had some success. Now that at least one of them has managed to develop his powers, the Guild is entitled and obliged to deal with them. I have included information on this group with this letter. You will find your relationship with the scholar, Tayend of Tremmelin, helpful in persuading them that you can be trusted. It is possible the rebels will try to use this personal information against you once you have arrested them. I will ensure that it is understood that I asked you to give them this information in order to achieve your goal.*'"

As Dannyl expected, the other magicians exchanged little puzzled looks.

'I assume he meant your working relationship with this scholar?' Sarrin asked.

Dannyl spread his hands. 'Yes and no. I guessed he was also referring to rumours about our personal one. Tayend is, as the Elynes say, a lad.' Sarrin's eyebrows rose, but neither he nor the Higher Magicians looked mystified by the term, so Dannyl continued. 'The Elynes have been speculating whether there is more to our association than scholarly interest since he began assisting me with my research.'

'And you allowed the rebels to believe this was true, so they felt they could blackmail you should you prove troublesome?' Sarrin asked.

'Yes.'

'Akkarin was not very specific. He could have meant for you to encourage them to think you and your assistant would face expulsion and execution if you were discovered to be teaching magic.'

Dannyl nodded. 'I considered that, of course, and

324

realised that it would not have been enough to persuade the rebels to trust me.' To Dannyl's relief, Kito nodded.

'So Akkarin was going to tell the Guild that he had asked you to pretend to be involved with your assistant,' Vinara said, 'but when you arrived he had been arrested. Administrator Lorlen suggested you claim the deception was your idea.'

'That is right.'

The Healer's eyebrows rose. 'Has this worked?'

Dannyl shrugged. 'In general, I believe. What are your impressions?'

She nodded. 'Most have accepted your story.'

'And the rest?'

'Are known to be rumour-mongers.'

Dannyl nodded. Thinking back to Lord Garrel's questions in the Night Room, he wondered if Vinara would include the Warrior among her 'rumour-mongers'.

Lorlen leaned forward to rest his elbows on the desk. 'So, tell us how you came to meet the rebels.'

Dannyl continued his story, relating how he had arranged a meeting with the Dem Marane, and a visit to the Dem's home. He described teaching Farand, and how the book Tayend had borrowed had convinced him to arrest the rebels.

'I was considering whether to wait and see if they continued to consult me after Farand had learned Control,' Dannyl told them. 'I thought I might learn the names of other rebels. When I saw what was in the book, though, I knew it was too great a risk. Even if the Dem allowed me to keep it, the rebels might have others. If they did disappear after Farand had learned Control, they might have taught themselves black magic and we would have worse than rogue magicians on our hands.' Dannyl paused and grimaced. 'I never would have guessed we already had.'

Sarrin shifted in his seat and frowned. 'Do you think Akkarin knew of this book?'

'I don't know,' Dannyl replied. 'I don't know how he knew of the rebels in the first place.'

'Perhaps he had detected Farand's powers in the same way that he detected Sonea's before she learned Control,' Vinara suggested.

'From as far away as Elyne?' Sarrin asked.

Vinara's shoulders lifted. 'He has many unique abilities, no doubt gained through the use of black magic. Why not one more?'

Sarrin frowned. 'You speak of undertaking research with this scholar, Ambassador. What research is that?'

'Research into ancient magic,' Dannyl replied. He looked around the room. As his eyes met Lorlen's, the magician smiled faintly.

'I have told them you began it under my instruction,' Lorlen said.

Dannyl nodded. 'Yes, though I do not know why.'

'I wanted to retrieve some of the knowledge that Akkarin lost,' Lorlen said. 'But Akkarin learned of the research, and made it clear he didn't approve. I told Lord Dannyl that his help was no longer needed.'

'And you didn't obey that order?' Sarrin asked Dannyl.

'It wasn't an order,' Lorlen said. 'I said only that the research was no longer needed. I believe Dannyl continued out of his own interest.'

'I did,' Dannyl confirmed. 'Later, Akkarin heard that I had continued and called me back to the Guild. He seemed pleased by my progress and encouraged me to continue.

Unfortunately, I made little further progress. The only sources I hadn't explored were in Sachaka, and he had made it clear I must not go there.'

Sarrin leaned back in his chair. 'Interesting. He discouraged the research, then encouraged it. Perhaps you had already found something he didn't want you to find, but you hadn't understood its significance. Then he would have felt safe allowing you to continue.'

'I have considered that, too,' Dannyl agreed. 'It wasn't until I saw the rebel's book that I realised the ancient magic I'd been researching was actually black magic. I don't think he intended me to know that.'

Sarrin shook his head. 'No. If that is so, he would not have wanted you to read that book. So he probably didn't know that Dem Marane possessed it, and the arrest of the rebels was not an exercise designed to bring it into his possession.' He frowned. 'And it may contain information that he does not know. How very interesting.'

Dannyl looked from face to face while the magicians considered this.

'May I ask a question?'

Lorlen smiled. 'Of course, Ambassador.'

'Have you discovered anything that proves Akkarin's story is true?'

The Administrator sobered. 'Not yet.' He hesitated. 'Despite Akkarin's warning, we can see no other way to learn the truth but to send spies into Sachaka.'

Dannyl nodded. 'I suppose their identity will be a secret, even to members of the Guild.'

'Yes,' Lorlen replied. 'But some, like yourself, will be permitted to know, because they will probably guess the real reason for the absence of certain magicians.'

Dannyl straightened. 'Really?'

'One of the spies will be your mentor, Lord Rothen.'

The climb into the mountains seemed endless.

The morning sun had revealed steep, heavily forested slopes on either side. Though the road was well maintained, and showed signs of recent repair, all else appeared to be wilderness. If the escort had passed any houses during the night, they had been well hidden in the darkness.

The road followed the curve of the mountainous slopes and climbed through steep ravines. Sonea occasionally caught a glimpse of rocky outcrops above. The air grew steadily colder, until she was forced to keep a barrier of warmth about herself all the time to stop from shivering.

She longed for the end of the journey, yet dreaded it. The constant uphill climb altered her position in the saddle subtly, and a whole new range of muscles had begun to protest. In addition, the coarse material of her trousers had chafed her skin raw and she had to Heal herself every few hours to ease the pain.

'Halt!'

At Balkan's order, Sonea sighed with relief. They hadn't stopped since the morning, and then only briefly. She felt her horse draw in a deep breath as it came to a halt, then gust it out again.

Several of the escort dismounted to tend to the horses. Akkarin stared into the distance. Following his gaze, she saw that the land below the mountain was visible through a gap in the trees. Hills rolled outward, gradually smoothing out into a flat plain in the far distance. Narrow rivers and streams glittered in the creases between them. Everything glowed with the warm light of the late afternoon sun. The horizon was a misty edge. Somewhere over it lay Imardin. Her home.

At every step in the journey, she moved further away from everything she had ever known: her family, her old friends, Cery, Rothen, Dorrien. The names of people she had grown to like in the last few years ran through her mind: Tania, Dannyl, Tya, and Yikmo – and even some of the novices. She might never see any of them again. She hadn't even had a chance to say goodbye to most of them. Her throat tightened, and she felt her eyes begin to sting.

Closing her eyes, she forced herself to breathe slowly and normally. *This is not the time or place to start crying. Not now, with Balkan and the other magicians watching – and especially not Akkarin*. She swallowed hard and forced herself to turn away from the view.

As she opened her eyes again, she saw Akkarin's expression shift. For a moment, before the familiar mask settled over his face, she glimpsed a look of intense frustration and bitterness. She looked down, disturbed by what she had seen.

Osen began handing out bread, cold cooked vegetables and chunks of salted meat. Akkarin accepted his share silently, and returned to his brooding. Sonea chewed slowly, determined to force thoughts of the Guild out of her head, and concentrate instead on the days ahead. Where would they find food in Sachaka? The area beyond the pass was wasteland. Perhaps they could buy food. Would Balkan give them money?

Osen returned to her side and offered a mug full of watered wine. She drank it quickly and handed back the cup. He paused, as if he wanted to say something, and she quickly straightened and looked away. She heard a sigh, then footsteps retreating as he walked back to his horse.

'Onward,' Balkan called.

Breaks in the trees became more common as they continued on. In the spaces, great sheets of bare rock were exposed. A chill wind whipped the horses' tails. The sun steadily descended toward the horizon, then the road straightened and passed between two tall, smooth walls of rock. Ahead, stained orange by the setting sun, was an enormous, squat column of stone punctured by rows of tiny square holes.

The Fort.

Sonea stared up at the building as they drew closer. In history lessons, she had learned that the Fort had been built soon after the Sachakan War. It was taller than she had imagined, probably two or three times taller than the main University building. The huge cylinder of rock filled the narrow gap between the two high rock walls. Nothing could pass this way without going through the building.

There was no sign of cracks or mortar, yet the Fort had been made long before Lord Coren had discovered how to meld rock. She shook her head in wonder. Those long-dead builders must have carved the Fort out of the mountain itself.

A pair of large metal doors at the base of the building began to swing open as they approached. Two figures stepped out. One wore the uniform of a captain of the guard, the other wore red Warrior robes. Sonea blinked in surprise, then stared at the magician in disbelief.

'Lord Balkan,' Fergun said as the captain bowed respectfully, 'this is Captain Larwen.'

Of course, she thought. *Fergun was sent away to a distant Fort as punishment for blackmailing me. I hadn't realised it would be this Fort.*

As the Captain addressed Lord Balkan, Sonea looked down at her hands and cursed her luck. No doubt Fergun had been looking forward to this moment. He had risked much in his efforts to convince the Guild that they should not admit anyone from outside the Houses. *Now his claims that slum dwellers are not to be trusted have been proven true*, she thought.

But that was wrong. She had only learned and used black magic to save the Guild and Kyralia.

He, too, had believed he was saving the Guild. She felt an uncomfortable sympathy for him. Was there really any difference between her and her former enemy?

Yes, she thought. *I'm trying to save* all *of Kyralia. He only wanted to prevent lower-class Kyralians learning magic.*

In the corner of her eye, she saw that he was staring at her.

Ignore him, she told herself. *He's not worth it.*

But why should she? He was no better than her. Steeling herself, she lifted her head and returned his stare. His lips curled with contempt and his eyes gleamed with satisfaction.

You think you're so superior, she thought at him, *but consider this. I am stronger than you. Even without the forbidden magic I have learned, I could beat you in the Arena any day, Warrior.*

His eyes narrowed, and his jaw stiffened with hatred. She returned his stare coldly. *I have killed a magician who, like you, preyed on the helpless. I would kill again, if it were the only way to protect Kyralia. You do not frighten me, magician. You are nothing, a petty fool, a . . .*

Fergun suddenly turned to regard the Captain, as if the man had said something significant. She waited for him to meet her gaze again, but he didn't. The formalities ended, and the Captain stepped aside and blew on a whistle. The escort began to move into the Fort.

As they did, the wide corridor beyond filled with the echoing clatter of hooves. The escort continued for several paces, then slowed as it approached a wall of stone blocking half the passage. Passing this in single file, they then stopped before a pair of closed metal doors a hundred paces further along the corridor. These swung open slowly. They passed through and crossed a wooden section of floor that echoed hollowly under the horses' hooves, then filed past another stone wall.

Sonea felt cool air on her face. She looked up and saw a pair of open metal doors leading to another walled ravine. Night had already descended on the other side of the Fort. Steep walls were illuminated by two rows of lamps. Beyond them, the road continued into darkness.

As the escort moved into the open, Sonea found that her heart was beating fast. If they had passed through the Fort, then her horse was now walking on Sachakan soil. She looked down.

Rock is a better description, she amended.

She turned in her saddle and looked back up at the Fort. Lights beyond some of the windows made silhouettes of the watching occupants.

The sound of hoofbeats faded. Her horse stopped.

'Dismount.'

As Akkarin swung out of the saddle, Sonea realised that Balkan's order had been solely for her and Akkarin. She slid to the ground, wincing at the stiffness in her legs. Lord Osen leaned down to take the reins and led the horses away.

With the horses and Osen gone, only she and Akkarin remained standing within the ring of Warriors. A globe of light flared above Balkan's head, flooding the area with brightness.

'Remember the faces of these two magicians,' Balkan called. 'They are Akkarin, former High Lord of the Magicians' Guild, and Sonea, former novice of the High Lord. They have been cast out of the Guild and exiled from the Allied Lands for the crime of practising black magic.'

A chill entered Sonea's blood. At least this was the last time she would hear those ritual words. She glanced at the darkened road beyond the lamplight.

'Wait!'

Her heart skipped. Osen stepped forward.

'Yes, Lord Osen?'

'I would speak to Sonea once more before she leaves.'

Balkan nodded slowly. 'Very well.'

Sonea sighed as Osen climbed down from his horse. He approached her slowly, his expression tense.

'Sonea, this is your last chance.' He spoke quietly, perhaps so the escort would not hear. 'Come back with me.'

She shook her head. 'No.'

He turned to regard Akkarin. 'Would you have her turn down this opportunity?'

Akkarin's eyebrows rose. 'No, but she seems determined to discard it. I doubt I could change her mind.'

Osen frowned and turned to regard Sonea again. He opened his mouth, then thought better of it and merely shook his head. He looked at Akkarin again.

'You had better look after her,' he muttered.

Akkarin stared impassively at the magician. Osen scowled and turned on his heel. He strode back to his horse and stepped up into the saddle.

At a signal from Balkan, the escorts blocking the road into Sachaka fell back.

'Be gone from the Allied Lands,' Balkan said. His voice was neither angry, nor regretful.

'Come, Sonea,' Akkarin said quietly. 'We have a way to go yet.'

She looked at him. His expression was distant and hard to read. As he turned away and started walking, she followed a few steps behind.

A voice murmured behind them. She listened carefully. It was Lord Osen.

'. . . lands again. I cast you out, Sonea. Do not enter my lands again.'

She shivered, then set her gaze upon the darkening road before her.

As the last of the sun's rays left the garden, Lorlen turned from the window of his office and began to pace. The route took him around the room, from chair to chair, then back to his desk. He stopped, looked down at the mass of paper, and sighed.

Why, of all places, did they have to send Akkarin to Sachaka?

He knew why. He knew, with a cold certainty, that the King hoped Akkarin would perish in Sachaka. Akkarin had broken one of the most serious Guild laws. No matter how much the King had liked the High Lord, he knew there was nothing more dangerous than a magician who would not obey laws, and was too powerful to control. If the Guild could not execute Akkarin, then they must send him to the only magicians who could: the Ichani.

Of course, the Ichani might *not* exist. If they didn't, the

Guild was about to free a magician who had learned black magic willingly. He might come back, stronger than ever.

That couldn't be helped, however.

If the Ichani did exist, it seemed foolish to send to his death the only magician who could tell them about their enemy. Akkarin wasn't the only one, though. There was Sonea.

That was where the King had misjudged the situation badly. He had assumed the ex-slum girl, who'd been guided and manipulated by more than one magician, would be easily swayed. Lorlen smiled wryly as he remembered her angry refusal.

'*If you send High Lord Akkarin into exile, you must send me too. Then, when you come to your senses, he might still be alive and able to help you.*'

The King had been angry at her defiance. *What do you expect?* Lorlen had wanted to say. *Loyalty? From one who once lived among those you drive out of the city during the Purge each year?* Eventually the King had concluded that, if she would not accept the judgment of the Guild and her ruler, then perhaps exile was for the best.

Lorlen sighed and began pacing again. In truth, the Guild didn't need Sonea to tell them about the Ichani so long as he had Akkarin's ring . . . and Akkarin remained alive. But if Lorlen began relaying information from Akkarin to the rest of the Guild, he would eventually have to admit how he was receiving it. The ring was a tool of black magic. How would the Guild react to the news that their Administrator owned and continued to use such a thing?

I should throw it away, he thought. But he knew he wouldn't. He took out the ring and considered it, then slipped it on a finger.

—Akkarin? Are you there?

Nothing.

Lorlen had tried to contact Akkarin through the ring several times. Occasionally he thought he had detected a faint feeling of anger or fear, but had decided this was only his imagination. The silence tortured him. If it wasn't for Osen's mental reports on the journey, Lorlen might have worried that Akkarin was dead.

Lorlen finished his circuit of the room, then stepped behind his desk and collapsed into his chair. He removed the ring and put it back in his pocket. A moment later, there was a sharp knock on the door.

'Come in.'

'A message from the King, my lord.'

A servant entered, bowed, and placed a wooden cylinder on Lorlen's desk. The King's incal was imprinted on the stopper and the wax was dusted with gold powder.

'Thank you. You may go.'

The servant bowed again, then retreated from the room. Lorlen broke the seal and pulled out a rolled sheet of paper.

So the King wants to talk about Sachaka, Lorlen mused as he read the formal script. He let the letter curl back into a roll, returned it to the cylinder and stowed it inside a box he kept for royal messages.

A meeting with the King was unexpectedly appealing. What he had longed for most was just to be able to *do* something. For too long he had been restrained and helpless to act. He stood up, then froze as he heard his name echo at the edge of his senses.

—Lorlen!

Osen. Lorlen sensed the minds of other magicians, attracted by the call, fade as they turned their attention away.

—Yes, Osen?

—It is done. Sonea and Akkarin are in Sachaka.

Lorlen felt his heart sink.

—Could you ask Fergun and the Captain if anyone in the Fort or surrounding locality has noticed anything unusual going on in Sachaka?

—I will ask and tell you his reply tomorrow. He has requested that some magicians remain here in case Akkarin and Sonea try to return.

—Did you explain that it would make no difference?

—No, I didn't want to make them more nervous than they already are.

Lorlen considered the Captain's request.

—I'll leave that decision to Balkan.

—I'll tell him. There was a pause. *I must go.* The image of a hall with a large open fire and magicians taking seats at a long dining table reached Lorlen's mind. He smiled.

—Enjoy your meal, Osen. Thank you for informing me.

—Thank you for informing me, another voice replied. Lorlen blinked in surprise.

—Who was that? Osen asked.

—I don't know, Lorlen replied. He thought back over their conversation and shivered. If someone was waiting over the border, ready to ambush visitors, then they now knew Akkarin and Sonea were on their way.

Then he considered what might have been discussed by magicians in the last few days and his heart sank even further. *We've been fools*, Lorlen thought. *Not one of us has really considered what it might mean if Akkarin's story is true.*

—Balkan, he called.

—Yes?

—Please tell your men that all mental communication must cease from this moment. I will inform the rest of the Guild.

As Osen and Balkan's presence withdrew, Lorlen drew Akkarin's ring out of his pocket. His hands shook as he slipped it over his finger.

—Akkarin?

But silence was his only reply.

CHAPTER 21

A DANGEROUS ROAD

Ninth day of the fifth month.
We were forced to stop this morning when we encountered a landslip that had blocked the road. The servants have spent the day digging, but I fear we will not move on until tomorrow. I have climbed to the top of a hill. The mountains are now a dark line across the horizon. Looking ahead, I see dusty hills continuing to the north. These wastelands seem endless. Now I understand why Kyralian merchants do not often trade with Sachaka. It is an impossible journey, and Riko tells me it is easier for the Sachakans to trade with lands in the north-east. And, of course, they distrust the Guild . . .

A knock at the door interrupted Rothen. He sighed, lowered the book and willed the door open. Dannyl stepped into the room, his brow creased with a frown.

'Dannyl,' Rothen said, 'would you like some sumi?'

Dannyl closed the door, walked to Rothen's chair, and stared down at him. 'You *volunteered* to go to Sachaka?'

'Ah.' Rothen closed the book and set it down on the table. 'So they told you.'

'Yes.' Dannyl seemed to struggle for words. 'I want to ask why, but I don't have to. You're going to look for Sonea, aren't you?'

Rothen shrugged. 'In a way.' He gestured to a seat. 'Sit

down. Even *I* feel uncomfortable when you're towering over me like that.'

Dannyl sat down and stared across the table at Rothen. 'I'm surprised the Higher Magicians agreed. They must have realised finding Sonea might become more important to you than discovering if the Ichani exist.'

Rothen smiled. 'Yes, they did consider that. I told them that if there was a choice between saving Sonea and completing the mission, I would choose to save Sonea. They accepted that condition because I have a better chance of persuading her to return – and because I am not the only spy.'

'Why didn't you tell me about this?'

'I only volunteered this morning.'

'But you must have been thinking about it before then.'

'Only since last night. After I watched you dealing with Garrel, I came to the conclusion that you don't really need my help.' Rothen smiled. 'My support, perhaps, but not my help. Sonea, however, does need my help. I've been unable to do anything for her for so long. Now I finally can.'

Dannyl nodded, but he did not look happy. 'What if Akkarin's story *is* true? What if you walk into a land ruled by black magicians? He said any Guild magician entering Sachaka would be killed.'

Rothen sobered. It *was* going to be a dangerous mission. He was not a little frightened by the possibility he would encounter the magicians Akkarin had described.

If the Ichani were not real, however, then Akkarin must have had a reason to invent them. Perhaps he'd done so simply to ensure the Guild allowed him to live. Perhaps it had been part of some greater deception. If that were so, he would be anxious to hide the truth. He might be the black magician who killed any Guild magician who entered Sachaka.

But surely he expected the Guild to investigate his claims. By telling them this story, he had ensured they *would* send spies into Sachaka. Rothen frowned. What if Akkarin had spun the tale so he could hunt down the magicians who entered Sachaka, kill them one by one for their strength?

'Rothen?'

Looking up, Rothen managed a wry smile. 'I know it's going to be dangerous, Dannyl. We're not going to blunder into Sachaka wearing robes and flaunting our magical abilities. We'll do everything we can to remain unnoticed.' He pointed to the book. 'Every record of journeys into Sachaka has been copied for us to study. We'll be questioning merchants and their servants. We're going to be trained by a professional spy, sent by the King, who will teach us to speak and behave like commoners.'

A reluctant smile pulled at Dannyl's mouth. 'Sonea would find that amusing.'

Rothen felt a familiar pang of grief. 'Yes. She would have, once.' He sighed. 'Well then, tell me about your meeting with the Higher Magicians. Did they ask any awkward questions?'

Dannyl blinked at the change of subject. 'A few. I don't think they approve of Tayend, but that was no surprise.'

'No,' Rothen agreed. He considered Dannyl closely. 'But you approve of him.'

'He is a good friend.' Dannyl met Rothen's gaze. There was a hint of defiance in his expression. 'Will I be expected to avoid him now?'

Rothen shrugged. 'You know what the gossips will say if you don't. But you can't let gossips run your life, and

Elyne is Elyne. Everyone knows the social rules are different there.'

Dannyl's eyebrows rose slightly. 'Yes. What may be considered prudent here, would be considered rude there.'

'Now, did you want a cup of sumi?'

Dannyl smiled and nodded. 'Yes, thank you.'

Standing up, Rothen took a step toward the cabinet where the sumi cups and leaves were kept, then froze.

—All magicians, listen to me!

Rothen blinked in surprise at Lorlen's mental voice.

—All mental communication must cease from now on, unless in an emergency. If you are unable to avoid conversing in this way, be mindful of what you reveal. If you hear another magician communicating mentally, please inform him or her of this restriction.

'Well,' Dannyl said after a moment. 'I hate to say it, considering what you've set out to do, but every day I grow more worried.'

'Of what?'

'That what Akkarin told us is the truth.'

As Cery refilled Savara's glass, she stiffened and stared into the distance.

'What is it?' he asked.

She blinked. 'Your Guild has made its first good decision.'

'Oh?'

She smiled. 'Orders to stop speaking mind to mind.'

Cery topped up his glass. 'Will that do them much good?'

'It might have, had they done it a week ago.' She shrugged and picked up her glass. 'But it is good the Ichani won't learn about the Guild's plans now.'

'You won't either.'

She shrugged. 'No. But that does not matter any more.'

Cery considered her. She had found a gloriously well-fitted dress somewhere, made of fine, soft material dyed a rich purple. The colour complemented her skin. Her eyes, when she looked at him, seemed to glow with a rich golden warmth.

But those eyes were downcast now, and her expressive mouth set in a thin line.

'Savara—'

'Do not ask me to stay.' She looked up and fixed him with a direct stare. 'I must go. I must obey my people.'

'I just—'

'I cannot stay.' She rose and began pacing the room. 'I wish I could. Would you leave and go to my land with me, knowing what your country will face? No. You have your own people to protect. I have—'

'Hai! Let me get a word in!'

She stopped and gave him a rueful smile. 'I am sorry. Go on, then.'

'I was just going to tell you that I get what you're saying. I'd rather you stayed, but I won't stop you going.' He smiled wryly. 'I'd wager I'd never have a chance of stopping you anyway.'

Her eyebrows rose. She gestured to the table. 'But you invited me to dinner so you could try to talk me into it.'

He shook his head. 'I just wanted to thank you for your help – and I had to make up for not giving you the chance to do one of these slaves.'

She gave a little pout. 'That would take more than a meal.'

He chuckled. 'Really? Hmmm, we Thieves don't like to break a deal, you know. Would you forgive me if I made up for it another way?'

Her eyes flashed and her smile became sly. 'Oh, I will

think of something.' She walked to him, bent forward and kissed him. 'Hmmm, that gives me an idea or two.'

He smiled, caught her waist and pulled her down so she was sitting across his knees. 'Are you sure I can't talk you into staying?' he asked quietly.

She tilted her head to the side and considered. 'Perhaps just one more night.'

The road into Sachaka was dark and silent. Akkarin had spoken only once, to caution Sonea against making a light or speaking any louder than a murmur. Since then the only sound had been the echo of their footsteps, and the distant howl of the wind somewhere far above.

She looked down at her boots, the only items left of her novice uniform. Would the Ichani recognise them? She considered asking Akkarin if she should discard them, but the idea of walking without any shoes in this cold and rocky terrain was unappealing.

As her eyes had adjusted to the dark, she had begun to make out more of the road ahead. Two vertical walls of rock hung on either side, curving and folding like heavy drapes. Looking up, she saw that they stretched several hundred paces toward the sky, but were growing steadily shorter.

After several turns, the wall on the left ended abruptly. A great dark expanse came into view. They stopped and stared at the land below.

A black, endless darkness spread from the foot of the mountains to a glow at the horizon. As Sonea watched, the glow began to brighten. A sliver of white appeared and began to swell upward. Light flooded across the land as the moon – no longer quite full – slowly escaped the horizon. Sonea sucked in a breath. The mountains now shone like jagged lumps of silver. Ridges clawed down into the plain below like thick tree roots. Where rock ended, a treeless, desolate land began. In places, water from the mountain had eroded the soil, creating branched and twisted fissures that stretched toward the horizon. Further away, she could see strange crescent-shaped hills, like the ripples in a pond frozen in time.

This was the wasteland of Sachaka.

She felt a hand grasp her arm. Surprised, she let Akkarin pull her back into the shadow of the wall.

'We might be seen,' he murmured. 'We must leave the road.'

Looking ahead, she could not see how that was possible. The road curved to the right, cut into the face of the mountain. Steep, almost vertical walls of rock rose on either side.

Akkarin's hand was still around her arm. She realised her heart was beating quickly, and not entirely from fear. His attention was on the cliff above, however.

'We can only hope there aren't watchers up there,' he said.

He let her go, and strode back up the road. Sonea followed. When they had reached a point where the left-hand wall shadowed most of the right, he spun about and took hold of her shoulders.

Guessing what he was going to do, Sonea braced her legs. Sure enough, they began to rise upward, supported by a disk of magic below their feet. She made herself look away, suddenly too conscious of how close Akkarin was.

He stopped their ascent near the top so he could peer over the lip of the wall. Satisfied that the area was safe, he levitated them over the edge and set them down on the stony surface.

Sonea looked around in dismay. The slope was not as

precipitous as the rock wall below, but it was still frighteningly steep. Cracks and jagged outcrops broke the surface, and in other places the ground was so smooth she could not see how they could walk across it without sliding off the mountain. How could they navigate this, when all they had to light the way was the moon?

Akkarin started forward and began picking his way across the slope. Sonea drew in a deep breath, then followed. From then on, climbing over or around outcrops, leaping over crevasses and keeping her balance on the treacherous slope occupied her mind. She lost all sense of the time passing. It was easier to just follow Akkarin, and think only of making it past the next obstruction.

The moon had risen much higher in the sky, and she had Healed the weary muscles in her legs several times, when Akkarin finally stopped at the crest of a ridge. She assumed at first that he had encountered a particularly large crevasse or some other difficulty on the other side, but when she looked up at him, he was staring back over her shoulder.

Abruptly, he grabbed her arms and pulled her into a crouch. Her heart skipped.

'Keep low,' he said urgently. He glanced behind. 'We might be visible against the sky.'

She squatted beside him, her pulse racing. He stared back the way they had come, then pointed back across the rugged slope they had crossed. She searched for something new. Finding nothing, she shook her head.

'Where?'

'He's behind that rock shaped like a mullook,' he murmured. 'Wait a moment . . . there.'

She saw a movement perhaps five or six hundred paces

away — a shifting shadow. It leapt and strode along the mountain slope with practised surety.

'Who is he?'

'One of Kariko's allies, no doubt,' Akkarin muttered.

An Ichani, Sonea thought. *So soon. We can't face one yet. Akkarin's not strong enough.* Her heart was beating too quickly and she felt ill with fear.

'We must move fast now,' Akkarin said. 'He is an hour behind us. We need to increase that distance.'

Remaining in the crouch, he moved along the ridge to where a slab of rock overlapped another, leaving a narrow gap. Slipping through, he straightened and all but ran down the other side of the ridge. Sonea hurried after, somehow keeping her balance despite the stones that shifted and rolled under her boots.

It took all her concentration to keep up with him now. He hurried around boulders, jogged across slopes slippery with rubble, and barely paused before leaping over gaps in their path. Every step tested Sonea's reflexes and balance.

When Akkarin stopped again, in the shadow of an enormous round boulder, she almost stumbled into him. Seeing that he was staring behind again, she turned to search for their pursuer. After a moment, she found him. The man was no further away, she saw with dismay.

At least he is no closer, she told herself.

'Time to put him off our track,' Akkarin murmured. He walked around the boulder. Sonea caught her breath as she saw the deep crevasse at their feet. It was about twenty strides across where they stood, but widened to form a huge ravine with sheer walls that descended into darkness.

'I will go to the left for about a quarter hour and then to the edge. He'll assume we descended into the ravine.

You levitate to the other side, then make your way parallel to the mountains. Keep in the shadows as much as possible, even if it means slowing down.'

She nodded. He turned away and stalked into the night. For a moment she felt a terrible fear of being left alone, but she took a deep breath and pushed it aside.

Standing up, she created a disk of magic and lifted herself into the air. As she moved over the crevasse, she looked down. It was very deep. She fixed her gaze on the other side and moved across. When her feet met solid ground again, she sighed with relief. She had never been afraid of heights, but the drop into the ravine made the tallest buildings in the city look like the steps of the University.

From there, she concentrated on navigating the craggy mountainside. Keeping to the shadows was remarkably easy. The moon was now directly above, but the slope of the mountain had cracked or eroded to form several giant steps. The nearest seemed to be the obvious one to follow, so she descended to the one below.

Keeping to the shadows meant it was harder to see, however. She nearly stumbled into a hole or crevasse more than once. After an endless stretch of leaping and jogging, she glanced up to see that the moon had nearly reached the peaks above.

She felt a stirring of fear again as she realised how much time had passed since Akkarin had left her. She considered what he had said he would do. A quarter hour down the left side of the ravine plus another quarter back to the boulder meant he was half an hour behind her. What if Akkarin had miscalculated? What if the pursuer had been only half an hour behind them, not an hour? Akkarin might have returned to the crevasse at the same time as the Ichani.

She found she had slowed down, and pushed herself onward again. Akkarin wasn't dead. If he'd been captured, he would have called to her, to warn her to keep running.

But what if he'd tricked her into leaving him?

Don't be ridiculous, she told herself. *He wouldn't abandon you to the Ichani.*

Unless . . . unless he had led the pursuer away, knowing that he would be caught and killed, to save her.

She stopped and looked behind. The terrain curved around the mountain, and she could not see far behind her. Sighing, she forced herself to continue on. *Don't speculate*, she thought. *Concentrate.*

The words repeated themselves in her mind and became a chant. After a while she found herself silently mouthing them. The rhythm carried her on, from one step to the next. Then she charged around an outcrop and found herself stepping out into an abyss.

Throwing her arms out, she managed to grab the outcrop, swing herself against it, and stop herself falling.

Her heart pounded as she pulled herself back from the brink. An enormous ravine blocked her path. Panting with fright and exertion, she stared at the opposite wall and tried to decide what she should do now. She could levitate across, but while she did she would be in plain sight.

The sound of hurried footsteps close behind her was all the warning she had. She started to turn, but something slammed into her back and a hand clamped over her mouth to smother her scream. She fell forward, over the edge of the precipice.

Then magic surrounded her, and she felt her descent slow. At the same time she recognised a familiar scent.

Akkarin.

His arms held her tightly. They turned in the air and began to rise. The creased and cracked wall of the ravine rushed past, then a larger slash of blackness appeared. They moved into it.

Her feet met an uneven floor and, as Akkarin released her, she staggered and threw out her arms. A hand met a wall, and she managed to regain her balance. She felt light-headed and giddy, and fought a strange urge to laugh.

'*Give me your power.*'

Akkarin was a shadow in the darkness, and his voice held both urgency and command. She struggled to regain some control of her breathing.

'I—'

'Now!' he said urgently. 'The Ichani can sense it. Quickly.'

She held her hands out. His fingers brushed against hers then wrapped around her hands. Closing her eyes, she sent out a steady stream of energy. As the significance of what Akkarin had said sank in, she quickened the flow until power was rushing from her.

'Stop, Sonea.'

She opened her eyes and a wave of exhaustion swept over her.

'You gave too much,' he said. 'You've tired yourself.'

She yawned. 'It's no use to me.'

'No? How are you going to continue on now?' He sighed. 'I could Heal you, I suppose, but . . . maybe we should stay here. If he had seen where we went, he would have followed us by now. And we haven't slept for days.'

She shivered and looked up. 'He was *that* close to me.'

'Yes. I took a different path to yours and his, so I could watch him. I noticed how he followed you unerringly, but did not pick up my trail even when I crossed yours several times. Then I got close enough to watch him and I realised from his behaviour that he could sense you. So I looked closer, and found I could, too. You are unused to holding extra power, and were allowing a sense of it to slip past your control.'

'Oh.'

'Fortunately, I was able to catch up with you just as you reached this ravine. A moment more, and he would have found you.'

'Oh.'

'You shall sleep here, while I keep watch.'

She sighed with relief. She had been bone-weary before she had given him all her strength. A tiny globe light appeared, revealing that the crack extended a little way into the rock wall. The base was filled with a jumble of large stones. Though Sonea wanted desperately to lie down and sleep, she regarded the floor with dismay.

Finding a relatively even area, she shifted a few of the rocks, filled in a few holes between them with smaller stones, then lay down. It was not very comfortable. She smiled wryly, remembering how she had once slept on the floor of Rothen's spare room so long ago, because she had been unused to soft beds.

Akkarin sat down near the entrance. As his globe light blinked out again, she wondered how she would ever sleep when she knew an Ichani was searching for her above.

But exhaustion blunted the rock's sharp edges and her fear, and her thoughts soon drifted away from all the concerns of the moment.

CHAPTER 22

AN EXCHANGE OF VIEWS

From the outside, only the towers of the Palace were visible over the high round wall that surrounded it. As the Guild carriage turned onto the circular road ringing the wall, Lorlen looked up and felt a twinge of anxiety. It had been many years since he had entered the Palace. Matters between the King and the Guild were always dealt with by the High Lord. Though two magicians – the King's Advisors – attended the monarch on a daily basis, their role was to protect and counsel, not to receive or attend to orders regarding the Guild. Now, with Akkarin gone, the responsibilities of the High Lord fell to the Administrator.

As if I don't already have enough to do, Lorlen thought. The King had asked for all Higher Magicians to attend him today, however. Lorlen looked at the other occupants of the carriage.

While Lady Vinara looked calm, Lord Sarrin wore a frown of worry. Expatriate Administrator Kito was tapping the fingers of one hand against the other. Lorlen was unsure if this indicated nervousness or impatience. Not for the first time, he wished that Kito's duties didn't require him to be absent from the Guild so often. If he had known Kito better, he might have been able to read the man's mood from this little mannerism.

The carriage slowed, then turned toward the Palace entrance. The two enormous blackened iron gates swung inward, each guided by a pair of guards. Several more guards, standing on either side of the entrance, bowed as Lorlen's carriage entered a large enclosed courtyard.

Statues of previous kings stood proudly around the courtyard. The carriages drew to a halt in front of the grand Palace doors. A guard stepped forward and bowed as Lorlen climbed out of the carriage.

Lorlen glanced at the second Guild carriage pulling up behind the first, then stepped forward to meet the greeter at the Palace doors. The task of the greeters was to welcome every visitor to the Palace with appropriate formality and later compose a report. Lorlen had been fascinated to learn, as a child, that the greeters had developed their own shortened form of writing to speed the process.

The man bowed gracefully.

'Administrator Lorlen. An honour to meet you.' His alert eyes moved from magician to magician as he greeted each. 'Welcome to the Palace.'

'Thank you,' Lorlen replied. 'We have been summoned by the King.'

'So I have been informed.' The man was holding a small board in one hand. He drew a square of paper out of a slot in the side and made several quick marks on it with an ink stick. A boy standing nearby dashed forward, bowed, and took the slip of paper.

'Your guide,' the greeter said. 'He will take you to King Merin now.'

The boy dashed to one of the huge Palace doors and hauled it open, then stepped aside. Lorlen led the other magicians into the Palace entrance hall.

The hall was based on the one in the University and was filled with fragile-looking spiral staircases. There were many more of them, however, and they were decorated with gold and illuminated by several hanging lamps. An elaborate clockwork timepiece clicked and whirred in the centre of the room. They followed their young guide up a staircase to the second level.

A complicated journey followed. Their guide led them through large doorways and along wide corridors and halls. After a long climb up a narrow staircase, they arrived at an ordinary-sized door, blocked by two guards. The boy asked them to wait, then slipped past the guards. After a short pause, he reappeared and announced that the King would see them.

As Lorlen stepped into the room beyond, his attention was immediately drawn to the tall, narrow windows. They gave a view of the entire city and beyond. He realised they were in one of the Palace towers. As he looked to the north, he almost expected to be able to see a dark line of mountains, but of course, the border was far beyond the horizon.

The King was sitting in a large, comfortable chair on the far side of the room. The King's Advisors stood on either side, their expressions watchful and serious. Lord Mirken was the older of the pair. Lord Rolden was closer to the King's age, and, Lorlen knew, was considered as much a friend as protector.

'Your Majesty,' Lorlen said. He dropped to one knee, and heard the rustle of robes behind him as the other Higher Magicians followed suit.

'Administrator Lorlen,' the King replied, 'and Higher Magicians of the Guild. Be at ease.'

Lorlen and the others rose.

'I wish to discuss the claims of the former High Lord with you and your colleagues,' the King continued. His gaze shifted from one magician to another, then he frowned. 'Where is Lord Balkan?'

'The Head of Warriors is at the Northern Fort, Your Majesty,' Lorlen explained, 'with the magicians who escorted Akkarin to the border.'

'When will he return?'

'He intends to remain in case Akkarin attempts to return that way, or his story proves to be true and these Ichani he spoke of try to enter Kyralia.'

The King's frown deepened. 'I need him here, where I can consult with him.' He hesitated. 'My Advisors tell me you have given orders that all mental communication cease. Why is that?'

'Last night I heard the mental voice of a magician unknown to me.' Lorlen felt a chill as he remembered. 'He appeared to have been listening in to a conversation I was having with my assistant.'

The King's eyes narrowed. 'What did this stranger say?'

'I thanked Lord Osen for informing me that Akkarin and Sonea had entered Sachaka. The stranger repeated the thanks.'

'That is all this stranger said?'

'Yes.'

'You don't know if this stranger is Ichani, however.' The King tapped his fingers on the arm of his chair. 'But if the Ichani do exist, and have been listening to your conversations, they may have learned a great deal in the last few days.'

'Unfortunately, yes.'

'And if I order Lord Balkan home, they will hear of it.

Will his Warriors be capable of defending the Fort against attack if he leaves them and returns?'

'I do not know. I could ask him, but if his answer is no and he leaves, anyone listening will know the Fort is vulnerable.'

The King nodded. 'I understand. Speak to him. If he feels he cannot leave, then he must stay.'

Lorlen sent out a mental call to Balkan. The response was immediate.

—Lorlen?

—If you return to Imardin, will your men be able to defend the Fort?

—Yes. I have taught Lord Makin how to co-ordinate them against a black magician.

—Good. Come back immediately. The King wants your advice.

—I'll leave in an hour.

Lorlen nodded and looked at the King. 'He is confident they can defend the Fort. He should arrive in two or three days.'

The King nodded, satisfied. 'Now, tell me about your investigations.'

Lorlen clasped his hands behind his back. 'In the last few days we have located a few merchants who visited Sachaka in the past, and one does remember the term "Ichani". He said it meant "bandit" or "robber". Merchants and their possessions have been known to disappear in the wastes. It was assumed they had lost their way. That is all we know. We are sending three magicians into Sachaka to seek more information. They will leave in a few days.'

'And what defensive preparations have you made in case Akkarin's story is true?'

Lorlen turned to regard his fellow magicians. 'If what

he says is true, and these Ichani are hundreds of times stronger than a single Guild magician, I don't know if there is anything we can do. There are over three hundred of us, if we include magicians living in other lands. Akkarin estimated there were ten to twenty Ichani. Even if there were only ten, we would have to increase our numbers more than threefold to meet a force that strong. Though there is magical potential in the underclasses, I doubt we would find seven hundred new magicians – and we certainly couldn't train them quickly enough.'

The King had grown a little pale. 'Is there no other way?'

Lorlen hesitated. 'There is one way, but it has its own dangers.'

The King gestured for Lorlen to continue.

Lorlen turned to look at Lord Sarrin. 'The Head of Alchemists has been studying Akkarin's books. What he has learned has been both disturbing and enlightening.'

'How so, Lord Sarrin?'

The old magician stepped forward. 'They reveal that black magic was not forbidden by the Guild until five centuries ago. Before then, it was in common use and was known as "higher magic". After it was banned, records were rewritten or destroyed to eliminate reference to it. The books Akkarin possessed were buried under the University as a precaution against Kyralia facing a powerful enemy again.'

'So your predecessors intended for the Guild to relearn black magic if it was under threat?'

'It appears so.'

The King considered that. Lorlen was pleased to see wariness and fear in the monarch's expression. No ruler would like the idea of giving magicians potentially limitless power.

'How long would it take?'

Sarrin spread his hands. 'I don't know. More than a day. I believe Sonea learned it in a week, but with guidance from Akkarin. Learning from books may prove more difficult.' He paused. 'I would not recommend attempting such an extreme measure unless there was no other way.'

'Why not?' the King asked, though he seemed unsurprised.

'We could save ourselves only to end up fighting the corrupting effects of black magic on our own people.'

The King nodded. 'Yet black magic does not appear to have corrupted Akkarin. If he had intended to overpower the Guild, and myself, he could have done it at any time in the last eight years.'

'That is true,' Lorlen agreed. 'Akkarin was my closest friend, from the day we met as novices, and I never found him to be dishonourable. Ambitious, yes, but not immoral or lacking in compassion.' He shook his head. 'The Guild is large, however, and I cannot guarantee that all magicians would be as restrained if they had access to limitless power.'

The King nodded. 'Then perhaps only a few might learn it, those who were judged trustworthy . . . but only if the situation proves desperate, as you say. Proof is the key, here. You must discover whether Akkarin's story is true or untrue.' He looked at Lorlen. 'Is there anything else that I should know?'

Lorlen glanced at the others, then shook his head. 'I wish we had more significant or reassuring news, Your Majesty, but we do not.'

'Then the rest of you may go. Stay with me a while,

Administrator. I would question you further about Akkarin and his novice.'

Lorlen stepped aside and nodded to the others. They knelt briefly, then left the room. At a gesture from the King, the Advisors quietly moved away to chairs beside the door. He rose and crossed to the northern window.

Lorlen followed at a respectful distance. The monarch leaned on the sill and sighed.

'I have never found Akkarin to be anything but honourable,' he murmured. 'For the first time I find myself hoping that I was wrong about him, and have been proven a fool.'

'As do I, Your Majesty,' Lorlen replied. 'If he was telling the truth, we have just sent our best ally into the hands of our enemy.'

The King nodded. 'Yet it had to be done. I do hope that he survives, Administrator, and not just because we may need him. I, too, valued him as a good friend.'

Pain was the first sensation Sonea became aware of when she woke. It was at its worst in her legs and back, but her shoulders and arms also felt bruised and sore. Concentrating on it, she realised it was the ache of muscles unused to exercise, and the cramping of others that had tried to brace themselves against the hard surface she was lying on.

Drawing on her power, she Healed away the discomfort. As the ache receded, she grew aware of a nagging hunger. She wondered when she had last eaten, and memories of the previous night flooded in.

Last thing I remember, I was in a cave with Akkarin.

She opened her eyes slightly. Two walls of stone

stretched up above her, drawing closer until they met. The cave. Keeping her eyes mostly closed, she looked toward the entrance. Akkarin was sitting a few steps away. As she watched, he looked at her and his mouth curled into that wry, half-smile she knew so well.

He's smiling at me.

She didn't know if he could see she was awake, and she didn't want him to stop smiling, so she stayed still. He continued to regard her, then looked away, sighed and the smile was replaced with a frown of worry.

She closed her eyes again. She ought to get up, but she did not want to move. Once she did, the day would begin and there would be more walking and climbing and running away from Ichani. And Akkarin would turn cold again.

She opened her eyes fully and regarded him again. The skin of his face seemed tight, and looked bruised under his eyes. The shadow of stubble accentuated the angles of his jaw and cheekbones. He looked thin and tired. Had he slept at all? Or had he sat up all night watching her?

His eyes snapped to hers and his expression became disapproving.

'So. You're awake at last.' He climbed to his feet. 'Get up. We must get as much distance as possible between us and the Pass.'

Good morning to you, too, Sonea thought. She rolled and pushed herself unsteadily to her feet.

'What time is it?'

'Nearly dusk.'

She had slept all day. She considered the shadows under his eyes again.

'Did you sleep?'

'I kept watch.'

'We should watch in turns.'

He didn't reply. She moved to the entrance of the cave. The drop into the ravine made her head spin. He put a hand on her shoulder, and she felt the vibration of magic under her feet.

'Let me do that,' she offered.

He ignored her. Magic lifted them both from the cave floor. She watched his face as they moved upward, noting the tension in his face. Tomorrow night she would insist on taking the first watch, she decided. Clearly she would not be able to rely on him to wake her up so he could sleep.

As he set them down at the top of the cliff, his hand left her shoulder. She followed as he began searching the ground. Guessing he was looking for signs of the Ichani's passing, she hung back a little. After moving uphill for a few hundred paces, he stopped, walked back past her, and started in the opposite direction.

Turning to follow, she looked up and drew in a short breath in amazement. The wasteland spread before her. Despite the muting of the dusk light, the colours of the land were still vivid.

Dark, rust-coloured soil lapped at the base of the mountains, but where rivers had eroded the land away, bands of black and pale yellow could be seen. If she looked closely, she could see a speckling of tussocky grass on the surface and, here and there, scraggly groves of trees grown twisted by the wind.

It was a bleak landscape, yet there was a wild beauty to it. The colours were so intense and strange. Even the sky was a different blue.

'It is as I feared. He continued southward instead of descending toward the wastes.'

She blinked in surprise as she saw that Akkarin was walking toward her again. He passed her and continued up the slope again. She sighed and hurried after.

A demanding climb followed. Akkarin seemed reluctant to levitate, preferring to climb up the stepped shelves of rock. He did not stop to rest, and by the time the last rays of the sun had left the mountains above, she was sore and weary again.

She soon craved the relief of standing still. Or just to be able to keep up with his long strides. Perhaps, if she got him talking, he would slow down for a little while.

'Where are we going?'

Akkarin hesitated, but didn't stop or turn.

'Away from the Pass.'

'And then?'

'Somewhere safe.'

'Do you have a place in mind?'

'Somewhere far from Sachaka and the Allied countries.'

Sonea halted and stared at his back. Away from Sachaka and Kyralia? He did not intend to stay close so he could help the Guild when the Ichani invaded? Surely he wasn't going to *abandon* Kyralia.

It made sense, though. What else could they do? They weren't strong enough to fight the Ichani. Neither was the Guild. And the Guild wasn't going to accept their help anyway. What was the point of staying?

Yet she could not believe he would give up so easily. *She* could not give up so easily. She would fight, even if it meant she would probably lose.

But what if that meant leaving Akkarin . . . ?

Akkarin glanced back at her. 'Actually, I intend to find Kariko's group and do a little spying myself,' he said. 'When I find them I will send images of what I see to the Guild.'

Sonea blinked, then shook her head. He had been testing her, then. The realisation brought both relief and anger. Then she considered what he was saying, and felt her blood turn cold.

'The Ichani will hear you. They'll know you're watching,' she said. 'They'll—'

He stopped and turned to regard her.

'Why did you come, Sonea?'

Sonea stared at him. His eyes glittered dangerously. She felt a stab of hurt, then a growing anger.

'You need me more than the Guild does,' she told him.

His eyes narrowed. 'Need you? I don't need a half-trained, disobedient novice to protect.'

Disobedient. So that is what he is so angry about. She straightened. 'If that ill-considered plan you just told me is what you're truly intending to follow, then obviously you *do* need me,' she retorted.

His gaze flickered, but his expression did not soften.

'Ill-considered or not, why should I include you in my plans when you're so disinclined to follow them?'

She held his gaze. 'I'm only disinclined to follow plans that will get you killed.'

He blinked, then stared at her intently. She made herself hold his gaze. He abruptly turned away and resumed climbing.

'Your presence has complicated things. I cannot do what I intended. I will have to reconsider what I . . . *we* will do now.'

Sonea hurried after. 'You didn't really intend to spy on

the Ichani and communicate what you saw to the Guild, did you?'

'Yes and no.'

'If they hear you, they will be able to work out where you are hiding.'

'Of course,' he replied.

And if they caught him, they would not enslave him. They would kill him. Suddenly Sonea understood what he had intended to show the Guild. A chill rushed through her.

'Well, I guess showing them *that* will definitely convince the Guild the Ichani exist.'

He paused and straightened. 'I did not mean to imply that I intended to sacrifice myself,' he said stiffly. 'The Ichani will not hear if I communicate through Lorlen.'

Lorlen's ring. She felt her face warm. 'I see,' she replied. *I'm a fool*, she thought. *Well, I just managed to sound like one anyway. Perhaps it would be better if I kept my mouth shut.*

But as they continued to climb, she considered his plan. There was no reason why they couldn't still try it. She looked at his back and considered whether she should broach the subject again, but decided to wait. When they stopped next, she would ask if it could still work.

Just as the growing darkness was beginning to make it difficult to see their way, they reached the base of a sheer cliff. Akkarin stopped and turned to regard the land below. He lowered himself to the ground and rested his back against the cliff. Sitting beside him, she caught the faint smell of his sweat. Suddenly she was very aware of his presence, and of the silence between them. Now was the time to ask about spying on the Ichani, yet she could not make herself speak.

What is wrong with me? she asked herself.

Love, a voice in her head whispered.

No. Don't be ridiculous, she answered. *I'm not in love. And he clearly isn't. I'm a half-trained, disobedient novice. The sooner I put these silly notions out of my mind, the better.*

'We have company.'

Akkarin lifted a hand and pointed. Following the direction of his finger, Sonea found herself searching the land she had travelled the night before.

A dark shape detached itself from the shadow of a boulder far below. It was hard to estimate how far away it was. She had never needed to guess such distances in the city.

The distant movements were strange, and definitely not human.

'It's an animal,' she said.

'Yes,' Akkarin replied. 'A yeel. They are a smaller, domestic breed of limek. The Ichani train them to track and hunt. See, its owner follows.'

A figure stepped into the moonlight, pursuing the limek.

'Another Ichani?'

'Probably.'

She realised her heart was pounding, but not from any foolish notions of love. One Ichani in front, one behind.

'Will he be able to track us?'

'If her yeel finds our scent.'

Her? Sonea watched the figure. There was something about the walk that did seem feminine, she decided. She looked at Akkarin. He was frowning.

'What now?'

He looked up at the cliff. 'I don't like wasting power levitating, but we will be safer higher up. We must find a crack or fold in the cliff to hide within as we go up.'

'And then?'

'We find water and food.'

'Up there?' she asked sceptically.

'It may seem desolate, but a little life can be found if you know where to look. It will grow easier the further south we go.'

'So we're going south?'

'Yes. South.'

He rose and extended a hand. She took it and let him pull her to her feet. As he turned away, his fingers slid from hers, leaving her skin tingling where he had touched her. Sonea looked down at her hand and sighed.

Getting these silly notions out of her head was not going to be easy.

Dannyl sighed with relief as the door to his room closed. He sat down in one of his guestroom chairs and reduced his globe light to a faint glow.

At last he was alone. Now that he was, however, he found he didn't feel any better. He moved around the room restlessly, examining the furniture and the framed maps and plans he'd collected and hung on his walls years ago.

I miss Tayend, he thought. *I miss sharing a bottle of wine, and talking for hours. I miss sitting in our room working on our research. I miss . . . everything.*

He longed to tell Tayend about Akkarin's story. The scholar would work his way through every detail of it, teasing out hidden inconsistencies or meanings. He would see possibilities that others had never considered.

But Dannyl was glad that the scholar wasn't here. If Akkarin's story proved to be true, Dannyl would rather

Tayend was as far away from the Guild as possible.

He considered everything he had been told about black magic in preparation for his position as Ambassador, and what he had learned from the Dem's book. By using it, a magician could draw magical strength from others. A person gifted with magical talent had more power to take than one without it – but that did not mean that a magician was the better target. A magician, once defeated, would have little magic left to take. It was the person gifted with magical talent who *hadn't* been trained to use it who would be the most attractive victim.

Which was exactly what Tayend was.

Dannyl sighed. He felt as if he were being pulled in two directions. Though he longed to return to Elyne to make sure Tayend was safe, he did not want to abandon Kyralia and the Guild either.

He thought of Rothen and smiled grimly. *I might have joined this group of spies once. Now I hesitate, because I know how I would feel if Tayend left on such a dangerous mission. I wouldn't do that to him unless there was no other choice.*

Sitting down at his desk, Dannyl drew out a sheet of paper, ink and a pen. He paused to consider what he could risk putting onto paper.

To Tayend of Tremmelin

As you have no doubt heard, the Guild is in a state of upheaval. I arrived to learn that the High Lord had been arrested for using black magic. You will appreciate how unfortunate the timing was in relation to our work, but while it created some problems, none have proven too troublesome so far.

He went on to relate Akkarin's story, then explained that he could not return to Elyne until he knew the Guild was safe.

I will be surprised, and not a little annoyed, if I am not free to return within the next few months. While it is good to speak to Rothen again, I don't feel like I belong here now. Instead, I feel like a visitor waiting for the chance to return home. When this matter is settled, I will ask Lorlen if I may continue in the role of Guild Ambassador to Elyne permanently.

Yours in friendship, Ambassador Dannyl.

Sitting back in his chair, Dannyl considered the letter carefully. It was more formal than he would have liked, but he was not about to put on paper anything more personal. If there were people like Farand in the Allied Lands, employed to listen to magicians' mental conversations, there must also be people employed to intercept and read mail.

He rose and stretched. It might be months before he could leave Kyralia. If Akkarin's claims proved to be true, the Guild would want to keep as many magicians in Kyralia as possible. He could be stuck here for a long time.

If Akkarin was telling the truth, he thought with a shiver, *I might never return to Elyne again.*

CHAPTER 23

SPIES

While outside the summer heat was slowly rising to its peak, the rooms inside the University were still pleasantly cool. Rothen relaxed in one of the large comfortable chairs in the Administrator's office and regarded his companions. Lord Solend, the historian, seemed a strange choice for a spy, but who would suspect the sleepy-looking old man of gathering intelligence for the Guild? The other spy, Lord Yikmo, was the Warrior Skills teacher who had trained Sonea.

Solend was an Elyne, and Yikmo a Vin, making Rothen the only Kyralian magician chosen for the task. Rothen expected this would make it harder for him to get information out of the Sachakans – if they did dislike Kyralians as much as Akkarin claimed.

Lorlen drummed his fingers on the arm of his chair. They were waiting to meet a professional spy, sent by the King, who would instruct them in the art of disguise and intelligence-gathering before they left for Sachaka in a few days. At a knock on the door, all turned to see who entered. A messenger strode into the room, bowed, and informed Lorlen that Raven of House Tellen would be late and offered his apologies.

Lorlen nodded. 'Thank you. You may go.'

The messenger bowed again, then hesitated and glanced around the room.

'Does this room often suffer from unexplained drafts, my lord?'

Lorlen looked at the man sharply. He opened his mouth to reply, paused, then smiled and leaned back in his chair.

'Raven.'

The man bowed again.

'Where did you get the uniform?'

'I collect them.'

So this is what a professional spy looks like, Rothen mused. He had expected someone sly and clever-looking. Instead, Raven's appearance was surprisingly ordinary.

'A useful habit, in your profession,' Lorlen commented.

'Very.' The man shivered. 'Would you like me to find the source of this draft?'

Lorlen nodded. The spy crossed the room and began examining the walls. He stopped, pulled out a nose cloth, and wiped the frame of a painting, then smiled and slipped his hand behind it.

A section of the wall slid open.

'The source of your draft,' Raven announced. He turned to regard Lorlen, and a look of disappointment crossed his face. 'But I see you already knew about it.' His hand moved again and the panel slid back into place.

'Everyone here knows of the passageways in the walls of the University,' Lorlen said. 'Not everybody knows where the entrances are, however. Using them is forbidden, though I suspect the former High Lord often ignored that rule.'

Rothen resisted a smile. Despite Lorlen's unconcerned manner, there was a crease between his eyebrows and he kept glancing at the painting. Rothen supposed the Administrator was wondering if Akkarin had ever spied on him.

Raven approached the Administrator's desk. 'Why is using them forbidden?'

'They are unsafe, in places. If novices observed magicians using them, they would be tempted to do the same – before they are capable of protecting themselves against cave-ins.'

Raven smiled. 'That is your official reason, of course. In reality, you don't want magicians or novices spying on each other.'

Lorlen shrugged. 'I'm sure that possibility was considered by my predecessor when he invoked that rule.'

'You might want to revoke it if your former High Lord's predictions come true.' Raven looked at Solend, then Yikmo. As Rothen was given the same calculating look, he wondered what the spy made of him. The man's expression betrayed nothing of his thoughts. 'They may prove to be valuable escape routes,' Raven added. He turned to face Lorlen. 'I have examined all the books, reports and maps you sent to me. Confirming whether these Ichani exist should not be difficult, particularly if they do live as the former High Lord described. You don't need to send three magicians into Sachaka.'

'How many do you suggest we send?' Lorlen asked.

'None,' Raven replied. 'You should send non-magicians. If the Ichani do exist and capture one of your magicians, they will learn too much about you.'

'No more than what they will learn if they capture Akkarin,' Lorlen pointed out.

'It sounds as if he knows enough about Sachaka to look after himself,' Raven replied. 'Whereas these magicians do not.'

'That is why we have employed you to educate them,'

Lorlen answered calmly. 'And there is one advantage to sending magicians. They can communicate what they discover in an instant.'

'And if they do, they will reveal themselves.'

'They have been instructed to communicate only as a last resort.'

Raven nodded slowly. 'Then I would make one strong recommendation.'

'Yes?'

He glanced at Rothen. 'Send only one of these, and choose two others. Your spies should not know who else you've sent. If one is captured, he will reveal the identity of the others.'

Lorlen nodded slowly. 'Which would you choose, then?'

Raven turned to Yikmo. 'You are a Warrior, my lord. If they capture you and read your mind they will learn too much of the Guild's fighting skills.' He turned to Solend. 'Forgive me for pointing this out, my lord, but you are old. No merchant would take a man of your age with him on an arduous journey through the wastes.' He looked at Rothen and frowned. 'You are Lord Rothen, am I right?'

Rothen nodded.

'If your former novice is captured and her mind read, the Ichani might recognise you. She doesn't know you are intending to enter Sachaka, however, and it probably makes little difference that she knows you so long as you don't encounter the Ichani who captured her.' He paused, then nodded. 'You have a face that inspires trust. You would be my choice.'

As Raven turned to regard Lorlen, Rothen did too. The Administrator considered the three magicians and the spy, then nodded.

'I will take your advice.' He looked at Solend and Yikmo. 'Thank you for volunteering. I will speak to you both later. For now, we had best ensure only Rothen hears what Raven has to say.'

The two magicians rose. Rothen searched their faces for signs of annoyance, but read nothing more than disappointment. He watched them walk to the door and leave, then turned back to find Raven watching him closely.

'So,' Raven began, 'what would you prefer? Lose the grey in your hair, or go completely white?'

As Sonea paused to catch her breath, she looked around. The sky was streaked with wispy ribbons of orange clouds, and the air was growing steadily colder. She guessed Akkarin would decide to rest soon.

For three nights since escaping the Ichani, she had followed Akkarin along the mountain range. They began at dusk every day, walked until it grew too dark to see, then rested until the moon rose. Travelling as quickly as they dared, they stopped only when the moon had disappeared behind the peaks.

When they had stopped at the darkest hours of the second morning, she had told Akkarin to take the magical strength she had regained. He had hesitated before accepting the power. Afterwards, she had told him she would watch for the first half of the day. When he had begun to argue, she had told him bluntly that she didn't trust him to wake her up when her turn came. The Healers had lectured novices often on the dangers of using magic to stay awake for too long, and Akkarin was looking more worn and haggard each day.

At first, when he didn't lie down to sleep, she had

assumed this was his way of refusing. She had waited until midday before giving in to weariness. The next morning, when she took the first watch again, he had fallen asleep leaning against a boulder, but woke again with a start long before midday and remained awake.

The third morning, she discovered the real reason he was resisting sleep.

They had both put their backs to a sloped wall warmed by the sun. She noted a little later that he had fallen into a doze, and felt some satisfaction and relief that he was finally sleeping. Soon after, however, he had begun to move his head slowly from side to side, his eyes roving under his eyelids. His face had tightened into an expression of pain and fear that sent a shiver down her spine. Then he woke with a start, stared at the stony landscape before him, and shuddered.

A nightmare, she guessed. She had wished she could comfort him somehow, but read from his expression that the last thing he wanted was sympathy.

Besides, she told herself, *he doesn't smell so good now*. The scent of sweat, which had once been pleasant, was now the stale stink of an unwashed body. And she was sure she smelled no better. They had found the occasional small puddle of water to drink from, but nothing large enough to wash in. She thought wistfully of hot baths and clean robes, and of fruit and vegetables – and raka.

A squawk brought her attention back to the present, and she felt her heart skip. Akkarin had stopped walking and was looking up at several birds circling above. As she watched, a small shape dropped from the sky.

He caught the bird easily, then another. By the time she caught up with him, he had removed their feathers

374

and had begun the less pleasant task of gutting them. He worked quickly and efficiently, obviously having once been well practised at the task. It seemed strange to see him using magic for such a menial task, but then she had never seen a magician hesitate to use it to open and close doors and move objects they were too lazy to collect.

Every time he caught and roasted an animal, or she purified stagnant water, she wondered how they could have survived in this place without magic. They could not have travelled as quickly for a start. An ordinary man or woman would have needed to detour around the deep crevasses they had encountered, and scale the sheer cliffs in their path. Though Akkarin avoided using his magic as much as possible, without levitation they couldn't have kept ahead of the Ichani woman tracking them.

As Akkarin began roasting the birds in a globe of heat, Sonea realised she could hear a faint pattering nearby. Moving away, she walked along the rock wall towards the sound. Seeing a glistening patch of stone, she drew in a sharp breath. A small trickle of water was running down a crack in the rock, surrounded by several birds.

She hurried to the wall, sending the birds fluttering away, and cupped her hands under the dribbling water. Hearing footsteps behind her, she turned and smiled at Akkarin.

'It's clean.'

He held up the two birds he'd caught, now reduced to a small, steaming handful of brown meat.

'They're ready.'

She nodded. 'Just give me a moment.'

Sonea hunted around until she had found a suitable rock, then began to work. Remembering her lessons on moulding stone, she shaped the rock into a large bowl, then set it below the trickle of water to fill. Akkarin made no comment on her use of magic.

They sat down to eat. The small mountain birds did not yield much meat, but they were tasty. She sucked on the thin rib bones and tried to ignore the nagging hunger that remained. Akkarin rose and moved away. The sky had rapidly darkened to a deep blue-black and she could barely see him. She heard a faint splash and a swallow, and guessed he was drinking from the bowl of water.

'Tonight I will attempt to spy on our pursuers,' he said.

Sonea looked toward his shadowy figure, her pulse quickening.

'Do you think they're still following us?'

'I don't know. Come here.'

She rose and approached him.

'Look down and to the right a little. Can you see it?'

The slope of the mountain dropped steeply down from their position. Where it began to split into ridges and ravines, Sonea could see a small point of light. Something was moving about in the light. Something on four legs . . .

A small limek, she realised. Another movement brought her attention to a figure.

'They're much further away now,' she observed.

'Yes,' Akkarin agreed. 'I believe they've lost our trail. We're safe, for the time being.'

Sonea stiffened as another shadow moved near the distant light.

'There are two of them now.'

'It appears the one who nearly caught you has met with the woman.'

'Why have they made the light?' she wondered aloud.

'They can be seen from all around. Do you think they're trying to trick us into coming closer?'

He paused. 'I doubt it. Most likely they do not know we are so high above them. They have stopped within a cluster of boulders. If we were lower on the slopes, we would not have seen the light.'

'It is going to be a big risk, approaching them just for the sake of showing Lorlen the truth.'

'Yes,' he agreed. 'But that is not the only reason to do it. I may also learn how the Ichani plan to enter Kyralia. The North Pass is blocked by the Fort, but the South Pass is open. If they enter from the south, the Guild won't have any warning of their approach.'

'The South Pass?' Sonea frowned. 'Rothen's son lives near there.' That put Dorrien in considerable danger, she realised.

'Near, but not on the road or in the Pass. The Ichani would appear to be a small band of foreign travellers. Even if they were noticed, Dorrien may not hear about it from the local people for a day or so.'

'Unless Lorlen instructs him to keep an eye on the road, and question travellers.'

Akkarin did not reply. He remained silent, watching the distant Ichani. The sky brightened beyond the horizon, heralding the rise of the moon. When the first sliver of light appeared, he spoke again.

'We will have to approach from downwind, or the limek will smell us.'

Sonea glanced back at the bowl of water. It was full to the brim and overflowing.

'Then, if we have the time, there is something we ought to do first,' she said.

He watched as she walked over to the bowl. She warmed

the water with a little magic, then glanced up at him. 'Turn around – and no peeking.'

A faint smile curled his lips. He turned his back and crossed his arms. Keeping him in sight, Sonea pulled off her clothes a piece at a time, washing them and herself, then drying off with magic. She had to wait for the bowl to refill a few times as her clothes soaked up the water. Finally, she emptied the bowl over her head. She scrubbed at her scalp and sighed with relief.

Straightening, she shook her hair out of her eyes.

'Your turn.'

Akkarin turned, then approached the bowl. Moving away, Sonea sat down with her back to him. A nagging curiosity stole over her as she waited. She pushed it aside and concentrated on drying her hair with magic while combing out the knots with her fingers.

'That's better,' he said eventually.

Glancing back, she froze as she saw that his shirt was lying on the ground beside him. Seeing his bare chest, she felt her face flush and turned away.

Don't be ridiculous, she told herself. *You've seen plenty of bare chests before*. The workmen in the markets wore little more than short trousers in the summer heat. That had never embarrassed her before.

No, a voice in the back of her mind answered, *but you'd have felt differently about those workmen if you'd fancied any of them*.

She sighed. She did not want to feel like this. It made the situation more difficult than it needed to be. She drew in a deep breath and let it out slowly. For once, she wanted to be moving, so that all her attention was focussed on traversing the rough terrain of the mountains.

She heard footsteps behind her. Looking up, she saw with relief that he was fully dressed again.

'Come along then,' Akkarin said.

She rose and followed as he started down the mountain slope. The journey did seem to clear her mind. They descended quickly, taking a direct route to the Ichani and their light. After more than an hour had passed, Akkarin slowed and stopped. His eyes were fixed on a distant point.

'What is it?' she asked.

'Lorlen has put on the ring,' he said after a long pause.

'He isn't wearing it all the time, then?'

'No. Until now, it has remained a secret. Sarrin was reading the books and would have recognised it for what it was. Lorlen usually slips it on a few times each evening.' He started moving again. 'I wish I had some glass,' he murmured. 'I would make you a ring.'

Sonea nodded, though she was heartily glad he hadn't. A blood ring would have revealed too much of her thoughts. Until she managed to rid herself of this foolish attraction to him, she did not want Akkarin knowing what was going on in her mind.

They continued slowly. After several hundred paces, he pressed a finger to his lips. They crept forward slowly, pausing many times as Akkarin noted the direction of the wind. Sonea saw a glimmer of light between two boulders ahead of them, and knew they had arrived.

Faint voices grew more audible as she and Akkarin approached the boulders. They stopped and crouched behind the rocks. The first voice Sonea heard was male and thickly accented.

'. . . better chance than I had, with a yeel.'

'She's a smart girl,' the woman replied. 'Why don't you have one, Parika?'

'I did once. Last year I picked up a new slave. You know how the new ones can be. She took off on me and when the yeel found her she killed him. He'd torn her legs up, though, so she didn't get far after that.'

'You killed her?'

'No.' Parika sounded resigned. 'As tempting as it was. Too hard to find good slaves. She can't run now, so she isn't as much trouble.'

The woman made a low noise. 'They're all trouble – even when they're loyal. Either that or they're stupid.'

'But necessary.'

'Hmmm. I hate travelling on my own, with nobody to serve me,' the woman said.

'It's faster, though.'

'These Kyralians would have slowed me down. I'm almost glad I didn't find them. I don't like the idea of keeping magicians prisoner.'

'They're weak, Avala. They wouldn't have been much trouble.'

'They'd be less trouble dead.'

A chill ran down Sonea's spine, then prickled over her skin. Suddenly she wanted to get as far from this place as she could, as quickly as possible. It was not a comfortable feeling, knowing that two powerful magicians who wanted her dead sat just a dozen or so strides away.

'He wants them alive.'

'Why doesn't he hunt them himself?'

The male Ichani chuckled. 'He's probably itching to, but he doesn't trust the others.'

'I don't trust *him*, Parika. He might have sent us to find the Kyralians to get us out of the way.'

The man didn't answer. Sonea heard a soft rustle of clothing, then the sound of footsteps.

'I did what I could to find them,' Avala declared. 'I won't be excluded. I'm going back to join the others. If he wants these two, he'll have to hunt them himself.' She paused. 'What will you do?'

'Return to the South Pass,' Parika replied. 'I will see you again soon, I'm sure.'

Avala gave a soft grunt. 'Good hunting, then.'

'Good hunting.'

Sonea heard footsteps, growing faintly softer. Akkarin looked at her, jerked his head in the direction they had come. She followed him slowly and silently away from the boulders. When they had walked several hundred paces, he quickened his stride. Instead of heading to the higher slopes of the mountain, he set off in a southerly direction.

'Where are we going?' Sonea murmured.

'South,' Akkarin replied. 'Avala was anxious to get back to the others, as if she feared she might miss something. If she is travelling back to meet Kariko without Parika, who is heading to the Southern Pass, that suggests Kariko intends to enter via the North Pass.'

'Yet they said they'd meet soon.'

'In Kyralia, most likely. It has taken us four days to reach here, and it will take Avala the same time to return. If we hurry, we'll reach the South Pass before Parika. We must hope it is not guarded by other Ichani.'

'So we're going back into Kyralia?'

'Yes.'

'Without the Guild's permission?'

'Yes. We will enter Imardin in secret. If they ask for my help, I want to be close enough to act quickly. But we have a long way to go yet. Save your questions. We must try to put some distance between ourselves and Parika tonight.'

'I think that is all we're going to get,' Lorlen said. He unclasped his hands from Balkan and Vinara's, and leaned back in his chair. As the pair released Sarrin's hands, the three magicians turned to stare at Lorlen.

'Why haven't you told us about this ring before?' Sarrin asked.

Lorlen took off the ring and set it on the desk before him. He regarded it a moment, then sighed.

'I could not decide what to do about it,' he told them. 'It is a thing of black magic, yet it does no harm and it is our only safe means of contacting Akkarin.'

Sarrin picked up the ring and examined it, taking care to touch only the band. 'A blood gem. Strange magic. It allows the maker access to the wearer's mind. He sees what the wearer sees, hears what the wearer hears, and absorbs what the wearer thinks.'

Balkan frowned. 'That does not sound like a harmless magical object to me. Whatever you know, he learns.'

'He can't search my mind,' Lorlen said. 'Only read my surface thoughts.'

'That can be damaging enough, if you happen to think about something he shouldn't know.' The Warrior frowned. 'I don't think you should wear this ring again, Lorlen.'

The others shook their heads. Lorlen nodded reluctantly.

'Very well, if you all agree.'

'I do,' Vinara replied.

'Yes, so do I,' Sarrin added. He put the ring down. 'What shall we do with it?'

'Put it somewhere only we four know of,' Balkan said. 'Where?'

Lorlen felt a stab of alarm. If they locked it away, it had better be in a place they could get to quickly if they needed to call on Akkarin.

'The library?'

Balkan nodded slowly. 'Yes. The cupboard of old books and plans. I'll put it away on the way back to my rooms. For now,' he looked up at each of them in turn, 'let's consider this conversation Akkarin relayed to us. What have we learned?'

'That Sonea is alive,' Vinara replied. 'That she and Akkarin have overheard a woman named Avala and a man named Parika discussing a third man.'

'Kariko?' Lorlen suggested.

'Possibly,' Balkan replied. 'The pair did not mention his name.'

'Inconsiderate of them,' Sarrin muttered.

'This unseen pair discussed slaves, so that much about them is true,' Vinara said.

'They also discussed hunting for Kyralians.'

'Sonea and Akkarin?'

'Probably. Unless this is a ruse Akkarin has arranged,' Balkan said. 'He could have employed two people to have that discussion, so he could relay it to us.'

'Why such an ambiguous message, then?' Sarrin asked. 'Why not have them mention Kariko, or his intention to invade Kyralia?'

'I'm sure he has his reasons.' Balkan yawned, then apologised. Vinara gave him a penetrating look.

'Have you slept since you returned?'

The Warrior shrugged. 'A little.' He glanced at Lorlen. 'Our meeting with the King continued late into last night.'

'Is he still considering asking one of us to learn black magic?' Sarrin asked.

Balkan sighed. 'Yes. He would rather that, than call Akkarin back. Akkarin has proven himself untrustworthy by breaking the Guild's law and his vow.'

'But if one of us learned it, he or she would also be breaking that law and the Magicians' Vow.'

'Not if we make an exception.'

Sarrin scowled. 'There should be no exceptions where black magic is concerned.'

'Yet we may have no choice. It may be the only way we can defend ourselves against these Ichani. If one of us was voluntarily strengthened by a hundred magicians each day, that magician would be strong enough to fight ten Ichani in just two weeks.'

Sarrin shuddered. 'No-one should be trusted with that much power.'

'The King knows you feel this way,' Balkan said. 'Which is why he believes you would be the best candidate.'

Sarrin stared at the Warrior in horror. 'Me?'

'Yes.'

'I couldn't. I . . . I'd have to refuse.'

'Refuse your King?' Lorlen asked. 'And watch the Guild and all of Imardin fall before a handful of barbarian magicians?'

Sarrin stared at the ring, his face white.

'It would not be an easy burden to shoulder,' Lorlen said gently, 'and not one to take on unless we were sure there was no other choice. The spies will leave in a few days. Hopefully they will discover, once and for all, whether Akkarin spoke the truth.'

Balkan nodded. 'We should consider sending reinforcements to the Fort, too. If this overheard conversation is real, it suggests that this woman is meeting a group of Ichani in the north.'

'What about the South Pass?' Vinara asked. 'Parika was returning there.'

Balkan frowned. 'I will have to consider that. It is not as defendable as the Fort, but their conversation suggests a larger gathering in the north. We should have the road to the South Pass watched, at the least.'

The Warrior yawned again. Clearly he was struggling against weariness. Lorlen caught a meaningful look from Vinara.

'It is late,' he said. 'Shall we meet here, early, to discuss it?' The others nodded. 'Thank you for coming here so promptly. I will see you in the morning.'

As the trio rose and bid him good night, Lorlen could not shake a feeling of disappointment. He had hoped Akkarin would show them something that would prove his story was true. The conversation between the Sachakans hadn't revealed much, but it had pointed out some flaws in Kyralia's defence.

But now the ring was gone, and with it went his only link to Akkarin.

CHAPTER 24

SECRETS REVEALED

The whisper of robes and the shuffle of booted feet was a constant background noise in the Guildhall, even during Lorlen's short speech. *We're all restless*, Dannyl mused. *Too few questions were answered this Meet.*

There was a collective sigh as Lorlen announced the Meet concluded.

'There will be a short break before the Hearing to judge the Elyne rebels begins,' the Administrator told them.

At the announcement, Dannyl's stomach flipped over. He looked at Rothen.

'Time for me to face the rumour-mongers.'

Rothen smiled. 'You'll be fine, Dannyl. You've gained quite an air of competence since you left for Elyne.'

Dannyl looked at his mentor in surprise. Competence? 'You mean I didn't have one before I left?'

Rothen chuckled. 'Of course you did, or you would not have been chosen for the position. It's just stronger now. Or did you bring back some of that awful Elyne scent with you?'

Dannyl laughed. 'If you thought scent might give me an air of competence, you should have suggested it earlier. Not that I would have taken your advice. There are some habits best left to the Elynes.'

The older magician nodded in agreement. 'Well go on,

then. Get yourself down there before they start without you.'

Dannyl rose and made his way to the end of the seats. As he moved to the front of the hall, he noted that Expatriate Administrator Kito was descending to the floor in preparation to lead the proceedings. The magician glanced to one side, where a row of men and women were entering with an escort of guards. Dannyl recognised Dem Marane's group of friends and co-conspirators. Royend walked beside his wife. He looked up at Dannyl and narrowed his eyes.

Dannyl returned the man's gaze steadily. The hatred in Royend's eyes was new. The Dem had been angry on the night of the arrest, but during the journey to Kyralia and the wait for the Hearing that anger must have matured into something stronger.

I can understand his hatred, Dannyl thought. *I tricked him. He doesn't care that I was acting under Akkarin's orders or that he was breaking the law. He just sees me as the man who ruined his dreams.*

Farand stood on the other side of the room, beside two Alchemists. The young man looked nervous, but not frightened. A heavy clunk drew eyes to the rear of the hall, where one of the great doors was swinging open. Six Elynes strode down the aisle. Two were the magicians from the ships that had brought the rebels to Kyralia, Lords Barene and Hemend. The others were representatives of the Elyne King.

As Kito directed the newcomers to the seats at the front of the room, Dannyl considered where he should position himself. He decided to stand near Farand, knowing that this would be taken as a gesture of support for the young man. When all were settled, Lorlen rang a small gong, and the hall quickly fell silent. Kito glanced around and nodded.

'We have called this Hearing today to judge Farand of Darellas, Royend and Kaslie of Marane, and their co-conspirators . . .'

Catching a noise from an unexpected direction, Dannyl looked up to the topmost tier of the seats for the Higher Magicians. He blinked in surprise when he saw that one of the King's Advisors was present.

But of course, he thought, *our King would want to be sure that anyone from another land caught trying to start their own magicians' guild was appropriately punished.*

'. . . Farand of Darellas has been accused of learning magic outside of the Guild,' Kito continued. 'These men and women have been accused of seeking to learn magic. The Dem Marane has also been accused of possessing knowledge of black magic.'

Kito paused to look around the room. 'The evidence to support these accusations will be presented for us to judge. I call forth the first speaker, Second Guild Ambassador to Elyne, Dannyl.'

Dannyl drew in a deep breath and stepped forward to stand beside Kito.

'I swear that all I speak in this Hearing will be the truth.' He paused. 'Seven weeks ago I received orders from the former High Lord to find and arrest a group of rebels who were seeking to learn magic outside the influence and guidance of the Guild.'

The audience was silent as Dannyl told his tale. He had considered for weeks how much he ought to reveal when it came to explaining how he had convinced the rebels to trust him. The entire Guild had probably heard of the Dem's claims by now, so Dannyl didn't need to go into great detail. But he couldn't avoid that part of the story completely.

So he told them he had arranged for the Dem to learn of a 'false secret' so the man thought he could blackmail Dannyl. He then went on to describe his meeting with Farand. The Elyne courtiers' faces grew tense as he explained that Farand had been denied entrance into the Guild after he had learned something the Elyne King wanted concealed. Dannyl explained, for their benefit, that Farand had been in danger of losing control of his powers, and what the consequences would have been if that happened.

Dannyl then described the book that Tayend had borrowed from the Dem. He told how the contents had convinced him to arrest the rebels immediately, rather than continuing to visit the Dem in the hope of identifying more of them. Finally, he finished with a warning that he may not have found all of the members of the group.

Kito turned to Lord Sarrin for a confirmation of the book's contents, then asked for Farand to be brought forward. The young man was ushered to the front.

'Farand of Darellas, do you swear that you will speak the truth during this Hearing?' Kito asked.

'I swear.'

'Is Ambassador Dannyl's story true in regard to your part in it?'

The young man nodded. 'Yes.'

'How did you come to be a part of Dem Marane's rebel group?'

'My sister is his wife. He thought it was a waste that

389

I wasn't able to become a magician. He encouraged me to listen into mind conversations again.'

'And this, I understand, is how you learned to release your magic.'

'Yes. I overheard a discussion about it.'

'Did you hesitate before trying what they said?'

'Yes. My sister didn't want me to learn magic. Well, she did at first, but then she started to worry that we didn't know enough and it might be dangerous.'

'So what overcame your hesitation?'

'Royend said, once I started, it would get easier.'

'How long have the Dem and his accomplices been meeting with the intention of learning magic?'

'I don't know. Longer than I've known him.'

'How long have you known him?'

'Five years. Since my sister was engaged to him.'

'Are there any other members of the group who are missing today?'

'There are more, but I don't know who they are.'

'Do you believe Dem Marane sought to learn magic himself?'

Farand hesitated, then his shoulders drooped. 'Yes.'

Dannyl felt a pang of sympathy for the young man. He had chosen to help, knowing that the Dem and his friends would be punished regardless, but it must not be easy.

'And the others in the group?'

'I'm not sure. Some probably did. Some came along just for the excitement, I think. My sister was there because of Royend, and me.'

'Is there anything else you wish to add?'

Farand shook his head.

Kito nodded, then turned to face the hall. 'I wish to

add that I have truth-read Farand, and can confirm that all he has revealed is true.'

A low murmur followed. Dannyl looked at Farand in surprise. Allowing a truth-read was an indication of how willing Farand was to co-operate.

Kito turned to regard the Higher Magicians. 'Any comments or questions?' Heads were shaken. 'Return to your place, Farand of Darellas. I now call on Royend of Marane to be questioned.'

The Dem walked forward.

'Royend of Marane, do you swear to speak the truth during this Hearing?'

'I do.'

'Is Ambassador Dannyl's story true in regard to your part in it?'

'No.'

Dannyl suppressed a sigh and braced himself for the inevitable.

'In which way is it incorrect?'

'He says he made up this story about his secret affair with his assistant. I believe it to be true. Anyone who has seen the two together would know there was more to it than just . . . just a trick. No-one pretends that well.'

'Is this the only part of his story that is incorrect?'

The Dem stared at Dannyl. 'Even Dem Tremmelin, Tayend of Tremmelin's father, believes it to be true.'

'Dem Marane, please answer the question.'

The Dem ignored him. 'Why don't you ask him if he's a lad. He swore that he'd tell the truth. I want to hear him deny it.'

Kito's eyes narrowed. 'This Hearing has been called to judge whether the law against the learning of magic outside the restrictions of the Guild has been broken, not whether Ambassador Dannyl has been involved in dishonourable and perverse practises. Please answer the question, Dem Marane.'

Dannyl just managed to stop himself wincing. Dishonourable and perverse. No doubt the Guild's opinion of him – and his story – would change completely if they knew the truth. And the Dem knew it.

'If he's lied about that, then he could have lied about everything,' the Dem spat. 'Remember that, after you've put me in my grave. I will not answer your questions.'

'Very well,' Kito said. 'Return to your place. I call Kaslie of Marane to be questioned.'

The Dem's wife was nervous but co-operative. She revealed that the rebels had been meeting for ten years, but assured the Guild that their interest had been purely academic. As the other rebels were questioned, only small details about the group were revealed. They all claimed they had not intended to learn magic, only learn about it.

A short discussion followed in which Farand's poisoning was considered. Dannyl was not surprised to learn that the Elyne magicians' investigations had not revealed the poisoner. From the look on Lady Vinara's face, Dannyl guessed the matter would not end there.

Kito asked for the accused to be enclosed in a barrier of silence as the Guild discussed their punishment. The hall filled with voices. After a long break, Kito called for all magicians to return to their places and for the barrier of silence to be removed.

'It is time to make our judgment,' he declared. He held out a hand and a globe light appeared above it, then floated upward. Dannyl created his own, and sent it up to join those from the rest of the Guild.

'Do you judge that Farand of Darellas is undoubtedly guilty of learning magic outside of the Guild?'

All of the globe lights turned red. Kito nodded.

'Traditionally, punishment for this crime is execution,' he said, 'but the Higher Magicians feel that, under the circumstances, an alternative ought to be offered. Farand of Darellas is a victim of circumstances and the manipulations of others. He has been helpful at all times and has submitted to a truth-read. I recommend he be offered a place in the Guild with the condition that he remains within the grounds for the rest of his life. Please change your lights to white if you agree with my recommendation.'

Slowly the lights shifted to white. Only a few remained red. Dannyl breathed a sigh of relief.

'Farand of Darellas will be offered a place in the Guild,' Kito announced.

Looking at Farand, he saw that the young man was grinning with relief and excitement. But as Kito continued, the smile vanished.

'Next: do you judge that Royend of Marane is undoubtedly guilty of seeking to learn magic, and of possessing knowledge of black magic, outside of the Guild?'

The Guildhall filled with an eerie glow as the globe lights all turned red.

'Again, the Higher Magicians feel they must offer an alternative to execution,' Kito said. 'The crime is a serious one, however, and we believe nothing less than imprisonment for life would be appropriate. Please change your lights to white, if you wish to reduce the punishment to imprisonment.'

Dannyl changed his globe light to white, but felt a chill

as he realised that fewer than half the magicians had done the same. *It must be years since the Guild has elected to execute someone*, he thought.

'Royend of Marane will be executed,' Kito announced heavily.

A gasp came from the rebels. Dannyl felt a stab of guilt and forced himself to look at the group. The Dem's face was white. His wife gripped his arm tightly. The rest of the rebels looked pale and uneasy.

Kito glanced at the Higher Magicians, then turned back to face the hall and spoke another rebel's name. The rest were granted the lesser punishment of imprisonment. Clearly, the Guild saw Dem Marane as the leader of the group and wanted to make an example of him. *His refusal to co-operate had done him no favours either*, thought Dannyl.

When it was Kaslie's turn, Kito surprised Dannyl by speaking out in her defence. He urged the Guild to consider her two children. His words must have sufficiently moved the magicians, because they granted the Dem's wife a pardon, allowing her to return to her home.

The Elyne magicians then asked if they could mentally communicate the judgments to the Elyne King. Lorlen agreed, on the condition that no other information was communicated. He then announced the Hearing concluded.

Released from his role at last, Dannyl felt an over-whelming relief. He looked for Rothen in the crowd of magicians descending from the seats, but before he had located his friend, a voice spoke his name. He turned to find Administrator Kito approaching.

'Administrator,' Dannyl replied.

'Are you satisfied with the result?' Kito asked.

Dannyl shrugged. 'Mostly. I have to admit, I did not think the Dem deserved his punishment. He is an ambitious man, but I doubt he would ever succeed in learning magic in a prison.'

'No,' Kito replied, 'but I think the Guild resented his attack on your honour.'

Dannyl stared at the magician. Surely that was not the sole reason for the Guild choosing execution?

'You find this disturbing?' Kito asked.

'Of course.'

Kito's gaze was unwavering. 'It would be particularly disturbing, if his claims were true.'

'Yes, it would be,' Dannyl replied. He narrowed his eyes at the man. Was Kito baiting him?

Kito grimaced apologetically. 'I'm sorry. I did not mean to insinuate that they were. Will you be returning to Elyne soon?'

'Unless Lorlen decides otherwise, I will stay here until we are sure there is no threat from Sachaka.'

Kito nodded, then glanced away as his name was called. 'I will speak to you again soon, Ambassador.'

'Administrator.'

Dannyl watched the man move away. Was what Kito had suggested true? Had the Guild voted for execution out of anger at Dem Marane's accusation?

No, he thought. *The Dem's defiance had swayed the vote. He had dared to seek what the Guild felt it has the sole right to, and he obviously felt no respect for laws or authority.*

All the same, Dannyl could not find it in himself to agree with the Guild's vote. The Dem did not deserve to die. But there was nothing Dannyl could do about that now.

* * *

Walking back through the underground passages of the Thieves' Road, Cery considered his latest conversation with Takan. Akkarin's former servant was difficult to read, but his mannerisms had betrayed both boredom and anxiety. Unfortunately, Cery could do little about the former, and nothing about the latter.

Cery knew that being cooped up in a hidden underground house, no matter how luxurious, was bound to become tedious and frustrating. Sonea had lived in a similar place when Faren had first agreed to hide her from the Guild. She had grown restless after a week. For Takan it was even more frustrating because he knew his master was facing dangers elsewhere and there was nothing he could do about it.

Cery also remembered how solitude and being unable to help someone he cared for had once made his every moment a torture. He still dreamed, though now only occasionally, about the weeks he had spent imprisoned under the University by Fergun. When he remembered that Akkarin had found and freed him, he was even more determined to help Takan in any way he could.

He had offered to provide any sort of entertainment Takan might crave – from whores to books – but the man had politely declined. Cery asked the guards to chat with his guest now and then, and he tried to visit every day, as Faren had once done for Sonea. Takan was not a talkative man, however. He avoided discussing his life before becoming Akkarin's servant, and spoke little of the years after. Cery eventually drew out some humorous stories that servants liked to tell about the magicians. It seemed even Takan didn't mind indulging in a little gossip.

Akkarin had only communicated with Takan a few times

in the last eight days. When he did, Takan always reassured Cery that Sonea was alive and unharmed. Cery was both amused by and grateful for these updates on Sonea's welfare. Obviously the servant had learned from Akkarin about Cery's former interest in Sonea.

That's in the past, Cery thought wryly. *Now I have Savara to mope about.* Had *Savara to mope about*, he corrected. He was determined there would be no pining, this time. *We are both sensible adults*, he told himself, *with responsibilities that can't be neglected.*

They reached the beginning of the maze of passages around his own rooms. Bricks whispered against bricks as Gol opened the first hidden door. Cery nodded at the guards as he strolled through.

She said she might come back, Cery reminded himself. *To 'visit'.* He smiled. *That sort of arrangement has its advantages. No expectations. No compromises . . .*

And he had bigger concerns. Imardin faced a probable invasion by foreign magicians. Cery had to consider what he would do about them – if he *could* do anything about them. After all, if the Guild was too weak to face these Ichani, what hope did non-magicians have?

Not a lot, he thought. *But that's better than nothing. There must be ways ordinary people can kill a magician.*

He thought back to a conversation he'd had with Sonea over a year and a half ago. They had jokingly discussed how to get rid of a novice who was bothering her. He was still thinking about it when one of his messenger boys informed him that a visitor was waiting to meet him.

Entering his office, Cery sat down, checked his yerim were still in his drawer, then sent Gol out to meet the visitor. When the door opened again, Cery looked up and felt his heart skip. He rose from the chair.

'Savara!'

She smiled and sauntered to his desk. 'I have surprised you this time, Ceryni.'

He dropped down into his seat again. 'I thought you left.'

She shrugged. 'I did. But halfway to the border my people spoke to me. They decided, at my urging, that someone should stay and witness the invasion.'

'You don't need my help for that.'

'No.' She sat on the edge of the desk and tilted her head to one side. 'But I did say I would visit if I came back. It could be some time before the Ichani come, and I might get bored while I am waiting.'

He smiled. 'We can't have that.'

'I did hope you would think so.'

'What are you offering me in return, then?'

Her eyebrows rose. 'There is a price for visiting you, now?'

'Maybe. I just want a little advice.'

'Oh? What advice?'

'How can ordinary people kill magicians?'

She gave a short laugh. 'They can't. At least, not if a magician is competent and vigilant.'

'How can we tell if he isn't?'

Her eyebrows rose. 'You are not joking – but of course you are not.'

He shook his head.

She pursed her lips thoughtfully. 'So long as I don't reveal my people's hand in this, I see no reason why I shouldn't help you.' She smiled crookedly. 'And I am sure

398

you will find a way, even if I don't. You might get killed trying, though.'

'I'd rather avoid that,' Cery told her.

She grinned. 'I'd rather you did, too. Well, then, if you keep me informed of what's going on in the city, I'll give you advice on killing magicians. Does that sound reasonable?'

'It does.'

She crossed her arms and looked thoughtful. 'I cannot tell you a sure way to kill an Ichani, however. Only that they are no different from ordinary people in that they make mistakes. You can trick them, if you know how. All it takes is courage, bluff, and some considerable risks.'

Cery smiled. 'Sounds like the sort of work I'm used to.'

'I hear water.'

Akkarin turned to regard Sonea, but his face was in shadow and she couldn't see his expression.

'Go on, then,' he replied.

She listened carefully, then moved toward the sound. After so many days in the mountains, she could now recognise the faintest noise of water trickling over rock. Drawn to the shadows of a recess in the rock wall they had been following, she stared intently into the darkness and felt her way forward.

She saw the tiny stream of water at the same time as she saw the break in the wall. A narrow gap led to an open space. Rock scraped across her back as she squeezed through. When she'd made her way out to the other side of the gap, she gave a low exclamation of surprise.

'Akkarin,' she called.

She stood at the edge of a tiny valley. The sides sloped

gently up to steeper rocky walls. Stunted trees, bushes and grass grew along a narrow stream that gurgled cheerfully down to disappear into a crack several strides away.

Hearing a grunt, she turned to see that Akkarin was having some difficulty forcing himself through the gap in the rock wall. He freed himself, then straightened and gazed at the valley appreciatively.

'Looks like a good place to spend the night – or the day,' she said.

Akkarin frowned. They had continued walking toward the South Pass long into the morning for the last three days, conscious of the Ichani travelling behind them. Sonea worried constantly that Parika would catch up, but she doubted that he would travel at such a punishing pace unless he had good reason to.

'It may be a dead end,' Akkarin observed. He did not move back to the gap, however. Instead he started toward the trees.

A loud squawk rang out, echoing in the valley. Sonea jumped as a large white bird arced out of a nearby tree. The bird suddenly twisted in the air. Sonea heard a faint snap, then watched it plummet to the ground.

Akkarin chuckled. 'I guess we will be staying.'

He strode forward and picked up the creature. As Sonea saw the huge eyes of the bird, she gasped in surprise.

'A mullook!'

'Yes.' Akkarin smiled crookedly. 'Ironic. What would the King say if he knew we were eating his House incal?'

He continued up the stream. After several hundred paces, they reached the end of the valley. Water trickled over a looming cliff overhang to form the stream.

'We'll sleep under that,' Akkarin said, pointing to the

overhang. He sat down by the stream and began pulling the feathers from the bird.

Sonea looked down at the springy grass under her feet, then up at the hard stone under the overhang. Dropping into a crouch, she began tearing up handfuls of grass. As she carried armloads to their sleeping place, the smell of roasting meat drifted to her nose and set her stomach rumbling.

Leaving the mullook cooking in a floating globe of heat, Akkarin moved to one of the trees. He stared up at the branches, and they began to shake. Sonea heard a dull patter, then saw Akkarin crouch and examine the ground. She moved to his side.

'These nuts are hard to open, but quite tasty,' he told her, holding one out. 'Keep gathering them. I think I saw some stingberries further down.'

The moon hung low in the sky. In the growing darkness, it was hard to find the nuts. She resorted to groping around until she felt their smooth roundness under her fingers. Gathering them in the front of her shirt, she carried them to the cooking mullook, and soon worked out how to crack the shells without crushing the soft nuts inside.

Akkarin returned soon after, carrying a rough stone bowl filled with berries and a few stalks. The berries were covered in nasty looking spines.

Between shelling nuts, Sonea watched as Akkarin lifted the berries with magic and carefully peeled off the skin and spines. Soon the bowl was half filled with the dark flesh of the fruit. Next he set to work on the stalks, peeling away the fibrous outer layer.

'I think we're ready for our feast,' he said. He handed her two of the stalks. 'This is shem – Not particularly tasty, but edible. It's not good to live on just meat.'

Sonea found the inside of the stalks pleasantly juicy, if not flavoursome. Akkarin divided up the mullook, which contained more meat than any of the other birds they had eaten. The nuts proved to be as delicious as he had promised. Akkarin crushed the berries, then added water to the pulp to make a tart drink. When they had finished, Sonea felt full for the first time since they had entered Sachaka.

'It's amazing how something as simple as a meal can be so good.' She sighed contentedly. The valley was almost completely hidden in darkness now. 'I wonder what this place looks like in the daylight.'

'You'll find out in an hour or so,' Akkarin replied.

He sounded tired. She looked at him, but his face was in shadow.

'Time to sleep, then,' she said. She drew on enough Healing power to chase away her own weariness, then held out her hands. He didn't take them at first, and she wondered if he could see her in the darkness. Then she felt his warm fingers wrap around hers.

She drew in a deep breath, then sent power to him, taking care not to exhaust herself. Not for the first time, she wondered if he had accepted her decision to take the first watch to ensure she didn't give him too much power. If she exhausted herself, she wouldn't be able to stay awake.

As she felt her power ebb, she stopped and pulled her hands away. Akkarin remained still and silent, making no move toward the grass bed she had prepared.

'Sonea,' he said suddenly.

'Yes?'

'Thank you for coming with me.'

She caught her breath, then felt her heart swell with

pleasure. He remained silent for several minutes, then drew in a short breath.

'I regret separating you from Rothen. I know he was more like a father than a teacher.'

Sonea stared at his shadowed face, searching for his eyes.

'It was necessary,' he added softly.

'I know,' she whispered. 'I understand.'

'But you didn't understand then,' he said wryly. 'You hated me.'

She chuckled. 'That's true. I don't any more.'

He said no more, but after a short pause he rose and moved to the overhang and lay down on the grass bed. For a long time she sat in darkness. Eventually the sky began to lighten and the stars fade and disappear. She wasn't bothered by sleepiness, and she knew her Healing power wasn't solely responsible for that. Akkarin's sudden thanks and apology had stirred up the hopes and wishes she had been trying to smother for days.

Little fool, she scolded herself. *He's just being kind. Just because he has finally acknowledged your help, and regrets what he did to you, doesn't mean he considers you as anything more than a useful but unwanted companion. He's not interested in you otherwise, so stop torturing yourself.*

But no matter how hard she had tried to stop herself, she couldn't help feeling a thrill every time he touched her, or even looked at her. And it didn't help that she kept catching him watching her.

She wrapped her arms around her knees and drummed her fingers on her calves. When she had lived in the slums, she had assumed she knew everything she needed to know about men and women. Later, Healing lessons had shown her how little she had really understood. Now she found that even the Healers hadn't taught her anything useful.

But then, perhaps they hadn't told her how to stop feeling this way because it wasn't possible. Perhaps . . .

A low noise, like a growl, echoed through the valley. Sonea froze, her mind now suddenly still, and stared out into the gloom. The sound came again, from behind, and she rose and spun about in one movement. As she realised the sound had come from somewhere near Akkarin, she felt a flash of fear. Was some night creature stalking him? She hurried forward.

Reaching the overhang, she peered into the gloom and saw no creature poised to attack. Akkarin's head was rolling from side to side. As she drew closer, he moaned.

She stopped and regarded him with dismay. He was having another nightmare. Relief and concern filled her. She wondered if she should wake him, but it had always been so clear from his expression after waking that he didn't like her witnessing these moments of weakness.

For that matter, she thought, *I don't either.*

Another moan escaped him. Sonea winced as it echoed loudly in the valley. Sound carried far in the mountains, and she did not like to imagine who might be listening. As he uttered another low cry, she came to a decision. It didn't matter if he liked it or not, she had to wake him up before he attracted unwanted attention.

'Akkarin,' she whispered hoarsely. He stilled and she thought she had woken him, but then he tensed all over. '*No!*'

Alarmed, Sonea drew closer. His eyes roved under his eyelids. His face contorted in pain. She reached toward him, intending to shake him awake.

The sting of a shield met her fingers. She saw his eyes fly open, then felt a force slam into her, throwing her up into the air. Something hard slammed into her back, then she dropped to the ground. Pain lanced down her arms and legs.

'*Ow!*'

'Sonea!'

She felt hands pushing her over onto her back. Akkarin stared at her.

'Are you hurt?'

She examined herself. 'No, just bruised, I think.'

'Why did you wake me?'

She looked down at his hands. Even in the gloom she could see they were shaking. 'You were dreaming. A nightmare . . .'

'I am used to them, Sonea.' he said quietly, his voice controlled and calm. 'They are no reason to wake me.'

'You were making a lot of noise.'

He paused, then straightened.

'Go to sleep, Sonea,' he said in a low voice. 'I will watch.'

'No,' she said irritably. 'You've barely slept – and I know you won't wake me up when it's your turn to sleep.'

'I will. I give you my word.'

He leaned forward and offered her a hand. Taking it, she let him haul her to her feet. A bright light dazzled her, and she realised that the rising sun was just beginning to crest the rock wall at the base of the valley.

Akkarin stilled. Sensing that something had caught his attention, she squinted at him, but he was a dark shape against the brightness. Instinctively, she sought him with her mind instead. At once she saw an image.

A face, framed by hair shining in the morning sunlight.

Eyes . . . so dark . . . and pale, perfect skin . . .

It was her own face, but it was unlike any reflection she had seen in a mirror. Her eyes held a mysterious shine, her hair seemed to ripple as if moving in a breeze, and her lips surely did not curve so invitingly . . .

He snatched his hand away and took a step back.

This is how he sees me, she thought suddenly. There was no mistaking the desire she had sensed. She felt her own heart racing. *All this time, I resisted because I thought it was just me*, she thought. *And so has he.*

She took a step toward him, then another. He watched her intently, frowning. She willed him to see beyond her eyes, to sense her own thoughts, and that she knew his. His eyes widened with surprise as she stepped very close. She felt his hands encircle her arms, then tighten as she rose up on the balls of her feet, and kissed him.

He went very still. Leaning against him, she felt his heart beating quickly. His eyes closed, then he pulled away.

'Stop. Stop this,' he breathed. He opened his eyes and stared at her intently.

Despite the words, his hands still held her arms tightly as if reluctant to let go of her. Sonea searched his face. Had she read him wrong? No, she was sure of what she had sensed.

'Why?'

He frowned. 'This is wrong.'

'Wrong?' she heard herself ask. 'How? We both feel . . . feel . . .'

'Yes,' he said softly. He looked away. 'But there is more to consider.'

'Like?'

Akkarin released her arms and took a step back. 'It would not be fair – to you.'

Sonea considered him carefully. 'Me? But—'

'You're young. I am twelve – no, thirteen – years older than you.'

Suddenly his hesitation made sense. 'That is true,' she answered carefully. 'But women in the Houses are matched with older men all the time. *Much* older men. Some when they're as young as sixteen. I'm nearly twenty.'

Akkarin seemed to struggle with himself. 'I am your guardian,' he reminded her sternly.

She could not help smiling. 'Not any more.'

'But if we return to the Guild—'

'Will we cause a scandal?' She chuckled. 'I think they're getting used to that.' She hoped he would smile at that, but he only frowned. She sobered. 'You speak as if we'll go back and everything will be the same again. Even if we return, nothing will ever be as it was for us. I am a black magician. So are you.'

He winced. 'I am sorry. I should never have—'

'Don't apologise for *that*,' she exclaimed. 'I *chose* to learn black magic. And I didn't do it for you.'

Akkarin regarded her silently.

She sighed and turned away. 'Well, this is going to make things awkward.'

'Sonea.'

She looked back and stilled as he stepped closer. He brushed a strand of hair away from her face. She felt her pulse quicken at the touch.

'Either of us could die in the next few weeks,' he said quietly.

She nodded. 'I know.'

'I'd be happier knowing you were safe.'

Sonea narrowed her eyes at him. He smiled.

'No, I will not start that argument again, but . . . you test my loyalties, Sonea.'

She frowned, not understanding. 'How?'

He reached out and ran a finger across her brow. 'It doesn't matter.' The corner of his mouth curled upward. 'It's too late, anyway. I started to fail that test the night you killed the Ichani.'

She blinked in surprise. *Did that mean . . . ? For that long . . . ?*

He smiled. She felt his hands slip around her waist. As he pulled her closer, she decided her questions could wait. She reached up and traced the curl in his lips with the tip of her finger. Then he leaned forward and his mouth met hers, and all questions were forgotten.

CHAPTER 25

A CHANCE ENCOUNTER

Gorin, Rothen had discovered, were frustratingly slow walkers. The enormous beasts were the favourite of merchants, however. They were strong, docile and easy to handle and direct, and much more resilient than horses.

But they were impossible to hurry. Rothen sighed and glanced back at Raven, but the spy was dozing among the sacks of cloth in the cart, a wide-brimmed hat covering his face. Rothen allowed himself a smile and turned his attention back to the road. The previous night, they had hired rooms above a bolhouse in a town called Coldbridge. The spy, posing as Rothen's cousin, had drunk more bol than anyone ought to be able to, then spent the night swaying from his bed to the piss drain and back again.

Which probably meant Raven was doing a much better job at playing the part of intrepid merchant than Rothen was. *Or am I supposed to be the sensible older cousin?*

Rothen adjusted his shirt. The closely fitting garment was much less comfortable than robes. He was grateful for his traveller's hat, however. Though it was early morning, the day was promising to be a hot one.

A haze of dust hung in the air over the road and blurred the horizon. No mountains had appeared in the distance, though he had been travelling for two days. Rothen knew that the road ran near-straight to Calia, where it split into two. Turn left and it took you north to the Fort; turn right and you headed north-east to the South Pass. That was where he and Raven were headed.

It seemed strange to be travelling north-east to a *southern* pass, Rothen mused. The route was probably named for its location in the mountains, not for its general position in Kyralia. He had come close to it once, while visiting his son during the summer break five years ago.

He frowned as he thought of Dorrien. His son was watching the road to the Pass, and a meeting was inevitable. Rothen would have to explain where he was going, and why, and Dorrien wasn't going to like it.

He will probably try to join us. Rothen snorted quietly. *That's an argument I'm not looking forward to.*

It would be several days before he faced his son, however. Raven had said it took six or seven days to reach the South Pass by cart. *By then Sonea will have been in Sachaka for fifteen days*, Rothen thought. *If she stays alive that long.*

He had been relieved to hear from Lorlen that Akkarin had contacted the Higher Magicians, now five days ago. Sonea had been alive. Lorlen had also described an overheard discussion between two Sachakans that disturbed Rothen greatly. Whether the strangers were Ichani or not, they clearly wanted Akkarin and Sonea dead.

'They called them "the Kyralians",' Lorlen had said. *'I hope this doesn't mean they'll treat all Kyralians entering Sachaka the same way. Kyralian merchants have been making the journey to and from Arvice safely for years, though, and say they see no reason why that might have changed recently. Just be careful.'*

'Someone's approaching,' Raven said. 'From behind us.'

Rothen glanced at the spy. The man shifted slightly, and one eye appeared beneath the brim of his hat. Looking down the road, Rothen realised that he could see movement beyond the dust stirred up by their passing. Horses and riders emerged from the cloud, and Rothen felt his pulse quicken.

'Magicians,' he said. 'Balkan's reinforcements for the Fort.'

'Better move to one side of the road,' Raven advised. 'And keep your head down. You don't want them recognising you.'

Rothen pulled gently on the reins. The gorin tossed their heads halfheartedly, and slowly moved to the left side of the road. The sound of drumming hoof beats drew nearer.

'Feel free to gawk, though,' Raven added. 'They'll expect that.'

The spy was sitting up now. Rothen turned and peered under the rim of his hat at the approaching magicians. The first to pass the cart was Lord Yikmo, the Warrior who had been Sonea's special tutor last year. The magician did not even glance at Rothen and Raven as he passed.

The other magicians thundered by, kicking up a dense cloud of dust in their wake. Raven coughed and waved a hand.

'Twenty-two,' he said, climbing onto the seat beside Rothen. 'That'll double what's at the Fort. Is the Guild sending magicians to the South Pass?'

'I don't know.'

'Good.'

Rothen looked at Raven, amused.

'The less you know, the less an Ichani can learn from you,' the spy said.

Rothen nodded. 'I do know that the South Pass is being

watched. If the Ichani enter there, the Guild will be alerted. Those at the Fort should have time enough to ride back to Imardin and join the Guild. The distance is about the same, from either pass.'

'Hmmm.' Raven clucked his tongue, as he had a habit of doing when he was thinking hard. 'If I were these Ichani, I would use the South Pass. There are no magicians there, and no Fort, so they can enter without using any power in fighting. That doesn't bode well for us, I'm afraid. Though . . .' He frowned. 'These Ichani do not know how to fight as one. If the entire Guild faces them, it may be able to kill one or two. If the Guild is split, however, there is no danger of that. The Fort may be the better option.'

Rothen shrugged and turned his attention to guiding the gorin back from the side of the road. Raven spent a little time in thoughtful silence.

'Of course, the Ichani may be an invention of the former High Lord,' he said eventually, 'created simply to convince the Guild to let him live. And your former novice believed him.'

Seeing his companion's sidelong look, Rothen scowled. 'So you keep reminding me.'

'If we are to work effectively together, I need to know what is between you and Sonea, and her companion,' Raven said. His tone was respectful but also determined. 'I know it is not simple loyalty to the Guild that motivated you to volunteer for this mission.'

'No.' Rothen sighed. Raven would keep prying until he was satisfied he had all the information he could get. 'She means more to me than just another novice. I took her from the slums and tried to teach her how to fit in.'

'But she didn't.'

412

'No.'

'Then Akkarin took her hostage, and you couldn't do anything about it. Now you can.'

'Maybe. It would be nice if I could just slip into Sachaka and take her back.' Rothen glanced at the spy. 'Somehow I don't think it's going to be as easy as that.'

Raven chuckled. 'It never is. Do you think Sonea might be in love with Akkarin?'

Rothen felt a flash of anger. 'No. She hated him.'

'Enough to learn forbidden magic and follow him into exile, to ensure he survived long enough for, as she put it, the Guild to come to its senses?'

Taking a deep breath, Rothen pushed away a nagging fear. 'If she believes these Ichani exist, it would have been easy for him to convince her to do all those things for the sake of the Guild.'

'Why would he, if the Ichani weren't real?'

'So she would follow him. He needs her.'

'What for?'

'Her strength.'

'Why teach her black magic, then? That gained him nothing.'

'I don't know. She said she asked him to. Perhaps he could not refuse without losing her support.'

'So now she's potentially as powerful as he. If she discovered he was lying, why wouldn't she return to Imardin, or at least tell the Guild?'

Rothen closed his eyes. 'Because . . . just because . . .'

'I know this is distressing,' Raven said in a low voice, 'but we must examine all the possible motivations and consequences before we meet them.'

'I know.' Rothen considered the question, then

grimaced. 'Just because she has learned black magic, doesn't mean she is powerful. Black magicians grow stronger by taking energy from others. If she hasn't had the opportunity to do that, Akkarin may be much more powerful than her. He may also be keeping her weaker by taking all her strength from her each day – and he may have threatened to kill her if she communicates with the Guild.'

'I see.' Raven frowned. 'That doesn't bode well for us either.'

'No.'

'I hate to say it, but I am hoping we find your novice in such a situation. The alternative is much worse, for Kyralia.' He clucked his tongue. 'Now, tell me about your son.'

As Akkarin stopped, Sonea breathed a sigh of relief. Though she had grown used to the long days of walking, every rest was welcome. The morning sun was warm and made her feel sleepy.

Akkarin stood at the top of a short slope, waiting as she trudged up to meet him. Reaching the top, Sonea saw that their way was blocked by another crevasse. This one was broad and shallow. Looking down, she caught her breath.

A ribbon of blue ran down the middle. Water rushed around boulders and cascaded down short drops in the ravine floor before running away toward the wasteland. Trees and other vegetation crowded the banks of this little river, and in places extended out to the rock walls on either side.

'The Krikara River,' Akkarin murmured. 'If we follow it, we will reach the road to the South Pass.'

He looked at the mountains. Sonea followed his gaze

and noted how the gap between the peaks on either side of the ravine was much wider than the rest. She felt a twinge of excitement and longing. Kyralia lay beyond that gap.

'How far to the Pass?'

'It is a long day's walk.' He frowned. 'We should get as close as possible to the road, then wait until darkness.' He looked down at the ravine. 'Though Parika must be at least a day's travel behind us now, his slaves will be there, watching it for him.'

He rose, then turned to face her. Guessing what he intended to do, she grasped his hands.

'Let me do it,' she said, smiling.

Drawing magic to her will, she created a disk beneath their feet, then lifted them up and over the lip of the ravine. She lowered them down between the trees and they landed on a patch of grass.

Looking up, she found Akkarin regarding her closely.

'What are you looking at me like that for?'

He smiled. 'No reason.' He turned away and started walking along the river. Sonea shook her head and followed.

After so long walking in the dry slopes of the mountains, the sight of so much clean running water and vegetation lifted her spirits. She imagined rain falling high up, gathering into streamlets and then streams, all joining to form the river that flowed through this ravine. Glancing behind, she wondered where it ended. Did it continue though the dry wasteland below?

The trees and undergrowth made travelling a little harder, however. Akkarin moved to the shadows by one wall, so they could avoid the vegetation as much as possible. After an hour, they encountered a thick forest that seemed to stretch from one side of the ravine to the other, blocking the river from view. In single file, they pushed their way through undergrowth, and as they walked on, the sound of water splashing over stone grew ever louder. When they emerged into the sunlight again, they found their way blocked by a wide pool.

Sonea drew in a breath. Above them stood a rock wall over which the river fell in wide sheets of water to fill the pool below. The sound of it was deafening after the silence of the mountain slopes. She turned to Akkarin.

'Can we stop?' she asked eagerly. 'We can stop, can't we? I haven't had a real bath for *weeks*.'

Akkarin smiled. 'I guess a short stop won't hurt.'

She grinned at him, then sat on a nearby rock and pulled off her boots. As she stepped into the shallows of the pool, she let out a gasp.

'It's freezing!'

She focussed her mind and sent heat out into the water. Her ankles began to warm. Moving slowly, she waded deeper. She found that she could keep the water around her comfortably heated if she did not move too abruptly and stir up eddies of cold.

As her trousers soaked up the water, they grew heavier. She could see that the pool was much deeper at the middle. When the water was just past knee-deep, she stopped and sat down, immersing herself to the neck.

The rock floor was a little slimy, but she didn't care. Leaning back, she slowly let her head fall beneath the surface. As she came up for air, she heard a sloshing nearby. She turned to see Akkarin wading into the water. He stared intently at the pool then suddenly dived under the surface. A splash of icy cold water engulfed her, and she cursed.

She watched him glide under the water. When he

416

surfaced, his long hair was plastered to his face. He flicked it back and turned to regard her.

'Come here.'

She could see his feet kicking beneath the water. The pool was deep. She shook her head.

'I can't swim.'

He glided a little closer, then rolled onto his back. 'My family used to spend every summer by the sea,' he told her. 'We swam nearly every day.'

Sonea tried to picture him as a boy, swimming in the ocean, and failed. 'I lived near the river a few times, but nobody swims in *that*.'

Akkarin chuckled. 'Not willingly, anyway.'

He turned over again and swam toward the waterfall. As he reached it, his shoulders rose out of the water and he stood regarding the fall. He ran a hand through the curtain of water, then stepped through it.

A faint shadow of him was visible for a moment, then nothing. She waited for him to return. After several minutes she grew curious. What had he found behind there?

She stood up and made her way around the pool. It was little more than ankle deep at first, then grew steadily deeper as she neared the waterfall. By the time she had reached the beginning of the curtain, the pool was past waist deep, but she could feel that the rock slope angled upward under the fall.

She ran a hand through the falling water. It was heavy and cold. Bracing herself, she moved through the curtain and felt her knees meet rock.

A ledge had formed behind the fall, at about shoulder height. Akkarin was sitting in it, his back against the wall and his legs crossed. He smiled at Sonea.

'It's quite private in here, if a bit cramped.'

'And noisy,' she added.

Hoisting herself up onto the ledge, she turned and put her back to the wall. The greens and blues of the outside world coloured the curtain of water.

'It's beautiful,' she said.

'Yes.'

She felt fingers curl around her hand and looked down.

'You're cold,' he said.

He lifted her hand and covered it with both of his. His touch sent a warm shiver down her spine. She looked at him, noting that the stubble on his chin and jaw had grown into thick hair. *He might not look too bad with a beard*, she mused. *And his clothes certainly leave less to the imagination when they're wet.*

He lifted one eyebrow.

'What are you looking at me like that for?'

She shrugged. 'No reason.'

He laughed, then his gaze dropped from her own. She looked down, then felt her face warm as she realised that her own clothes were plastered against her body. She moved to cover herself, but felt his hands tighten about hers. Looking up, she saw the mischievous glint that had entered his gaze, and smiled.

He chuckled and drew her close.

All thoughts of time, the Ichani, and decently dry attire slipped out of her mind. More important matters demanded her attention: the heat of bare skin against skin, the sound of his breathing, pleasure flaring up like fire through her body, and then how comfortable it was, curled up together on the ledge.

Magic has its uses, she thought. *A cold, cramped space can be made warm and cosy. Muscles tired from walking can be revived. To think I once would have given this away, out of hatred for magicians.*

If I had I wouldn't be with Akkarin now.

No, she thought as reality struck hard, *I'd be a blissfully ignorant slum dweller, completely unaware that immensely powerful magicians were about to invade my home. Magicians who will make the Guild look humble and generous.*

She reached out to the falling water. As her fingers met the curtain it parted. In the gap she saw the trees and pool outside . . . and a figure.

She stiffened and snatched her hand away.

Akkarin stirred.

'What is it?'

Her heart was racing. 'Someone is standing beside the pool.'

He drew himself up onto his elbows, then frowned.

'Be quiet a moment,' he murmured.

The muffled sound of voices reached them. Sonea felt her blood turn to ice. Akkarin scanned the wall of water, his eyes halting at a natural gap in the curtain further along the ledge. He slowly pushed himself onto his hands and knees and crept toward the gap.

As he reached it he paused, then his face hardened into a scowl. He turned to her and mouthed a word: Parika.

Reaching for her shirt and trousers, Sonea struggled into them. Akkarin appeared to be listening. She crept to his side.

'. . . no harm. I only sought to be ready for your return,' a woman said meekly. 'See, I have gathered stingberries and tiro nuts.'

'You should not have left the Pass.'

'Riko is there.'

'Riko is asleep.'

'Then punish Riko.'

There was a wordless protest, then a thump. 'Forgive me, master,' the woman whimpered.

'Get up. I don't have time for this. I haven't slept for two days.'

'Are we going straight into Kyralia, then?'

'No. Not until Kariko is ready. I want to be well rested before then.'

Silence followed. Through the curtain of water, Sonea saw movement. Akkarin crept away from the gap to her. She felt his arm circle her waist, and she leaned against the warmth of his chest.

'You're shaking,' he observed.

Sonea drew in a deep, shuddering breath. 'That was too close.'

'Yes,' he said. 'Lucky I hid our boots. Sometimes it pays to be overly cautious.'

Sonea shivered. An Ichani had stood less than twenty strides away. If she hadn't decided to bathe, and Akkarin hadn't discovered the alcove behind the falls . . .

'He's in front of us now,' she said.

Akkarin's grip tightened a little. 'Yes, but it sounds as if Parika is the only Ichani at the Pass. It also sounds as if Kariko plans to invade in the next few days.' He sighed. 'I tried to reach Lorlen, but he isn't wearing the ring. He hasn't put it on in days.'

'So we wait until Parika enters Kyralia, then follow?'

'Or we try to sneak past him tonight, while he sleeps.' He paused, then pushed her away a little so he could regard her. 'It isn't far to the coast from here. From there it would only be a few days' ride to Imardin. If you were to go that way while I—'

'No.' Sonea was surprised by the force of her own voice. 'I'm not leaving you.'

His expression grew stern. 'The Guild needs you, Sonea. They don't have time to learn black magic from my books. They need someone who can train them, and fight for them. If we both go through the Pass, we might both be caught and killed. At least, if you went south, one of us might reach Kyralia.'

Sonea pulled away. It made sense, but she didn't like it. He moved past her and began to dress.

'You need my strength,' she said.

'One more day's strength from you will make no difference. I could never have gained enough power in these last weeks to face an Ichani. I'd need ten or twenty of you.'

'It would not be one more day. It will take another four or five days to get from the Pass to Imardin.'

'Four or five days will make little difference. If the Guild accept my help, I will have hundreds of magicians to draw from. If they don't, they are doomed anyway.'

She shook her head slowly. 'You're the valuable one. You have the knowledge and the skill, and the power we've collected. You should go south.' She looked up at him and frowned. 'If it's safer, why don't we both go south?'

Akkarin picked up his shirt and sighed. 'Because I would not get there in time.'

She stared at him. 'So I wouldn't, either.'

'No, but if I failed, you could help what was left of the Guild regain Kyralia. The rest of the Allied lands will not like having Sachakan black magicians as neighbours. They would—'

'No!' she exclaimed. 'I'm not going to stay away until the battle is over.'

Akkarin pulled his shirt over his head, shrugged into the sleeves, then moved to her side. He took her hand and regarded her intently.

'It would be easier for me to face the Ichani if I did not have to worry about what they might do to you if I fail.'

She stared back at him. 'Do you think it's any easier for me,' she asked softly, 'when I know what they will do to you?'

'At least one of us would be safe if you went south.'

'Why don't you go, then?' she retorted. 'I'll stay and fix the Guild's little Ichani problem.'

His jaw tightened, then his mouth widened into a smile and he chuckled.

'No good. I'd have to come with you to see that for myself.'

She grinned, then grew serious again. 'I'm not going to let you do all the fighting and take all the risks. We face them together.' She paused. 'Well, we should probably avoid facing this one in the Pass. I'm sure, between the two of us, we'll come up with an alternative.'

The stack of letters on Lorlen's desk slowly toppled over. Osen caught them in time, then divided them into two piles.

'This ban on mental communication will generate some extra employment for couriers,' the young magician observed.

'Yes,' Lorlen agreed. 'And pen makers. I'll probably wear them out twice as fast now. How many more letters do we have to answer?'

'This is the last,' Osen replied.

Lorlen signed it with a flourish, then busied himself cleaning the pen.

'It's good to have you back, Osen,' he said. 'I don't know how I would manage without you.'

Osen smiled. 'You wouldn't. Not with the responsibilities of both Administrator and High Lord to look after.' He paused. 'When will we elect a new High Lord?'

Lorlen sighed. It was a subject he had been avoiding. He just couldn't imagine someone other than Akkarin in the role. Yet it would have to be filled eventually – and the sooner the better, if Akkarin's predictions came true.

'Now that the Elyne rebels have been taken care of, candidates will probably be nominated at the next Meet.'

'A month from now?' Osen grimaced and looked at the pile of letters. 'Can't you begin earlier than that?'

'Perhaps. None of the Higher Magicians has suggested we tackle the matter sooner, however.'

Osen nodded. He had been unusually distracted this morning, Lorlen noted.

'What's bothering you?'

The young magician glanced at Lorlen, then frowned.

'Will the Guild reinstate Akkarin if his story does prove to be true?'

Lorlen grimaced. 'I doubt it. Nobody will want a black magician as High Lord. I'm not sure Akkarin would even be accepted back into the Guild.'

'What about Sonea?'

'She defied the King. If the King allows a black magician in the Guild, he will want someone he knows he, or the Guild, can control.'

Osen scowled and looked away. 'So Sonea will never finish her training.'

'No.' As Lorlen said it, he realised it was true and felt a pang of grief.

'The bastard,' Osen hissed, rising from his chair. He paused. 'I'm sorry. I know he was a friend, and you still feel some regard for him. But she could have been . . . something amazing. I knew she was unhappy. It was so obvious he was part of the reason, but I didn't do anything.'

'You couldn't have,' Lorlen said.

Osen shook his head. 'If I'd known, I would have taken her away. Without her as hostage, what could he have done?'

Lorlen looked down at his hand, at the finger the ring had encircled. 'Taken over the Guild? Killed you and Rothen? Don't torture yourself, Osen. You didn't know, and couldn't have helped her if you had.'

The young magician didn't reply. 'You're not wearing that ring any more,' he said suddenly.

Lorlen looked up. 'No. I grew tired of it.' He felt a twinge of anxiety. Had Osen heard enough about blood gems to suspect what it was? If he did, and he remembered that Lorlen had been wearing the ring for a year and a half, he might realise that Lorlen had been aware of Akkarin's secret for much longer than he had admitted.

Osen picked up the two piles of letters and smiled crookedly. 'You don't need me to start lamenting the past. I guess I should make myself useful and arrange couriers for these.'

'Yes. Thank you.'

'I'll be back as soon as I'm done.'

Lorlen watched his assistant stride across the room.

When the door had closed, he regarded his ringless hand again. For so long he had wished he could get rid of it. Now he desperately wanted it back. It was securely locked within the Magicians' Library, however. He could retrieve it at any time . . .

Or could he? He knew what Balkan would say. It was too dangerous. The other Higher Magicians would agree.

Did Balkan, or the others, have to know?

Of course they do. And they're right: it is too dangerous. I just wish I knew what was going on.

Sighing, Lorlen turned his attention back to the requests and letters on his desk.

CHAPTER 26

THE SOUTH PASS

As they approached one of the exits from Cery's rooms, Gol paused and looked back.

'Do you think you ought to tell the other Thieves about these magicians?'

Cery sighed. 'I don't know. I'm not sure if they'd believe me.'

'Perhaps later, when you got proof.'

'Perhaps.'

The big man climbed a ladder to a hatch in the roof. He unbolted it, then cautiously pushed it up. The sound of voices reached Cery's ears. Gol climbed through, then signalled that it was safe for Cery to follow.

He entered a small bol storeroom. Two men sat at a table, playing tiles. They nodded at Cery and Gol politely. Though they knew they were employed to guard one of the entrances to the Thieves' Road, they did not know it led to the lair of a Thief.

The following journey was short, but Cery stopped at a baker and a few other crafters' shops on the way. The owners were as oblivious to their customer's identity as the guards. Cery made a few subtle enquiries about whether they were happy with their arrangements with 'the Thief', and all but one behaved favourably.

'Get someone to check what's up with the matmaker

when we're done,' Cery said to Gol when they had descended into the underground passages again. 'He's not happy about something.'

Gol nodded. When they arrived at their destination, he stepped forward to haul open a heavy metal door. A thin man sat in the short corridor beyond.

'Ren. How's our guest?' Cery asked.

The man stood up. 'He been pacing. Worried, I think.'

Cery frowned. 'Open the door, then.'

Ren stooped and grabbed a chain on the floor. He pulled and a vibration ran through the floor. The far wall slid sideways, revealing a luxurious room.

Takan stood a few paces away, the sound having warned him of their arrival. He looked tense and eager. Cery waited until the door had closed behind Gol before he spoke.

'What is it?'

The Sachakan let out a short breath. 'Akkarin has spoken to me. He has asked me to explain some things to you.'

Cery blinked in surprise, then gestured to the chairs.

'Let's sit, then. I've brought some food and wine.'

Takan moved to a guestroom chair and perched himself on the edge of the seat. Cery sat down opposite him, while Gol disappeared into the kitchen to find plates and glasses.

'You know that these murderers Akkarin employed you to find were Sachakan magicians,' Takan began. 'And you know that Akkarin and Sonea were exiled for using black magic.'

Cery nodded.

'The murderers were former slaves,' Takan explained, 'sent by their masters to spy on Kyralia and the Guild – and kill Akkarin if they had the chance. Their masters are powerful magicians known as the Ichani. They use black magic to draw magical strength from their slaves – or their victims. The people in my country call this higher magic, and have no law against its use.'

'This magic makes them stronger?' Cery asked. Though he knew all this from Savara, he must pretend it was all new.

'Yes. Akkarin learned black magic in my country. I returned to Kyralia with him, and he has been taking strength from me so he could fight the spies.'

'You were a slave?'

Takan nodded.

'You say these murderers – spies – were once slaves. Yet they used black magic, too.'

'They were taught the secret of higher magic so that they might survive long enough to gather information about Kyralia's defences.'

Cery frowned. 'If they were free, why did they continue to do what their masters wanted?'

Takan looked down at the floor. 'Servitude is a hard habit to break, especially when you are born to it,' he said quietly. 'And the spies feared the Guild as much as they feared the Ichani. They saw only two choices: to hide in the enemy's land, or return to Sachaka. Until Akkarin and Sonea were so publicly exiled, most Sachakans believed the Guild still used higher magic. All previous spies had been killed. Sachaka seemed a safer place. The dangers there are familiar. But they knew the Ichani would kill them if they returned without completing their mission'

Gol returned carrying wine, glasses, and a plate laden with meat-filled savoury buns. The big man offered Takan a glass of wine, but the servant shook his head.

'The Ichani know the Guild do not use higher magic now,' Takan continued. 'They know they are stronger. Their leader, a man named Kariko, has been trying to unite them for years. Now he has succeeded. Akkarin contacted me this morning, and told me to tell you this: they plan to enter Kyralia in the next few days. You must warn the Guild.'

'And they'll believe me?' Cery asked dubiously.

'The message must be anonymous, but its recipient will know from the content who it is from. Akkarin has told me what it should contain.'

Cery nodded, then sat back in his chair and took a sip of the wine.

'How much does the Guild know?'

'All but this latest news. They do not believe any of it, but Akkarin hopes they will prepare in case it proves true.' Takan hesitated. 'You do not seem alarmed to learn that your country is about to face a war.'

Cery shrugged. 'Oh, I am. But I am not surprised. I had a feeling something big was about to happen.'

'You are not concerned?'

'Why? It is magicians' business.'

Takan's eyes widened. 'I wish, for your sake, that it was so. But when these Ichani have removed the Guild and the King, they will not leave ordinary people to continue their lives as if nothing happened. Those they do not enslave, they will kill.'

'They have to find us first.'

'They will collapse all your tunnels and tear down your houses. Your secret world will not survive.'

Cery smiled as he thought of Savara's suggestions for killing magicians.

'They won't find it as easy as they think,' he said darkly. 'Not if I have any say in it.'

* * *

Dannyl stepped out of the University and considered the busy courtyard. Midbreak had just begun, and the grounds were full of novices enjoying the summer warmth. He decided to follow their example and take a stroll through the gardens.

As he entered the shady walkways, he considered his interview with Lord Sarrin. Now that the fate of the rebels had been decided, and Rothen had left for Sachaka, Dannyl had very little to do, so he had volunteered to help in the construction of the new Lookout. The Head of Alchemists had been surprised by Dannyl's proposal, as if he had forgotten all about the project.

'The Lookout. Yes. Of course,' Sarrin had said distractedly. 'It'll keep us occupied, unless . . . but then it won't matter. Yes,' he repeated, in a firmer tone. 'You may ask Lord Davin how you may assist.'

On the way out of the University, Dannyl had glimpsed Lord Balkan leaving the Administrator's office. The Warrior had looked worried. That was to be expected, but his manner suggested he had something new on his mind.

I wish I knew what was going on, Dannyl thought. He looked around, noting the tense expressions of a group of novices gathered together nearby. *It looks like I'm not the only one.*

He turned a corner and noted a lone novice sitting on a garden seat. The boy was older, probably a fifth year, and very thin and sickly. He looked strangely familiar.

Dannyl stopped as he realised this was no boy. It was Farand. He stepped off the path and approached the garden seat.

'Farand.'

The young man looked up, then smiled self-consciously.

'Ambassador.'

Dannyl sat down. 'I see they've got you a set of robes. Have you started training yet?'

Farand nodded. 'Private lessons for now. I'm hoping they're going to spare me the humiliation of joining the younger novices.'

Dannyl chuckled. 'And miss all the fooling around?'

'From what I've heard, you didn't have an easy time as a novice.'

'No.' Dannyl sobered. 'Not in the first few years. But don't let my experiences put you off. I've heard some magicians say their years in the University were their most enjoyable.'

The young man frowned. 'I was hoping it would all be easier from here, but I'm beginning to wonder. I've heard it said that the Guild is facing a war. We're going to either fight Akkarin, or Sachakan magicians. Either way, nobody is sure if we'll win.'

Dannyl nodded. 'You may have joined the Guild at the worst possible time, Farand. But if you hadn't, you would not have escaped the strife for long. If Kyralia falls to either enemy, Elyne would fall soon after.'

'Better that I'm here, then. I'd rather be a help, than gain a few safe months at home.' Farand paused, then sighed. 'I have only one regret, however.'

'Dem Marane.'

'Yes.'

'It is my one regret, too,' Dannyl admitted. 'I had hoped the Guild would be more forgiving.'

'I think, perhaps, this strife with your High Lord influenced the decision. The Guild ought to have noticed that its leader had learned black magic. It hadn't, so it didn't want to make the same mistake twice. And it should have executed Akkarin, but it couldn't. So it dealt out the full punishment to the next man to break that law, to show itself and the world that it would not condone such crimes.' Farand paused. 'I'm not saying that each magician was aware of this, just that the situation may have influenced their thinking.'

Dannyl glanced at Farand, surprised at the young man's perceptiveness. 'So we have Akkarin to blame.'

Farand shook his head. 'I'm done with blaming people. I am here, where I was supposed to be all along. I'm expected to put all political matters behind me, and that is what I will do.' He hesitated. 'Though I am not sure I could have if my sister hadn't been pardoned.'

Dannyl nodded. 'Did you see her before she left?'

'Yes.'

'How is she?'

'She grieves, but the children will give her something to hold to. I will miss them all.' He looked up as the gong signalling the end of midbreak rang out. 'Time to go. Thank you for stopping to talk to me, Ambassador. Will you be returning to Elyne soon?'

'Not for a while. Administrator Lorlen wants as many magicians to remain here as possible, until he knows more about Sachaka.'

'Then I hope I have an opportunity to talk to you again, Ambassador.' Farand bowed, then strode away.

Dannyl watched the young man leave. Farand had been through so much, and faced the prospect of death three times – through loss of control, poisoning, and possible execution. Somehow he managed to view it all without resentment.

It was humbling. And his thoughts on the reason for Dem Marane's execution were interesting.

He might make a good Ambassador one day, Dannyl mused. *If he gets the chance.*

But for now, the Guild could only go on as it always had. Dannyl sighed, stood up and went in search of Lord Davin.

Something brushed against Sonea's lips. She blinked her eyes open and stared at the face hovering above hers. Akkarin.

He smiled and kissed her again. 'Wake up,' he murmured, then he straightened, took her hand and pulled her to her feet. She looked around. An eerie half-light had turned everything to grey. The sky was covered in cloud, but she guessed it was too early for the sun to have dropped below the horizon yet.

'We should find the road now, before the sun sets,' Akkarin said. 'It will be very dark until the moon rises, and we can't afford to stop.'

Sonea yawned and looked up at the gap between the two peaks. They had left the waterfall after the Ichani's visit that morning, and continued up the ravine as far as they dared. A small space between some boulders and the rock wall had provided enough shelter to hide them as they slept. While it was not as concealed as the ledge behind the waterfall, there was no reason for the Ichani or his slaves to visit it.

Now, as the ravine narrowed and the light faded, the way became steadily more difficult. The small river filled most of the ravine, and the banks were strewn with huge rocks. After an hour or so, Akkarin stopped and pointed up at the ravine wall. In the fading light, Sonea could only see that a steep rock slope continued up from just beyond the top. Then Sonea blinked in surprise as she made out the stone steps hewn into the wall.

'The road runs alongside the ravine from here,' Akkarin murmured.

He started toward the stairs. They reached the base, then began to climb. When they finally reached the top, the darkness was like a thick smoke all around, and Akkarin a warm shadow within it.

'Be as silent as you can,' he murmured into her ear. 'Put one hand to the rock wall. If you want to speak, take hold of my hand so we can communicate mind to mind without the Ichani hearing us.'

A persistent wind tugged at them now that they were out of the shelter of the ravine. Akkarin walked in front, setting a steady pace. She let her right hand brush the rock wall, and tried to keep her footsteps light. The occasional stone clattered across the ground as she or Akkarin disturbed it, but the sound was blown away by the wind.

After a long stretch of walking, Sonea found she could make out another wall several hundred paces to their left. She wondered how she could see it, then looked up. The peaks above were glowing faintly, bathed in moonlight filtering through the clouds.

The ravine was gone and the road continued along the floor of a narrow valley. Sonea moved to Akkarin's side, and they strode on. As the hours passed, the left-hand wall drew closer, then fell back out of sight again. It returned, and the right-hand wall withdrew. The moon rose higher, then dipped down toward the peaks.

Much later the road started to twist and turn. It began to follow the curve of a rocky slope. The higher they climbed, the steeper the slope became, and soon they were walking with a cliff wall on one side and a precipice on the other. Still they strode onward.

Then she heard a faint noise ahead and Akkarin stopped. The sound came again.

A sneeze.

They crept forward to the next turn in the road. Akkarin reached out and squeezed her hand.

—*That must be Riko*, Akkarin sent.

In the faint moonlight, Sonea made out the dark shape of a man sitting on a rock beside the road. She could hear him shivering. As he rubbed his arms, something glinted on his finger. A blood ring, she guessed.

—*Parika probably took his outer clothing from him to ensure he stayed awake*, Akkarin added.

—*This makes things difficult*, Sonea replied. *How are we going to get past the slave as well as his master? Do we trick both of them?*

—*Yes and no. The slave can be our bait. Are you ready?*

—*Yes.*

It was not easy forcing herself to step past the turn in the road, knowing that the man would see them. Riko was too wrapped up in his misery to see them at first. Then he looked up, leapt to his feet and fled.

Akkarin stopped, cursed loudly, then propelled Sonea backward.

'A slave!' he said, loud enough for Riko to hear. 'There must be someone in the Pass. Come on.'

They ran back down the road. Akkarin slowed and stared up at the rock walls on either side. He pulled Sonea to a halt. She felt the ground shift, then they were rising up in the air.

The cliff face sped past, then slowed and they moved into a shadow. Sonea felt her feet touch solid rock. The ledge Akkarin had set them upon was barely wide enough for her boots. She leaned back against the wall, her heart hammering.

A long silence followed in which the only sound was their breathing. Then a figure appeared below, walking cautiously around the turn in the road. It stopped. Akkarin's hand tightened around hers.

—*He needs a little encouragement*, Akkarin observed.

From the distance came the sound of a rock skittering against the road. The figure took a step forward, then a light blazed into existence, flooding the area. Sonea caught her breath. The man was dressed in a fine coat and his hands glittered with jewels and precious metals.

—*Great*, she replied. *Now he has only to look up and he'll see us.*

—*He won't.*

A thin, hunched man shuffled up behind the Ichani.

'I saw—'

'I know what you saw. Go back and stay with—'

The Ichani suddenly broke into a half run. Looking down the road, Sonea saw that a light was visible behind the next turn, several hundred paces down the road. It was fading, as if moving away. She looked at Akkarin, guessing that he was the source of the light. His forehead was creased with a frown of concentration.

The Ichani hurried on, passed the turn and disappeared. When Sonea looked down again, the slave was gone. Akkarin drew in a deep breath.

—*We haven't got much time. Let's hope Riko obeys his master promptly.*

They descended to the road, then hurried on toward the Pass. At every step, Sonea was sure they would catch up with the slave, but it wasn't until several hundred paces later that they saw the man ahead of them.

Soon after, they saw a flickering light in the distance. A fire, Sonea saw with relief. She had dreaded that they would discover another Ichani. Riko reached the fire and sat down beside a younger woman.

Akkarin and Sonea drew closer, keeping to the shadows. The fire lit steep rock walls on either side of the road.

—We can't slip past without them noticing, Akkarin sent. *Are you ready to run?*

Sonea nodded.

—As ready as I'm going to get.

Akkarin did not move, however. She glanced at him, and saw that he was frowning.

—What is it?

—I should take the opportunity to divest Parika of his slaves. They will only be used against us later.

Sonea felt her blood go cold as she realised what he intended to do.

—But there is no time . . .

—Best make it quick, then.

He let go of her hand and started forward.

She bit back a protest. Killing the slaves made sense. Their strength would be used to kill Kyralians. Yet it seemed so cruel to kill people who had been victims all their lives. They hadn't chosen to be Ichani tools.

The woman was the first to notice Akkarin. She jumped up then flew backward as a force slammed into her. She landed on the ground and lay still.

Riko had bolted down the road. As Akkarin broke into

a run, Sonea dashed after him. Somewhere behind them, Parika would have seen the attack through the slave's blood ring. She paused only to look at the woman. Her eyes stared sightlessly at the sky.

At least it was quick, Sonea thought.

A light flared above Akkarin's head and he lengthened his stride. The road twisted about, but sloped downward now. Sonea caught no glimpses of the slave running ahead of them. She could not help hoping he would remain out of sight. Akkarin could not kill someone he could not see.

Then they heard a scream from the road ahead. Akkarin checked, then ran faster. He drew ahead of Sonea easily, rounding the next corner several strides before she did. As he reached the turn, she saw that the road ahead twisted sharply. It left the confining walls of the Pass, and hugged the steep side of a mountain. Akkarin was standing at the turn, looking over the precipice. She stopped beside him and peered over the edge, but saw only darkness below.

'He fell?'

'I think so,' he panted. He looked at the road ahead. It curved along the side of the mountain for several hundred paces before it turned out of sight. 'Nowhere . . . to hide. He was . . . not that far ahead.' He glanced behind, and his face hardened. 'We must . . . keep going. If Parika follows . . . we'll be as exposed.'

He started forward. They pounded along the road. When they passed the next turn, Sonea's relief turned to dismay when she saw another long stretch of exposed road. They kept running. Her back prickled, and she resisted the urge to glance over her shoulder.

Time stretched out as they sprinted on. The road descended steadily. The sense of urgency and fear faded.

Weariness grew until it dominated all her thoughts. She healed it away.

Surely we can stop now, she thought, over and over. *Parika wouldn't follow us into Kyralia, would he?*

But Akkarin continued on.

How many times can I Heal myself like this? Can I damage my body doing it too often?

When Akkarin finally slowed to a walk, she let out a great sigh of relief. He chuckled, then put an arm around her shoulder. She looked around and realised they were walking between trees. The moon was gone. Akkarin reduced his globe light to a faint glow. They walked for another long hour or more, then Akkarin steered her off the road.

'I think we've come far enough,' he murmured.

'What if he follows us?'

'He won't. He won't enter Kyralia until Kariko does.'

She felt soft, uneven ground beneath her feet. They walked for several minutes, then Akkarin stopped and sat down, his back to a tree. Sonea collapsed beside him.

'What now?' she asked, staring at the trees around them.

Akkarin pulled her close to his chest, and wrapped his arms around her.

'Sleep, Sonea,' he whispered. 'I will watch. We'll decide what to do next tomorrow.'

CHAPTER 27

A SURPRISE MEETING

*N*o. *It's too soon to wake up*, Sonea thought. *I'm still too tired*.

But a growing feeling of unease would not let her slip back into sleep. Her back leaned against something warm; she was sitting mostly upright. She drew in a deep breath and felt the weight of arms around her. Akkarin's arms. She smiled, then opened her eyes.

Four slim, hair-covered legs stood before her. Horse's legs. Her heart skipped a beat and she looked up.

Familiar blue eyes stared back at her. Green robes, half-covered by a heavy black cloak, shone in the late morning sunlight. She felt her heart fill with joy and relief.

'Dorrien!' she gasped. 'You have no idea how good it is to see you.'

His expression was cold, however. The horse shifted its feet and shook its head. Sonea heard the snort of another nearby. She looked to one side and saw that four more riders waited several strides away, dressed in plain clothes.

Akkarin stirred, then drew in a deep breath.

'What are you doing here?' Dorrien demanded.

'I . . . we . . .' Sonea shook her head. 'I don't know where to start, Dorrien.'

'We are here to warn you,' Akkarin replied. She felt the

vibration of his voice against her back. 'The Ichani plan to enter Kyralia in the next few days.'

His hands caught her shoulders and pushed her gently forward. She rose and stepped aside as he climbed to his feet.

'You are exiles,' Dorrien's voice was low. 'You cannot return to this land.'

Akkarin's eyebrows rose. 'Cannot?' he asked, straightening and crossing his arms.

'Do you intend to fight me?' Dorrien asked, his eyes glittering dangerously.

'No,' Akkarin replied. 'I intend to help you.'

Dorrien's eyes narrowed. 'We do not require your help,' he snapped. 'We require your *absence*.'

Sonea stared at Dorrien. She had never seen him like this, so cold and full of hatred. He sounded like a stranger. A foolish, angry stranger.

Then she remembered how passionate he was about caring for the people in his village. He would risk everything to protect them. And if he still regarded her as he once had, finding her sleeping in Akkarin's arms would not put him in the best of moods . . .

'Dorrien,' she said. 'We would not have come back if we hadn't felt we must.'

Dorrien glanced at her and scowled. 'Whether you must return or not is for the Guild to judge. I have been ordered to watch the road and turn you back if you try to return,' he said. 'If you intend to remain, you will have to kill me first.'

Sonea's heart skipped a beat. A memory of the dead slave flashed though her mind. Surely Akkarin wouldn't . . .

'I don't have to kill you,' Akkarin replied.

Dorrien's eyes were like two chips of ice. He opened his mouth to speak.

'We'll go back,' Sonea said quickly. 'But at least let us deliver our news first.' She laid a hand on Akkarin's arm.

—*He's thinking with his heart. If we give him time to think this over, he may be more reasonable.*

Akkarin frowned at her, but did not argue. She turned back to find Dorrien regarding her closely.

'Very well,' he said with obvious reluctance. 'Tell me your news.'

'You're watching the pass, so no doubt Lorlen has informed you of the threat from Sachaka. Yesterday morning, Sonea and I narrowly avoided capture by an Ichani named Parika,' Akkarin said. 'From his conversation with his slave, we learned that Kariko and his allies plan to enter Kyralia in the next few days. Sonea and I intended to stay in Sachaka until the Guild satisfied itself that the Ichani were real and a threat, but time is running out. If the Guild want us to return and assist in the coming battle, we must be close enough to Imardin to reach it before the Ichani do.'

Dorrien regarded Akkarin impassively. 'Is that all?'

Sonea opened her mouth to tell him about the Ichani in the South Pass, but then she pictured Dorrien riding up into the mountains to investigate for himself. The Ichani would kill him. She choked back the words.

'At least let us rest here for today,' she pleaded. 'We are exhausted.'

Dorrien's eyes slid to Akkarin and narrowed, then he glanced over his shoulder at the other riders.

'Gaden. Forren. Might the Guild loan your horses for a day?'

Sonea peered over the flank of Dorrien's horse at the men. They exchanged glances, then two began to dismount.

'I have no authority to grant you a day or even an hour in Kyralia,' Dorrien said stiffly, as the men led their horses forward. 'I will escort you to the Pass.'

Akkarin eyes burned dangerously. Sonea felt him tense. She tightened her grip on his arm.

—*No! Let me talk to him on the way. He will listen to me.*

He turned to regard her, his expression sceptical. Sonea felt her face warm.

—*We were almost intimate once. I think he is angry because you took me away.*

Akkarin's eyebrows rose. He regarded Dorrien appraisingly.

—*Really? Then see what you can do. Just don't take too long.*

As one of the men drew near, Akkarin stepped forward and took the offered reins. The man shrank away, glancing nervously up at Dorrien. The young magician said nothing as Akkarin swung up into the saddle. Sonea approached the other horse and managed to haul herself up onto its back. Akkarin turned back to regard Dorrien.

'After you,' the Healer said.

Sonea's horse followed as Akkarin turned his mount and urged it toward the road. They travelled single file, making private conversation impossible. All the way through the forest she could feel Dorrien's eyes on her back.

When they reached the road, Sonea pulled back on the reins so that her horse slowed. When it was walking beside Dorrien's, she glanced at the Healer, but suddenly could not think of what she should say. It would be so easy to anger him further.

She thought back to the days she had spent with him in the Guild. It seemed a long time ago. Had he hoped he would regain her interest one day? Though she had made no promises, she felt a pang of guilt. Her heart was Akkarin's. She had never felt this strongly about Dorrien.

'I did not believe Rothen when he first told me,' Dorrien murmured.

Sonea turned to look at him, surprised that he had broken the silence.

He was watching Akkarin. 'I still can't.' His eyebrows knit together. 'Once he told me Akkarin's reasons for taking your guardianship from him, I understood why you put a distance between us. You thought I might see how unhappy you were and start to ask questions.' He looked at her. 'That was it, wasn't it?'

She nodded.

'What happened? When did he turn you away from us?'

She felt another pang of guilt. 'About . . . two months ago he asked me to come with him into the city. I didn't want to go, but I thought I might learn something that the Guild could use against him. He took me to see a man – a Sachakan man – and taught me how to read the man's mind. What I saw in it could only be the truth.'

'Are you sure? If the man believed things that were wrong, you—'

'I am no fool, Dorrien.' She held his gaze. 'That man's memories could not have been false.'

He frowned. 'Go on.'

'Once I knew about these Ichani, and that their leader only needed to prove that the Guild was weak to gather enough allies to invade, I couldn't stand by and let Akkarin do all the work. I asked – no, I insisted – that he let me join him.'

'But . . . *black magic*, Sonea. How could you learn such things?'

'It was not an easy choice. I knew it was a terrible responsibility, and a great risk. But if the Ichani attacked, the Guild would be destroyed. I'd probably die anyway.'

Dorrien's nose wrinkled as if he had smelled something foul. 'But it is evil.'

She shook her head. 'The early Guild didn't think so. I'm not sure I do either. On the other hand, I wouldn't want the Guild to begin using it again. If I imagine Fergun or Regin wielding that kind of power . . .' she shuddered. 'Not a good idea.'

'But you consider yourself worthy?'

She frowned. The question still bothered her. 'I don't know. I hope so.'

'You admitted to using it to kill.'

'Yes.' She sighed. 'Do you believe I'd do something like that just for the sake of making myself stronger? Or do you think I had a good reason?'

He looked away, at Akkarin. 'I don't know.'

She followed his gaze. Akkarin's horse walked about twenty paces ahead.

'But you think Akkarin would kill for power, don't you?'

'Yes,' Dorrien admitted. 'He admitted that he has killed many times before.'

'If he hadn't, he'd still be a slave in Sachaka – or dead – and the Guild would have been attacked and destroyed years ago.'

'If he speaks the truth.'

'He does.'

Dorrien shook his head and looked away into the forest.

'Dorrien, you must tell the Guild that the Ichani are coming,' she urged. 'And . . . let us remain this side of the mountains. The Ichani know we came through last night. If we go back, we will be killed.'

He turned to stare at her, his expression wavering between alarm and disbelief.

Then a figure stepped out onto the road in front of them.

Sonea reacted instinctively, but the shield she threw around herself and Dorrien crumpled before a powerful forcestrike. She felt herself thrown backward, then the ground knocked the air from her lungs. She heard Dorrien curse nearby, then hooves thundered around her head and she threw up another shield. A shrill whinny was followed by the rapid beat of receding hoof beats as the horses fled.

Get up, she told herself. *Get up and find Akkarin!*

She rolled and scrambled to her feet. In the corner of her eye she saw Dorrien crouching nearby. Akkarin stood several strides away.

Between her and Akkarin stood Parika.

Sonea felt her stomach sink and twist with fear. Akkarin was not strong enough to fight an Ichani. Not even with her help, and Dorrien would make little difference.

The air flashed as Akkarin attacked the Ichani. Parika retaliated with powerful strikes.

'Sonea.'

She glanced at Dorrien as he moved to her side.

'This is an Ichani?'

'Yes. His name is Parika. Do you believe me now?'

He did not reply. She grabbed his wrist.

—Akkarin is not strong enough to fight him. We have to help.

—Very well. But I will not kill unless I am sure he is what you say he is.

They struck together, battering the Ichani's shield. The Ichani paused, then looked over his shoulder. His lips curled into a disdainful sneer as his gaze settled on Dorrien. Then his eyes shifted to Sonea. His sneer changed to a malicious smile. He turned his back on Akkarin, and started toward her.

Sonea backed away. She attacked with strike after strike, but they did not stop him advancing. Flashes came from Dorrien but his efforts appeared to have no effect either. Akkarin continued pounding Parika's shield, but the Ichani ignored him.

Dorrien began to move away from her, and Sonea realised he was hoping to draw Parika's attention aside. The Ichani paid him no attention. As his strikes grew more powerful, she allowed him to drive her down the road.

Think, she told herself. *There must be a way out of this. Remember Lord Yikmo's lessons.*

She attacked Parika's shield from all directions, and found it whole and impenetrable. She considered all kinds of false strikes and tricks she'd used in classes, but most relied on the adversary trying to save power by weakening his shield. All she could do was try to trick him into using up his strength.

Then Dorrien stepped between her and the Ichani. Parika's expression darkened. He stopped and sent several blasts of power at the Healer. Dorrien staggered backward, his shield wavering. Sonea hurried forward and extended her shield over his. As she did, she felt her own powers beginning to dwindle. Dorrien caught her arm.

—He is so strong!

—Yes, and I can't do this much longer.

—We have to get away. He grabbed her arm and pulled her down the road.

—But Akkarin—

—Is doing well enough. We can't do anything more.

—He isn't strong enough.

—Then we're all doomed.

Another blast shook her. She let Dorrien pull her into a run. The next strike propelled them on. She reached for more power and knew it was the last of her strength.

As the next strike shattered her shield, she gasped. Glancing over her shoulder, she saw Parika striding toward her. Akkarin was hurrying after them. She began to run.

Then a force hit her side. She felt the air rush from her lungs and felt the ground smash into her shoulder. For a moment, she could only lie still on her back, stunned by the twin blows. Then she forced herself up onto her elbows.

Dorrien lay several paces away, still and pale. Alarmed, she tried to stand up, but another blow sent her sprawling again. She felt the sting of a shield slide over her and her heart froze with terror. A hand grabbed her arm and pulled her to her knees. Parika stared down at her, his mouth twisting into a cruel smile. She stared back in horror and disbelief.

It can't end this way!

The Ichani's shield vibrated as it was struck over and over. She glimpsed Akkarin standing only strides away, his expression terrible. The Ichani shifted his grasp from her arm to her wrist, then reached into his coat.

As she saw the curved knife he drew out, her mind went blank with fear. She struggled uselessly. Then the pain of the blade slicing open her skin brought a memory of another cut that she had made.

'Heal yourself,' Akkarin instructed. 'Always heal yourself without delay. Even half-healed cuts are a break in your barrier.'

She had no power left, but while she was alive, there was always a little energy left. And Healing such a small cut only took . . . there!

Parika went still. He stared at her arm. The blade slowly descended and touched her skin again. She focussed her will and felt the pain fade. The Ichani's eyes widened. He cut her again, deeper, and made a disbelieving noise as the wound sealed before his eyes.

They do not know how to Heal. She felt a moment's triumph, but it faded quickly. She couldn't keep Healing herself forever. She would eventually grow too exhausted even for that.

But perhaps there was another way to turn this skill to her advantage?

Of course there is.

He was holding on to her wrist. Skin against skin. That made him almost as vulnerable to her Healing powers as she was to black magic. Closing her eyes, she sent her mind outward, into his arm. She almost lost her concentration as she felt the sting of another cut. Pausing only to Heal herself, she dove deeper into his body. To his shoulder. Into his chest. She felt the pain of another cut . . .

There, she thought in triumph. His heart. With the last of her strength, she took hold and twisted.

The Ichani gave a half scream, half gasp, and let her go. She fell backward and scrambled away as he fell to his knees, clutching at his chest.

He remained frozen. Poised on the brink of death. She watched, fascinated, as his face slowly turned blue.

'Get away from him!'

Sonea jumped at Akkarin's shout. He dove forward and scooped up the Ichani's knife from where the man had dropped it. With a sweep of his arm, he slashed at the back of the man's neck, then pressed his hand to the wound.

Realising what he was doing, Sonea relaxed. Akkarin might as well take Parika's remaining power. The Ichani was going to die anyway, and he might even have quite a bit of strength left . . .

Then the significance of Akkarin's words came to her. If Parika died with magic still stored within his body, that power would consume his body and probably blast everything around it. She scrambled to her feet and backed away.

Akkarin straightened then. He dropped the knife and let Parika slump to the ground. A few steps later he was gathering her close, his arms squeezing the air out of her lungs.

'I thought I'd lost you,' he whispered hoarsely. He drew in a deep, shuddering breath. 'You should have run as soon as he appeared.'

She felt bruised and exhausted, but as Healing magic flowed from Akkarin she felt strength return. 'I told you. I won't leave you. If we die, we die together.'

He drew back a little and looked down at her, amused. 'That's very flattering, but what about Dorrien?'

'*Dorrien!*'

He muttered a curse and turned to regard Dorrien, lying several paces away. They hurried to the Healer's side. Dorrien's eyes were open and glazed with pain.

Akkarin placed a hand on the Healer's head.

'You're badly wounded,' he said. 'Stay still.'

Dorrien's eyes shifted to Akkarin. 'Save your strength,' he whispered.

'Don't be ridiculous,' Akkarin replied.

'But—'

'Close your eyes and help me,' Akkarin said sternly. 'You know this discipline better than I.'

'But—'

'You are more useful to me alive than dead, Dorrien,' Akkarin said dryly, with a hint of command. 'You can replace the strength I use to heal you later, if you wish to.'

Dorrien's eyes widened with understanding.

'Oh.' He paused, then looked at Sonea. 'What happened to the Sachakan?'

Sonea felt her face warm. Using Healing power to kill seemed like the worst abuse of the discipline.

'He's dead. I'll tell you later.'

Dorrien closed his eyes. Watching closely, Sonea saw colour slowly come back to his face.

'Let me guess,' Akkarin said quietly. 'You stopped his heart.'

She looked up to find him watching her. He nodded at Dorrien. 'He is doing all the Healing now. I'm just supplying the strength.' He looked toward the Sachakan. 'Am I right?'

Sonea glanced at Dorrien, then nodded.

'You said Parika would not enter Kyralia.'

Akkarin frowned. 'Perhaps he wanted revenge for the deaths of his slaves. Strong slaves are rare, and Ichani do get angry if one is killed or taken from them. It's like losing a prize horse. I don't know why he'd bother, though. It's been hours since we arrived, and he must have known it would be difficult to find us once we left the road.'

Dorrien stirred and opened his eyes. 'That will do,' he said. 'I feel like I've been smashed into small pieces, then put together again, but I'll live.'

He gingerly pushed himself up onto his elbows. His gaze slid to the dead Ichani. A shudder ran through him, then he looked at Akkarin.

'I believe you. What do you want me to do now?'

'Get away from the Pass.' Akkarin helped Dorrien to his feet. 'And send a warning to the Guild. Do you have any—'

—Lorlen!

—Makin?

—Strangers are attacking the Fort!

Sonea stared at Akkarin. He gazed back at her. An image of a road flashed through Sonea's mind, seen from above. She recognised it as the road on the Sachakan side of the Fort. Several men and women, dressed in similar clothes to Parika's, stood in a line. The air blazed with their strikes.

'Too late for warnings,' Dorrien muttered. 'They're here already.'

CHAPTER 28

THE INVASION BEGINS

As Cery looked around at the crowds, he felt a small pang of jealousy. The two Thieves whose territory included the Market, Sevli and Limek, were very rich men, and today it was not hard to see why. Bright sunlight glinted off an endless stream of coins passed from customers to stallholders, and a small part of that income taken in exchange for services would quickly add up to a fortune.

A server approached the table and set down two mugs. Savara sipped at hers, closed her eyes and sighed.

'You do have good raka here,' she said. 'Almost as good as ours.'

Cery smiled. 'I ought to get some in from Sachaka, then.'

An eyebrow lifted in warning. 'That would be expensive. Not many merchants risk travelling across the wastes.'

'No? Why is that?'

She gestured around them. 'We have nothing like this. No markets. Each Ashaki owns many hundred slaves—'

'Ashaki?'

'Powerful free men. Slaves provide almost everything they need. They tend the fields, make cloth, cook, clean, entertain, almost anything the Ashaki needs. If a slave has a special talent, like making beautiful pottery, or the Ashaki owns a mine or produces more of a crop than he can use, he will trade with other Ashaki.'

'So why do merchants bother going there?'

'If they do manage to attract a buyer, they can make a considerable profit. Selling luxuries, mostly.'

Cery considered the cloth in the next stall. It had appeared in markets the year before, after one of the crafters had invented a way to make the surface glossy. 'Sounds like there'd be no profit in Sachakans coming up with a better way to make something.'

'No, but a slave might, if he has ambition or if he wants to be rewarded. He might try to attract attention by creating something beautiful and unusual.'

'So only pretty things get better.'

She shook her head. 'Ways of processing or making ordinary products do improve, if the change is simple. A slave might work out a quicker way of harvesting raka if his master wanted it done faster and would beat him if he failed.'

Cery frowned. 'I like our way better. Why beat someone, when greed or having to feed a family will get a man to work smarter and faster?'

Savara laughed quietly. 'That's an interesting view, coming from a man in your position.' Then she sobered. 'I like your way better, too. Aren't you going to drink your raka?'

Cery shook his head.

'Are you afraid someone will recognise you and slip in some poison?'

He shrugged.

'It's gone cold now, anyway.' She stood up. 'Let's move on.'

They walked down to the end of the row of stalls, where she stopped at a table covered in jars and bottles.

'What is this for?'

The vessel she had picked up held two preserved sevli, floating in a green liquid.

'A key to the doors of delight,' the stall owner replied. 'One sip and you will have the strength of a fighter.' His voice lowered. 'Two, and you will experience pleasure that lasts a day and a night. Three, and the dreams you will have shall—'

'Turn into nightmares, which don't stop for days,' Cery finished. He took the jar from her hands and put it back on the counter. 'You couldn't pay me to . . . Savara?'

She was staring into the distance, her face pale.

'It's started,' she said, so quietly he barely heard her. 'The Ichani are attacking the Fort.'

He felt a chill run down his spine. Taking her arm, he pulled her away from the stall and anyone who might overhear them.

'You can see this?'

'Yes,' she said. 'The Guild magicians there are sending out mental images.' She paused, and her eyes focussed beyond the market. 'The first gate just fell. Can we go somewhere quiet so I can watch uninterrupted? Somewhere close by?'

Cery looked for Gol and found his second standing nearby, eating a pachi. He signalled rapidly in the Thieves' sign language. Gol nodded and started in the direction of the Marina.

'I have the perfect place,' Cery told Savara. 'I think you'll like it. Ever been on a boat?'

'You have a *boat*?' She smiled. 'But of course you do.'

An image of eight richly dressed men and women, seen

from above, flashed into Dannyl's mind. Each was striking at a point somewhere below Lord Makin, the magician sending the image.

The scene shifted beyond the attackers to a crowd of men and women standing several paces behind them. They were dressed in plain, worn clothes, and some held ropes tied to the collars of small limek-like animals.

Are these people the slaves Akkarin spoke of? Dannyl wondered.

The scene blurred, then the attackers were in view again. They had stopped striking the Fort, and were approaching it cautiously.

—*The Captain says the first gate has been destroyed. The Sachakans are moving into the Fort. We're heading down to meet them.*

In the pause that followed Makin's call, the images stopped and Dannyl became aware of his surroundings again. He glanced around the room. For the last hour he had been entertained by an argument between Lord Peakin, Head of Alchemic Studies, and Lord Davin, the magician who had proposed rebuilding the Lookout. The pair were now staring at each other in dismay, their argument forgotten.

—*We are in position*, Makin reported. *They are attacking the inner door now.*

The image that followed was of a darkened corridor blocked by a wall of stone. The corridor vibrated with the sound of two impacts. Makin and the warriors beside him held a shield ready.

Then the wall exploded inward. The shield was pelted with rubble, then covered by a cloud of dust. Through the haze came strikes, then another explosion battered the corridor.

—We have attacked the Sachakans from below a false floor, Makin explained.

Confusing images followed. Flashes of light brightened the dust beyond the shield, but revealed nothing. Then a shadow appeared in the cloud and the attack on the Warriors' shield resumed. Two magicians staggered backward, clearly exhausted.

—Back away. To the door.

The Warriors retreated hastily through a set of metal doors. Makin propelled the doors shut and used magic to draw huge bolts out of the walls to lock them in position.

—Report, Makin ordered.

A jumbled mix of images and messages followed.

—Most of us are dead . . . I can see five . . . no six bodies and . . .

—They're inside the Fort! An image of a door hanging from one hinge flashed into Dannyl's mind, then he saw a Sachakan striding down a corridor toward him.

—Run!

—Come back! I'm trapped!

Hands reached through the dust. In one was a curved blade. A sense of overwhelming panic followed . . . then nothing.

Names of the Warriors were called, as friends and family in the Guild ignored the ban on mental communication. A confusion of mental voices followed.

—Please be silent! Balkan called above the panic. *I cannot help them if I cannot hear them. Makin?*

An image of the metal doors cut through the other magicians' communications. They were glowing red, filling the corridor with heat. Slowly the centre melted away.

—Back, Makin ordered. *Behind the wall. Let them waste their strength.*

The Warriors hurried past a wall half blocking the corridor. They gathered beyond it. The stone slab slowly began to move. It slid across to slot into a gap in the wall. There was a heavy thump as a mechanism within the side walls fell into place.

The magicians waited.

—If they get through this, Makin sent, *we hit them with everything we have left.*

Mental calls from other magicians punctuated the tense silence of the corridor. Dannyl winced as, one by one, the three remaining magicians in the Fort were killed.

Then, without warning, the stone wall erupted. The Warriors had let their shield drop to save their strength. Makin's communication wavered as something struck his temple, but strengthened again when he spared himself a little Healing power. He joined with those who had thrown up a shield, then glanced around to see that two of the Warriors lay on the floor.

The attack on their shield was no weaker than before. The Warriors staggered backward as each succumbed to exhaustion. Makin felt an awful disbelief as his own strength failed. The shield shattered, and two more magicians fell to strikes.

—Get away, Balkan called. *You've done all you can.*

Figures strode out of the dust cloud. Makin stepped aside as the first reached him. The man gave Makin a dismissive glance and walked past.

—If the guard have followed orders, the last door should have been secured when the first one fell, Makin sent.

The lead Sachakan stopped before the door. Six more

Sachakans strode past Makin to join the first. It took one blast to fling the doors off their hinges. The Sachakans stepped out into the sunlight.

'Welcome to Kyralia,' the leader said, glancing at his companions. Then he turned and regarded the corridor. His eyes snapped to Makin. 'You. You're the one sending this.'

An invisible force pushed Makin forward. Dannyl felt Makin's fear, then the magician's communication abruptly stopped.

Dannyl blinked and found himself staring at his surroundings again. Peakin staggered to a chair and collapsed into it.

'It's true,' he gasped. 'Akkarin was right.'

There was a crackle of paper. Dannyl looked at Davin. The magician was regarding a rolled plan. It was crushed in the middle where he had gripped it tightly. He unrolled it and smoothed the plan out, then let it spring into a half-crumpled roll again.

Seeing the glitter of tears in the Alchemist's eyes, Dannyl turned away. The man had worked for years to have his weather-predicting methods accepted. What point was there in building the Lookout now?

Dannyl stared out of the window. Novices and magicians stood alone or in groups in the gardens below, frozen like statues. Only a few servants were still moving about, looking both puzzled and unnerved by the strange behaviour of the magicians.

Then a new image of the Fort reached those gifted with the ability to see it.

When Makin's communication ended, Lorlen found

himself gripping the rail of the balcony tightly. His heart was pounding in reaction to the Warrior's last moment of terror.

'Administrator?'

Lorlen turned to regard the King. The man was pale, but his face was stiff with anger and determination.

'Yes, Your Majesty?'

'Summon Lord Balkan.'

'Yes, Your Majesty.'

Balkan responded to Lorlen's mental call immediately.

—*The King wants you to come to the Palace.*

—*I thought he might. I'm already on my way.*

'He's coming,' Lorlen said.

The King nodded. He turned and walked back into the Palace tower. Lorlen followed, then froze as a new image of the Fort flashed into his mind. He felt something sharp against his throat. Forcing his attention back to his real surroundings, he saw that the King's Advisors had both put their hands to their throats.

The King glanced at the three of them.

'What is it?'

'Lord Makin is still alive,' Lord Rolden replied.

The King grabbed the magician's hand and pressed it to his forehead.

'Show me,' he ordered.

The image Makin was sending was of the Fort again, but viewed from the outside. A small crowd of plainly dressed Sachakans were hurrying out of the building, some leading the small limek-like animals.

A voice spoke in Makin's ear.

'That's right. Tell them this. I will—'

'Kariko! Look what I've found,' a woman called.

This voice came from within the Fort. A Guild magician staggered from the corridor and fell to his knees. Lorlen recognised Lord Fergun with a jolt. *Of course*, he thought. *Fergun was sent away . . .*

Makin felt surprise, then anger. The attack had happened so fast, he hadn't noticed the disgraced Warrior's absence.

A Sachakan woman in a glittering coat strode out of the building. She stopped beside Fergun and looked toward Makin.

'Pretty, isn't he?'

'You can't keep him, Avala,' said the voice at Makin's ear.

'But he's *weak*. I can't believe they bothered to teach him. He probably can't even boil water.'

'No, Avala. He might be weak, but he can send them information.'

The woman reached down and ran her fingers through Fergun's hair, then yanked his head backward.

'I could break his ears. He wouldn't be able to hear us.'

'And burn out his pretty eyes, too?'

She pulled a face. 'No. That would spoil him.'

'Kill him, Avala. You'll find other pretty men in Imardin.'

Avala pouted, then shrugged. She pulled out a knife and slashed it across Fergun's throat. His eyes widened and he tried to pull away, but he was clearly too weak to break her hold. She slapped a hand over the cut and he went limp. After a moment the woman let go and he slumped to the ground.

She stepped over his body and approached Makin, though her eyes were fixed on the Sachakan behind him.

'So where next?'

'Imardin,' Kariko replied. The knife pressed harder against Makin's throat. 'Now listen, magician. Tell your Guild I will see them soon. If they open the gates for me I might let them live. Well, some of them, anyway. I expect a big welcome. Gifts. Slaves. Gold . . .'

The knife moved. There was a flash of pain . . .

Lorlen gasped as his awareness returned abruptly to his surroundings. *We just lost twenty magicians in less than an hour! Twenty of our finest Warriors . . .*

'Sit down, Administrator.'

Lorlen looked up at the King. His voice had been unexpectedly kind. He allowed himself to be ushered to a chair. The King and his Advisors took the seats on either side.

The ruler rubbed his forehead and sighed. 'That was not the way I would have chosen to learn that Akkarin's claims were true.'

'No,' Lorlen agreed. Memories of the battle still flashed through his thoughts.

'I must make a choice,' the King continued. 'Either I allow one or more magicians to learn black magic, or I ask Akkarin to return and help us. Which would you choose, Administrator?'

'I would call Akkarin back,' Lorlen replied.

'Why?'

'We know he spoke the truth.'

'Do we?' the King asked quietly. 'He may have given us only part of the truth. He could have formed an alliance with these magicians.'

'Why would he send a message warning of their attack?'

'To fool us. He said they would attack in a few days, not today.'

Lorlen nodded. 'He might simply have been mistaken.' He leaned forward and met the monarch's gaze. 'I believe Akkarin is honourable. I believe he would leave again after helping us, if we asked him to. Why have one of our own learn black magic, who we could not then justify sending away, when we can call on someone who already has that skill?'

'Because I don't trust him.'

Lorlen felt his shoulders slump. There was no arguing with that.

'I have put this question to your Heads of Disciplines,' the King said. 'They agree with me. Lord Sarrin is my preference, but I will not make that decision for the Guild. Put it to a vote.'

He rose and walked to the open door of the balcony.

'There is another, more practical reason for my choice,' he continued. 'Akkarin is in Sachaka. He may not be able to reach us in time. Lord Sarrin believes Sonea learned black magic in a week, despite lessons and other activities taking up her time. If a magician dedicates all his or her time to the task, he should learn it faster. I – ' A knock at the door interrupted him. 'Enter.'

A boy hurried inside and dropped to one knee.

'Lord Balkan to see you, Your Majesty.'

The King nodded and the boy hurried out. Balkan strode in and knelt before the King.

'At ease.' The King smiled grimly. 'A well-timed visit, Lord Balkan.'

'I thought you might want to speak to me, Your Majesty,' Balkan replied as he stood up. He glanced at Lorlen and nodded politely. 'You have heard that the Fort has fallen?'

'Yes,' the King replied. 'I have decided that one magician

must be allowed to learn black magic. The Guild will nominate candidates and choose one by vote. If the Sachakans draw close to Imardin before the magician you select has learned black magic, the reinforcements you sent to the Fort will engage them.'

Lorlen stared at the monarch. He was sending those magicians to their deaths. 'We need them here, Your Majesty, so that the magician who is chosen can increase his or her strength as quickly as possible.'

'You will not order them to attack the Sachakans until it is clear we require the delay.' The King turned to Balkan. 'Can you suggest any strategy that might otherwise slow or weaken the enemy?'

The Warrior nodded. 'We can take advantage of the city's defences. Every obstacle the Sachakans overcome will use up some of their strength.'

'What of the Guard? Can they be used?'

Balkan shook his head. 'I fear they would be easily turned against us.'

The King frowned. 'How so?'

'Any non-magician with latent magical ability is a potential source of strength. I recommend keeping all non-magicians well out of the way.'

'Perhaps I should send them out of Imardin.'

Balkan paused, then nodded. 'If that is possible.'

The King gave a short laugh. 'Once the news spreads that several Sachakan black magicians are about to attack Imardin, the city will empty itself without any urging from me. I will employ the Guard to keep order, and to ensure that any ship leaving the Marina carries a reasonable number of evacuees, then I will send them away. Do you have any other recommendations?'

Balkan shook his head.

'Stay with me. I want you to discuss fortification with the Guard.' The King turned to regard Lorlen. 'Administrator. Return to the Guild and arrange the selection of a black magician. The sooner he or she begins, the better prepared we will be.'

'Yes, Your Majesty.'

Lorlen rose, knelt, then strode out of the room.

'What will you do now?'

Rothen turned to regard Raven. The spy's expression was grim.

'I don't know,' Rothen confessed. 'Obviously, I don't need to enter Sachaka now.'

'But finding out if the Ichani exist was not your only reason for going. You might still search for Sonea.'

'Yes.' Rothen looked away to the north-east. 'But the Guild . . . Kyralia . . . will need every magician it has to fight these Sachakans. Sonea . . . Sonea might need my help but helping her won't save Kyralia.'

Raven watched Rothen silently and expectantly. Rothen felt a pain in his chest, as if his heart were being pulled in two directions.

The Ichani exist, he thought. *Akkarin wasn't lying. Sonea hasn't been deceived.* He felt a flood of relief, then, knowing that the decisions she had made were for good reasons, even if they weren't the right ones.

Sonea is in Sachaka. The Ichani are here. She is safe, perhaps, for now. If I help the Guild, maybe she will have a home to return to.

'I will stay,' he said aloud. 'I will return to Imardin.'

Raven nodded. 'We can trade the cart and the goods in

Calia for two fresh horses – if the reinforcements didn't take them all.'

The reinforcements. Lord Yikmo and the others would not have reached the Fort yet. They would probably return to Imardin to join the rest of the Guild.

'I may as well wait in Calia and join the reinforcements on their return,' Rothen said.

The spy nodded. 'Then we will part there. It has been an honour working with you, Lord Rothen.'

Rothen managed a wan smile. 'I have enjoyed your company, and your lessons, Raven.'

The spy snorted at Rothen's comment. 'You lie well, Lord Rothen.' Then he shrugged. 'But then, I trained you. Pity those lessons won't be put into practise. But now you must do what you have been trained to do as a magician.' He glanced at Rothen. 'Defend Kyralia.'

When the tiny house appeared between the trees, Sonea assumed it was another farmer's cottage, but as they left the track Dorrien gestured proudly at the building.

'My home.'

He reined his horse in before the house. The other riders watched nervously as Akkarin and Sonea dismounted. Sonea led her mount to one of the men.

'Thanks for the loan,' she offered.

He gave her a distrustful look before taking the reins. She returned to Akkarin's side and watched as Dorrien thanked the men and sent them away.

'They're worried,' Dorrien said as he returned. 'One moment I'm escorting you out, the next there's a dead Sachakan on the road and I've changed my mind about you two.'

'What did you tell them?' Akkarin asked.

'That we were attacked and you saved us. That I've decided you deserve a night's rest and a meal in return, and I'd appreciate it if they kept that to themselves.'

'Will they?'

'They're no fools. They know something important is happening, even if they don't know the details. But they'll do as I ask.'

Akkarin nodded. 'We are in their debt. If they hadn't caught the horses and come back for us, we'd still be walking. That took courage.'

Dorrien nodded. 'Go on inside. The door is unlocked. If you're hungry, there's some fresh bread and a pot of left-over soup. I'll be with you once I've tended to my horse.'

Sonea followed Akkarin through the cottage door. They entered a room as wide as the building. A bench and shelves ran along one side. From the baskets of vegetables and fruit, and the pots and utensils scattered about, Sonea guessed this was where he prepared his meals. Several wooden chairs and a large, low table filled the rest of the room. Shelving covered the walls, and every space was filled with jars, bottles, boxes and books.

Two doors led to other rooms. One was open, allowing a glimpse of an unmade bed.

As Akkarin moved to the cooking area, Sonea sat down in one of the chairs and gazed about at everything. *It's so messy*, she mused. *Not like Rothen's rooms at all.*

She felt strangely calm. The images Makin had sent from the Fort had filled her with horror, but now, hours later, she felt only numb and bone weary. She also felt a peculiar relief.

They know, she thought. *The Guild – Rothen – everyone – knows that we spoke the truth.*

Not that it will do any good, now.

'Hungry?'

She looked at Akkarin. 'Silly question.'

He picked up two bowls, poured soup from a pot into them, then broke off two fistfuls of bread from a large loaf on the bench. As he carried the bowls to the table they began to steam.

'Real food,' Sonea murmured as Akkarin put a bowl in her hands. 'Not that I didn't like your cooking,' she added. 'You had somewhat limited ingredients.'

'Yes, and I don't have Takan's gifts.'

'Even Takan couldn't have done better.'

'You'd be surprised. Why do you think Dakova kept him so long?'

They ate in silence, savouring the simple meal. Dorrien entered the room just as Sonea put down her empty bowl. He glanced at it and smiled.

'Good?'

She nodded.

He collapsed into a chair.

'You should get some sleep,' Akkarin said.

'I know,' Dorrien replied, 'but I don't think I can. I have too many questions.' He shook his head. 'That magician . . . how did you get through the Pass if he was guarding it?'

'A little deception,' Akkarin replied. As he began to explain, Sonea watched him closely. He seemed different. Not as aloof and distant. 'I thought Parika had entered Kyralia with the intention of finding us, but once the Fort was attacked I knew it was part of the invasion.'

'He was so strong.' Dorrien looked at Sonea. 'How did you stop him?'

She felt heat rush to her cheeks. 'I stopped his heart. With Healing magic.'

Dorrien looked surprised. 'He didn't resist?'

'The Ichani don't know how to Heal, so he didn't know I could do that to him.' She shuddered. 'I didn't think I'd ever do something like that to someone.'

'I would have done the same in your place. He was trying to kill you, after all.' He looked at Akkarin. 'Was Parika the only Sachakan in the Pass?'

'Yes. That does not mean others won't come later, however.'

'Then I should warn the locals.'

Akkarin nodded. 'The Ichani will prey on non-magicians, particularly those with latent magical potential.'

The Healer's eyes widened. 'So they'll hunt down farmers and villagers all the way from the Fort to Imardin.'

'If the Guild is sensible, it will evacuate all the villages and farms on the road. Kariko won't let the other Ichani waste too much time on the journey, however. He will be worried that the Guild will change their mind about me, and allow Sonea and me to return so I can strengthen myself in time to face him.'

Dorrien paused and stared at Akkarin. He seemed to struggle with himself, then he glanced at Sonea.

'What will happen if the Guild does not call you back? What can they do?'

Akkarin shook his head. 'Nothing. Even if they do call me back and allow me to use black magic, I don't have enough time to grow as strong as eight Ichani. If I were High Lord now, I would have the Guild leave Imardin. I would teach black magic to a selected few, then return and take Kyralia back.'

Dorrien stared at him in horror. 'Abandon Kyralia?'

'Yes.'

'There *must* be another way.'

Akkarin shook his head.

'But you came back. Why would you do that, if you did not intend to fight?'

Akkarin smiled wanly. 'I don't expect to win.'

Dorrien's eyes shifted to Sonea. She could almost hear him thinking: *And you are in this, too?*

'What will you do?' he asked quietly.

Akkarin frowned. 'I haven't decided. I had hoped to return to Imardin in secret and wait for the Guild to call me.'

'We can still do that,' Sonea interjected.

'We have no horses and no money. Without them, we cannot reach Imardin before the Ichani.'

Dorrien smiled thinly. 'I can help you with that.'

'You would disobey the Guild's orders?'

The Healer nodded. 'Yes. What will you do once you reach the city?'

'Wait for the Guild to call me back.'

'And if they don't?'

Akkarin sighed. 'Then I can do nothing. I gained some power from Parika today, but not enough to face an Ichani.'

Sonea shook her head. 'We weren't strong enough to face an Ichani this morning either, but we still managed to kill one. Why don't we do the same thing to the others? We can pretend to be exhausted, let them catch us, then use our Healing powers to kill them.'

Akkarin frowned. 'That would be very dangerous. You have never experienced the drawing of power. Once it begins, you cannot use your own magic. You would not be able to Heal.'

'Then we'll have to be quick.'

Akkarin's expression darkened further. 'The other Ichani will see what you have done. Even if they don't understand it, they will be cautious. It would only take a barrier at the skin to stop you using Healing power on them.'

'Then we have to make sure they don't see.' Sonea leaned forward. 'We get them when they're alone.'

'They may stay together.'

'Then we'll have to trick them into separating.'

Akkarin looked thoughtful. 'They are unused to city surrounds, and the slums are quite a labyrinth.'

'We could enlist the Thieves.'

Dorrien looked at her, then narrowed his eyes. 'Rothen said you had broken all connections with them.'

She winced at Rothen's name. 'How is he?'

'I haven't heard from him since before Lorlen's order to cease mental communication,' Dorrien replied. He looked at Akkarin. 'He would be relieved to know Sonea is still alive. If I tell the Guild that I have seen you, I can tell them that you are willing to help.'

'No.' Akkarin's expression was distant and thoughtful. 'If Sonea and I are to ambush Ichani in the city, they must not know we are there. If they do, they will band together and hunt us down.'

Dorrien straightened. 'The Guild would keep your presence a—'

'The Ichani will read it from the mind of the first magician they kill.' Akkarin looked at Dorrien, his eyes dark. 'Where do you think I learned that trick?'

Dorrien paled. 'Oh.'

'The Guild must not know we are in the city,' Akkarin said, a note of determination entering his voice. 'So you must not tell them you have met us, or of your encounter with Parika today. The fewer who know of our return, the less chance of the Ichani discovering what we plan.'

'So we have a plan now?' Sonea asked.

Akkarin smiled at her. 'The beginning of one, perhaps. Your suggestion may work, though perhaps not on Kariko. Dakova learned to Heal from me, but he kept that secret to himself. I'm not sure if he ever taught the skill to his brother, but even if he didn't, Kariko is more likely to know Healing is possible and have considered how it might be used to harm another.'

'So we avoid Kariko,' she said. 'That leaves us seven Ichani to kill. I think that will keep us occupied for a while.'

Dorrien chuckled. 'Sounds like you do have a plan. I might be able to drop a hint or two here and there when the Guild are debating strategy. If there's anything you'd have me say . . . ?'

'I don't imagine anything you say will persuade them to hide,' Akkarin replied.

'But they might, once they've fought and exhausted themselves,' Sonea pointed out.

Akkarin nodded. 'Suggest they focus their power on one Ichani. The Sachakans are not used to helping and supporting each other. They don't know how to shield together.'

Dorrien nodded. 'Anything else?'

'I will consider on the way. The sooner we leave, the better.'

The Healer rose. 'I'll saddle up again and find horses for you both.'

'Could you get us some clean clothes, too?' Sonea asked.

'We should travel in disguise,' Akkarin added. 'A servant uniform would be ideal, but anything plain should do well enough.'

Dorrien's eyebrows rose. 'You're going to pose as my servants?'

Sonea shook a finger at him in warning. 'Yes. Just don't get used to it.'

CHAPTER 29

LEGACY OF THE PAST

The Guildhall fell utterly silent as Lorlen rose from his seat.

'I have called this Meet at the request of the King. As you must all know, the Fort was attacked and breached by eight Sachakan magicians yesterday. All but two of the twenty-one Warriors at the Fort were killed.'

A whispering rose from the audience. The discovery that two of the Warriors had escaped the Fort had been the only good news Lorlen had received in the last day.

'It appears that some of the former High Lord's claims and predictions are right. We have been invaded by Sachakan magicians of immense strength. Magicians who use black magic.'

Lorlen paused and looked around the hall. 'We are unable to avoid the possibility that we are too few and too weak to defend the Allied Lands. In these circumstances, the King has asked that we set aside our laws. He has asked us to choose one among us, one we consider unfailingly trustworthy, to learn black magic.'

The hall filled with voices. Lorlen read a mixed reaction from the crowd. Some magicians voiced protests, while others looked resigned.

'I ask you now to suggest candidates for this role,' he called out over the noise. 'Consider carefully. Strict rules will curtail the activities of this magician. They must remain within the Guild grounds for the rest of their life. They may not hold a position of authority within the Guild. They will not be allowed to teach. These rules may become more restrictive. as we consider the consequences of creating this position.' Lorlen was pleased to see no sign of eagerness on any magicians' face. 'Any questions?'

'Can the Guild refuse to do this?' a voice called.

Lorlen shook his head. 'The King has ordered it.'

'The Council of Elders would never agree to this!' a Lonmar magician declared:

'According to the Allied agreement, the Kyralian King is obliged to undertake whatever measures necessary to protect the Allied Lands from a magical threat,' Lorlen replied. 'The Higher Magicians and I have discussed this with the King many times. Believe me, he would not have made this decision if he did not feel there was no better option.'

'What about Akkarin?' another magician called. 'Why not call him back?'

'The King considers this the wiser path,' Lorlen replied stiffly.

No more questions came. Lorlen nodded.

'You have half an hour to consider. If you wish to nominate someone, please speak to Lord Osen.'

He watched as magicians left their seats and gathered in small groups to discuss the King's order. Some approached Lord Osen directly. The Higher Magicians were uncharacteristically silent. Time seemed to slow. When the half-hour had ended, Lorlen rose and struck the gong beside his seat.

'Please be seated.'

As the magicians returned to their places, Osen climbed the stairs to Lorlen.

'This will be interesting,' Director Jerrik murmured. 'Who do they consider worthy of this dubious honour?'

Osen's shoulders lifted. 'No surprises. They suggest Lord Sarrin, Lord Balkan, Lady Vinara or,' he looked at Lorlen, 'Administrator Lorlen.'

'Me?' Lorlen exclaimed, before he could stop himself.

'Yes.' Osen looked amused. 'You're very popular, you know. One magician suggested that a King's Advisor should take on the burden.'

'Interesting idea.' Balkan chuckled, then quite deliberately looked up at the topmost row of chairs. Lord Mirkan blinked down at him, his face changing from watchfulness to sudden anxiety. 'Let the King face whatever consequences this may lead to.'

'He would find himself a new Advisor within a day,' Vinara said flatly. She looked at Lorlen. 'Let's get this over with, then.'

Lorlen nodded and turned to the Hall. 'Nominations for the role of . . . black magician are as follows: Lord Sarrin, Lord Balkan, Lady Vinara, and myself.' *Surely they won't choose me*, he thought. *What if they do?* 'Nominees will abstain from the vote. Please create your lights.'

Hundreds of globe lights floated up to the ceiling. Lorlen's heart was beating too fast. He kept hearing Osen's comment, repeating in his mind. *'You're very popular, you know.'* The possibility that he might lose his position as Ambassador and force himself to learn what Akkarin had admitted was evil magic turned his blood to ice.

'Those in favour of Lord Sarrin, change your lights to purple,' he ordered. 'Those in favour of Lord Balkan, choose red. For Lady Vinara, choose green.' He paused and swallowed. 'For myself, blue.'

Some of the globe lights had begun to take on colour before he had finished, as magicians anticipated that Lorlen would suggest the colour of each candidate's robes. Slowly, the remaining white globe lights changed.

It's close, Lorlen thought. He started counting . . .

'Sarrin,' Balkan said.

'Yes, I get that result, too,' Vinara confirmed. 'Though you were their second choice.'

Lorlen breathed a sigh of relief as he realised they were right. He looked down at Sarrin, then felt a pang of sympathy. The old magician looked pale and ill.

'Lord Sarrin will be our defender,' Lorlen announced. Looking closely at the audience, he saw reluctant acceptance on most faces. 'He will relinquish his role as Head of Alchemy and begin learning black magic immediately. I now declare this Meet ended.'

'Wake up, little Sonea.'

Sonea grew aware of her surroundings with a start. She saw with surprise that her horse had stopped. Looking around, she found Dorrien watching her with an odd look on his face. They had pulled up by a road leading to a house, and Akkarin was nowhere to be seen.

'He's gone to get us some food,' Dorrien explained.

She nodded, then yawned and rubbed her face. When she looked at Dorrien again, he was still watching her thoughtfully.

'What are you thinking?' she asked.

He looked away and smiled crookedly. 'I was thinking that I should have kidnapped you from the Guild while I had the chance.'

She felt a familiar pang of guilt. 'The Guild wouldn't have let you. *I* wouldn't have let you.'

He lifted an eyebrow. 'No?'

'No.' She avoided his eyes. 'It took a lot before I really decided I wanted to stay and learn magic. It would take a lot more to make me change my mind.'

He paused. 'Do you . . . do you think you would have been tempted?'

She thought back to the day they went to the spring together, and his kiss, and she couldn't help smiling. 'A little. But I hardly knew you, Dorrien. A few weeks isn't enough time to be sure about someone.'

His eyes flickered over her shoulder. She turned to see that Akkarin was riding toward them. With his short beard and simple clothing, she doubted he would be recognised. Anyone looking closely would notice he rode too well, however. She would have to point this out.

'And you're sure now?'

She turned back to Dorrien. 'Yes.'

He let out a long breath, then nodded. Sonea looked at Akkarin again. His expression was grim and hard.

'Though it took a lot to convince *him*,' she added.

Dorrien made a choking noise. She turned, cursing herself for making such a thoughtless comment, only to have him burst into laughter.

'Poor Akkarin!' he said, shaking his head. He looked at her sideways and shook his head. 'You're going to be a formidable woman one day.'

Sonea stared at him, then felt her face grow hot. She

tried to think of a retort, but the words refused to come. Then Akkarin reached them and she gave up.

As he handed her a bread roll, Akkarin looked at her closely. She felt her face warming again. His eyebrows rose, and he looked at Dorrien speculatively. The Healer smiled, tapped his heels against his horse's flank and started forward.

They moved on, eating as they rode. An hour later, they arrived at a small village. She and Akkarin dismounted and handed the reins of their horses to Dorrien, and the Healer left to find fresh mounts.

'So what were you and Dorrien discussing before?' Akkarin asked.

She turned to regard him. 'Discussing?'

'Outside the farmhouse when I was buying the food.'

'Oh. Then. Nothing.'

He smiled and nodded. 'Nothing. Amazing subject, that one. Produces such fascinating reactions in people.'

She regarded him coolly. 'Perhaps it's a polite way of saying it's none of your business.'

'If you say so.'

She felt a flash of irritation at the knowing look on his face. Was she so easy to read? *But if I can guess his moods now, he can probably read mine just as easily.*

He yawned, then closed his eyes. When he opened them again, he looked more alert. *When was the last time we slept?* she thought. *The morning after we slipped through the Pass. Before then? A few hours' sleep each day. And for the first half of our journey, Akkarin hadn't slept at all . . .*

'You haven't had any more nightmares,' she said suddenly.

Akkarin frowned. 'No.'

'What did you dream about?'

He gave her a sharp look, and she instantly regretted the question.

'Sorry,' she said, 'I shouldn't have asked.'

Akkarin drew in a deep breath. 'No, I should tell you. I dream of events that happened when I was a slave. Mostly events concerning one person.' He paused. 'Dakova's slave girl.'

'The one who helped you, in the beginning?'

'Yes,' he said quietly. He paused, and looked away. 'I loved her.'

Sonea blinked in surprise. Akkarin and the slave girl? He had *loved* her? He had loved *another*? She felt a growing uncertainty and annoyance, then guilt. Was she jealous of a girl who had died years before? That was ridiculous.

'Dakova knew it,' Akkarin continued. 'We dared not touch each other. He would have killed us if we had. As it was, he enjoyed tormenting us any way he could. She was his . . . his pleasure slave.'

Sonea shivered as she began to understand what that must have been like. To always see each other, yet never be able to touch. To watch as the other was tormented. She could not imagine what Akkarin had felt, knowing what the girl endured.

Akkarin sighed. 'I used to dream about her death every night. In my dreams, I tell her that I'll distract Dakova so she can get away. I tell her I'll stop him finding her. But she always ignores me. She always goes to him.'

She reached out and touched the back of his hand. His fingers curled around hers.

'She explained to me that the slaves considered it an honour to serve a magician. She said the slaves' sense of honour made their life easier to bear. I could understand that they might allow themselves to think that way when they had no choice, but not when they did have a choice – or when they knew their master intended to kill them.'

Sonea thought of Takan, of how he had called Akkarin 'master', and of the peculiar way he had handed the Ichani knife to Akkarin across his upturned wrists, as if he was offering something more than the blade. Perhaps he was.

'Takan has never stopped thinking that way, has he?' she asked quietly.

Akkarin glanced at her. 'No,' he said. 'He could not let go of a lifetime of habits.' He paused to chuckle. 'I think in the last few years he persisted with the rituals just to infuriate me. I know he would never go back to that life willingly.'

'Yet he stayed with you, and would not let you teach him magic.'

'No, but there were practical reasons for that. Takan could not join the Guild. Too many questions would have been asked. Even if we invented a past for him, it would have been difficult for him to avoid those lessons that involve mind sharing. It would have been too risky to teach him magic secretly. If he had returned to Sachaka, he would not have survived unless he knew black magic. I don't think he trusted himself with that knowledge, in that place. In Sachaka, there are only masters and slaves. To survive as a master, he would need his own slaves.'

Sonea shuddered. 'It sounds like an evil place.'

Akkarin shrugged. 'Not every master is cruel. The Ichani are outcasts. They are the magicians the King has banished from the city – and not just for being overly ambitious.'

'How did the King make them leave?'

'His own powers are considerable, and he has supporters.'

'The Sachakan King is a magician!'

'Yes.' Akkarin smiled. 'Only the Allied Lands have laws preventing magicians from ruling, or having too much influence in politics.'

'Does our King know this?'

'Yes, though he does not understand how powerful the Sachakan magicians are. Well, he does now.'

'What does the Sachakan King think of the Ichani invading Kyralia?'

Akkarin frowned. 'I don't know. If he knew of Kariko's plan, he would not have liked it, but he probably believed it would never work. The Ichani were always too busy fighting each other to think of forming an alliance. It will be interesting to see what the Sachakan King will do when he has a neighbouring land ruled by Ichani.'

'He'll help us?'

'Oh, no.' Akkarin laughed grimly. 'You forget how much Sachakans hate the Guild.'

'Because of the war? But that was so long ago.'

'To the Guild it is. The Sachakans cannot forget, not with half their country a wasteland.' Akkarin shook his head. 'The Guild should never have ignored Sachaka after it had won the war.'

'What should it have done?'

Akkarin turned his head and gazed at the mountains. Sonea followed his eyes. Only a few days before, they had been on the other side of that jagged line.

'It was a war between magicians,' Akkarin murmured. 'There is never any point in sending armies of non-magicians against magicians, especially magicians who use black magic. Sachaka was conquered by Kyralian magicians, who promptly returned to their rich homes. They knew the Sachakan empire would eventually recover and become a danger again, so they created the wasteland to keep the country poor. If some of the Guild magicians had taken up residence in Sachaka instead, freed the slaves and shown that magicians can use their powers to help the people, the Sachakans might have been guided toward becoming a more peaceful, free society, and we might not be facing this situation today.'

'I see,' Sonea said slowly, 'but I can also see why it never happened. Why would the Guild help ordinary Sachakans when they don't help ordinary Kyralians?'

Akkarin regarded her speculatively. 'Some do. Dorrien, for instance.'

Sonea held his gaze. 'Dorrien is an exception. The Guild could do a lot more.'

'We can't do anything if nobody volunteers to do it.'

'Of course you can.'

'Would you force magicians to work against their will?'

'Yes.'

His eyebrows rose. 'I doubt they would co-operate.'

'Perhaps their income should be reduced if they don't.'

Akkarin smiled. 'They would feel they were being treated like servants. No-one will want their children to join the Guild if it means they must work like commoners.'

'No-one from the Houses,' Sonea corrected him.

Akkarin blinked, then chuckled. 'I knew you'd be a disruptive influence the moment the Guild proposed teaching you. They ought to be grateful I took you away.'

She opened her mouth to reply, but stopped as she

realised Dorrien was approaching. He was riding a new horse and was leading two others.

'They're not the best,' he said, handing them the reins, 'but they'll have to do. Magicians all over the country are hurrying to Imardin, so the supply of fresh horses at resthouses is dwindling fast.'

Akkarin nodded grimly. 'Then we must hurry or the supply will run out.' He moved around to the side of a horse and swung up into the saddle. Sonea hauled herself up onto the other horse. As she slipped her other boot into the stirrup, she watched Akkarin closely. He had called her a disruptive influence, but that didn't mean he disapproved. He might even agree with her.

Did it matter? In a few days there might not be a Guild, and the poor would discover there were worse things to endure than the Purge.

Sonea shivered and pushed that thought from her mind.

The corridor of the Magicians' Quarters was almost as busy as the University at midbreak, Dannyl mused. He walked with Yaldin past knots of magicians, their wives, husbands and children. All were discussing the Meet.

As Yaldin reached the door to his rooms, the old magician looked up at him and sighed.

'Come in for a cup of sumi?' he asked.

Dannyl nodded. 'If Ezrille doesn't mind.'

Yaldin chuckled. 'She likes to tell people I'm in charge, but you and I – and Rothen – know better.'

He opened the door and ushered Dannyl into his guestroom. Ezrille was sitting in one of the chairs, dressed in a gown of shimmering blue material.

'That was a quick Meet,' she said, frowning.

'Yes,' Dannyl replied. 'You are looking beautiful today, Ezrille.'

She smiled, the skin around her eyes crinkling. 'You should come home more often, Dannyl.' Then she shook her head. 'With manners like yours, I'm amazed you still haven't found yourself a wife. Sumi?'

'Yes, please.'

She rose and busied herself with cups and water. Dannyl and Yaldin sat down. The old magician's brow furrowed.

'I can't believe they've decided to allow black magic.'

Dannyl nodded. 'Lorlen said that *some* of Akkarin's claims have proven to be true.'

'The worst ones.'

'Yes, but I wonder if that means some of his claims were proven to be *untrue*.'

'Which ones?'

'Obviously not the ones about Sachakan black magicians invading Kyralia,' Ezrille said as she laid a tray on the table before the chairs. 'What will Rothen do? He doesn't need to go to Sachaka now.'

'He'll probably come back.' Dannyl took the cup she offered and sipped at the steaming brew.

'Unless he decides to go on in the hope of finding Sonea.'

Dannyl frowned. *Rothen might just do that . . .*

They looked up at a knock on the door. Yaldin waved a hand and the door opened. A messenger bowed, glanced around the room, then stepped inside when he saw Dannyl.

'Ambassador. A man is here to see you. All the places for receiving visitors are in use, so I brought him to your rooms. Your servant was present and admitted him.'

A visitor? Dannyl put down his cup and rose. 'Thank

you,' he said to the messenger. The man bowed and retreated from the room.

Dannyl smiled apologetically at Yaldin and Ezrille. 'Thanks for the sumi. I had better find out who my visitor is.'

'Of course,' Ezrille replied. 'You must come back later and tell us about him.'

The corridor was a little quieter now that most magicians had returned to their rooms or duties after the Meet. Dannyl strode to his door and opened it. A young man with blond hair rose from one of his guestroom chairs and bowed. For a moment Dannyl didn't recognise him, as he was dressed in the sober fashion preferred by Kyralians.

Then he hastily stepped inside and let the door close.

'Greetings, Ambassador Dannyl.' Tayend grinned. 'Did you miss me?'

CHAPTER 30

DELAYING THE ENEMY

At first Imardin appeared as a shadow against the yellow-green of the fields. Then, as they drew nearer, the city sprawled out on either side of the road like outstretched arms welcoming them back. Now, hours later, a thousand lamps burned before them, lighting their way through the rain and the darkness to the Northern Gates.

When they were close enough to hear the rain beating on the glass of the first lamp, Dorrien drew his horse to a halt and looked back at Akkarin and Sonea. His eyes strayed to the other people using the road. They must make their farewells quick, and be careful what they said. People would think it strange, if he spoke to his 'commoner' companions with too much familiarity.

'Good luck,' he said. 'Be careful.'

'You be in more rub than us, my Lord,' Sonea replied, speaking with the typical slum dweller drawl. 'Thanks for your help. Don't let those foreign magicians get you.'

'You either,' he replied, smiling at her accent. He nodded at Akkarin, then turned away and urged his horse forward.

Sonea's stomach clenched with anxiety as she watched him ride away toward the gates. When he had disappeared, she glanced at Akkarin. He was a tall shadow, his face hidden in the hood of his cloak.

'Lead on,' he said.

She directed her horse off the main road and into a narrow street. Dwells eyed them and their bedraggled horses. *Don't try anything*, she thought at them. *We might look like simple country people oblivious to the dangers of the city, but we aren't. And we can't afford to draw attention to ourselves.*

After winding their way through the slums for half an hour, they reached the horse sellers at the edge of the Market. They stopped in front of a sign with a painting of a horseshoe on it. A wiry-looking man limped through the rain toward them.

'Greetings,' he said in a gruff voice. 'You looking to sell your horses?'

'Maybe,' Sonea replied. 'Depends on the price.'

'Let me have an eye, then.' He beckoned. 'Come on in out of the rain.'

They followed the man into a large stable. Stalls had been built on either side, some occupied. They dismounted and watched as the man examined their horses.

'What's this one's name, then?'

She paused. They had changed horses three times, and she had given up remembering their names.

'Ceryni,' she said. 'After a friend of mine.'

The man straightened and turned to stare at her.

'Ceryni?'

'Yes. Do you know him?'

Then from one of the stalls came the sound of laughter.

'You named your horse after *me*?'

A stable door opened and a short man in a grey coat strode out, followed by Takan and a large, muscular man. Sonea looked closer at the speaker, then gasped as she recognised him.

'Cery!'

He grinned. 'Hai! Welcome back.' Then he turned to the horse seller and the grin disappeared. 'You didn't see this.'

'N-no,' the man agreed. His face was white.

'Take the horses and leave,' Cery ordered.

The man grabbed the reins of the horses, and Sonea watched, bemused, as he hurried away. Akkarin had told her that Takan was hiding with a Thief. If Cery was also working for this Thief, then was it the Thief Faren, or had Cery started working for another? In any case, it seemed he had gained some influence in the last few years, if the horse seller's reaction was any indication. Sonea turned to see Takan drop to his knees before Akkarin.

'Master.'

Takan's voice was laden with emotion. Akkarin pushed back his hood and sighed.

'Get up, Takan,' he said quietly. Though his voice was all command and tolerance, Sonea recognised signs of embarrassment in his face. She smothered a smile.

The servant climbed to his feet. 'It is good to see you again, master, though I fear you have returned to a dangerous and impossible situation.'

'Nevertheless, we must do what we can,' Akkarin replied. He turned to Cery. 'Has Takan explained what we intend to do?'

Cery nodded. 'There'll be a meeting of the Thieves tomorrow. Seems most of them have heard something's up, even if it's just that the Houses are all packing up and leaving the city. You need to tell me how much you want them to know.'

'Everything,' Akkarin replied, 'if that will not damage your standing among them.'

Cery shrugged. 'It won't, in the long term — and I get the feeling we'll have no city left to deal in if these Sachakan magicians win. Now, before we get to the grit of it, I'll take you somewhere better than a stable. I'm sure you'd like a bit of food, too.'

As he strode back to the stall he had emerged from, Sonea watched him closely. There was a sureness about the way he carried himself that she hadn't seen before. He had expressed none of the fear or awe of Akkarin that she had expected. They spoke as if they had dealt with each other before.

No doubt he was one of the men helping Akkarin find the spies. But why didn't Akkarin tell me Cery was involved?

Cery unlocked a hatch at the back of the stall and held it open.

'Lead the way, Gol.'

The large, silent man bent double and stepped through, then began to descend a ladder. Takan followed, then Akkarin. Sonea paused to look at Cery. He grinned.

'Go on. We'll catch up when we get to my place.'

She climbed down the ladder into a large passage. Gol held a lamp. Familiar smells brought back old memories of the Thieves' Road. As Cery joined them, he nodded to Gol, and they set off through the passage.

They travelled for several minutes, then passed through a large metal door into a luxuriously furnished guestroom. A low table at the centre was covered in several plates of food, glasses, and bottles of wine.

Sonea collapsed into a chair and helped herself to a few morsels of food. Akkarin sat down beside her and picked up one of the bottles. His eyebrows rose. 'You live better than magicians do, Ceryni.'

'Oh, I don't live here,' Cery said, taking another of the seats. 'This is one of my guest places. Takan's been staying here.'

'The Thief has been generous,' Takan said quietly, nodding at Cery.

The Thief? Sonea choked, swallowed, then stared at Cery. Catching her look, he grinned. 'Only just clicked, did it?'

'But . . .' She shook her head. 'How is that possible?'

He spread his hands. 'Hard work, clever moves, good connections . . . and a little help from your High Lord.'

'So you're the Thief who helped Akkarin find the spies?'

'That's right. I started after he helped you and me with Fergun,' Cery explained. 'He wanted someone to find the murderers for him. Someone with the right connections and influence.'

'I see.' *So Akkarin has known about this since my guardianship Hearing.* She turned to glare at him. 'Why didn't you tell me?'

Akkarin's lips curled into a faint smile. 'Initially, I couldn't. You would have believed I had forced or tricked Cery into helping me.'

'You could have told me after I had learned the truth about the Ichani.'

He shook his head. 'I am always wary of revealing more than I need to. If you were captured by the Ichani, they might discover Cery's connection to me from your mind. As it turns out, I do need the association to remain a secret.' He turned to Cery. 'It is important that our presence in Imardin does not become common knowledge. If the Ichani read it from someone's mind, our only chance of winning the battle will be lost. The fewer who know we are here, the better.'

Cery nodded. 'Only Gol and I know you are here. The other Thieves think we're just going to talk about what's stirring up the city.' He smiled. 'They'll be surprised to see you.'

'Do you think they will agree to keep our presence a secret?'

Cery shrugged. 'Once they know what's going on and see that they'll lose everything they've got if the Sachakans win, they'll mind you like their own children.'

'You told Takan you had been considering ways of killing magicians,' Akkarin said. 'What were you—'

—Balkan?

Sonea straightened in her seat. The mental voice belonged to—

—Yikmo? Balkan replied.

—The Sachakans are nearing Calia.

—I will advise you shortly.

'What is it, master?' Takan asked.

'A communication,' Akkarin replied. 'Lord Yikmo reported that the Ichani are approaching Calia. He must be there.'

Sonea felt a shiver run down her spine. 'Surely the Guild hasn't gone out to meet them?' She looked at Cery. 'You'd have heard if they had left the city.'

Cery shook his head. 'Nothing like that has been reported.'

Akkarin frowned. 'I wish Lorlen would use the ring.'

'About twenty magicians left the city four days ago,' Gol interjected. 'In the morning.'

—Yikmo?

—Balkan.

—Take your time.

—We will.

Sonea frowned at Akkarin. 'What does that mean?'

His expression darkened. 'No doubt it's a prearranged code for an instruction. They can't tell Yikmo and his men what to do without giving away their intentions to the Ichani.'

'But what does it mean?'

He drummed the tips of his fingers together. 'Twenty magicians. Four days ago. They left before the Ichani attacked the Fort. What purpose could they have had?'

'A guard for the South Pass?' Sonea suggested. 'Balkan left our escort at the Fort. Perhaps he thought the South Pass needed guarding, too.'

Akkarin shook his head. 'We would have passed them on the road. They must have been north of Calia, where the road forks. Whatever the reason, they could not have travelled so far before the attack that they could have returned to Imardin again. They have remained in Calia for a reason.'

'To report the Ichani's position?' Cery suggested.

'All twenty of them?' Akkarin's frown deepened. 'I hope the Guild hasn't planned something foolish.'

'That would be a surprise,' Takan remarked dryly.

Cery looked down. 'We better eat this, before it goes cold. Wine anyone?'

Sonea opened her mouth to reply, but froze as an image flashed into her mind. Three carts trundled down a village main road. Several men and women rode in each cart, some of them splendidly dressed.

The horses pulling the first cart halted, and their driver slowly turned to face the viewer. Sonea recognised Kariko with a shiver. He handed the reins to a man sitting beside him, then jumped to the ground.

'Come out, come out, Guild magician,' he called.

A strike flashed from the window of a house on the other side of the street, followed by several more from both sides. They struck an invisible shield around each cart.

'An ambush,' Sonea heard Akkarin mutter.

Kariko turned full circle, surveying the houses and street, then looked at his allies.

'Who wants to hunt?'

Four of the Ichani stepped down from the carts. They separated and started toward the houses on either side. Two brought yeel with them, the animals barking with excitement.

Then the view shifted. She caught a glimpse of a window frame, a room, and a Guild magician.

'Rothen!' she gasped. The images stopped, and she stared at Akkarin in horror. 'Rothen is with them!'

It has been far too many years since I had a Warrior lesson or a bout in the Arena, Rothen thought as he hurried across the yard to the back door of the house.

Yikmo's strategy was simple. If the Sachakans could not see their attackers, they could not fight back. The Guild magicians would strike from concealed places, then change position and strike again. When they had no more power, they were to hide and rest.

Rothen hurried as fast as he could through the house to the front room. The villagers had been sent away hours before, and the doors and windows had all been unlocked in preparation for the ambush. Peering out, he saw a Sachakan man reach out to the door of the next house. He threw a powerful strike, and was gratified to see the man stop.

Then his heart sank as the man turned and started toward him. He stumbled over a chair and hurried out of the room.

The town was large, and most of the houses were built close to each other. Rothen crept about, watching the Sachakans and striking when they were far enough away that he had time to escape from them. Twice he held his breath as one of them passed only a few strides away from his hiding place. Other Guild magicians were less fortunate. One of the animals led a Sachakan to a young Warrior hiding in a stable. Though Rothen and another Alchemist emerged to strike at the Sachakan, the man ignored them. The Warrior fought until he was too weak to stand. Then, as the Sachakan drew out his knife, Rothen heard the sound of approaching footsteps from another direction nearby and was forced to flee.

From then on, Rothen was frighteningly aware that his attempts to save the young Warrior had depleted most of his strength. Not all of it, though. After coming across two bodies half an hour later, he decided he would strike at a Sachakan one more time before he slipped away to hide.

More than an hour had passed since the carts had arrived, and he was far from the main street. Balkan's orders had been to delay the Sachakans as long as possible. He was not sure how long or how far the enemy would continue to hunt for Guild magicians.

Not all night, he thought. *They'll eventually head back. And they won't expect anyone to be there to attack them.*

Rothen smiled. Slowly and cautiously, he made his way back toward the main road. Entering one of the houses, he listened carefully for other movements inside. All was silent.

Moving to a window at the front of the house, he saw that the carts were still where they had been before. Several of the Sachakans were walking near them, stretching their legs.

A slave was inspecting one of the wheels.

A broken wheel would slow them down, Rothen mused. Then he grinned to himself. *Better still would be a few broken carts.*

He drew in a deep breath and reached for his remaining power.

Then he heard a floorboard squeak behind him and felt his blood go cold.

'Rothen,' a voice whispered.

He turned and let the breath out in a rush. 'Yikmo.'

The Warrior moved to the window.

'I heard one boasting that he had killed five of us,' Yikmo said grimly. 'The other claims he took three.'

'I was about to strike the carts,' Rothen murmured. 'They would have to replace them, and I think most vehicles here went with the villagers.'

Yikmo nodded. 'They were protecting them before, but they might not be n—'

He fell abruptly silent as two Sachakans sauntered into view from the houses on the other side of the street. A woman called out to them.

'How many, Kariko?'

'Seven,' the man replied.

'I got five,' his companion added.

Yikmo drew in a sharp breath. 'It can't be. If the two I heard on this side are telling the truth, we are the only two left.'

Rothen shivered. 'Unless they are exaggerating.'

'Did you get all of them?' the woman asked.

'Most,' Kariko replied. 'There were twenty-two.'

'I could send my tracker after them.'

'No, we have wasted enough time already.' He straightened and Rothen stiffened as he heard the man's mental voice.

—*Come back now.*

Yikmo turned to regard Rothen. 'This is our last chance to hit those carts.'

'Yes.'

'I'll strike the first. You take the second. Ready?'

Rothen nodded and drew on the last of his power.

'Go.'

Their strikes flashed to the carts. Wood shattered, then humans and horses screamed. Several of the plain-clothed Sachakans fell to the ground, cut and bleeding from flying splinters of wood. One horse kicked its way free and galloped away.

The Sachakan magicians whirled around to stare in Rothen's direction.

'Run!' Yikmo gasped.

Rothen made it halfway across the room before the wall behind him exploded. The force slammed into his back and threw him forward. As he slammed against a wall, pain shot through his chest and arm.

He fell to the floor and lay still, too stunned to move. *Get up!* he told himself. *You've got to get away!*

But when he moved, pain stabbed through his shoulder and arm. *Something's broken*, he thought. *And I have no strength left for Healing*. He gasped and, with a great effort, forced himself up onto one elbow, then his knees. Dust filled his eyes and he tried to blink it away. He felt a hand grasp his other arm. *Yikmo*, he thought. He felt a flood of gratitude. *He stayed to help.*

The hand hauled him to his feet, sending rips of agony through his upper body. He looked up at his helper and gratitude turned to horror.

Kariko stared at him, his face contorted with anger. 'I'm going to make you very sorry you did that, magician.'

A force pushed Rothen against the wall and held him there. The pressure sent pain shooting through his shoulder. Kariko grasped Rothen's head with both hands.

He's going to read my mind! Rothen thought, feeling panic rising. He instinctively struggled to block an intrusion, but felt nothing. For a moment, he wondered if mind reading was Kariko's intention, then a voice boomed within his head.

—What is your greatest fear?

Sonea's face flashed into Rothen's mind. He pushed it away, but Kariko caught and sent the image back again.

—Who is this, then? Ah, someone you taught magic to. Someone you care for. But she is gone. Sent away by the Guild. Where? Sachaka! Ah! So that's who she is. Akkarin's companion. Such a naughty girl, breaking Guild rules.

Rothen tried to still his mind, to think of nothing, but Kariko began sending tantalising images of Akkarin into Rothen's mind. He saw a younger Akkarin, in clothes like those of the slaves in the carts, cowering before another Sachakan.

—He was a slave, Kariko told him. *Your noble High Lord was once a pathetic, grovelling slave who served my brother.*

Rothen felt a pang of sympathy and regret as he realised that Akkarin had told the truth. The last of the anger he had felt toward Sonea's 'corruptor' melted away. He felt a wistful pride. She had made the right decision. A hard decision, but the right one. He wished he could tell her so, but knew he would never get the chance. *At least I did everything I could*, he thought. *And she is far from all this trouble, now that the Ichani have left Sachaka.*

—*Far from trouble? I have allies there still*, Kariko sent. *They will find her and bring her to me. When I have her, I will make her suffer. And you . . . you will be alive to see it, slave-killer. Yes, I see no harm in that. You are weak and your body is broken, so you will not reach your city in time to help your Guild.*

Rothen felt the hands against his head slide away. Kariko was looking at the floor. He stepped away and bent down to pick up a broken piece of glass.

Drawing close again, he ran the edge of the shard over Rothen's cheek. The touch of the glass was followed by a sharp pain, then the sensation of a warm trickle running down his face. Kariko cupped his hand under Rothen's chin, then pulled it away. His palm held a small pool of blood.

Kariko held the shard of glass in the air. The tip slowly began to glow and melt, until a small globule had formed. This fell from the tip of the shard into Kariko's palm.

Kariko closed his fingers around it and shut his eyes. Something stirred at the edge of Rothen's thoughts. He sensed another mind and caught a glimpse of what this strange ritual meant. His mind was linked to the glass now, and to anyone who touched it. Kariko intended to make it into a ring and—

Suddenly the link broke. Kariko smiled and turned away. Rothen felt the force holding him to the wall dissipate. He gasped as his shoulder flared with pain. Looking up, he watched in disbelief as the Sachakan walked away through the ruined front of the house toward the broken carts.

He let me live.

Rothen thought of the little sphere of glass. He thought back to Lord Sarrin's briefing about the uses of black magic, and realised that Kariko had just made a blood gem.

The sound of voices outside sent a chill through his veins. *I must get away now*, he thought, *while I still can.* Turning away, he hurried through the house to the back door, and stumbled out into the night.

Looking at Sonea, Cery felt unexpectedly calm.

He had expected to be tormented by conflicting emotions at the first sight of her. There had been no thrill of excitement and admiration, as in the early days, nor any of the painful longing that had lingered after she had joined the Guild. Mostly he felt fondness – and concern.

I suspect I'll always be worrying about her for one reason or another. Watching her now, he noted how her attention constantly returned to Akkarin. He smiled. At first he had assumed this was because Akkarin was her former guardian and she was used to obeying his every command, but he wasn't so sure now. She hadn't hesitated to confront him about concealing Cery's status. And Akkarin hadn't been too bothered by her defiance either.

They aren't Guild magicians any more, Cery reminded himself. *They probably had to abandon all that guardian-novice stuff.*

But he was beginning to suspect there was more to it than that.

'Do you have my knife?' Akkarin asked his servant.

Takan nodded, rose and disappeared into one of the bedrooms. He returned with a sheathed knife hanging on a belt, and offered it to Akkarin with his head bowed.

Akkarin took it solemnly. He draped the belt across his knees, then suddenly looked up at the far wall. At the same time Sonea drew in a sharp breath.

The room fell silent. Cery watched the pair gaze into the distance. Akkarin's brows came together and he shook his head, then Sonea's eyes widened.

'No!' she gasped. 'Rothen!' Her face drained of all colour, then she buried her face in her hands and began to sob.

Cery felt his heart twist with concern, and saw the same emotion on Akkarin's face. The magician pushed the belt to one side and slipped out of his chair to kneel beside her. He drew her against him and held her tightly.

'Sonea,' he murmured. 'I'm sorry.'

Clearly something terrible had happened. 'What is it?' Cery asked.

'Lord Yikmo just reported that all of his men have been killed,' Akkarin said. 'Rothen, Sonea's guardian before me, was among them.' He paused. 'Yikmo is badly injured. He said something about successfully delaying the Ichani. I think that may be why they ambushed them, but I don't know why the Guild needs the delay.'

The sound of Sonea's sobs changed. She was clearly trying to stop. Akkarin looked down at her, then glanced at Cery.

'Where can we sleep?'

Takan gestured to a room. 'Through there, master.' Cery noted that the servant had indicated the room with the larger bed.

Akkarin rose, drawing Sonea to her feet. 'Come on, Sonea. We've not slept a full night for weeks.'

'I can't sleep,' she said.

'Then lie there and warm the bed up for me.'

Well, that leaves no doubt, Cery thought.

They moved into the room. After a moment, Akkarin returned. Cery stood up.

'It's late,' Cery said. 'I'll return early tomorrow, so we can talk about the meeting.'

Akkarin nodded. 'Thank you, Ceryni.' He returned to the bedroom, shutting the door behind him.

Cery regarded the closed door. *Akkarin, eh? An interesting choice.*

'I hope this does not upset you.'

Cery turned to regard Takan. The servant nodded toward the bedroom.

'Those two?' Cery shrugged. 'No.'

Takan nodded. 'I thought not, since you are now occupied with another woman.'

Cery felt his blood turn cold. He glanced at Gol, who was frowning. 'How did you know about that?'

'I heard it from one of my guards.' Takan glanced from Cery to Gol. 'This was meant to be a secret, then?'

'Yes. It is not always safe being friends with a Thief.'

The servant looked genuinely concerned. 'They did not know her name. A young man like yourself would be expected to have a woman, or many women.'

Cery managed a grim smile. 'Perhaps you're right. I'll have to look into these rumours. Good night, then.'

Takan nodded. 'Good night, Thief.'

CHAPTER 31

PREPARATIONS FOR WAR

The guide led Lorlen into a spacious room. Early morning sunlight streamed through enormous windows on one side. A small crowd of men surrounded a large table in the centre. The King stood at the middle of this, Lord Balkan on his left and Captain Arin, his military advisor, on the right. The rest of the group was made up of captains and courtiers, some familiar, some not.

The King acknowledged Lorlen with a glance and a nod, then turned his attention back to a hand-drawn map of the city spread before him.

'And how soon until the Outer Wall gate supports are finished, Captain Vettan?' he asked of a grey-haired man.

'The Northern and Western Gates are ready. The Southern will be finished by this evening,' the Captain replied.

'A question, Your Majesty?' This came from a finely dressed young man standing on the other side of the table.

The King looked up. 'Yes, Ilorin?'

Lorlen regarded the young man with surprise. This was the King's cousin, a youth no older than a new novice, and a possible heir to the throne.

'Why are we fortifying the gates, when the Outer Wall has fallen into disrepair around the Guild?' the young man asked. 'The Sachakans only need to send scouts out to circle the city, to discover this.'

The King smiled grimly. 'We're hoping the Sachakans don't try that.'

'We are expecting the Sachakans to attack us boldly,' Balkan told Ilorin, 'and since these slaves are a source of power to them, I doubt they will risk sending them out as scouts.' Lorlen noted that Balkan did not mention the possiblity that the Sachakans had read this weakness from the minds of the Warriors at the Fort, or Calia. Perhaps the King had asked him to keep the true hopelessness of their position from his cousin.

'Do you believe these fortifications will stop the Sachakans?' Ilorin asked.

'No,' Balkan replied. 'Slow them, perhaps, but not stop them. Their purpose is to force the Sachakans to use up some of their power.'

'What will happen once they have entered the city?'

Balkan glanced at the King. 'We will continue to fight them for as long as we can.'

The King turned to one of the other captains. 'Have the Houses evacuated?'

'Most have left,' the man replied.

'And the rest of the people?'

'The gate guards report that the number of people leaving the city has increased fourfold.'

The King looked at the map again and sighed. 'I wish this map included the slums.' He looked at Lord Balkan. 'Will they be a problem during the battle?'

The Warrior frowned. 'Only if the Sachakan decide to conceal themselves there.'

'If they do, we could set the buildings alight,' Ilorin suggested.

'Or burn them now, to ensure they don't use them to their advantage,' another courtier added.

'They will burn for days,' Captain Arin warned. 'The smoke will help conceal the enemy, and falling embers might set the rest of the city alight. I recommend leaving the slums standing unless we have no other choice.'

The King nodded. He straightened, then looked at Lorlen.

'Leave me,' he ordered. 'Administrator Lorlen and Lord Balkan may stay.'

The guard promptly left the room. Lorlen noted that the two King's Advisors remained.

'Do you have good news for me?' the King asked.

'No, Your Majesty,' Lorlen replied. 'Lord Sarrin has not been able to discover how to use black magic. He sends his apologies and says he will continue trying.'

'Does he feel he is even close?'

Lorlen sighed and shook his head. 'No.'

The King looked down at the map and scowled.

'The Sachakans will be here in a day, two if we are lucky.' He looked at Balkan. 'Did you bring it?'

The Warrior nodded. He drew a small pouch from his robes, opened it and tipped its contents on the table. Lorlen drew in a quick breath as he recognised Akkarin's ring.

'Do you intend to call Akkarin back?'

The King nodded. 'Yes. It is a risk, but what difference will it make if he betrays us? We will lose this battle without him anyway.' He picked the ring up by its band, and held it out to Lorlen. 'Call him back.'

The ring was cool. Lorlen slipped it on his finger and closed his eyes.

—*Akkarin!*

He waited, but no answer came. After counting to a hundred, he called again. Still no reply. He shook his head.

'He isn't responding.'

'Perhaps there is something wrong with it,' the King said.

'I'll try again.'

—*Akkarin*!

No answer came. Lorlen tried a few more times, then sighed and took off the ring.

'Perhaps he's asleep,' he said. 'I could try again in an hour.'

The King frowned. He looked up at the windows. 'Call him without the ring. Perhaps he will answer that.'

Balkan and Lorlen exchanged worried glances.

'The enemy will hear us,' the Warrior pointed out.

'I know. Call him.'

Balkan nodded, then closed his eyes.

—*Akkarin*!

Silence followed. Lorlen sent out his own call.

—*Akkarin! The King bids you return.*

—*Ak*—

—*AKKARIN! AKKARIN! AKKARIN! AKKARIN!*

Lorlen gasped as another mind thundered against his own like a striking hammer. He heard other mental voices shouting Akkarin's name mockingly before he drew away with a shudder.

'Well, that was unpleasant,' Balkan muttered, rubbing his temples.

'What happened?' the King asked.

'The Sachakans answered.'

'With mindstrike,' Lorlen added.

The King scowled, then turned away from the table

and clenched his fists. He paced for a few minutes, then turned to regard Lorlen.

'Try again in an hour.'

Lorlen nodded. 'Yes, Your Majesty.'

The house Tayend's directions led Dannyl to was a typical magician-designed mansion. Impossibly fragile balconies fronted the street. Even the door was magician-made – a sheet of delicately sculpted glass.

A long moment passed before there was any response to Dannyl's knock. Footsteps could be heard approaching, then a shadowy figure appeared beyond the glass. The door opened. Instead of a doorman, Tayend greeted Dannyl with a grin and a bow.

'Sorry for the slow service,' he said. 'Zerrend's entire household has left for Elyne, so there's no-one here but . . .' He frowned. 'You look terrible.'

Dannyl nodded. 'I was up all night. I—' He choked as emotion welled up and cut off the words.

The scholar ushered Dannyl inside and closed the door. 'What happened?'

Dannyl swallowed hard and blinked as his eyes began to sting. All night he had remained in control, comforting Yaldin and Ezrille, then Dorrien. But now . . .

'Rothen is dead,' he managed. He felt tears spill out of his eyes. Tayend's eyes widened, then he stepped close and embraced Dannyl.

Dannyl froze, then hated himself for doing so.

'Don't worry,' Tayend said. 'As I said, no-one is here except me. Not even servants.'

'I'm sorry,' Dannyl said. 'I just—'

'Worry that we'll be seen. I know. I'm being careful.'

Dannyl swallowed hard. 'I *hate* that we have to be.'

'So do I,' Tayend said. He leaned back and looked up at Dannyl. 'But that is how it must be. We'd be fools to think otherwise.'

Dannyl sighed and wiped his eyes. 'Look at me. I am such a fool.'

Tayend took his hand and pulled him through the guestroom. 'No, you're not. You just lost an old and close friend. Zerrend has some medicine for that, though my dear second – or is it third – cousin might have taken the best vintages with him.'

'Tayend,' Dannyl said, 'Zerrend left for a good reason. The Sachakans are only a day or two away. You can't stay here.'

'I'm not going home. I came here to see you through all this, and I will.'

Dannyl pulled Tayend to a halt.

'I'm serious, Tayend. These magicians kill to strengthen themselves. They'll fight the Guild first, because it is their strongest opponent. Then they'll look for victims to replace the power they've lost. Magicians will be useless to them, as we'll have exhausted our strength fighting them. It's ordinary people they'll target, particularly those with undeveloped magical ability. Like you.'

The scholar's eyes widened. 'But they won't get that far. You said they'd fight the Guild first. The Guild will win, won't it?'

Dannyl stared at Tayend and shook his head. 'From the instructions we've been given, I don't think anyone believes we can. We might kill one or two of them, but not all. Our orders are to abandon Imardin once we've exhausted ourselves.'

'Oh. You'll need help getting out, if you're exhausted. I'll—'

'No.' Dannyl took Tayend's shoulders. 'You must leave *now*.'

The scholar shook his head. 'I'm not leaving here without you.'

'Tayend—'

'Besides,' the scholar added. 'The Sachakans will probably invade Elyne next. I'd rather spend a few days here with you and risk an early death, than return home and hate myself for abandoning you for a few extra months of safety. I'm staying, and you will just have to make the best of it.'

After the darkness of the sewers, the sunlight was dazzling. As Sonea climbed out of the hatch, she felt something under her boot and stumbled, then heard a muffled curse.

'That was my foot,' Cery muttered.

She couldn't help smiling. 'Sorry, Cery, or should I call you Ceryni now?'

Cery made a noise of disgust. 'I've been trying to shake that name all my life, and now I *have* to use it. I'm sure a few of us would like to say some rough words to the Thief who decided we should all go by animal names.'

'Your ma must have been able to tell the future when she named you,' Sonea said. She stepped aside as Akkarin emerged from the tunnel.

'She could tell from one look which cappers would run off without paying,' Cery said. 'And she always said my da would get into some rub.'

'My aunt must have the gift, too. She always said *you* were trouble.' She paused. 'Have you seen Jonna and Ranel, lately?'

'No,' he said, bending to lift the sewer hatch back into place, 'not for months.'

She sighed and felt the knowledge of Rothen's death like a weight lodged somewhere inside her body. 'I'd like to see them. Before all this—'

Cery held up a hand – a signal for silence – then pulled her and Akkarin back into a recessed doorway. Gol hurried back from the alley entrance to join them. Two men entered the alley and moved quietly toward them. As they drew near, Sonea recognised the darker of the faces. She felt a hand push her gently in the small of her back.

'Go on,' Cery whispered in her ear. 'Give him the fright of his life.'

Sonea glanced back to see his eyes glittering with mischief. She waited until the two men drew level with her, then stepped into their path and pulled back her hood.

'Faren.'

The two men dropped into a crouch and stared at her, then one drew in a quick breath.

'*Sonea?*'

'You still recognise me, after all this time.'

He frowned. 'But, I thought you . . .'

'Left Kyralia?' She crossed her arms. 'I decided to come back and settle a few debts.'

'Debts?' He glanced at his companion nervously. 'Then you have no business with me.'

'No?' She moved closer to him, and was gratified to see him take a step back. 'I seem to remember a little arrangement we had once. Don't tell me you've forgotten, Faren.'

'How could I forget?' he muttered. 'I remember that you never upheld your end of the deal. In fact, you burned down more than one of my houses while I was protecting you.'

Sonea shrugged. 'I suppose I didn't prove to be all that useful. But I don't think a few burned houses justified selling me to the Guild.'

Faren took another step backward. 'That was not my idea. I had no choice.'

'No choice?' she exclaimed. 'From what I've heard, you made quite a profit. Tell me, did the other Thieves take a commission out of the reward? I heard you got all of it.'

Faren swallowed audibly, backed away even further.

'As compensation,' he said in a strangled voice.

Sonea took another step toward him, but then a spluttering came from the doorway. It quickly turned into a laugh.

'Sonea,' Cery said. 'I should hire you as a messenger. You're quite scary when you want to be.'

She managed a grim smile. 'You're not the only one who's said that to me lately.' But thinking of Dorrien only brought Rothen to mind again. She felt the weight of grief again, and struggled to ignore it. *I can't think about that now*, she told herself. *There's too much to do.*

Faren's yellow eyes were narrowed at Cery. 'I should have known you were behind this little ambush.'

Cery smiled. 'Oh, I only suggested she have a bit of fun with you. She deserves it. You did hand her over to the Guild, after all.'

'You're taking her to the meeting, aren't you?'

'That's right. She and Akkarin have lots to tell them.'

'Akkarin . . . ?' Faren repeated in a small voice.

Sonea heard footsteps behind her and turned to see that Akkarin and Gol had emerged from the doorway. Akkarin had shaved off the short beard and tied his hair back, and looked like his former, imposing self again.

Faren took another step backward.

'It is *Faren*, isn't it,' Akkarin said smoothly. 'Black, eight-legged and poisonous?'

Faren nodded. 'Yes,' he replied. 'Well, except for the legs.'

'Honoured to meet you.'

The Thief nodded again. 'And you.' He looked at Cery. 'Well. This meeting should be entertaining. Follow me.'

Faren started toward the end of the alley, his companion giving Sonea and Akkarin a curious glance before hurrying after. Cery glanced at Sonea, Akkarin and Gol, then beckoned. They followed him into a narrow gap between two buildings at the end of the alley. Halfway down, a large man stepped out to block Faren's way.

'Who are these?' the man demanded, pointing at Sonea and Akkarin.

'Guests,' Cery replied.

The man hesitated, then reluctantly stepped into a doorway. Faren followed him inside the building. A short corridor followed, then a staircase. At the top Faren stopped outside a door and turned to regard Cery.

'You should ask first, before bringing them in.'

'And let them argue about it for hours?' Cery shook his head. 'We don't have the time.'

'Well, I warned you.'

Faren opened the door. As Sonea followed the pair, she took in luxurious surrounds. Cushioned chairs had been arranged in a rough circle. She counted seven occupied chairs. The seven men standing behind them were the Thieves' protectors, she guessed.

It was not hard to guess which Thief was which. The

thin, bald man was obviously Sevli. The woman with a pointy nose and red hair was probably Zill and the man with the beard and bushy eyebrows had to be Limek. Looking around, Sonea wondered if the physical similarities to the animals had produced the Thieves' names, or if they had groomed themselves to look like a creature they favoured. Perhaps a little of both, she decided.

The occupants of the chairs were staring at her and Akkarin, some with expressions of anger and outrage, others with puzzlement. One face was familiar. Sonea smiled as she met Ravi's eyes.

'Who are these people?' Sevli demanded.

'Cery's friends,' Faren said. He moved to one of the empty chairs and sat down. 'He insisted on bringing them.'

'This is Sonea,' Ravi answered for the other Thieves' benefit. His eyes shifted to Akkarin. 'Which means you must be the former High Lord.'

Outrage and puzzlement changed to shocked surprise.

'It is an honour to meet you all at last,' Akkarin replied. 'Especially you, Lord Senfel.'

Sonea looked up at the man standing behind Ravi's chair. The old magician had shaved off his beard, which was probably why she hadn't recognised him at first glance. The last time she had seen him, when Faren had tried to blackmail him into teaching her magic, he had worn a long white beard. She had been drugged, in a vain atempt to control her magic, and had thought she'd dreamed the encounter until Cery had spoken at the meeting later. He stared at Akkarin, his face pale.

'So,' he said, 'you've finally found me.'

'Finally?' Akkarin's shoulders lifted. 'I've known about you for a *very* long time, Senfel.'

The old man blinked in surprise. 'You *knew?*'

'Of course,' Akkarin replied. 'Your faked death was not very convincing. I'm still not sure why you left us.'

'I found your rules . . . stifling. Why didn't you do anything?'

Akkarin smiled. 'Now, how would that have made my predecessor look? He didn't even notice you were missing. You were not doing any harm here, so I decided to let you stay.'

The old magician laughed, a short, unpleasant bark. 'You do make a habit of breaking the rules, Akkarin of Delvon.'

'And I was waiting until I had need of you,' Akkarin added.

Senfel sobered. 'The Guild have been calling you,' he said. 'It would seem *they* have need of *you*. Why don't you answer?'

Akkarin looked around the circle of Thieves. 'Because the Guild must not know we are here.'

The Thieves' eyes sharpened with interest.

'Why is that?' Sevli asked.

Cery stepped forward. 'Akkarin's story isn't quick. Can we get some more chairs?'

The man who had met them at the door left the room, then returned with two simple wooden chairs. When all were seated, Akkarin glanced around the circle of faces, and drew in a deep breath.

'First let me tell you how I encountered the Sachakans,' he began.

As he briefly described his encounter with Dakova, Sonea watched the Thieves' faces. At first they listened calmly, but when he described the Ichani their expressions changed to alarm and concern. He told them of the spies, and how he had recruited Cery to hunt for them; at that they looked at Sonea's old friend with surprise and interest. Then, as he told of their exile in Sachaka, Sevli exclaimed in disgust.

'The Guild are fools,' he said. 'They should have kept you here until they knew if the Ichani were real.'

'It may be fortunate that they did not,' Akkarin said. 'The Ichani do not know I am here, and that gives us an advantage. While I am stronger than any Guild magician, I am not strong enough to defeat eight Ichani. Sonea and I might be able to defeat one, if he is separated from the others. If the Ichani know we are here, however, they will band together and hunt us down.'

He looked around the circle. 'That is why I have not answered the Guild's calls. If the Guild knows I am here, the Ichani will read it from the mind of the first magician they capture.'

'But you have allowed *us* to know this,' Sevli observed.

'Yes. It is a risk, but not a great one. I expect the people in this room will keep themselves well out of the Sachakans' way. Any other rumours of our presence that reach the general population may be dismissed as wishful thinking.'

'So what do you want from us?' Ravi asked.

'They want us to help them separate a Sachakan from the others,' Zill answered.

'Yes,' Akkarin confirmed. 'And to give us access and guides to the Thieves' Road throughout the entire city.'

'It doesn't cover all parts of the Inner Circle,' Sevli warned.

'But the buildings are mostly empty,' Zill said. 'They're locked, but we can fix that.'

Sonea frowned. 'Why are the buildings empty?'

The woman looked at Sonea. 'The King told the Houses to leave Imardin. We were wondering why, until Senfel told us of the defeat at the Fort and Calia just now.'

Akkarin nodded. 'The Guild will have realised that everybody in Imardin is a potential source of magic for the Ichani. They will have advised the King to empty the city.'

'But he has only told the Houses to leave, hasn't he?' Sonea said. As the Thieves nodded, she felt a flare of anger. 'What about the rest of the people?'

'With the Houses leaving, everyone else has figured out that something's up,' Cery told her. 'From what I hear, thousands of people have been packing up and heading out into the country.'

'What about the dwells?' she asked.

'They'll dig in,' Cery assured her.

'In the slums, outside the city walls, where the Ichani will arrive first.' She shook her head. 'If the Ichani decide to stop and strengthen themselves, the dwells won't have a chance.' She felt her anger rising. 'I can believe the King would be this stupid, but not the Guild. There has to be hundreds of potential magicians in the slums. *They* are the ones who should be evacuated first.'

'Potential magicians?' Sevli frowned. 'What do you mean?'

'The Guild only look for magical potential among the children of the Houses,' Akkarin said, 'but that does not mean that people among the other classes don't have magical potential. Sonea is the proof of that. She was only allowed to join the Guild because her powers were so strong that they developed without assistance. There are

516

probably hundreds of potential magicians in the lower classes.'

'And they're more attractive victims to the Ichani than magicians,' Sonea added. 'Magicians use up their powers fighting back, so by the time they're defeated there's not much power to take.'

The Thieves exchanged glances. 'We thought we'd be ignored by the invaders,' Ravi muttered. 'Now it seems we are going be harvested like some kind of magic crop.'

'Unless . . .' Sonea caught her breath and looked at Akkarin. 'Unless someone takes their power before the Ichani do.'

His eyes widened as he realised what she was suggesting, but then he frowned. 'Would they agree to it? I will not take the strength of any Kyralian by force.'

'I think most would, if they understood why we wanted it.'

Akkarin shook his head. 'But it would be impossible to organise. We'd have to test thousands of people, and explain what we're doing to all of them. We may have only a day to prepare.'

'Are you considering what I think you're considering?' Senfel asked.

'Which is what?' Sevli looked confused. 'If you understand this, Senfel, explain it to me.'

'If we can find the slum dwellers who have magical potential, Akkarin and Sonea can take their power,' Senfel said.

'We not only rob the Ichani of their harvest, but *our* magicians grow stronger,' Zill said, sitting straight in her seat.

Our magicians? Sonea suppressed a smile. *Looks like the Thieves have accepted us.*

'But will the dwells agree to it?' Akkarin asked. 'They have no great liking for magicians.'

'They will if *we* ask them to,' Ravi said. 'No matter what the dwells think of us, they do acknowledge that we fought for them during and after the first Purge. If we call for helpers in the fight against the invaders, we'll have thousands of volunteers by the end of the day. We can tell them we have a few magicians of our own. If they think you're not from the Guild, they'll be even more likely to agree to help you.'

'I see one problem,' Sevli said. 'If we do this, thousands of dwells are going to see you. Even if they don't know who you are, they'll have seen your face. If the Ichani read their minds . . .'

'I can help there,' Senfel said. 'I will test all of the volunteers. Only those that have potential will see Sonea and Akkarin. That will mean only a hundred or so will know they're here.'

Cery smiled. 'See, Senfel. You did come in useful.'

The old magician gave Cery a withering look, then regarded Akkarin again. 'If we encourage these volunteers to stay in one place – a safehouse with comfortable beds and a generous supply of food – they will recover their strength and you will be able to increase your power again tomorrow.'

Akkarin stared at the magician, then nodded. 'Thank you, Senfel.'

'Don't thank me yet,' Senfel replied. 'They may take one look at me and run.'

Sevli chuckled. 'You might have to try being charming for once, Senfel.' He ignored the old man's glare, and looked around the circle. 'Now that we know the nature of these Ichani, I can see the suggestions I was going to make for fighting them will not work. We should keep out of the way as much as possible.'

'Yes,' Faren agreed. 'And warn the dwells to keep out of sight, too.'

'Better still,' Ravi said, 'bring the dwells into the passages. It will be a tight squeeze, and the air might get a bit thin, but,' he glanced up at Senfel, 'magicians' battles don't take long, from what I'm told.'

'So how are we going to lure an Ichani away from the main group?' Zill asked.

'I hear Limek has a good tailor,' Cery said, giving the bushy-haired Thief a meaningful look.

'Fancy yourself in robes?' the man said in a deep voice.

'Oh, they'd never believe a magician could be so short,' Faren scoffed.

'Hai!' Cery protested. He pointed at Sonea. 'There are short magicians.'

Faren nodded. 'I suppose you might be convincing in novices' robes.'

Sonea felt something brush against her arm, and looked down to find Akkarin's fingers lightly touching her skin.

—*These people are braver than I thought*, he sent. *They appear to understand how dangerous and powerful the Ichani are, yet they are still willing to fight them.*

Sonea smiled and sent him a fleeting image of dwells throwing stones at magicians during the Purge, then of the sewer system that had enabled Cery to bring them into the city.

—*Why wouldn't they? They've been fighting and outwitting magicians for years.*

CHAPTER 32

A GIFT

Something was tickling Rothen's nostril. He snorted, then opened his eyes.

He was lying face down on dried grass. As he rolled over, he felt a twinge of pain in his shoulder. Memories of the previous night rushed back: the carts arriving, the young Warrior cornered by an Ichani, Lord Yikmo at the window of the house, blasting the carts, Kariko, the blood gem, hurrying away . . .

Looking around, he saw that he was in a barn. From the angle of the beams of light streaming between the slats of wood, it was close to midday.

As he pushed himself into a sitting position, he felt a stronger twinge of pain. He slipped a hand under his robes and touched his shoulder. It sat a little higher than it should. Closing his eyes, he sent his mind inward and regarded his shoulder with dismay. As he had slept, his body had used his returning powers to begin Healing the broken bones in his arm and shoulder. But something wasn't quite right.

He sighed. Unconscious self-Healing was a benefit of being a magician, but it wasn't a reliable reflex. The bones had set themselves at twisted, crooked angles. An experienced Healer could break and set them again, but for now he would have to put up with discomfort and restricted movement.

Standing up brought a short spell of dizziness, and hunger. He walked to the door of the barn and peered out. Houses surrounded the barn, but all was silent. The building closest to him looked familiar. He felt a chill as he realised it was the house where he had faced Kariko.

He felt a strong reluctance to leave the protection of the barn. The Sachakans might still be in the village, looking for replacement vehicles. He should wait until nightfall, then slip away under the cover of darkness.

Then he saw the magician lying by the back door of the house. There had been no body there the night before. It could only be one magician: Lord Yikmo.

Rothen stepped into the sunlight and hurried to the red-robed figure. He grasped Yikmo's shoulders and rolled him over. The magician's eyes stared sightlessly at the sky.

Streaks of blood had dried on the Warrior's chin. His robes were torn and covered in dust. Thinking back, Rothen recalled the moment when the front of the house had exploded inward. He had assumed that Yikmo had escaped. Instead, it seemed he had been fatally injured by the blast.

Rothen shook his head. Yikmo had been respected and admired in the Guild. Though he hadn't been strong magically, his sharp mind and ability to teach novices with learning difficulties had gained him the high regard of both Balkan and Akkarin.

Which was why Akkarin chose him as Sonea's teacher, Rothen thought. *She liked Yikmo, I think. She'll be upset when she hears of his death.*

As would the rest of the Guild. He considered communicating the news, but something made him hesitate. The Guild must know, from the silence following the battle, that all had perished. The Sachakans could not be sure. *Best not tell them anything they don't already know*, he thought.

Getting to his feet, Rothen turned to the house. He entered cautiously and approached the front room. A gaping hole opened onto the road. The shattered remains of two carts formed two piles in the centre of the thoroughfare.

They've gone.

Three bodies lay among the mess. Rothen looked closely at the houses on either side, then cautiously stepped out.

'Magician!'

Rothen spun around, then relaxed as a teenage boy ran toward him. He remembered the boy from the evacuation of the village. It had taken some firm words from Yikmo to dissuade the youngster from hanging about to watch the fight.

'What are you doing here?' Rothen asked.

The boy stopped, and the unpractised bow he gave was almost comically awkward. 'Came back to see what happened, my lord,' he replied. His eyes strayed to the carts. 'That the enemy?'

Rothen moved to the bodies and examined them. All were Sachakan. He noted the numerous scars on their arms. 'Slaves,' he said. He looked closer. 'Looks like they were injured when we struck the carts. They're bad wounds, but nothing that couldn't have been Healed, and nothing that would have killed them quickly.'

'You think the Sachakans killed their own people?'

'Maybe.' Rothen straightened and looked from one dead Sachakan to another. 'Yes. Those cuts on their wrists aren't from splinters of wood.'

'I guess they didn't want their slaves slowing them down,' the boy said.

'Have you looked around the village?' Rothen asked.

The boy nodded.

'Seen any other Guild magicians?'

The boy nodded again, then lowered his eyes. 'All dead, though.'

Rothen sighed. 'Are there any horses left?'

The boy grinned. 'Not here, but I can get you one. My da trains racehorses for House Arran. The estate isn't far away. I can run there and back in half an hour.'

'Then go fetch a horse.' Rothen looked around at the houses. 'And some men to take care of the bodies, too.'

'Where you want them put? In the Calia cemetery?'

A cemetery. Rothen thought of the mysterious cemetery in the forest behind the Guild, then of Akkarin's claims that black magic had been in common use before it was banned. Suddenly the reason for the existence of the graves was all too clear.

'For now,' Rothen replied. 'I will stay to identify them, then ride to the city.'

Like so many of the people before her, the woman who entered the room hesitated when she saw Sonea.

'I know, the veil's a bit much,' Sonea said, speaking with the slum accent. 'They say I got to wear this so nobody know who the Thieves' magicians are.' The veil had been Takan's idea. Wearing it meant that even the hundred or so potential magicians she took power from would not see her. Akkarin, who was meeting people in another room, was wearing a mask.

'Sonea?' the woman whispered.

Sonea felt a stab of alarm. She looked closer, then pulled the veil off as she recognised the woman.

'Jonna!'

Sonea hurried around the table and hugged her aunt tightly.

'It's really you,' Jonna said, leaning back to stare at Sonea. 'I thought the Guild sent you away.'

'They did.' Sonea grinned. 'I came back. We can't let these Sachakans make a mess of our city, can we?'

Different emotions crossed the woman's face. Concern and fear were followed by a crooked smile. 'You sure know how to get yourself into a lot of rub.' She looked around the room. 'They made me wait for hours. I thought I'd be cooking or something, but they told me I had some sort of magical ability, and I should help their magician.'

'Really?' Sonea ushered her aunt to the chair, then moved back to her own seat on the other side of the table. 'I must get my abilities from my mother's side, then. Give me your hand.'

Jonna offered her hand. Sonea took it and sent out her senses. She detected a small source of power. 'Not much. That's why they made you wait. How's Ranel and my little cousins?'

'Kerrel's growing fast. Hania's a crier, but I keep telling myself she'll grow out of it soon. If Ranel knew you were here, he would have come, but he thought he'd be no use because of his limp.'

'I'd love to see him. Perhaps after all this . . . I'm going to make a little cut on the back of your hand, if that's okay with you.'

Jonna's shoulders lifted. Sonea opened a box on the table and brought out the tiny knife that Cery had given her. He had reasoned that a small blade wouldn't frighten the dwells as much as a larger one. This one was so tiny, it had earned a few laughs.

Sonea nicked the back of Jonna's hand with the knife, then laid a finger over the cut. Like all the previous dwells, Jonna relaxed as Sonea drew energy from her. When Sonea stopped and healed the cut, the woman straightened.

'That felt . . . very strange,' Jonna said. 'I couldn't move, but I felt so sleepy that I didn't want to.'

Sonea nodded. 'That's what most people say it's like. I'm not sure I could do it if I knew it was unpleasant. Now, tell me what you and Ranel have been doing lately.'

The problems Jonna related seemed wonderfully simple and ordinary. Sonea listened, then told her aunt of everything that had happened since their last meeting, including some of her doubts and fears. At the end of the story, Jonna regarded her speculatively.

'It's hard to believe that the quiet little child I had to raise has grown into such an important person,' she said. 'And you with this Akkarin, the High Lord of the Guild and all.'

'He isn't any more,' Sonea reminded her.

Jonna waved a hand. 'Even so. How sure of him are you? Do you think you'll marry?'

Sonea felt her face heat. 'I . . . I don't know. I . . .'

'Would you agree?'

Marriage? Sonea hesitated, then slowly nodded.

'But you haven't talked about it, have you?' Jonna frowned leaned forward. 'You are being careful?' she murmured.

'There are . . .' Sonea swallowed. 'I know there are ways, with magic, of being sure a woman doesn't . . . It's one of the advantages of being a magician. Akkarin wouldn't want that.' She felt her face grow hotter. 'Not now, anyway. It wouldn't be wise, with all the fighting.'

Jonna nodded and patted Sonea's hand. 'Of course. Perhaps later, then. When all this is over.'

Sonea smiled. 'Yes. And when I'm ready. Which wouldn't be straightaway.'

The woman sighed. 'It's good to see you, Sonea. It's such a relief knowing you're back.' She sobered. 'But it isn't, too. I wish you were somewhere far away and safe. I wish you didn't have to fight these Sachakans. You . . . you will be careful?'

'Of course.'

'Don't try anything foolish.'

'I won't. I don't much like the idea of dying, Jonna. That's a strong deterrent against foolishness.'

A knock at the door interrupted them.

'Yes?' Sonea called.

The door opened, and Cery slipped inside carrying a large sack. He was grinning widely.

'Catching up?' he said.

'Did you arrange this?' Sonea asked.

'I might have,' Cery replied slyly.

'Thank you.'

He shrugged. Jonna rose. 'It's late. I must get back to my family,' she said. 'I've been gone too long already.'

Sonea stood and stepped around the table to hug her aunt again. 'Take care of yourself,' she said. 'Give Ranel a kiss for me. And tell him not to say anything about us being here. Not to anyone.'

Jonna nodded, then turned away and left the room.

'That was the last of them,' Cery said. 'I'll take you back to your rooms.'

'What about Akkarin?'

'He's waiting for you there. Come on.'

Moving to a door at the back of the room, he led her out into a corridor. At the end of it they entered a small cupboard. Cery untied a rope hanging from a hole in the roof and as he let it slip through his hands, the floor of the cupboard slowly descended.

'You make a good pair,' Cery said.

Sonea turned to frown at him. 'Me and Jonna?'

He grinned and shook his head. 'You and Akkarin.'

'You think so?'

'I hope so. I'm not sure I like him getting you into all this rub, but he seems just as worried about you surviving it as I am.'

The floor stopped before another door. Cery pushed it open and they stepped into a familiar passage. A few steps later, they were passing the large metal door to his guest rooms. Akkarin sat before a table laden with plates of fresh food, a glass of wine in his hand. Beside him sat Takan.

Akkarin looked up at Sonea and smiled. She noticed that Takan was regarding her closely, and began to wonder what they had been talking about before she arrived.

'Ceryni,' Akkarin said. 'Once again, you've provided for us generously.' He lifted his glass. 'Anuren dark, no less.'

Cery shrugged. 'No expense spared for the city's defenders.'

Sonea sat down and began eating. Though she was hungry, the food sat like stones in her belly and she soon lost her appetite when they began discussing their plans for tomorrow. They had not been talking long before Akkarin stopped and looked at her closely.

'Your power is detectable,' he said quietly. 'I need to teach you to hide it.'

Akkarin held out his hand. As she took it, she felt his presence grow strong at the edge of her mind. She closed her eyes.

—*This is what I can sense.*

At once she felt the power within him radiating out, like a glowing mist.

—*I see it.*

—*You're letting power leak through the barrier that surrounds your natural area of magical influence. You need to strengthen the barrier. Like this.*

The glow faded to nothing. Concentrating on her own body, she sensed the store of power within her. She hadn't had the opportunity to consider how much strength she had gained from the dwells. She had tried to keep track of the volunteers, but lost count after thirty.

Now she marvelled at the immense power she held, contained by the barrier at her skin. But that barrier was only strong enough to contain her natural level of power. She must use some of the extra magic to strengthen it. Concentrating, she began sending a steady trickle of power to the barrier.

—*That's it.*

Instead of retreating, Akkarin's mind lingered.

—*Look at me.*

She opened her eyes. A shiver ran down her spine as she realised she could see and sense him at the same time. His expression was the thoughtful one he always wore when she caught him watching her . . . and now she knew with certainty what he was thinking of at those times. She felt her face flush, and the corner of his mouth curled upward.

Then his mind faded and he let her hand go. When he looked away, she felt a vague disappointment.

'We should make blood gems for each other. There will be times we'll need to be able to communicate privately in the next few days.'

Blood gems. Her disappointment faded and was replaced by interest.

'We need some glass.' He looked at Takan. The servant rose and entered the kitchen, then returned and shook his head.

'Nothing there . . .'

Akkarin picked up a wineglass, then glanced at Cery. 'Do you mind if I break this?'

Cery shrugged. 'No. Smash away.'

The glass shattered as Akkarin struck it against the table. He picked up a sliver and handed it to Sonea, then took one for himself. Cery watched, clearly bursting with curiosity.

Together, Sonea and Akkarin melted the glass fragments into tiny spheres. Akkarin took another sliver of glass and cut his palm. Sonea did the same. Once more he held her hand and she sensed his mind touch hers. She followed his instructions on how to apply the blood and magic to the hot glass.

When the gems had cooled, Takan set a small square of gold on the table. It rose and hovered before Akkarin's face, then curled and twisted into two rings. As Akkarin dropped his blood gem into the setting of one ring, Sonea placed hers in the other. She noted how the gem protruded from the inner side of the band, allowing it to touch the skin of the wearer.

The gold claws of the settings closed over the gems.

Akkarin plucked the two rings out of the air, holding them by their bands, then turned to regard Sonea solemnly.

'With these rings, we will be able to see into each others' minds. This has some . . . disadvantages. Sometimes, hearing and knowing exactly how another person regards you can be an unpleasant experience. It can end friendships, turn love to resentment, and destroy self-regard.' He paused. 'But it can also deepen understanding. We should not wear these any more than we must.'

Sonea took his ring and considered his words. Turn love to resentment? But he had never *said* he loved her. She thought of Jonna's words. '*But you haven't talked about it, have you?*'

We haven't needed to, she told herself. *Just the occasional fleeting glimpse of his thoughts has been enough.*

Or was it?

She looked at the ring and found herself caught between two possibilities: either he loved her and was afraid the rings would spoil everything, or he didn't, and was afraid the rings would reveal the truth.

But when his mind had lingered just now, she was sure she had sensed more than just desire.

She put the ring on the table. Tomorrow they would need them. Tomorrow they would discover how much it cost them. For now, she did not need to see any more than what she had glimpsed in his mind.

Cery abruptly rose. 'I'd like to stay, but I've got other things to get around to.' He paused, then waved at the sack, which he had left on a chair. 'Some more clothes. I thought they might suit better than what you've got.'

Akkarin nodded. 'Thank you.'

'Good night.'

After Cery had gone, Takan also stood. 'It is late,' he said. 'If you do not need me . . .?'

Akkarin shook his head. 'No. Get some sleep, Takan.' He looked at Sonea. 'We should get some rest, too.'

He rose and moved into the bedroom. Sonea started to follow, then she paused as she saw the sack on the chair. Grabbing it, she carried it into the bedroom.

Akkarin glanced at the sack as she dropped it on the bed. 'What disguise has Cery come up with, then?'

Sonea opened the sack and turned it upside down. A cascade of black cloth spilled out. She glanced at Akkarin, then spread the garments over the bed.

They were robes. *Magicians'* robes.

Akkarin stared at them, his expression grim.

'We can't wear these,' he said quietly. 'We are not Guild magicians. It is a crime.'

'Then the Guild is going to be too busy arresting people to fight the Ichani tomorrow,' she said. 'There will be hundreds of non-magicians on the streets wearing robes, trying to lure the Sachakans into separating.'

'This is . . . different. We were cast out. And these are black. There will be no mistaking us for ordinary magicians.'

Sonea looked at the sack. It was still half full. Reaching inside, she pulled out two pairs of trousers and two shirts. Both were a generous fit.

'Strange. Why would he give us two sets of clothes?'

'An alternative.'

'Or we're supposed to wear the robes underneath these.'

Akkarin's eyes narrowed. 'And remove the outer clothing at a specific time?'

'Perhaps. You have to admit, it would be intimidating. Two black magicians . . .'

She drew in a breath and looked down at the bed, then felt a strange chill as she realised she was looking at two sets of full-length robes – the robes of a graduated magician.

'I can't wear these!' she protested.

Akkarin chuckled. 'Now that you agree with me, I find my mind is changing. I think, perhaps, your friend is being as subtle and clever as I've come to expect.' He bent to run a hand over the cloth. 'We would not show these unless our identities had been discovered. But once they have, it may appear to the Sachakans that the Guild has accepted us. The implications of that will give Kariko reason to pause.'

'And the Guild?'

He frowned. 'If they truly want us to return, they will have to accept everything we are,' he murmured. 'After all, we cannot unlearn what we have learned.'

She looked down. 'So they are black robes for black magicians.'

'Yes.'

She frowned. The thought of parading about in black robes in front of Rothen . . . she felt a sharp pang of grief. *But Rothen is dead.*

She sighed. 'I'd like it better if they called black magic higher magic, but if the Guild were ever to accept us I guess they couldn't call us Higher Magicians. That term is already in use.'

Akkarin shook his head. 'No, and black magicians should be discouraged from thinking that they are higher than others.'

Sonea looked at him closely. 'Do you think they'll accept us?'

Akkarin's eyebrows knitted together. 'Even if it survives, the Guild will never be the same.' He gathered up the robes and draped them over the back of a chair. 'For now, we should sleep. We might not get another chance for some time.'

As he began to strip off his clothes, Sonea sat on the edge of the bed and considered his words. The Guild had already changed. With so many dead . . . she felt her throat tighten again as she thought of Rothen.

'I've never seen anyone sleep well sitting up,' Akkarin said.

Sonea turned to find him sliding under the covers. She felt a strange mix of excitement and shyness. Waking to find herself in a bed with him that morning had changed something. *It was certainly more comfortable than rock*, she mused, *but being here, together, felt so much more . . . deliberate.*

She put the sack and remaining clothes aside, then undressed and slipped into the bed. Akkarin's eyes were closed, and his breathing was the deep steady rhythm of sleep. She smiled and reached over to the lamp to extinguish it.

Despite the darkness and the long day, she remained wakeful. She created a tiny, weak globe light and rolled over to watch Akkarin, content to just examine all the details and contours of his face.

Then his eyes fluttered open and looked into hers. A tiny frown creased his forehead.

'You're supposed to be asleep,' he murmured.

'I can't sleep,' she told him.

His lips curled up into a smile.

'When have I heard that before?'

* * *

As Cery entered his rooms he drew in a deep breath. A warm, spicy scent hung in the air. He smiled and followed it to the bathing room, where he found Savara relaxing in a tub of water.

'In the bath again?' he asked.

She smiled slyly. 'Care to join me?'

'I think I'll stay a safe distance away, for now.'

Her smile widened. 'Then tell me what I've missed.'

'I'll just get a chair.'

He returned to the guestroom, stopped in the centre and took several deep breaths.

Once again, he had felt a strong desire to tell her everything. He had made a deal with her: keep her informed in exchange for suggestions on killing Ichani. Part of him was sure he could trust her, but another whispered a warning.

How much did he know about her, really? She was Sachakan. She had sought out and identified her countrymen – and women – for him, knowing that they would be killed. That did not mean she had Kyralia's best interests in mind, however. She had told him she worked for another 'faction' of Sachakan society, and it was clear that her loyalties lay with her people.

He had made a deal, and so far she had kept her side of it . . .

But he couldn't tell her that Akkarin and Sonea had returned. Should news of their arrival and preparations get out, the Ichani would win. If he trusted Savara, and she betrayed them, Kyralia's fall would rest on his shoulders.

And Sonea might be killed. He felt vaguely guilty about withholding information from the new woman in his life for the sake of the old. *But if I endangered the life of the old by mistakenly trusting the new*, he reasoned, *I'd feel far worse than I do now.*

But Savara would find out eventually. Cery's heart raced with a strange, unfamiliar fear when he considered how she might react.

She will understand, he told himself. *What sort of Thief would I be if I so easily gave away the secrets entrusted to me? And it's not like she's going to stay here long. Once it's over, she'll leave me anyway.*

Taking a deep breath, he picked up a chair and carried it into the bathing room. She folded her arms over the edge of the tub, and rested her chin on them.

'So what have the Thieves decided?'

'They liked our ideas,' he told her. 'Limek set his people working on making robes.'

She grinned. 'I hope these people can run fast.'

'They'll use the Thieves' Road to get away again. We've also got people out looking for good places to lay traps.'

She nodded. 'The Guild sent out a mental call for Akkarin today.'

He feigned surprise. 'What did he say?'

'He didn't reply.'

Cery frowned. 'You don't think he's . . .?'

'Dead?' Her shoulders lifted slightly. 'I don't know. Maybe. Or maybe it's too dangerous to answer. He might attract the wrong kind of attention.'

He nodded and found it all too easy to look worried. Unfolding her arms, she beckoned to him.

'Come here, Cery,' she murmured. 'You leave me here all alone, all day long. A girl could get bored.'

He stood and crossed his arms. 'All day? I heard you slipped out to the Market.'

She chuckled. 'I thought you might. I wanted to pick up something I had a jeweller make for me. Look.'

A small box sat on the lip of the tub. She picked it up and handed it to him.

'A gift for you,' she said. 'Made with a few gems from my knives.'

Lifting off the lid, Cery caught his breath at the strange silver pendant inside. Intricate, veined wings sprouted from an elongated body. Twin glints of yellow formed the eyes of the insect, and green stones dotted its curved tail. The abdomen was a large, smooth ruby.

'In my country it's considered good luck for an inava to land on you just before a battle,' she told him. 'It is also the messenger of separated lovers. I've noticed Kyralian men don't wear jewellery, but you could keep it underneath your clothes.' She smiled. 'Close to your skin.'

He felt a pang of guilt. Lifting the pendant out of the box, he slipped the chain over his head.

'It's beautiful,' he told her. 'Thank you.'

She looked away for a moment, as if suddenly embarrassed by the sentimentality of her gift. Then she smiled slyly.

'How about coming in here and thanking me properly?'

Cery laughed. 'All right. How can I say no to that?'

CHAPTER 33

THE ICHANI ARRIVE

The morning sun crept slowly over the horizon as if reluctant to face the coming day. The first rays touched the towers of the Palace, painting them a vivid orange-yellow. Slowly the golden light spread across the rooftops, starting at the edge of the city and drawing ever closer to the Outer Wall, until it bathed the faces of the magicians standing along the top.

They had left the Guild as soon as scouts had reported that the Sachakans were on the move. Climbing to the top of the Outer Wall, they had spread themselves out in a long line. It was a formidable sight, so many hundreds of magicians gathered together – unlike the two overloaded carts trundling slowly toward the city. Lorlen had to remind himself that the occupants of those carts had already killed more than forty of the Guild's best Warriors and were several times stronger than the magicians on the wall.

The Ichani had found a replacement for the carts Yikmo's men had destroyed, but it had delayed them by half a day. The Guild hadn't benefited from the Warriors' sacrifice, however. All Sarrin's attempts to learn black magic had failed. The old magician had said that he could not quite make sense of the descriptions and instructions on black magic in the books. He had grown increasingly distressed as each day passed. Lorlen knew that the likelihood that Yikmo and his men had died for nothing weighed on Sarrin's conscience as much as his failure to become Kyralia's saviour.

Lorlen glanced at the Alchemist, who was standing several strides away. Sarrin looked haggard and tired, but regarded the advancing enemy with grim determination. Lorlen then looked at Balkan, who stood with his arms crossed, somehow managing to appear confident and at ease. Lady Vinara seemed as calm and resolute.

Lorlen regarded the approaching carts again. Scouts had reported the location of the enemy the night before. The Sachakans had broken into an abandoned farmhouse beside the road, only an hour's travel from the city. When it appeared that they intended to delay their attack until the next day, the King had been pleased. He still hoped that Sarrin would succeed.

One of the King's counsellors had pointed out that the Ichani would not rest unless they needed it. Lorlen had recognised this man as Raven, the professional spy who had accompanied Rothen on the first days of his abandoned mission.

'If they want to sleep, we should prevent it,' Raven had said. 'You don't need to send magicians. Ordinary men may be of no use in a magical confrontation, but don't underestimate our ability to be annoying.'

So a handful of guards had slipped out into the night to release swarms of sapflys into the farmhouse, rouse the Sachakans with loud noises, and finally set the building on fire. The last was done with more than the usual relish, after the Ichani had caught one of the guards. What they did to the man did not bode well for those citizens who hadn't left Imardin yet.

Looking over his shoulder, Lorlen considered the city. The streets were empty and silent. Most members of the Houses had sailed for Elyne, taking their families and servants with them. A line of carts had flowed through the Southern Gate for the last two days as the rest of the population fled toward the outlying villages. Guards had kept order as best they could, but there weren't enough of them to curtail some of the looting that had occurred. As soon as the sun had set the previous evening, the Gates had been closed and fortifications fixed in place.

Of course, the Ichani might ignore the gates. They might head straight for the gap in the Outer Wall where it had once surrounded the Guild grounds.

There was nothing the Guild could do to prevent that. They already knew they would lose this battle. They only hoped to kill one or two Ichani.

Still, he hated to think of the destruction they could wreak on the grand old buildings. Lord Jullen had packed up and sent away the most precious books and records, and sealed the rest in a room underneath the University. Patients within the Healers' Quarters, servants and family had been sent out of the city.

Similar precautions had been taken at the Palace. Lorlen turned to regard the towers, just visible over the Inner Wall. The city's walls had been built to protect this central building. Over the centuries the Palace had been modified to indulge the tastes and whims of Kyralia's royalty, but the wall around it had remained intact. The best of the Guard waited within, ready to fight if the Guild was defeated.

'They've reached the slums,' Osen murmured.

Facing north again, Lorlen looked down at the slums.

The labyrinth of unplanned streets spread before him. All were deserted. He wondered where the dwells had gone. Far away, he hoped.

The carts had reached the first buildings and the occupants were tiny figures now. As Lorlen watched, they drew to a halt. Six men and one woman stepped down from the vehicles and started walking toward the Northern Gates. The slaves drew the carts away into the slums.

One Ichani has gone with them, Lorlen noted. *One less to fight us. Not that it will make much difference.*

'The King has arrived,' Osen murmured.

Lorlen turned to see the monarch approaching. Magicians knelt and quickly rose again as the King passed. Lorlen followed suit.

'Administrator.'

'Your Majesty,' Lorlen replied.

The King looked down at the advancing Sachakans.

'Have you tried to contact Akkarin again?'

Lorlen nodded. 'Every hour, since you first requested it.'

'No answer?'

'None.'

The King nodded. 'Then we face them alone. Let's hope he was wrong about their strength.'

Sonea had never seen the Northern Gates closed. The enormous sheets of metal had always been streaked with rust and the decorations obscured by centuries of dirt and grime. Now they were a clean, glossy black – restored, no doubt, out of pride and defiance.

A line of magicians stood on top of the wall. Brown robes were scattered among the red, green and purple ones.

She felt a pang of sympathy for her fellow classmates. They must be terrified.

The Ichani walked into view on the road below. Sonea's heart lurched and she heard Akkarin catch his breath. They were only a hundred or so paces away, and this time she was not seeing them through the eyes of another magician.

She, Akkarin, Cery and Takan were watching from a house beside the North Road. Cery had brought them there because the building had a little tower room above the second floor, which had the best view of the area before the gates.

'The one in front is Kariko,' Akkarin murmured.

Sonea nodded. 'And the woman must be Avala. What about the rest?'

'Remember the spy whose mind you read? The tall one there is Harikava, his master. The two at the far end are Inijaka and Sarika. I've seen them in the minds of the spies I've read. The other two, Rikacha and Rashi, are old allies of Kariko.'

'There are seven,' she said. 'One's missing.'

Akkarin frowned. 'Yes.'

The Ichani continued for several paces past the house, then stopped. They looked up at the row of robed figures standing along the top of the Outer Wall.

The voice that drifted down was unfamiliar.

'Go no further, Sachakans. You are not welcome in my land.'

Looking at the figures of the magicians on the wall above the gates, Sonea saw a finely dressed man standing beside Administrator Lorlen.

'Is that . . . the King?'

'Yes.'

She felt a reluctant admiration for the monarch. He had stayed in the city, when he could have fled with the Houses.

Kariko spread his hands. 'Is this how Kyralians treat a guest? Or a weary traveller?'

'A guest does not kill his host's family or servants.'

Kariko laughed. 'No. Welcome or not, I am in your land. And I want your city. Open your gates, and I will allow you to live and serve me.'

'We would die rather than serve your kind.'

Sonea's heart leapt as she recognised Lorlen's voice.

'Was that one of those who calls himself a "magician"?' Kariko laughed. 'I'm sorry. The invitation wasn't for you, or your Guild. I don't keep magicians. Dying is the only way your pathetic Guild can serve me.' He crossed his arms. 'Open your gates, King Merin.'

'Open them yourself,' the King replied. 'And we'll see if my Guild is as pathetic as you say.'

Kariko turned to regard his allies. 'Well, that's all the welcome we're going to get. Let's break the shell and feast on the egg.'

Their movements were casual as they spread out into a line. White streaks of light sprang toward the gates, striking at the sides and centre. Sonea heard Cery suck in a breath as the metal began to glow. Hundreds of strikes rained down on the figures below. All scattered against the Ichani's shields.

'See their weakness, Lorlen!' Akkarin hissed. 'Focus on one!'

Sonea jumped as the sound of something tearing filled the room. Akkarin's hand had been resting on the paper screen beside the window. He extracted his fingers from the torn paper and gripped the sill instead.

'That's it!' he said.

Looking outside again, Sonea saw that the Guild's strikes had shifted to a single Ichani. She held her breath, expecting the other Sachakans to blend their shields, but they did not.

'That man,' Akkarin jabbed a finger toward the Ichani under attack. 'He will be our first.'

'If he'll leave the group,' Cery added.

Kariko glanced toward his failing ally then looked up at the wall. A streak of light shot from him to the figures above the gate, but was blocked by the Guild's combined shield.

Then a cloud of white belched out of the gates. A glowing hole had formed in the metal, and more clouds were billowing up from behind.

'Houses must have caught fire on the other side,' Cery said darkly.

Akkarin shook his head. 'Not yet. That's steam, not smoke. The Guard are throwing water on the wooden fortifications to keep them from burning.'

It seemed a ridiculously feeble attempt to stop the Ichani, yet every obstacle the Sachakans overcame used some of their power. Sonea glanced up at the wall again. The King and the magicians over the gate were hurrying to either side, away from the billowing clouds of steam.

Then one of the gates moved. Cery muttered a curse as it sagged forward. There were several loud cracks before it broke loose from its hinges and slammed to the ground. Beyond, a scaffolding of wood and iron filled the gap. As guards hurried to climb off the structure, the second gate fell.

Kariko glanced at his companions.

'They think they can stop us with this?' He laughed and turned back to stare at the fortifications.

The air rippled, then the scaffolding buckled inward as if punched by enormous, invisible fists. The crack of breaking timber and tortured metal echoed out of the gap in the wall, then the fortifications collapsed to the ground.

Looking up, Sonea saw that the magicians on the wall had all but disappeared. She watched as the Ichani strode into the city. Strikes came from the houses on either side, but the Sachakans ignored them. They strode on toward the Inner Wall.

Akkarin stepped back from the window, then turned to Cery.

'We must get into the city quickly,' he said.

Cery smiled. 'No problem. Just follow me.'

It was not long before Farand was gasping for air. Dannyl caught the young man's arm and slowed to a fast walk. The young man glanced behind, his expression fearful.

'They won't follow us,' Dannyl assured him. 'They looked like they had their mind set on the Inner Circle.'

Farand nodded. The young magician had appeared beside Dannyl on the wall, perhaps seeking the reassurance of a familiar face. The magicians ahead drew further away and eventually turned out of sight.

'Will we . . . get there . . . in time?' Farand panted as they reached the West Quarter.

'I hope so,' Dannyl replied. Looking up at the Inner Wall, he could see that some magicians were already hurrying along the top. He glanced at Farand, who was still pale but struggling along valiantly. 'Maybe not.'

He turned down the next street. The wall was directly

ahead of them. When they reached it, Dannyl took hold of Farand's shoulders. He created a disc of power beneath their feet, and sent them upward as quickly as he dared. The sudden ascent made his stomach sink disconcertingly.

'I thought we weren't supposed to use any magic except in the fight,' Farand gasped.

They reached the top of the wall and Dannyl set them down. 'It's obvious you're still too weak for running,' he said. 'Better we got here soon enough for me to channel your power, than not get here in time at all.'

A magician hurried toward them, his face flushed from exertion, and they followed him along the wall. Looking down at the Inner Circle, Dannyl felt a flash of anxiety. Tayend was down there. Though the mansion the Scholar was hiding in was located on the other side of the Palace, it would not be any protection once the Ichani began to explore.

As they reached the line of magicians forming along the wall, Dannyl sent his power out to join the Guild's shield. He looked down at the Ichani. They were standing together before the gates, talking.

'Why haven't they attacked?' Farand asked.

Dannyl looked closer. 'I don't know. There's only six. One's missing.'

The Sachakan woman stepped out of a side street. She sauntered toward the Ichani. The leader crossed his arms and stepped forward to meet her. Dannyl watched their lips moving. The woman smiled, but when the leader turned away her expression changed to a sneer.

'She's rebellious,' Farand said. 'That might be useful, later.'

Dannyl nodded, then his attention was drawn back to

the Ichani as they attacked. Strikes flashed through the air and he felt a vibration under his feet.

'They're attacking the wall,' a Healer nearby exclaimed.

The vibration increased rapidly to a shaking. Dannyl looked ahead. The magicians closest to the gates were struggling to keep their balance. Some had dropped to a crouch. As the Guild's shield fragmented, a few magicians were blasted off the wall completely.

—Attack!

Responding to Balkan's mental voice, Dannyl straightened. His own strike joined the hundreds that rained on the Sachakans. A hand touched his shoulder, and he felt Farand's power added to his own.

The shaking and noise ceased abruptly. The Ichani backed away from the gates. Dannyl felt a little surge of hope, though he had no idea what they were retreating from.

Then the gates fell outward and slammed into the ground at the Ichani's feet. Rubble from the ruined wall rained down on top of it. Kariko looked up at the magicians on either side and smiled with obvious satisfaction.

—Leave the wall, Balkan commanded.

At once the magicians hurried to wooden staircases that had been built on the inside of the wall. Dannyl and Farand hastened down to the streets below.

'What next?' Farand panted as they reached the ground.

'We meet Lord Vorel.'

'And then?'

'I don't know. Vorel will have directions, I imagine.'

A few streets later, Dannyl found the Warrior waiting in the prearranged meeting place with several other magicians. All were quiet and subdued.

—Regroup.

Vorel nodded at Balkan's command. He looked at each of them, his expression sober and grim. 'That means we are to get close to them, without being seen. When the next command comes, we are to attack at once, focussing our strikes on one Sachakan. Follow me.'

As Vorel hurried away, Dannyl, Farand and the other magicians in their group followed. Not a word was spoken. *They all know this will be the last confrontation*, Dannyl thought. *After this, if we're still alive, we abandon the city.*

Cery watched as Sonea and Akkarin disappeared into the darkened passage, following their guide. Drawing in a deep breath, he began walking in the other direction. Takan followed close behind.

He had much to do. The other Thieves needed to know that Akkarin and Sonea had made it into the Inner Circle. The fake magicians could be let loose on the streets. The slaves needed to be found and dealt with. And he . . . he needed a strong drink.

The journey through to the Inner Circle had been terrifying, even for one used to the passages of the Thieves' Road. The roof had collapsed under the wall, leaving only enough room to squirm through in places. Sonea had assured him that she and Akkarin would be able to hold the roof up with magic if it started to fall again, but with every breath of dust Cery had found it far too easy to imagine himself being crushed and buried.

He reached a stretch of passage that ran parallel to an alley. Grates high in the wall gave glimpses of the street beyond. Hearing the sound of running feet, Cery paused and watched as a magician ran past. The man skidded to a halt.

'Oh, no,' he whimpered.

Bending close to a grate, Cery saw that the alley was a dead end. The magician was a novice – a mere youth. His robes were covered in dust.

Then, from somewhere just past the street entrance, came a woman's voice.

'Where are you? Where are you, little magician?'

The woman's accent was so like Savara's, that for a moment Cery thought it was her. But the voice was higher, and the laugh that followed was cruel.

The youth cast about, but this was the Inner Circle, and there were no crates or rubbish lying about to hide behind. Cery hurried down the passage to the grate closest to the boy, then pushed it open.

'Hai, magician!' he whispered.

The boy jumped, then turned to stare at Cery.

'Come in here,' Cery beckoned. 'Come on.'

The youth glanced toward the alley entrance once, then dived for the opening. He fell into the passage head first, landed awkwardly, then rolled over and scrambled to his feet. As the woman's voice came again, he backed against the far wall, panting with terror.

'Where did you go?' the woman called as she strode down the alley. 'This goes nowhere. You must be inside one of these houses. Let's have a look.'

She tested a few doors, then blasted one open. As she disappeared inside, Cery turned to grin at the novice.

'You're safe now,' he said. 'It'll take her hours to search all the houses. Likely she'll get bored, and go looking for easier prey.'

The youth's panting had slowed to long, deliberate breaths. He straightened and pushed away from the wall.

'Thank you,' he said. 'You saved my life.'

Cery shrugged. 'No rub.'

'Who are you – and why are you here? I thought everyone had been evacuated.'

'Ceryni is my name,' Cery told him. 'Ceryni of the Thieves.'

The youth blinked in surprise. Then he grinned.

'I am honoured to meet you, Thief. I am Regin of Winar.'

The rhythm of the horse's gait drove everything. Its breath gusted out in time with the pounding of its hooves. The pain in Rothen's shoulder flared at every jolt. He could soothe it away with a little Healing power, but he did not want to use any more of his strength than he must. The Guild needed every scrap of magic to fight the Ichani. He hadn't even drawn power to chase away the weariness he felt from riding all night.

Ahead, the city shone like a glittering treasure spread over a table. Each building shone like gold in the morning light. He might reach it in an hour, maybe less.

A burned-out house smoked in a charred field. Small groups of people, mostly families, hurried along the road carrying bags, boxes and baskets. They watched him pass with both hope and fear in their faces. The closer he came to the city, the more numerous they were, until they became an unbroken line of humanity fleeing Imardin.

None of this boded well for the fate of the Guild. Rothen cursed under his breath. The only mental calls he had heard had been Balkan's orders. He dared not call out to Dorrien or Dannyl.

An image flashed before his eyes. A glimpse of a city

street, then a Sachakan face. Kariko. He blinked several times, but the image did not fade.

I've been wishing to know what's happening so much, I'm starting to hallucinate, Rothen thought. *Or is it from lack of sleep?*

He gave in and sent a little Healing power into his body, but the vision remained. A feeling of terror swept over Rothen, but not his own. He caught a glimpse of green robes and a sense of identity. Lord Sarle.

Was the Healer sending this? It didn't feel deliberate.

Kariko was holding a knife. He smiled and leaned closer. 'Watch this, slave killer.'

Rothen felt a flash of pain, then a distant but terrible feeling of paralysis and fear. Slowly the sense of Lord Sarle's mind faded to nothing, and Rothen felt himself abruptly released.

He gasped and stared at his surroundings. The horse was stationary. Men and women beside the road hurried past, eyeing him nervously.

The blood gem! Rothen thought. *Kariko must have put it on Lord Sarle*. He shuddered as he realised he'd felt Sarle's death. *He's going to show me the death of every magician he kills*.

And next time it might be Dorrien or Dannyl.

Slapping his heels against the horse's flanks, Rothen sent it galloping toward the city.

CHAPTER 34

THE HUNT BEGINS

The city streets were still hazy with dust from the destruction of the wall. All was desolate and empty, but now and then Lorlen caught a glimpse of movement at the corner of a building or within a window. He and Osen had broken into one of the houses facing the Palace only a few minutes before. Now they were waiting for the Ichani to arrive, and Balkan's order to attack.

He didn't know how many magicians had survived or how much power they had left, but he would find out soon enough.

'Here. Sit down,' Osen murmured.

Lorlen glanced away from the window to find his assistant holding an antique chair. As Osen set the chair down, Lorlen managed a wry smile.

'Thank you. I doubt I'll be using it for long.'

The young magician's gaze shifted back to the street outside.

'No. They're here.'

Looking through the window again, Lorlen saw six figures emerge from the dust. The Sachakans walked slowly past, toward the Palace. Kariko gazed up at the wall.

No, we're not going to give you another chance to blast the stone out from under our feet, Lorlen thought as he moved to the door.

—Attack!

At Balkan's order, Lorlen flung open the door and stepped outside, Osen following. Other magicians were emerging to form a half-circle around the Sachakans. Lorlen added his strength to their shield, then struck at the Ichani.

The Sachakans spun around to face them. An image of one of the Ichani flashed into Lorlen's mind. At once, the Guild attacked the man. The force of their strikes sent the Ichani staggering backward toward the Palace wall, until the Sachakan's answering strikes forced the Guild to concentrate on shielding again.

The blasts that hit the Guild's shield were terrible. Lorlen felt a rush of fear and anxiety as the half-circle of magicians flinched away. The Guild would weaken quickly if it endured this battering for long.

—Retreat.

At Balkan's command, the Guild magicians backed away to the houses and alleys they had emerged from. The Ichani began to advance.

'We have to get at least *one* of them,' Osen gasped.

'You shield, I'll strike,' Lorlen replied. 'Let's just get closer to the house.'

They edged toward the door. As they reached it, Lorlen stopped.

'Now!'

Abandoning his shield, Lorlen threw all his remaining power into a strike at the weakened Ichani. The Sachakan staggered, and other strikes came as Guild magicians saw the man's weakness. The man gave a shout – a wordless cry of anger and fear – as his shield failed. The next strike threw him back against the Palace wall, which buckled around him. He sagged and crumpled to the ground.

Cheers came from all around, but they ended abruptly as the Ichani retaliated with powerful blasts. Osen made a strangled noise.

'Get . . . back . . . inside . . .' Osen said between gritted teeth.

Lorlen followed Osen's gaze and felt his stomach turn with dread as he saw that the Ichani leader, Kariko, was walking toward them, sending strike after strike at Osen's shield. Taking Osen's arm, Lorlen guided him back into the house. Wood and brickworks shattered as Kariko's strikes passed through the doorway. Then Osen's shield wavered.

'No,' Osen gasped. 'Not yet.'

Grabbing Osen's shoulders, Lorlen pushed him aside. There was a boom, and the front wall of the house collapsed inward. Cracks ran across the ceiling. Lorlen felt something slam across his shoulders and he staggered to his knees.

Then he was being battered to the floor. The ceiling had fallen in, he guessed. A weight pushed down on him from above. It crushed the air from his lungs. Then, as stillness finally came, he grew aware of pain. He sent his mind inward, and went cold as he saw the broken bones and ruptured organs, and realised what it would mean.

There was only one thing to do.

Dust and dirt cascaded down around him as he edged his hand toward the ring in his pocket.

The passages under the Inner Circle were quiet. Here and there volunteers waited by exits. Akkarin and Sonea's guide stopped as a messenger appeared and hurried toward them.

'Sachakan magician . . . stayed with . . . the slaves,' the man panted. 'They're in . . . slums. Northside.'

'So one of them has separated from the others already,' Sonea observed. 'Should we find him first?'

'It will take time to get there,' Akkarin said. He looked up in the direction of the Palace. 'I would like to see how the Guild fares, but . . . this lone Ichani may try to rejoin Kariko when he hears that the Guild has been defeated.' He nodded slowly and turned to the guide. 'Yes. Take us to the slums.'

'I'll let them know you're coming,' the messenger said. He sprinted away.

The guide led them back down the passage. Several minutes later they were stopped by a middle-aged woman.

'Tunnel's collapsed,' she reported. 'Can't go that way.'

'What is the fastest alternative route?'

'There's another tunnel close to the Guild wall,' the Guide told them.

Akkarin looked up. 'The gap in the wall is almost above us.'

'That would be faster,' the guide said, shrugging. 'But you may be seen.'

'The Guild and Ichani are outside the Palace. To anyone else, we will look like two more ordinary Imardians escaping the city. Take us to an exit as close to the wall as possible.'

The guide nodded and led them away. After a few turns, he stopped at a ladder bolted to a wall and pointed up at a hatch.

'That'll put you in a storeroom. There's a door to an alley.' He gave them instructions on finding an entrance to the passages on the other side of the wall. 'You'll find guides there. They know the North Quarter better than me.'

Akkarin began to climb. Following him, Sonea found herself in a large room filled with foodstuffs. They pushed through a door into a narrow, dead-end alley. Akkarin glided forward and stopped at the entrance. Drawing alongside, Sonea saw that they were on the other side of the road that followed the Inner Wall. Her heart sank as she took in the ruins.

A gust of wind chased away the dust and she saw familiar colours among the rubble. As she looked closer, she realised they were the robes of magicians.

'The way is clear,' Akkarin murmured. As they moved out of the ally, she took a step toward the magicians, and felt Akkarin's hand on her arm.

'They're dead, Sonea,' he murmured gently. 'The Guild would not have left them, otherwise.'

'I know,' she said. 'I just want to know who they are.'

'Not yet. There will be time for that later.'

Akkarin drew her toward the gap in the wall. Rubble covered the ground, forcing them to slow as they neared the gap. They had just reached the base of the fallen gates when he stopped. Sonea looked at him, and felt a stab of alarm. His face had turned white, and he was staring at a point somewhere far below the ground.

'What is it?'

'Lorlen.' He turned abruptly to face the Inner Circle. 'I have to find him. Go on ahead. Find this Ichani, but do nothing until I arrive.'

'But—'

'Go,' he said, turning to fix her with a cold stare. 'I must do this alone.'

'Do what?'

'Just do as I say, Sonea.'

She could not help feeling a pang of hurt and anger at the impatience in his tone. This was not a good time for him to be mysterious and secretive with her. If they parted, how would they find each other again? Then she remembered the ring.

'Should I put on your blood ring now? You said we should wear them if we're separated.'

A look of alarm crossed his face, then his expression softened. 'Yes,' he said, 'but I will not put yours on yet. I would not show you what I fear I may see in the next hour.'

She stared back at him. What would happen that he didn't want her to see? Did it have something to do with Lorlen?

'I must go,' he said. She nodded, then watched him stride away.

After he had disappeared, she hurried into the North Quarter. Reaching the shadows of an alley, she took his ring out of her pocket and considered it. His warning from the previous night repeated in her mind.

'*Sometimes, hearing and knowing exactly how another person regards you can be an unpleasant experience. It can end friendships, turn love to resentment . . .*'

But they had to be able to contact each other when apart. She pushed aside her doubts and slipped the ring onto her finger. No feeling of his presence appeared at the edge of her thoughts. She searched, but sensed nothing. Perhaps it wasn't working.

No, she thought, *the maker controls how much the wearer senses*. But the maker couldn't stop sensing the wearer's thoughts and experiences. That meant Akkarin was attuned to her every thought now.

Hello? she thought.

No answer came. She smiled and shrugged. Whatever

he was doing, he wouldn't want her distracting him – and the last thing she wanted to do was divert his attention when he most needed to concentrate.

She followed the guide's directions and found the passage entrance easily. To her surprise, Faren was waiting inside. His second, the silent man who had watched her approach the Thief only a day before, stood beside him.

'The Guild have killed an Ichani,' Faren told her excitedly. 'I thought I'd tell you myself.'

She smiled and felt her mood lighten a little. 'Now *that's* good news. What about the rest of the Ichani?'

'The woman is roaming about on her own. The one with the slaves was still in Northside at the last report. I expect the rest are heading for the Palace. Where's your constant companion?'

She frowned. 'Had to sort something out on his own. I'm to find the Ichani with the slaves, then sit.'

Faren grinned. 'Then let's go find him.'

After a short trip, they emerged in an alleyway. He led her to a high stack of boxes and stepped through a narrow gap. At the centre was a cramped space. He crouched and rapped on something metallic.

Sonea smothered a groan as a hatch opened and an unpleasant smell wafted out.

'The sewers again.'

'I'm afraid so,' Faren replied. 'They're the most direct route out of the city.'

They descended into the murky darkness. A man with a wide face stood by the ladder, a lamp in one hand and another casting a pool of light around his feet. The Thief took the lamp and started along the ledge that ran down one side of the tunnel. They passed several hatch guards.

At one point, Faren told her that they had just passed under the Outer Wall. When they climbed out of the sewer, she found herself in a familiar part of the slums. Faren quickly led her back through a grate in a wall to the Thieves' Road.

A boy waiting inside informed them that the lone Ichani and the slaves were now only a few streets away.

'They're headed for the main road,' the boy said.

'Tell everyone to be ready, then report back.'

The boy nodded, then hurried away.

After a short journey, they ascended into a house and climbed up a rickety staircase to the second floor. Faren led her to a window. Looking out, Sonea saw that the Sachakan slaves were standing in the street below. The Ichani was watching as two emerged from a bakery carrying trays of rolls. Several of the limek-like animals were fighting over a reber carcass. The carts were nowhere to be seen.

The boy from the Road entered the room. His eyes were bright with excitement.

'Everything's ready,' he announced.

Sonea looked at Faren questioningly. 'For what?'

'We set up a few traps for the Sachakans,' Faren explained. 'It was Cery's idea.'

She smiled. 'Of course. What's the plan?'

He moved to a side window. Below, a small walled court-yard backed onto a narrow alleyway. Two heavily built men held a long metal pole with a sharpened point to the wall. They glanced up at the window anxiously. Faren gave them the signal for 'wait'.

'Another two are on the other side of the alley,' Faren told her. 'There's a hole in each wall, filled with false mortar. One of our fake magicians will lure the Ichani into the alley. When he reaches the right place, the men will skewer him.'

Sonea stared at him in disbelief. '*That's* your plan? It will never work. The Ichani's shield will protect him.'

'Maybe he'll get lazy, and think the walls are enough protection.'

'Maybe,' she said, 'but there's only a slim chance he will. You're taking a terrible risk.'

'Do you think our helpers don't know that?' Faren said quietly. 'They know there's a good chance it won't work. They're just as determined to fight these Sachakans as you are.'

She sighed. Of course the dwells wanted to fight, even if it meant taking enormous risks. 'Well, if it doesn't work, I should be down there to—'

'Too late,' Faren's second said. 'Look.'

Moving to the street-side window, Sonea saw that the Ichani and his slaves were approaching. A group of youths ran out in front of them from the other side of the street and began throwing stones. As the Ichani stepped toward them, Sonea heard a muffled shout and saw a robed man walk out into the street from somewhere directly below her. He strode toward the Ichani, then stopped at the alley entrance. As the Ichani saw the fake magician, he smiled.

A strike flashed through the air. The fake magician dodged, narrowly avoiding it. He dashed into the alley.

Sonea hurried to the side window. The two men with the spear were poised and ready. Surely it wouldn't work . . . but if it did . . . She felt a stab of alarm as she realised what would happen.

'Faren, I have to get down there.'

'There's not enough time,' he told her. 'Watch.'

The Ichani strode into the alley. The robed man had stopped. Sonea could see the faint flare of a barrier blocking his path. When the Ichani was a step away from the hidden men, the fake magician yelled something. The spears burst through the wall . . .

. . . and sank deep into the Ichani's body. The Sachakan yelled in surprise and pain.

'It worked!' Faren crowed. Sonea heard similar triumphant cries from outside, muffled through the window. She shuddered in sympathy as she saw the agony in the Ichani's face. As he began to sag against the spears, she knew she would never have time to get to him before he died.

Nevertheless, she smashed the window and yelled at the men below.

'Get away from him!'

They stared up at her in surprise.

Then everything went white.

She threw a shield around herself, Faren and his second. A moment later, the wall of the room exploded inward. Searing heat radiated through her shield, forcing her to strengthen it further. She felt the floor tilt and drop away, and the sensation of falling. As she landed, she tumbled to her knees.

Then the released magic of the dead Ichani abruptly ended. She found she was crouched on top of a pile of bricks and smoking wood. Standing up, she saw she was surrounded by a circle of ruins.

Everything for a hundred paces in any direction was now charred, smoking rubble. Sonea looked toward the alley, but there was no sign of the men who had wielded the spears. She felt a terrible sadness. *I could have saved them, had I known what they'd planned.*

Faren and his second climbed to their feet. They stared at the destruction around them in dismay.

'Cery said something like this might happen,' Faren said. 'He said everyone should get away as quick as they could. He didn't say it would reach this far.'

'What happened?' his second asked in a small voice.

Sonea tried to speak, but her throat was too tight. She swallowed and tried again. 'What always happens when a magician dies,' she managed. 'Any magic he or she has left is released.'

He looked at her with wide eyes. 'Will . . . will that happen to you, too?'

'I'm afraid so. Unless I'm exhausted, or the Ichani take all my power.'

'Oh.' The man shivered and looked away.

'We were lucky you were here,' Faren said quietly. 'If you hadn't been, we'd be like those slaves down there.'

Sonea followed his gaze to the street. Several dark shapes lay on the ground. She shuddered. At least their deaths had been quick.

Faren chuckled. 'Well, we don't have to figure out what to do with them now, do we?'

'Help me!'

Dannyl looked up, startled out of his daze by the plea. Lord Osen was standing within a gaping hole in the side of a house. He was covered in dust, and his face was streaked with tears.

'Lorlen is buried,' Osen gasped. 'Do either of you have any strength left?'

Dannyl glanced at Farand, then shook his head.

'Then . . . then at least help me dig him out.'

They followed Osen into the house. A huge mound of rubble filled the inside. Light streamed down through dust.

Looking up, Dannyl saw that the floor above, and the roof, were missing.

'He's here, I think,' Osen said, stopping near the half buried front door. He dropped to his knees and began digging with his bare hands.

Dannyl and Farand joined him. There was nothing else they could do. They tossed rubble aside, but their progress was slow. Dannyl cut himself as he encountered shards of broken glass in the dust. He was just beginning to wonder how anyone could have survived being this thoroughly buried, when the whole mound suddenly shifted. Bricks, wooden beams and shattered glass began to roll back toward the far wall of the house.

Osen shook his head as if to clear it, then looked around the room. His eyes snapped to a point somewhere behind Dannyl, then widened.

Twisting around, Dannyl saw that a figure stood within the hole in the side wall of the house, silhouetted against the bright light outside. He could see that the man wore plain clothes, but the stranger's face was hidden in shadow.

The sound of shifting rubble dwindled to silence.

'You came back.'

This voice was familiar but weak. Dannyl turned back and felt his heart fill with hope as he saw that Lorlen had been uncovered. The Administrator's robes were covered in dust. His face was bruised, but his eyes were bright.

'Yes. I came back.'

Dannyl sucked in a breath as he recognised the voice. He turned to stare at Akkarin. The exiled magician moved into the room.

'No!' Lorlen said. 'Don't come . . . any closer.'

Akkarin stopped. 'You are dying, Lorlen.'

'I know.' Lorlen's breathing was laboured. 'I won't . . . I won't have you waste your power on me.'

Akkarin took another step. 'But it—'

'Stop. Or I'll be dead before you reach me,' Lorlen gasped. 'Just a little power left, keeping me conscious. All I have to do is use it up faster.'

'Lorlen,' Akkarin said. 'It would only take a little magic. Just enough to keep you alive until—'

'Until the Ichani come to finish me off.' Lorlen's eyes closed. 'I was a Healer, remember. I know what it would take to fix me. Too much magic. You will need everything to stop them.' He opened his eyes and stared at Akkarin. 'I understand why you did it. Why you lied to me. Kyralia's safety was more important than our friendship. It still is. I only want to know one thing. Why didn't you answer when I called you?'

'I couldn't,' Akkarin said. 'If the Guild knew I was here, the Ichani would read it from the mind of their first victim. They would stay together. Alone, they are vulnerable.'

'Ah,' Lorlen smiled faintly. 'I see.'

His eyes closed again. Akkarin took another step toward his friend. Lorlen's eyes fluttered open.

'No, you don't,' he whispered. 'Stay there. Tell me . . . tell me about Sonea.'

'She is alive,' Akkarin said. 'She is . . .'

Though Akkarin did not finish the sentence, Lorlen's mouth twitched into a crooked smile.

'Good,' he said.

Then his face relaxed and he let out a long sigh. Akkarin hurried forward and dropped into a crouch. He touched Lorlen's forehead and an expression of pain crossed his face.

Taking Lorlen's hand, he bowed his head, then removed a ring.

'Lord Osen,' he said.

'Yes?'

'You, Ambassador Dannyl and . . .' he glanced at Farand, 'his companion must not tell anyone I am here. If the Ichani discover that Sonea and I are here, any chance we have of defeating them will be lost. Do you understand?'

'Yes,' Osen said quietly.

'All but one Ichani are in the Palace. Get out of the city while you still can.'

Akkarin rose and turned away in one abrupt movement. He moved to the hole in the wall. For a moment, before he strode outside, Dannyl caught a glimpse of his face. Though his expression was hard and set, his eyes glittered brightly in the sunlight.

Several hundred paces from the outskirts of the slums, Rothen left the road. He could see the gaping hole where the Northern Gates had been. Through it, he had seen the wider gap in the Inner Wall.

He didn't need to enter the city that way, however. There was always the gap in the Outer Wall around the Guild grounds.

He wondered, then, why the Ichani had chosen to waste their power on destroying the city gates. They must have learned about the breach in the Outer Wall from the minds of the magicians they had caught and killed at the Fort and in Calia. Perhaps they had wanted to demonstrate their superior strength to the Guild. And maybe they intended to replace the magic they had lost by preying on ordinary Imardians.

Either way, they must feel sure that their strength, or their ability to replace it, would win them Kyralia. As Rothen urged his horse toward the forested hill behind the grounds, he felt a growing dread. Would he arrive too late? Would he find the Guild destroyed and Ichani waiting? He must approach the grounds carefully.

He let the horse slow as she reached the first trees. The forest grew rapidly denser, until he was forced to dismount and lead her. An image flashed before his eyes. *Not again . . .*

He kept walking as the experience of death overlaid his surroundings. This time it was a Palace guard. When the vision faded to nothing, Rothen sighed with relief.

How many has it been? he thought. *Twenty? Thirty?*

The slope grew steeper. He stumbled through low vegetation, over logs, rocks and holes. Reaching a bare stretch of ground, he looked up and saw glimpses of white through the trees ahead.

At the sight of the buildings, relief and happiness rushed over him. He hurried forward until he stood at the edge of the forest. Dozens of small houses filled a clearing below. It was like a tiny village.

A deserted village, he amended. Though Rothen had lived only a few hundred paces from this place, he had only seen it once before, as a novice. The collection of houses was known as the Servants' Quarters.

He started walking down to the buildings. As he did, a door opened. A man in a servant uniform hurried forward to meet him.

'My lord,' the man said, sketching a quick bow. 'How goes the battle?'

'I don't know,' Rothen replied. 'I just arrived. Why are you still here?'

The man's shoulders lifted. 'I volunteered to keep an eye on the houses until everyone comes back.'

Rothen glanced up at his horse. 'Anyone from the stables still here?'

'No, but I can take care of your horse for you.'

'Thank you.' Rothen handed the reins to the servant. 'If nobody comes back by the end of the day, leave. Take the horse, if you wish.'

The man looked surprised. He bowed, then patted the horse's nose and led her away. Rothen turned and started along the path to the Guild.

Three hours had passed since Cery had parted with Sonea and Akkarin. He'd received reports that she had gone to the slums to deal with the lone Ichani. Akkarin had disappeared in the Inner Circle, and Takan could not say what his master was doing.

A smuggler's den under the Inner Circle had been selected as a meeting place. It was a large room, filled to the roof with goods. As three figures began to walk down the aisle between the shelving, Cery smiled and walked forward to meet them.

'Your Guild killed one of the Ichani,' he said. 'One dead, seven to go.'

'No.' Sonea smiled. 'Two dead, six to go.'

He glanced at Faren. 'The one in the slums?'

'Yes, though none of my doing.'

He grinned and felt a glow of pleasure. 'One of my traps worked, then?'

'I think you should have a look at what's left of the

slums before you go boasting about it,' Faren replied dryly. His second nodded in agreement.

'What happened?' Cery asked, looking at Sonea.

'Faren can explain later.' She looked over his shoulder, and he turned to find Takan approaching. 'Do either of you know where Akkarin is?' she asked.

The servant shook his head. 'I have received no word from him for two hours.'

Sonea frowned. Finding the same expression on Takan's face, Cery guessed that, whatever Akkarin was doing, he wanted it to remain private. What was so important that Akkarin would hide it from his two closest companions?

'Where are the other Ichani?' Faren asked.

'Five in the Palace, one roaming around,' Cery told them.

'Let me guess,' Sonea said, 'the wanderer is the woman.'

'Yes.'

She sighed. 'I suppose I should wait here until Akkarin comes back.'

Cery smiled. 'I've got someone hidden down here I want you to meet.'

'Oh, and who might that be?'

'A magician. I saved him from the Ichani woman. He's very grateful. In fact, he's so grateful he's volunteered to be the bait for the next little trap we've set up.'

Cery led her around a stack of boxes to a small space filled with chairs. The novice was sitting in one of them. He looked up as they appeared, then rose and smiled.

'Greetings, Sonea.'

Sonea stared at him in dismay. As he'd expected, she replied with gritted teeth.

'Regin.'

CHAPTER 35

TRAPPED

'Sit down, Sonea,' Cery urged. 'You two stay here, while I fetch something to eat.'

Sonea stared at Cery. No doubt he had no inkling of the history between her and Regin. Then he winked at her and she realised he *had* remembered who Regin was.

'Go on,' he said. 'I'm sure you have plenty of catching up to do.'

Sonea sat down reluctantly. She looked at Faren, but the Thief had moved across the room and was having a murmured conversation with his second. Takan was pacing in another corner. Regin glanced at her, looked away, rubbed his palms together, then cleared his throat.

'So,' he said, 'you kill any of these Sachakans yet?'

Sonea resisted the urge to laugh. It was a strange, yet somehow appropriate, way to begin a conversation with her old enemy.

'A couple,' she said.

He nodded. 'The one in the slums?'

'No. One in the South Pass, and one before then, in the city.'

His gaze slipped to the floor. 'Was it hard?'

'Killing someone?' She grimaced. 'Yes and no. I guess you don't think about it, when you're trying to stop the other person killing you. You only think about it later.'

He smiled faintly. 'I meant, are they hard to kill?'

'Oh.' She looked away. 'Probably. I only succeeded with those two because I tricked them.'

'Probably? Don't you know how strong they are?'

'No. I'm not even sure how strong I am. I guess I'll find out when I have to fight one.'

'Then how do you know if you can win a battle?'

'I don't.'

Regin looked up at her, his expression incredulous. Then he flushed and looked away. 'Everyone's given you a hard time,' he said in a low voice. 'Lord Fergun, me and the novices, and the whole Guild when they found out you'd learned black magic – but you still came back. You're still willing to risk your life to save us.' He shook his head. 'If I'd known what was going on, I wouldn't have been so rough on you that first year.'

Sonea stared at him, caught between disbelief and surprise. Was this an apology?

He met her eyes. 'I just . . . if I live through all this, I'll try and make it up to you.' He shrugged. 'If I live through this, it's the least I can do.'

She nodded. Now it was even harder to think of something to say to him. She was saved from having to when a tall figure strode into view from between the stacks of boxes.

'Akkarin!' She leapt out of her seat and hurried to meet him. He smiled grimly as he saw her.

'Sonea.'

'Did you see what the dwells did?'

'Yes, I watched through the ring, and saw the consequences.'

She frowned. His expression was tight, as if he was hiding the pain of an injury.

'What's wrong,' she whispered. 'What happened?'

His eyes flickered over her shoulder toward Regin. Taking her arm, he drew her down the aisle for several paces, then looked down and sighed heavily.

'Lorlen is dead.'

Lorlen? Dead? She stared at him in horror, then as she read pain in his face she felt a wave of sympathy for him. Lorlen had been Akkarin's closest friend, yet Akkarin had been forced to lie to him, to blackmail him, and control him through the ring. The last few years had been terrible for them both. The weight that had dragged at her since hearing that Rothen had died felt suddenly unbearably heavy.

She wound her arms around Akkarin's waist and rested her forehead on his chest. He drew her closer and held her tightly. After a moment he took a deep breath and let it out slowly.

'I saw Dannyl and Osen,' he told her quietly. 'They were with Lorlen, so they know of our presence now. I warned them that they must not tell the others and I . . . I took Lorlen's ring.'

'What about the rest of the Guild?'

'I doubt any are left who are not exhausted or near it,' he said. 'The Thieves have taken some into the passages. Others have retreated to the Guild grounds.'

'How many are dead?'

'I don't know. Twenty. Fifty. Maybe more.'

So many. 'What do we do now?'

Akkarin held her for a little longer, then pushed her to arm's length.

'Kariko is in the Palace with four of the others. Avala still wanders the streets alone. We must find her before she joins them again.'

Sonea nodded. 'I wish I had known what the Thieves had planned to do to the Ichani in the slums. If either of us had been close by, we could have had all his power.'

'Yes, but there is one less Ichani for us to deal with now.' He let her go, then moved back into the aisle. 'Your friend Cery does have some interesting ideas. I think, if Kyralia survives, the Guild will find the Purge has become a dangerous exercise.'

Sonea smiled. 'I thought I had convinced them of that.'

'Not quite in the way Cery's friends might.'

As they reached the end of the room, Sonea saw that Cery had returned with the promised food. Takan was eating hungrily, no longer looking as worried as he had been. Regin was looking from her to Akkarin, his eyes glittering with interest.

'Regin of Winar,' Akkarin said. Sonea recognised the hint of dislike in his voice. 'I hear you were rescued by the Thieves.'

Regin rose and bowed. 'They saved my life, my lord. I hope to repay that favour.'

Akkarin nodded and glanced at Takan. 'I think you may have your chance very soon.'

'Where are we going?'

Dannyl glanced at Farand. The young magician hadn't spoken for the last half hour. He had trustingly followed Dannyl without question, until now.

'I have to meet a friend,' Dannyl replied.

'But your former High Lord said we should leave the city.'

'Yes.' Dannyl nodded. 'He said that the Ichani are in the Palace. I have to meet Tayend now, while I still can. He should be able to give us some ordinary clothes, too.'

'Tayend? He's in Imardin?'

'Yes.' Dannyl checked the next street and found it empty. Farand followed him around the corner. The mansion Tayend was staying in was only a dozen houses ahead. Dannyl felt his pulse quicken in anticipation.

'But he didn't come to the Hearing,' Farand said.

'No, he only arrived a few days ago.'

'That was badly timed.'

Dannyl chuckled. 'It certainly was.'

'Why didn't he leave again?'

They were halfway to the house now. Dannyl searched for an answer. *Because Tayend has some crazy idea he can help me survive the battle. Because he doesn't want me to face the destruction of the Guild alone. Because he cares about me more than his own safety.*

Dannyl sighed. 'Because he didn't understand how dangerous these Ichani are,' he told Farand. 'And I couldn't convince him that non-magicians would be in as much danger as magicians. Are all Elynes so obstinate?'

Farand gave a low laugh. 'From what I'm told, it's a national trait.'

They reached the door of the house. Dannyl drew out a key and reached out for the lock . . . and froze.

The door was open.

He stood staring at the gap between the door and the frame, his heart suddenly pounding. Farand touched his shoulder.

'Ambassador?'

'It's open. Tayend wouldn't leave it open. Somebody's been here.'

'We should go, then.'

'No!' Dannyl took a few deep, slow breaths and turned

to look at Farand. 'I have to know if he's all right. You can come with me, or you can wait somewhere close until I come out, or you can leave me and make your way out of the city.'

Farand looked up at the mansion. He took a deep breath and straightened his shoulders. 'I'll come with you.'

Dannyl pushed open the door. The guestroom inside was empty. He slowly and cautiously crept through the house, a room at a time, but found no sign of the scholar other than a travel chest in one bedroom, and several used wine glasses.

'Perhaps he went out to get some food,' Farand suggested. 'If we wait, he might come back.'

Dannyl shook his head. 'He wouldn't go out unless he was forced to. Not today.' He entered the kitchen, where a half-empty wine glass and a bottle sat on a large table. 'Is there anywhere I haven't checked?'

Farand pointed to a door. 'The cellar?'

The door opened onto a staircase, which descended to a large storeroom full of bottles and some food. The room was empty. Dannyl returned to the kitchen. Farand gestured to the half-empty glass of wine.

'He left in a hurry,' he murmured. 'From this room. So, if I was standing here and something caused me to flee the house, where would I go?' He looked at Dannyl. 'The servant's entrance is the closest.'

Dannyl nodded. 'Then we go that way, too.'

The Guild grounds were so empty and quiet, it might have been mid-year break. The silence was too complete, however. Even during those few weeks of the year when classes were closed and most magicians took the opportunity to visit family, it was never this quiet in the grounds.

As Rothen entered the University, he began to wonder if the Guild was the best place for him to be. All the way to Imardin, he had thought no further ahead than getting to familiar surroundings. But now that he had arrived, he found the Guild lacked the anticipated feeling of safety that had drawn him here.

He knew from the minds of Kariko's victims that the Guild had confronted the Ichani one last time outside the Palace. They had killed a Sachakan, but had exhausted themselves in the process. After that, Kariko's victims had been Palace guards, so Rothen could assume the Ichani were still in the centre of the city. Where would the Ichani go once they had gained control of the Palace? Rothen stopped at the entrance to the Great Hall as his blood turned cold.

The Guild grounds.

Balkan knows this, he thought. *He will have told everyone to flee the city. He will want us to gather together elsewhere, recover our strength, then start planning to regain Imardin. I should leave here and try to join them.*

Rothen looked up at the grand ceiling of the Hall and sighed heavily. No doubt this would all be destroyed in the next day or two. He shook his head sadly and turned to go.

Then froze as he heard voices behind him.

His first thought was that the Ichani had arrived, then he felt a shock as he recognised the voices. Turning back, he hurried down the hall.

Balkan and Dorrien stood in front of the Guildhall. They were arguing, but Rothen didn't pause to listen. Both looked up as he appeared.

'Father!' Dorrien gasped.

A wave of relief and affection swept over Rothen. *He's alive*. Dorrien ran forward and embraced him. Rothen stiffened as pain shot through his shoulder.

'Dorrien,' he said. 'What are you doing here?'

'Lorlen called everyone to Imardin,' Dorrien said. His eyes focussed on the scar where Kariko had cut Rothen's cheek. 'Father, we thought you were dead. Why didn't you contact us?' He frowned at Rothen's shoulder. 'You're injured. What happened?'

'I wasn't sure if I could risk mental communication. There was the ban and . . .' Rothen hesitated, reluctant to tell Dorrien about the ring. 'My shoulder and arm broke in the fight, and healed badly in my sleep. But you didn't answer me – or perhaps I'm not asking the right question. Why are you here in the grounds? Surely this is where the Ichani will come next.'

Dorrien looked at Balkan. 'I . . . I didn't fight with the rest of the magicians. I slipped away at the first opportunity.'

Rothen stared at his son in surprise. He could not imagine Dorrien avoiding a fight. His son was no coward.

A look of intense frustration crossed Dorrien's face. 'I have reasons,' he said. 'I can't tell you what they are. I've been sworn to secrecy. You just have to trust me when I say I must not risk being caught by the Ichani. If they read my mind our last chance of killing the Ichani will be lost.'

'Our last chance has come and gone,' Balkan said. Then his eyes narrowed. 'Unless . . .'

Dorrien shook his head. 'Don't speculate. I've said too much already.'

'If you are so concerned that the Ichani will read your

mind, why are you here, in the grounds, where they will probably come next?' Rothen asked.

'I have a clear view of the gates from the Entrance Hall,' Dorrien replied. 'I'll see them coming, and leave through the forest. If I enter the city, the chances of being caught increase.'

'Why not leave now?' Balkan asked.

Dorrien turned to regard him. 'I'm not leaving until I have to. If the secret I hold is discovered by another means, I'll be free to help.'

Balkan frowned. 'Surely, if we leave with you, you can afford to risk telling us what this secret is.'

The stubborn expression on Dorrien's face was all too familiar. Rothen shook his head.

'I don't like your chances of talking him around, Balkan. I do think we should leave at the first sign the Ichani are coming here, however. Which brings me to wonder, why are *you* here?'

The Warrior's frown changed to a scowl. 'Someone should witness the fate of our home.'

Rothen nodded. 'Then the three of us will stay until the end.'

'Sweet bloodweed,' Faren whispered, holding up a tiny bottle. 'Almost undetectable in wine or sweet dishes. It works quickly, so be ready.'

Sonea glanced at the Thief and rolled her eyes.

'What?' he asked.

'Somehow it doesn't surprise me that you know so much about poisons, Faren.'

He smiled. 'I must admit, I started learning about them out of a fancy to mimic my namesake. The knowledge has been useful, at times, but not nearly as often as you'd think. Your novice friend seems particularly interested in the subject.'

'He's not my friend.'

Sonea pressed her eye to the peephole again. Most of the room beyond was taken up by a large dining table. Silver cutlery glinted softly in the filtered light from two small windows. A half-eaten meal lay cold and congealed on the fine plates.

They were inside one of the large Inner Circle mansions. The dining room was a small, private one with two servant doors as well as the main entrance. Sonea and Faren stood behind one door; Akkarin was standing behind the other.

'Cery seemed to think you two had a special acquaintance,' Faren continued to prod.

She snorted softly. 'He offered to kill Regin once. It was tempting.'

'Ah,' he replied.

Sonea looked at the glasses on the table. They were filled with varying levels of wine. Bottles, opened and unopened, were arranged at the centre. All had been laced with poison.

'So what did our volunteer do that inspired such a generous offer from Cery?'

'None of your business.'

'Isn't it? How interesting.'

Sonea jumped as the main door of the dining room burst open. Regin leapt inside, then pushed the door shut again. He dashed around the table and ran to the servants' door that Akkarin was waiting behind. Grasping the handle, he paused.

The main door opened again. Regin pretended to

struggle with the doorhandle. Sonea felt her heart begin to race as one of the Ichani men stepped into the room. He looked at Regin, then down at the table.

'So I guess you won't be too eager to save him if the Ichani doesn't fall for the bait,' Faren whispered.

'Of course I'll save him,' Sonea muttered in reply. 'Regin might be a . . . a . . . whatever, but he doesn't deserve to die.'

As the Ichani looked at Regin again, the boy pressed his back to the door, his face deathly white. The Ichani moved around the table. Regin slid around the wall, keeping the table between him and the Sachakan.

The Ichani chuckled. Reaching out, he took one of the glasses and lifted it to his lips. He sipped and grimaced. Shrugging, he tossed the cup away. It shattered against the wall, leaving a splash of red.

'Is that enough?' Sonea murmured.

'I doubt it,' Faren replied. 'But he's got the idea, and might go for something fresher.'

The Ichani began to walk around the table. Regin edged away. Suddenly he leaped forward and grabbed a bottle of wine by its neck. The Ichani laughed as Regin brandished it threateningly. He made a quick gesture. Regin staggered forward as if struck a heavy blow from behind and sprawled face first on the table.

The Ichani grabbed Regin by the back of his neck and held him down. Sonea grasped the handle of the door, but Faren caught her wrist.

'Wait,' he whispered.

The Sachakan took the bottle from Regin's hand and regarded it. The cork slowly wriggled out and fell to the floor. He lifted the bottle to his lips and gulped several mouthfuls. Beside her, Faren let out a sigh of relief.

'Is that enough?' Sonea breathed.

'Oh, yes.'

Regin writhed on the table, knocking plates and cutlery flying as he struggled against the Ichani's grip. The Sachakan took another swig from the bottle, then smashed it against the table. He reached toward Regin with the broken end.

'That's not good,' Faren said. 'If he cuts Regin the poison will—'

The door behind the Ichani opened. Sonea's heart skipped a beat, but Akkarin didn't leap out. The corridor beyond was empty. Hearing the noise, the Ichani twisted around. He stared at the open door.

'Good. That'll delay him a little longer,' Faren muttered.

Sonea held her breath. The door handle was slippery with sweat in her grasp. If she and Akkarin revealed themselves to the Ichani, he would call out to Kariko. It would be much better if the man succumbed to the drug instead.

'Here we go,' Faren said quietly.

The Ichani suddenly released Regin and staggered away from the table. As he clutched at his stomach, Regin hauled himself up and ran through the main doors.

—Kariko!

—Rikacha?

—I have . . . I have been poisoned!

Kariko did not reply. The Ichani dropped to his knees and doubled over. A long, low moan escaped his mouth, then he vomited up red liquid. Sonea shivered as she realised it was blood.

'How long until he's dead?' she asked.

'Five, ten minutes.'

'You call that quick?'

'I could have used roin. It's faster, but bitter.'

Akkarin appeared in the open doorway. He stared at the man, then pulled off his shirt.

'What is he doing?' Faren asked.

'I think . . .' Sonea nodded as Akkarin stepped forward and wrapped the shirt around the man's head. The Ichani shouted in surprise and tried to pull it off.

—*Sonea.*

Akkarin's mental voice sounded different – clearer – through the ring. She opened the door and hurried to his side.

—*Hold this for me.*

She took hold of the shirt and held it tightly. The man continued to struggle, but there was no strength in his movements. Akkarin drew out his knife, cut the man's arm and pressed his hand to the wound.

Sonea felt the Ichani go limp. It did not take long before Akkarin released him. As she let go of the shirt, the dead man slumped to the floor. She felt a wave of nausea.

—*That was horrible.*

Akkarin looked at Sonea.

—*Yes. But at least it was quick.*

'It worked. Good.'

They both looked up as Regin entered the room. He regarded the dead Ichani with satisfaction.

'Yes,' Sonea agreed. 'But we won't be able to do it again. The other Ichani heard him say he was poisoned. They won't fall for the same trick.'

'But your assistance is appreciated,' Akkarin added.

Regin shrugged. 'It was worth it to see one of those bastards get it.' He put a hand to his throat and grimaced.

'But I'm not sad to hear I won't have to do *that* again. He nearly broke my neck.'

Every man ought to have an ambition, Cery told himself as he stepped between the broken gates. *Mine is quite simple: I just want to get inside all the important places in Imardin.*

He was proud of the fact that, though he hadn't quite turned twenty yet, he had managed to enter almost every major building in the city. The exclusive areas of the Racecourse had been easy enough to sneak into disguised as a servant, and his lock-picking skills had gained him entrance to some of the mansions within the Inner City. Thanks to Sonea, he had been inside the Guild, though he would have preferred to have succeeded because of his own skills rather than because he had been taken prisoner by a meddling, bigoted magician.

As he crossed the courtyard, he couldn't help smiling. The Palace was the one important place left in Imardin he had never been able to sneak into. Now, with the Guard defeated and the heavy Palace gates hanging from their supports, nobody was going to prevent him exploring.

Not even the Ichani. According to the watchers posted by the Thieves, the Sachakans had left the Palace an hour ago. They had been inside the building for only an hour or two, and could not have destroyed everything in that time.

He stepped over the charred bodies of guards and peered through the broken doors of the building. A large entrance hall lay beyond. Delicate staircases wound up toward the higher levels. Cery sighed with appreciation. Moving inside, he wondered why the Ichani hadn't destroyed them. Perhaps they didn't want to waste their powers. Or perhaps they had quite sensibly left the stairs standing so they could reach the upper floors.

Cery looked down at the mullook symbol on the floor. He doubted the King was still in the Palace. The ruler had probably left Imardin once the Inner Wall fell.

'Avala is going to be a problem.'

'Probably. She likes to wander. I expect she'll wander away from Kyralia soon enough.'

'Got her eye on Elyne, I suspect.'

Cery spun around. The voices were distinctly Sachakan, and were coming from beyond the Palace entrance. He cast about, then ran toward an archway at the back of the hall. Just after he had skidded through it, he heard their footsteps echo on the hall floor.

'We all heard Rikacha's call, Kariko,' a third voice said. 'We know how he died. He was a fool for eating their food. I don't see why we need to come back here to discuss his mistake, and Avala and Inijaka probably agree.'

Cery smiled. So Faren's nasty little trick had worked.

'Because we have lost three already,' Kariko replied. 'Any more, and it might be more than bad luck.'

'Bad luck?' the first Ichani scoffed. 'The Guild got Rashi because he was weak. And Vikara might still be alive. We can only be sure that our slaves are dead.'

'Perhaps,' Kariko agreed. He sounded distracted. 'But there is something else I want to show you. See these stairs? They look fragile, don't they? As if they shouldn't be able to hold their own weight. Do you know how they stop them falling down?'

There was no reply.

'They put magic in them. Watch this.'

Silence followed, then a tinkling sound. The sound grew

louder, until the hall suddenly filled with a crashing and shattering. Cery gasped and peered through the archway.

The staircases were collapsing. As Kariko touched one railing after another, the beautiful structures buckled and dropped to the floor, fragments scattering everywhere. One slid in Cery's direction. An Ichani glanced toward the archway, and Cery quickly ducked out of sight.

Leaning against the wall, Cery closed his eyes. His heart ached that something so beautiful could be so carelessly destroyed. From the hall he could hear Kariko laughing.

'Magician-made, they call it,' the Ichani said. 'They put magic in their buildings to strengthen them. Half the houses in the middle of the city are made this way. What does it matter that the city is deserted? We can gather all the magic we need from the buildings.' His voice lowered. 'Let the others wander for a while. If they had returned here, as I instructed, they would know this, too. Come with me and we'll see how much power the Guild has left us.' Footsteps followed, then stopped. 'Harikava?'

'I'm going to have a look around here. This place is probably full of magically strengthened structures.'

'Just don't eat anything,' the third Ichani said.

Harikava chuckled. 'Of course not.'

Cery listened as the footsteps retreated and faded away. One set remained, however, and his heart sank as he realised they were growing louder.

He's coming this way.

Looking around, he saw that he was in a large room. Several archways broke the walls on his left and right. He hurried through the closest one. A corridor ran parallel to the room and a passage intersected with it opposite each archway. Cery cautiously peered out.

The Ichani stood within the room. He glanced around, then looked in Cery's direction. As he started toward the archway, Cery felt his mouth go dry.

How does he know I'm here?

He didn't fancy waiting to find out. Turning from the archway, he dashed away into the Palace.

CHAPTER 36

AN UNLIKELY RESCUER

A distant boom echoed through the passage. Akkarin exchanged a glance with Sonea, then moved to a ventilation grille set into the wall. She looked out into the alley beyond and listened carefully. Normally there would have been a constant hum of activity, but instead there was only an eerie silence.

Akkarin frowned, then signalled for their guide to continue. For several minutes the only noises were the soft sound of breathing and the tap of booted feet on the floor. Then Akkarin stopped abruptly and his gaze shifted to the distance.

'Takan says messengers are reporting that Kariko has come back out of the Palace again. The Ichani are destroying buildings.'

Sonea thought of the faint boom she had heard, and nodded. 'They're wasting their strength.'

'Yes.' He smiled and his eyes gleamed with an old, familiar predatory light.

Approaching footsteps drew their attention to a shadowy figure further down the passages.

'Looking for the foreigner?' The voice was aged and female. 'He just broke into a house near here.'

Akkarin started toward the old woman. 'What can you tell me of the place?'

'Belongs to House Arran,' she said. 'Has a big stable, and a yard in front, and a house the other side. Walls around it. No passages under it. Have to get in from the street.'

'How many entrances?'

'Two. The main one at the front, and a gate to the yard. The foreigner got in through the front.'

'Which is closest?'

'The gate.'

Akkarin looked at Sonea. 'Then we'll go in that way.'

The old woman nodded. 'Follow me, then.'

As they started through the passages again, Sonea touched the ring on her finger.

—*What are you planning?*

—*I'm not sure, yet. But I think it might be time to use your method.*

—*My method? You mean Healing?*

—*Yes.*

—*Then I should do it. He'll probably recognise you, but he might not recognise me.*

Akkarin frowned, but didn't answer. The woman led them to a small door, which they squeezed through one by one. On the other side was a room full of barrels.

'We're inside a house on the other side of the street,' the woman explained. 'Just go up those stairs, and out the door at the end of the hall.' She smiled grimly. 'Good luck.'

Following the woman's instructions, Sonea and Akkarin reached a sturdy servants' door. The lock was broken. Akkarin peered out, then pushed through. They stepped out into a typical Inner Circle street. Across the road was a plain wall, broken by a pair of large wooden gates. Akkarin strode swiftly to them, and looked through the narrow gap between.

'There are two entrances to the house from the court-yard,' he said. 'We'll enter through the closest.'

He glanced at the lock, and it clicked open. Sonea followed him through and shut the gate behind her. A large rectangular yard spread before them. To the left was a long building with several wide doors – the stable. To the right was a two-storey house. Akkarin hurried to the house, manipulated the lock of a door, and they slipped inside.

A narrow corridor lay beyond. Akkarin gestured for silence. A distant creaking and footsteps from the floor above reached their ears.

Seeing a movement in the corner of her eye, Sonea glanced out a small window beside the door. She caught her breath as she glimpsed two magicians and a richly dressed man hurrying toward the stables.

Akkarin moved to her side. The three men reached one of the large stable doors. The magician's companion threw the door wide, obviously expecting it to be heavier than it was. Sonea caught her breath as it smacked against the wall.

Hurried footsteps sounded above her. The three men disappeared inside the stable, leaving the door open. Silence followed. Sonea felt her mouth go dry as more footsteps sounded above. There was a pause, then a door closed and an Ichani strolled out into the yard. He stopped at the centre of the courtyard and looked around carefully. Seeing the open stable door, he started toward it.

'I don't like it, but you're right. Inijaka will recognise me,' Akkarin murmured. He looked at Sonea. 'We don't have time to come up with a better plan.'

She felt a chill run down her spine. It was up to her,

then. All the possible ways the Healing trick could fail ran through her mind. If the Ichani shielded, and she couldn't touch him, and then she wouldn't be able to use her Healing powers, and . . .

'Will you be all right?'

'Yes,' she replied. She glanced outside and saw the Ichani disappear inside the stable.

Akkarin drew in a deep breath, then opened the door for her. 'I will be watching. If it doesn't work, shield. We'll fight him openly instead.'

Sonea nodded, then stepped out into the yard and hurried across to the stable entrance. Peering inside, she tried to make out details in the dim interior. A figure was walking down a wide aisle between stalls. The Ichani, she guessed. He moved through a door in the far wall and out of sight.

She stepped inside. As she started down the aisle, three figures hurried out of a stall. They saw her and froze. At the same time, Sonea saw the face of the richly dressed man and felt a shock of recognition and dismay.

—You didn't tell me it was the King!

Kyralia's ruler looked her up and down, his eyes widening in recognition. Watching him, she felt dislike and anger stirring. A memory rose of the Guildhall. Of the King endorsing the Guild's punishment of exile. Then she thought of the Purge and of her aunt and uncle being driven out into the slums. She thought of the dwells hiding in the passages, never warned of the coming invasion.

Why should I risk my life for this man?

The moment the question ran through her mind she hated herself for asking it. She could not abandon anyone to the Ichani, no matter how much she disliked them. Straightening, she stepped aside.

'Go,' she told them.

The three men hurried past. As they moved out of sight, Sonea heard a noise in the room beyond the far wall. Turning around, she saw the Ichani returning. His eyes met hers, and he smiled.

It was not hard to feign terror as he started toward her. She backed toward the doorway and felt the sting of a barrier. The Ichani waved a hand and she felt a force push her forward. Resisting the urge to throw it off, she allowed herself to stumble toward him. When he was a mere step away, he looked her up and down.

'So there *are* a few Kyralian women here,' he said.

Sonea struggled as the force enveloped her, holding her arms against her body. Her heart began to race as the Ichani moved closer until she could feel his breath on her face. He slid his hands under her shirt. She stiffened with alarm and horror as she saw his expression change to a lecherous sneer.

A wave of panic rushed over her. She couldn't move, so she couldn't touch him. If she couldn't touch him, she couldn't use her Healing powers on him. And if he proceeded much further, he would discover the black robes beneath her ordinary clothes.

—*Fight him*, Akkarin urged.

She sent out a wave of force. The Ichani's eyes widened in surprise as he was pushed away. Striding after him, she attacked quickly and rapidly. He planted his feet, raised his hands and sent a strike in return. She staggered backward as it pounded her shield.

He laughed. 'So they *were* robes I felt under that shirt. I wondered where all the magicians went.'

Sonea felt a surge of hope. He thought she was an

ordinary Guild magician. She could still attempt to trick him if she pretended to grow weak with exhaustion.

—*I'm outside the door*, Akkarin sent. *What do you want me to do?*

—*Wait*, she told him.

When the Ichani struck again, she let herself stagger away until her back met the wall. He advanced, and she cringed as he struck again. At the fourth strike, she let her shield waver. He smiled maliciously as it fell, took out his knife and held it between his teeth.

She moved as if to dodge as he reached for her. Catching her arm, he hauled her back and pressed her against the wall with one hand. She grabbed his wrist, closed her eyes and sent her mind into his body.

She found his heart at the same time as pain flashed across her arm. Deciding she could not Heal herself and harm him simultaneously, she concentrated on his heart. Once it stopped, what could he do?

His grip tightened as she exerted her will. She heard him gasp in pain and opened her eyes to see his face turning white. He glared at her accusingly. A hand shifted to her arm.

A terrible lethargy spread from her arm through her body. Though she tried to move, no muscle would obey her. At the same time, she felt magical strength draining from her at a frightening speed. A movement in the corner of her eye beckoned, but she could not even summon the strength to shift her gaze. Then the draining eased. The Ichani's expression had changed from anger to confusion and horror. She saw the knife slip from his hand. He let her go and clutched at his chest.

Control came back to Sonea in an instant. She picked

up the knife and slashed it across his neck. As blood sprayed down, she grabbed his throat and drew in his strength.

Power flooded into her, but not as much as she had gained from Parika. The fight with the Guild had weakened this Ichani. As his strength ebbed, he fell backward onto the floor and lay still.

Behind him stood Akkarin. He gazed at her with an odd expression. She looked down at her blood-splattered clothes and shuddered in disgust.

After it's all over, Sonea thought. *I will never use this power again. Never.*

'I felt the same when I returned from Sachaka.'

She looked up at him. He extended a hand.

'There's bound to be something in the house for you to change into,' he said. 'Come on, let's get you cleaned up.'

Getting up was difficult even with his help. Though she wasn't tired, her legs were shaky. She stood still for a moment, swaying. Looking at the dead Ichani, she felt shock change to relief. *It worked. And he didn't get a chance to call to Kariko.* She had survived, and had even saved . . .

'The King?' she asked.

'I sent him to the house across the road, and Takan warned Ravi to be prepared to receive him.'

As she imagined what that encounter would be like, Sonea felt her mood lighten a little. 'The King rescued by the Thieves. Now that's something I'd like to see.'

The corner of Akkarin's mouth curled upward. 'I'm sure there will be some interesting consequences.'

Cery ran down yet another corridor and skidded to a halt beside a door. He tested the handle. Locked. He moved to the next. The same. The sound of distant footsteps grew louder. He bolted for the door at the end of the corridor, and gasped with relief as the handle turned.

Beyond was a long room with windows facing the gardens at the centre of the Palace. Cery hurried past chairs decorated with gold and sumptuous fabrics to another door at the end of the room. Savara's pendant hammered against his chest under his clothes.

Please don't be locked, he thought. Please don't be a dead end.

He grabbed the handle and twisted, but it would not turn. A curse escaped him and he fumbled through his coat for picks. He drew them out, glad that he had never lost the habit of carrying them. Selecting two, he inserted them into the lock and began to feel for the mechanism.

Behind him, the faint sound of footsteps grew louder.

His breath rushed in and out of his throat. His mouth was dry and his hands sweaty. Taking a deep breath, he let it out slowly, then gave the picks a quick turn and push.

The lock clicked open. Cery grabbed the picks, pulled open the door and dashed through. He yanked the door behind him, stopping it just as it was about to slam, and drew it closed as quietly as he could.

A quick glance told him that he had entered a small room filled with mirrors and small tables and chairs. A dressing room for entertainers, Cery guessed. There was no other door or entrance to the room. He turned his attention back to the lock and set to work on closing it again.

The mechanism was easier to trigger now he knew the type. It closed with a satisfying click. Sighing with relief, Cery moved to a chair and sat down.

As he heard footsteps outside the room, his relief evaporated. If Harikava had been following him, he would guess that there was nowhere else that Cery could have gone but through the door – locked or not. Rising, Cery took a step toward the small windows on one side of the room. He had to get out somehow.

Then the lock clicked and his blood turned to ice.

The door swung open with a faint squeak. The Ichani peered inside. As he saw Cery, he smiled.

'There you are.'

Cery backed away from the door. Reaching inside his coat pockets, he felt the handles of his knives against his palms. He grasped them tightly.

This isn't good, he thought. He glanced toward the windows. *I won't get to them. He'll stop me.*

The Ichani took a step closer.

If he catches me, he'll read my mind. He'll find out about Sonea and Akkarin.

Cery swallowed hard and loosened the knives from their sheaths. *But he can't read my mind if I'm already dead.*

As the Ichani took another step, Cery felt his determination weaken. *I can't do it. I can't kill myself.* He stared at the Ichani. The man's eyes were cold and predatory.

What's the difference? I'm going to die anyway.

He took two quick breaths, then whisked out the knives.

—*No, Cery! Don't!*

Cery froze at the voice in his mind. Was this his fear speaking? If it was, it had a woman's voice. A voice much like . . .

Harikava turned to look out of the room and his eyes widened. Cery heard swift footsteps. As a woman stepped into the doorway, he caught his breath in surprise.

'Leave him, Harikava,' Savara said. Her voice was commanding. 'This one is mine.'

The Ichani backed way from her. 'What are your kind doing here?' he snarled.

She smiled. 'Not making our own claim on Kyralia, as you probably fear. No, we are merely watching.'

'So you say.'

'You are in no position to say otherwise,' she replied, stepping into the room. 'If I were you, I'd leave now.'

As she moved toward Cery, Harikava watched her carefully. When she was several steps away from the door, he strode to it and out of the room. Cery heard the man's footsteps stop outside.

'Kariko won't have your kind here. He will hunt you down.'

'I will be long gone before he has the time to spare.'

The footsteps moved away, then there was the sound of the door in the next room closing. Savara looked at Cery.

'He's gone. That was close.'

He stared back at her. She had saved him. Somehow she had known he was in trouble, and appeared just in time. But how was that possible? Had she followed him? Or had she been following the Ichani? Relief changed to doubt as he considered her words. The Ichani had been afraid of her. Suddenly he was sure he ought to be, too.

'Who *are* you?' he whispered.

Her shoulders lifted. 'A servant of my people.'

'He . . . he ran away. From you. *Why?*'

'Uncertainty. He has used a great deal of power today, and can't be sure he would defeat me.' She smiled and moved toward him. 'Bluff is always the most satisfying way to win a fight.'

Cery backed away. She had just saved his life. He ought to thank her. But there was something too strange about all this. 'He recognised you. You know his name.'

'He recognised what I am, not who I am,' she corrected.

'What are you, then?'

'Your ally.'

'No, you're not. You say you want to help us, but you won't do anything to stop the Ichani, even though you're strong enough to do it.'

Her smile vanished. She regarded him solemnly, then her expression hardened. 'I'm doing everything I can, Cery. What will it take to convince you of that? Would you trust me if I said I have known for some time that Akkarin and Sonea had returned? Obviously I haven't told the Ichani this.'

Cery's heart skipped a beat, then began to pound. 'How did you find out about that?'

She smiled and her eyes flickered to his chest. 'I have my ways.'

Why the glance at his chest? He frowned as he remembered the pendant. Reaching under his shirt, he pulled it out. Her eyes flickered and her smile faded.

What sort of magical properties did it have? Looking at the smooth ruby at the centre, he felt a chill go down his back as he remembered Sonea and Akkarin making their rings for each other. Rings with red glass baubles . . .

'*With these rings, we will be able to see into each others' minds* . . .'

He looked at the ruby. If this was a blood gem, then Savara had been reading his mind . . . and he had been wearing it since just after Akkarin and Sonea arrived.

How else could she know they were in the city?

Drawing the chain over his head, he tossed the pendant aside.

'I *have* been a fool to trust you,' he said bitterly.

She regarded him sadly. 'I have known about Sonea and Akkarin since I gave you that pendant. Have I revealed them to the Ichani? No. Have I used this information to bribe you? No. I have not taken advantage of your trust, Ceryni, you have taken advantage of mine.'

She crossed her arms. 'You told me you would keep me informed if I gave you advice on killing magicians, but you have kept much from me that I needed to know. My people have been looking for Akkarin and Sonea in Sachaka. They intended to help the former High Lord take back Kyralia from the Ichani. We do not want Kyralia ruled by Kariko and his allies any more than you do.'

Cery stared at her. 'How can I believe this?'

Savara sighed and shook her head. 'I can only ask you to trust me. It is too difficult to prove . . . but I think you have reached the limit of your trust.' She smiled ruefully. 'What are we to do with each other?'

He didn't know how to answer that. Looking at the pendant, he felt angry, foolish and betrayed. Yet when he looked at her, he saw a sadness and regret in her eyes that he did believe was real. He did not want them to part with ill feelings for each other.

But perhaps that was not possible.

'You and I have deals and secrets we can't give away, and people we must protect,' he said slowly. 'I respect that about you, but you didn't respect that about me.' He looked at the pendant again. 'You shouldn't have done that to me. I know why you did it, but that doesn't make it right. When you gave me that, you made it impossible for me to keep my promises.'

'I wanted to protect your people.'

'I know.' He managed a wry smile. 'And I can respect that, too. While our lands are fighting, we can't put each other's feelings before our people's safety. So let's see how this turns out. When it's all over, I might forgive you for doing that to me. Until then, I'm sticking to my own side. Don't expect anything more.'

She looked down, then nodded. 'I understand.'

The servants door to Zerrend's mansion opened onto an alley just wide enough for a delivery cart to pass through. The lock was undone, but the door was closed. Both ends of the alley met empty, silent streets.

There was no sign of Tayend – no sign of anyone at all.

'What shall we do now?' Farand asked.

'I don't know,' Dannyl admitted. 'I don't want to leave, in case he comes back. But he may have been forced to flee the city.'

Or he might be lying dead somewhere. Every time Dannyl thought about the possibility, his blood turned cold and he felt ill with dread. *First Rothen, then Tayend . . .*

No, he told himself. *Don't even consider it. Not until you see it for yourself.*

The thought that he might see Tayend's body only made it harder to think clearly. He had to concentrate, to decide where they should go. They had three choices: stay at the mansion and hope Tayend would eventually return, search the city for him, or give up and leave the city.

I'm not leaving the city until I know.

So that left the mansion or the search. Neither were very fair to Farand.

'I'm going to look for Tayend,' Dannyl said. 'I'll try the surrounding streets, and come back to check the house from time to time. You should leave the city. There's no point in us both risking our lives.'

'No,' Farand replied. 'I'll stay here in case he comes back.'

Dannyl regarded Farand in surprise. 'Are you sure?'

The young magician nodded. 'I don't know Imardin, Dannyl. I don't know if I'd find my way out. And you need someone to stay here in case Tayend comes back.' He shrugged, then took a few steps backward. 'I'll see you when you return.'

Dannyl watched Farand until he had entered the house, then moved back to the end of the alley and scanned the street beyond. All was still. He stepped out and hurried to the next alley.

At first Dannyl found only a few wooden crates in the alleys and streets. Then he began to encounter the bodies of magicians. Fear for Tayend's safety grew stronger.

He took a circular route, and had almost made his way back to the mansion again when a man stepped out in front of him. His heart jumped and began to pound, but it was only a rough-looking servant or crafter.

'In here,' the man said, pointing to an open garbage hatch in the wall. 'Safer for you magicians down there.'

Dannyl shook his head. 'No, thank you.' As he walked past, the man caught his arm.

'Sachakan was close, not long ago. You be safer out of sight.'

Dannyl pulled away. 'I'm looking for someone.'

The man shrugged and stepped back.

Continuing on, Dannyl reached the end of the alley. The street beyond was empty. He stepped out and hurried across the road toward the alley on the other side.

When he had nearly reached it, he heard a door close behind him. He turned, and felt his blood turn to ice.

'Ah, now that's better.' The woman striding toward him smiled slyly. 'I was beginning to think there were no other pretty magicians in Kyralia.'

He bolted for the alley, but slammed into an invisible barrier. Stunned, he staggered backwards, heart pounding.

'Not that way,' the woman said. 'Come here. I won't kill you.'

Dannyl took several deep breaths and turned to face her. As she drew closer he backed down the street. There was a malicious gleam in her eyes. He realised he had seen it before. She was the Ichani who had wanted to 'keep' Lord Fergun for herself.

'Kariko won't let you keep me alive,' he said.

She tossed her head. 'He might, now that we're here and most of your Guild is dead.'

'Why would you want to keep me, anyway?' he said, still backing away.

She shrugged. 'My slaves are dead. I need new ones.'

He must be getting close to the next alley. Perhaps, if he kept talking, she would not remember to block it.

'It could be very pleasant for you.' She smiled slyly, her eyes roaming from his neck to his feet. 'I like to reward my favourite slaves.'

He felt a mad urge to laugh. *What does she think she is?* he thought. *Some sort of irresistible seductress? She sounds ridiculous.*

'You're not my type,' he told her.

Her eyebrows rose. 'No? Well, it doesn't matter. You will do as I say, or—' She stopped and glanced around the street in surprise.

From doors and alleys on all sides, Guild magicians had emerged. Dannyl stared at them. He did not recognise any of the faces. Then a hand grabbed his arm and hauled him sideways.

He stumbled through a door. It closed behind him. Dannyl turned to stare at his rescuer, and felt his heart leap.

'Tayend!'

The scholar grinned up at him. Dannyl gasped with relief, pulled Tayend close and held him tightly.

'You left the house. Why did you leave the house?'

'That woman came in. I thought I'd wait in the alley until she left, but she came out that way. The Thieves saved me. I told them you would come looking for me, but they didn't reach the house in time.'

Dannyl heard a muffled cough, and froze as he realised they weren't alone. He turned to find a tall Lonmar regarding him curiously. His face went cold, then hot.

'I see you're good friends,' the man said. 'Now that you've caught up, we should—'

The door shuddered from a heavy blow. The man beckoned frantically.

'Quickly! Follow me.'

Tayend grabbed Dannyl's wrist and dragged him after the stranger. From behind them came a crash. The Lonmar began to run. Taking them down a staircase, he led them into a cellar and bolted the door behind them.

'That won't stop her,' Dannyl said.

'No,' the stranger replied. 'But it'll slow her down.'

He hurried between racks of wine bottles to a cupboard at the far wall. Opening the door, he tugged at shelves containing jars of preserves. The shelves swivelled forward, revealing another door. The stranger opened the door and stepped aside. Tayend and Dannyl squeezed through into a passage. A boy stood nearby, holding a small lamp.

The Lonmar followed and began pulling the shelves back in place. There was a faint sound beyond the cellar door, then an explosion.

'No time,' the Lonmar muttered. He left the cupboard half assembled and closed the inner door. Taking the lamp from the boy, he started to jog down the passage. Dannyl and Tayend hurried after.

'Not good,' the stranger said to himself. 'Let's hope she—'

From behind came another explosion. Dannyl glanced behind to see a globe light flare into existence where the secret door had been. The Lonmar drew in a sharp breath.

'Run!'

CHAPTER 37

A GLIMPSE OF THE ENEMY

The servant's dress Sonea had found to replace her bloodied shirt and trousers must have belonged to a taller woman. It covered her robes well, but the sleeves were so long she'd had to roll them up, and the hem kept getting under her feet. She was just catching her balance after stepping on it again when a messenger appeared in the passage before them. He saw them, and quickened his pace.

'I have . . . bad news,' he panted. 'One of . . . Sachakans . . . found passages.'

'Where?' Akkarin asked.

'Not far.'

'Take us there.'

The messenger hesitated, then nodded. He started back down the passage, his lamp throwing distorted shadows onto the walls.

—*We'll try the same deception*, Akkarin told Sonea. *This time, Heal yourself when the Ichani cuts you. Once he begins drawing strength, you will not be able to use your powers.*

—*Oh, I won't be making that mistake again*, she replied. *Not now that I know what it feels like.*

The guide continued through passages, stopping briefly now and then to question helpers posted by the exits. They encountered people fleeing, then a dark-skinned figure appeared. Faren.

'You're here,' he panted. 'Good. She's coming this way.'

So it's the woman, Sonea thought. *Avala*.

'How far?'

Faren nodded back the way he had come. 'Fifty paces, perhaps. Turn left at the intersection.'

He stepped out of the way as Akkarin started down the passage. Sonea took the lamp from the guide and followed, her heart beating faster at every step. They reached the intersection, stopped, and Akkarin peered into the left-hand passage. He stepped out, and Sonea hurried after him. At the next turn, they stopped again.

—*She's coming. Wait here. Let her think* she *found* you. *I won't be far away.*

Sonea nodded. She watched him stride away to the intersection and disappear into a side passage. From behind her came the faint sound of footsteps.

Slowly the footsteps grew louder. A faint light began to reflect around the turn. It brightened rapidly, and Sonea backed away. A globe light appeared. She blocked the brightness with a hand, then gasped in feigned horror.

The Ichani woman stared at her, then smiled.

'So it's you. Kariko will be pleased.'

Sonea turned to run, but as she did her foot caught the hem of her dress and she fell to her hands and knees. Avala laughed.

That would have been an impressive bit of acting, if I'd meant it, Sonea thought wryly as she struggled to stand up. She heard footsteps come closer, then a hand caught her arm. It took all her self-control not to blast the woman away.

The Ichani pulled Sonea around to face her. A hand reached toward Sonea's head. Grabbing the Ichani's wrists,

Sonea tried to send her mind out into the woman's body, but encountered a resistance.

Avala was shielding.

The barrier lay at the surface of the woman's skin. Sonea felt a moment's admiration for Avala's skill, but it was soon replaced by panic.

She would not be able to use her Healing powers on the woman.

—*Fight her*, Akkarin instructed. *Bring her down past the intersection. We must get her between us so she cannot escape.*

Sonea sent out a wave of force. Avala's eyes widened as she staggered backward. Sonea lifted her skirt, spun around, and ran down the passage.

A barrier flashed into existence before her. She smashed it down with forcestrike. A few steps later she passed the intersection. Another barrier appeared. She stopped and turned to face the Ichani.

The woman smiled triumphantly.

—*Kariko. Look what I've found.*

Sonea saw an image of herself looking thin and small in the long dress.

—*What a pathetic-looking creature she is!*

—*Ah! Akkarin's apprentice*, Kariko replied. *Search her mind. If one is here, the other might be close by – but don't kill her. Bring her to me.*

Sonea shook her head.

—*I'll decide when and where we meet, Kariko,* she sent.

—*I look forward to it*, Kariko replied, *as does your former mentor. Rothen, isn't it? I have a blood stone of his. He will watch you die.*

Sonea gasped. *Rothen?* But Rothen was dead. Why would Kariko bother making a gem of Rothen's blood?

—Does this mean Rothen is alive?

—Probably, if he does have a blood gem, Akkarin's mental voice whispered through her ring. *But he may be lying in order to upset and distract you.*

Avala was drawing closer. As she passed the intersection of passages, Sonea felt a mingled relief and anxiety. The woman was between her and Akkarin now. Once Akkarin stepped out, however, Avala would recognise him.

—Kariko can't be completely sure you're here until he or another Ichani sees you, she told Akkarin. *We could trick him into thinking I'm here alone. So if I fight Avala alone . . .*

—Yes, Akkarin agreed. *If you grow weak, I will take over. Just keep out of her reach.*

As the Ichani attacked, Sonea threw up a strong shield then retaliated with powerful strikes of her own. There was no strategy or trickery in Avala's attack and, as with the fight with Parika, Sonea realised she could use little of her own training to gain an advantage. It was, she decided, a brutal race to see who ran out of strength first.

The air grew hot in the passage, then the walls began to glow faintly. The woman took one step away, then suddenly everything turned a bright white. Sonea blinked, but she was too dazzled to see anything.

She's blinded me!

Sonea almost laughed aloud as she realised that Avala had used the same trick she had used to escape Regin's gang years before. Except the novices hadn't learned enough about Healing to . . .

Her sight returned slowly but steadily. She made out two figures in the passage before her. Avala was closest.

Behind her was Akkarin. He was attacking the Ichani with relentless savagery. Avala glanced back at Sonea, her expression fearful. Her shield abruptly disappeared, her strength gone, then Akkarin's last strike threw her against Sonea's shield. There was a sickening crack, then the woman slumped to the ground.

Sonea watched, heart still racing, as Akkarin slowly approached the woman. Avala's eyes opened. Her expression changed from pain and anger to a satisfied smile, then her gaze slid to somewhere beyond the walls and she let out a long, final breath.

'Is it just me,' Sonea said, 'or did she look a little too happy to be dying?'

Akkarin dropped into a crouch. He ran a finger under the collar of the woman's jacket. As he continued examining her clothes, Sonea saw that one of Avala's hands was slowly relaxing. As the fingers uncurled, a small red globe fell onto the floor.

'A blood gem,' Sonea hissed.

Akkarin sighed and looked up at Sonea. 'Yes. Whose it is, we can only guess, but I think we should assume the worst: Kariko knows I'm here.'

Rothen blinked in surprise as an image of a woman flashed into his mind. As he recognised her, he felt a fierce joy. *She's alive!*

'Sonea!' Balkan exclaimed. 'She's here!'

—*Ah! Akkarin's apprentice. Search her mind. If one is here, the other might be close by – but don't kill her. Bring her to me.*

—*I'll decide when and where we meet, Kariko.*

Sonea's reply was defiant and fearless. Rothen felt a surge of both fear and pride.

—I look forward to it, Kariko replied, *as does your former mentor. Rothen, isn't it? I have a blood stone of his. He will watch you die.*

Suddenly Rothen couldn't breathe. The image had been sent by the Ichani woman. Who must be trying to capture Sonea right now. And if she did . . .

'Rothen?'

He looked at Balkan and Dorrien, and found them staring at him.

'You made a blood stone?' Balkan asked in a low voice.

'Kariko did. At Calia . . .' Rothen forced himself to take a breath. 'He read my mind and saw Sonea there, then made the gem.' He shuddered. 'Since then, I've been seeing and . . . feeling the deaths of everyone he's killed.'

Balkan's eyes widened slightly, then he grimaced in sympathy.

'What is a blood stone?' Dorrien asked.

'It enables the maker to see into another's mind,' Balkan explained. 'Though Kariko actually made it, it is attuned to Rothen because he used Rothen's blood.'

Dorrien's stared at Rothen. 'He captured you. Why didn't you say?'

'I . . .' Rothen sighed. 'I don't know.'

'But what he did to you . . . can you stop yourself seeing these deaths?'

'No, I have no control over it.'

Dorrien's face was pale. 'And if they catch Sonea . . .'

'Yes.' Rothen looked at his son. 'And this is the secret you couldn't tell us, isn't it? She's here and so is Akkarin.'

Dorrien opened his mouth, but no words came out. He looked from Rothen to Balkan uncertainly.

'It will make no difference if you tell us now,' Balkan

said. 'They know about Sonea. They have probably guessed that Akkarin is with her, just as we have.'

Dorrien's shoulders slumped.

'Yes, they're here. Five days ago Sonea and Akkarin came through the South Pass. I brought them to the city.'

Balkan frowned. 'Why didn't you send them back to Sachaka?'

'I tried. In fact, they were co-operating when an Ichani attacked us. We barely survived. Then the Fort was attacked. After that, I knew everything Akkarin had said was true.'

'Why didn't you tell anyone about this?' Rothen asked.

'Because if the Guild knew Akkarin was here, the Ichani would read it from the minds of their victims. Akkarin knew he and Sonea had a better chance of killing them one by one, but if the Ichani knew he was here they would stay together.'

Balkan nodded. 'He knew we would be defeated. So what did he—'

A rumble came from the city. Rothen turned and walked toward the Entrance Hall, then glanced back at Balkan.

'Another one. Closer, too. What do you think is happening?'

The Warrior shrugged. 'I don't know.'

A cloud of dust billowed up from somewhere in the Inner Circle.

'We might see better if we go up onto the roof,' Dorrien suggested.

Balkan glanced at Dorrien, then started toward the stairs. 'Come on, then.'

The Warrior led them to the third level, then through the passages to a staircase. A short climb later, they reached the door to the roof. Balkan led them out and to the front of the University. A narrow raised walkway enabled them to see over the facade to the houses of the Inner Circle.

They watched in silence. After a long pause, another boom echoed from the city centre and dust billowed up.

'The whole front of that house has fallen,' Dorrien said, pointing.

'So they're destroying houses now,' Rothen said. 'Why waste their power?'

'To draw Akkarin out,' Balkan replied.

'And if destroying the Inner Circle doesn't work, they'll come here,' Dorrien added.

Balkan nodded. 'Then we'd better be ready to leave as soon as they arrive.'

The journey through the tunnels seemed endless. The further they travelled, the greater Dannyl's amazement. He had passed through passages under the slums, years before, when he had been negotiating with the Thieves for Sonea's release, and had assumed that they extended no further than the Outer Wall. Now he could see the Thieves had not only dug under the Quarters, but had even tunnelled under the Inner Circle.

He glanced back at his companions. Tayend looked as cheerful as ever. Farand wore an expression of astonishment. The young magician hadn't believed it at first, when Dannyl had returned to the house to tell him that Imardin's underworld had arranged to get them out of the city.

Their guide stopped before a large door guarded by two enormous men. At a word from the guide, one of the guards rapped on the doors. The sound of heavy bolts sliding out of their housings followed, then the doors silently swung open.

A short corridor followed, occupied by more guards. It ended at a second pair of doors. These were unbolted and pushed open to reveal a large, crowded room.

Dannyl gazed around the room, then chuckled. He'd had too many surprises in the last few hours to feel more than a mild amusement now.

The room was full of magicians. A few were lying on makeshift beds, Healers hovering beside them. Some were helping themselves to platters of food on large tables at the centre of the room. Others relaxed in comfortable-looking chairs.

So who has survived? Dannyl thought. He looked around and noted that, of the Higher Magicians, only Director Jerrik, Lord Peakin, Lady Vinara and Lord Telano were present. He continued searching, but could not see Rothen anywhere.

Perhaps he didn't make it back to the city, he thought. The brief mental communication between the Ichani and Sonea had filled Dannyl's heart with hope. He had found Tayend, and might still find his mentor alive, too.

Unless Kariko was lying.

Then as a few of the magicians moved away from the food tables, Dannyl saw the richly dressed man sitting at the end of the room, and found he was still capable of being surprised.

So this is where the King got to, he thought. Before he could decide what protocol required in this situation, the monarch looked at Dannyl, nodded once, then turned back to his companion. His expression clearly indicated he didn't want to be interrupted.

The enormous man he was speaking to looked familiar. Dannyl smiled as he realised where he had seen the large man before. This was Gorin, the Thief Dannyl had negotiated with over Sonea's release.

The King talking to Thieves. Dannyl chuckled to himself. *Now I've seen everything.*

'So,' Tayend said. 'Are you going to introduce me?'

Dannyl glanced at the scholar. 'I guess so. I should start with the Higher Magicians.'

He started toward Lord Peakin. The Alchemist was talking to Davin and Larkin.

'Ambassador,' Peakin said as he saw Dannyl approaching, 'do you have any news?'

'According to my guide, all but three Ichani are dead,' Dannyl replied. He turned to Tayend. 'This is Tayend of Tremmelin, who has been visiting Imar—'

'Have you seen Sonea? Is Akkarin with her?' Davin asked with barely restrained excitement.

'No, I haven't seen her,' Dannyl replied carefully. 'So I wouldn't know if Akkarin is with her.' He glanced at Farand, who gave an almost imperceptible nod. Akkarin had instructed them to keep his presence a secret, and Dannyl wasn't going to reveal anything until he had to.

Davin looked disappointed. 'Then how is it possible that so many Ichani are dead?'

'Perhaps it's just Sonea's work,' Larkin suggested.

The other magicians looked sceptical.

'I know the Thieves killed one on their own,' Tayend said. 'The one called Faren told me about it.'

Peakin shook his head. 'Thieves defeating Ichani. Doesn't *that* make us look incompetent.'

'Any other news?' Larkin asked.

Dannyl glanced around the room. 'Is Lord Osen here?'

The Alchemists shook their heads.

'Oh.' Dannyl glanced from one magician to another, then sighed. Then they didn't know about Lorlen. 'Then I do have news, but it is not good.'

The storeroom hummed with voices. A small crowd had formed in the last hour. The two Thieves, Ravi and Sevli, had arrived after the news came that the Ichani woman had entered the passages. Soon after, Senfel had recited a short mental communication between the woman, Kariko and Sonea. They had been waiting in tense silence for more news, when Takan announced that Akkarin and Sonea had killed the woman.

Everyone had forgotten the servant's presence, but now that he had reminded them of his link to Akkarin, he was being subjected to a stream of questions he clearly couldn't answer.

Gol caught Cery's eye. He looked sullen and unhappy. Cery knew it was because he had slipped away to visit the Palace alone. He felt a little guilty about that. Gol was supposed to be his protector.

Thinking back to his encounter with the Ichani, Cery considered what might have happened if Gol had been with him. He could have ordered his second to lure the Ichani away. Would he have been able to do so, knowing it would lead to Gol's death? Would Gol have obeyed, or even suggested it? Cery had found Gol to be nothing but loyal, but was he *that* loyal?

Interesting questions, Cery thought, *but I'm glad I didn't have to find out the answers.*

Cery frowned. *What would Gol think of Savara if he knew what she'd done?* They had parted outside the Palace gates, and he hadn't seen her since.

The voices in the room suddenly fell silent. Looking up, Cery saw that Sonea and Akkarin were striding down the room toward them. He stepped forward and grinned.

'Takan just told us you got the woman.'

'Yes,' Akkarin replied. 'She carried a blood gem, so Kariko probably knows we are here.'

'And about the passages under the city, too,' Faren added. 'We're not safe down here any longer.'

'Will the other Ichani enter the passages?' Ravi asked.

'Probably,' Akkarin replied. 'They will try to find and kill us as quickly as possible.'

Sevli crossed his arms. 'They won't find you. They don't know the ways, and no-one will show them.'

'All they need to do is capture a guide and read his mind to find their way around,' Akkarin reminded him.

The Thieves exchanged glances. 'Then we got to send the helpers away,' Cery said. He looked at Akkarin. 'I'll guide you from now on.'

Akkarin nodded in gratitude. 'Thank you.'

Sonea looked at Akkarin. 'If they come down here, they might split up to corner us. We could use that to our advantage by circling back and attacking them separately.'

'No.' Akkarin shook his head. 'Kariko will not risk parting from his allies.' He looked at Faren. 'What are the Ichani doing now?'

'Talking,' Faren replied.

'I bet they are,' Senfel rumbled.

'Not any more,' a new voice said.

All turned to regard a messenger hurrying toward them. 'They've gone back to wrecking buildings.'

Akkarin frowned. 'Are you sure?'

The man nodded.

'Do you think they're trying to get us to come out and stop them?' Sonea asked.

'Maybe,' Akkarin replied.

Akkarin doesn't know what the Ichani are doing, Cery thought. *But I do*. He resisted a smile.

'They're taking the magic from the buildings that have been strengthened with it.'

Akkarin regarded him in surprise. 'How did you work that out?'

'I overheard Kariko and two others talking, when I was in the Palace.'

Faren choked. 'The Palace? What were you doing there?'

'Just looking around.'

'Just looking around!' Faren repeated, shaking his head.

Akkarin sighed. 'This isn't good,' he muttered.

'How much power will they get?' Sonea asked.

'I'm . . . not sure. Some houses have more magic in them than others.'

'You could take this magic, too,' Senfel suggested.

Akkarin winced.

'I'm sure the owners won't mind if their homes are used to defend the city,' Cery added.

'They've wrecked a lot of them,' Ravi said. 'Not every building in the Inner City is magically enhanced. There can't be many left.'

'But they haven't been to the Guild yet,' Senfel pointed out.

Akkarin looked pained. 'The University. It's not the only magically enhanced structure in the Guild, but it contains more power than any other in the city.'

Sonea sucked in a breath. 'No, it doesn't. The Arena has got to be stronger.'

Senfel and Akkarin exchanged grave looks. The old magician cursed vehemently.

'Exactly,' Akkarin agreed.

Cery looked at the three magicians. 'That's bad, isn't it?'

'Oh, yes,' Sonea replied. 'The barrier around the Arena is strengthened by several magicians every month. It has to be strong enough to withstand stray magic from Warrior training sessions – some of them quite vigorous.'

'We have to stop the Ichani taking that power,' Akkarin said. 'If they do, we may as well hand the city over to them.'

'We take that power ourselves?' Sonea asked.

'If we must.'

Sonea hesitated. 'And then . . . confront them?'

His eyes rose to meet hers. 'Yes.'

'Are we strong enough?'

'We have taken power from four Ichani, if we include Parika. We have used little of our own, and we have taken strength from the volunteers.'

'And you could again,' Senfel reminded them. 'It is nearly a day since you tapped their reserves. They will have recovered most of their strength.'

'And there are only three Ichani left,' Faren pointed out.

Akkarin straightened. 'Yes, I think it is time to face them.'

Sonea went a little pale, but nodded in agreement. 'Looks like it.'

The group fell silent, then Ravi cleared his throat.

'Well, then,' he said. 'I had best get you to our volunteers as quickly as possible.'

Akkarin nodded. As the Thief turned toward the door, Cery looked at Sonea closely. He caught her arm.

'This is it, then. Are you scared?'

She shrugged. 'A little. Mostly relieved.'

'Relieved?'

'Yes. Finally we'll fight them properly, with no poison, traps, or even black magic.'

'It's fine wanting a fair fight, so long as they fight the same,' Cery said. 'Just be careful. I won't relax until this is all over, and I know you're all right.'

She smiled, squeezed his hand, then turned to follow Akkarin out of the room.

CHAPTER 38

THE BLACK MAGICIANS

For the last hour, messengers had reported that the Ichani were slowly making their way toward the Guild, destroying houses as they went. Sonea and Akkarin had hurried to the volunteers, who had dealt with their swift visit with admirable tolerance and courage, then raced back to the Inner Circle. During the journey Sonea had burned with impatience, but as she stepped through the secret door into Lorlen's office she began to wish the journey hadn't passed so quickly. Suddenly her knees were weak, her hands were shaking, and she could not help feeling there must be something they had forgotten to do.

Akkarin paused for a moment to look around the office. He sighed, then shrugged out of his shirt. Sonea pulled the dress over her head and dropped it to the floor. She looked down at herself and shivered. Full magician's robes . . . *black* magician's robes . . .

Then she looked at Akkarin. He stood straighter, taller. A little thrill ran down her back, similar to the fear he had once inspired.

Akkarin glanced at her and smiled. 'Stop leering at me.'

Sonea blinked innocently. 'Me? Leering?'

His smile widened, then it faded away. He walked up to her and pressed his hands gently against the sides of her face.

'Sonea,' he began, 'if I don't—'

She put a finger to his lips, then pulled his head down so she could kiss him. He pressed his lips hard to hers, then drew her close against him.

'If I could send you far away, I would,' he said. 'But I know you'd refuse to go. Just . . . don't do anything impulsive. I watched the first woman I loved die, I don't think I could survive losing the second.'

Sonea drew in a breath in surprise, then smiled.

'I love you, too.'

He chuckled, then kissed her again, but they both froze as a mental voice blared out.

—*Akkarin! Akkarin! What a pretty place you have here.*

An image of the Guild Gates, and the University beyond, flashed into Sonea's mind.

'They're here,' Akkarin muttered. His arms slid from her shoulders.

'The Arena?'

He shook his head. 'Only as a last resort.' His expression was hard as he strode across the room to the door.

Sonea straightened her shoulders, drew in a deep breath, and followed.

'So they've finally arrived,' Balkan murmured.

Rothen looked out at the city. The late afternoon sun sent long shadows across the streets. As he watched, three men stepped out and started toward the Guild Gates.

'What did Akkarin and Sonea plan to do once the Ichani knew they were here, Dorrien?' Balkan asked.

'I don't know. They never discussed it.'

Balkan nodded. 'Time for us to leave, then.'

Yet he did not move, and neither did Rothen and

618

Dorrien. They stood and watched as the three Ichani passed between the gates and strode toward the University.

Then, from below, came a hollow boom.

'What was that?' Dorrien exclaimed.

They leaned over the facade and looked down. Rothen caught his breath as he saw the pair on the steps below.

'Sonea! And Akkarin.'

'They've closed the University doors,' Balkan said.

Rothen shivered. The University doors hadn't been closed for centuries.

'Should we call out and let them know we're here?' Dorrien asked quietly.

'Knowing you two are watching could be a distraction to Sonea,' Balkan warned.

'But I can use my powers now. I can help them.'

'So can I,' Rothen added. Dorrien glanced at him in surprise, then grinned.

Balkan frowned. 'I would like to communicate the fight to the rest of the Guild.'

'Dorrien and I will keep out of sight until we have an opportunity to help,' Rothen suggested.

Balkan nodded. 'Very well. Just be mindful of the moment you choose.'

The forest surrounding the Guild was striped with golden light. Twigs cracked under Gol's feet so frequently, Cery began to wonder if his second was deliberately trying to make a lot of noise. He glanced back and couldn't help smiling at the big man's strained expression.

'Don't worry,' Cery said. 'I've been here before. We should be able to watch without being seen.'

Gol nodded. They continued on. As Cery saw glimpses

of buildings through the trees ahead, he quickened his stride. Gol fell a little behind.

Then Cery saw a figure crouching beside a tree trunk at the edge of the forest. He stopped and signalled to Gol to stay where he was and remain silent.

By the way Savara was cautiously peering around the tree, Cery knew she was anxious to avoid being discovered. *Too late*, he thought. He crept forward. When he was a few steps away from her, he straightened and crossed his arms.

'We can't seem to stop running into each other, can we?' he said.

It was gratifying to see her jump. She let out a sigh of relief as she saw him.

'Cery.' She shook her head at him disapprovingly. 'It's not wise to sneak up on magicians.'

'Isn't it?'

'No.'

'You've come to see the show, then?'

She smiled crookedly. 'That's right. Join me?'

He nodded. Beckoning to Gol, Cery crouched by the trunk of another tree. As he saw what lay beyond, he felt his heart sink.

The University doors were closed and Sonea and Akkarin stood on the steps. The three Ichani were less than a hundred paces from them, advancing confidently.

'You and your friends have done well,' Savara murmured, 'if this is all that remains of Kariko's allies. Perhaps you have a chance, after all.'

Cery smiled grimly. 'Perhaps we do. We'll just have to see.'

* * *

Sonea blinked as an image of herself and Akkarin, seen from above, entered her mind. From the angle of the view, the watcher must be behind them, on top of the University. She caught a sense of Balkan's personality, but no thoughts or emotions.

—*If we can sense this, so can the Ichani.*

—*Yes*, Akkarin replied. *Block out the images. They'll distract you.*

—*But it will alert us to any trick the Ichani try.*

—*And warn the Ichani of ours.*

—*Oh. Should you tell Balkan to stop?*

—*No. The Guild should see this. They might learn—*

'Akkarin.'

Kariko's voice echoed across the grounds.

'Kariko,' Akkarin replied.

'I see you've brought your apprentice. Do you intend to trade her for your life?'

A chill ran over Sonea's skin as the Ichani looked at her. She stared back, and he smiled maliciously.

'I might consider taking her,' Kariko continued. 'I never liked my brother's taste in slaves, but he did show me that Guild magicians can be surprisingly entertaining.'

Akkarin slowly started down the steps. As Sonea followed, she took care to stay within the blended magic of their shield.

'Dakova was a fool for keeping me,' Akkarin said, 'but he was always making stupid mistakes. It is hard to understand how a man with such power could have so little grasp of politics or strategy, but I guess that is why he was Ichani – and why he kept me.'

Kariko's eyes narrowed. 'You? I don't think so. If you

621

are such a master of strategy, why are you here? You must know you can't win.'

'Can't we? Look around you, Kariko. Where are all your allies?'

As Akkarin and Sonea reached the bottom of the steps, Kariko stopped. He was about twenty strides away.

'Dead, I suppose. And you killed them.'

'Some.'

'You must be worn out, then.' Kariko glanced at the other Ichani, then back at Akkarin. 'What a perfect end to our conquest. I will avenge my brother's death, and at the same time Sachaka will finally have revenge for what your Guild did to our land.'

He lifted a hand, and the other Ichani followed suit. Strikes flashed toward Sonea and Akkarin. She felt magic batter their shield, more powerful than any strike she had encountered before. Akkarin sent a trio of strikes in reply, but all curved inward to attack Kariko.

More exchanges followed, and the air hummed with power. As Akkarin continued striking at Kariko and ignoring the other Ichani, the leader frowned. He said something to his companions. They moved closer, leaving only a narrow gap between their shields.

—*Strike Kariko from beneath*, Akkarin instructed.

As Sonea sent heatstrike through the earth, Akkarin sent more curving down on Kariko from above. The other Ichani shifted their shields to meet Akkarin's strikes just as the ground began to steam beneath Kariko's feet.

Kariko glanced down, then said something quietly. His companions increased their attack.

—*Keep striking at Kariko from all directions.*

Kariko appeared to have resigned himself to being the main target. He concentrated on shielding, while the others attacked. Sonea resisted a smile. This was all to her and Akkarin's advantage. Shielding took more power, so Kariko would be tiring faster.

It seemed they would stand and blast each other until one side finally weakened. Then the ground shifted violently beneath her. She staggered and felt a hand grab her arm. Looking down, she saw a dark hole forming below her feet and sensed a disc of power.

—*Hold the shield.*

She forced her attention back to their barrier, taking the full brunt of the Ichani's attack so that Akkarin could concentrate on levitating. The air was full of grass and dirt and strikes. Akkarin moved them backward, but the shifting area of earth followed them. Through the dirt-filled air, Sonea saw the Ichani marching across the disturbed ground toward them.

Akkarin sent a dozen strikes at the Ichani. At the same time, a dozen weaker ones streaked from the direction of the gates. The Sachakans glanced to the side.

Sonea gasped as she saw the figure standing just inside the gates. Blue robes swirled around the man as he walked forward.

'Lorlen!' Sonea gasped. But how could that be? Lorlen was dead. Or was he . . .?

Kariko sent a blast of energy toward the Administrator. It flashed through the magician and struck the gates. The bars of metal shattered, filling the street beyond with glowing spears and fragments.

Lorlen had vanished. Sonea blinked. It had been an illusion. Hearing a chuckle, she looked up to see Akkarin smiling grimly. Kariko and his companions looked unimpressed. They resumed their assault with greater ferocity.

Akkarin threw a rain of strikes at Kariko, testing the Ichani's shield. Kariko sent powerful blasts back. Akkarin sent a great net of heatstrike out, curving around to hit Kariko from all sides, just as Sonea had done in her last bout against Regin in the Challenge. Sonea frowned as she remembered that battle. In the second fight Regin had saved his strength by shielding only when a strike hit. Could she do the same? It required concentration . . .

She focussed her will and refined her shield, leaving it weaker behind and above, but not so weak that she could not strengthen it quickly if she needed to.

—Be careful, Sonea.

She watched the Ichani closely, ready to react if any strikes should change course.

'LOOK TO THE GATES!'

The voice came from the top of the University. Looking up, she saw Balkan on the roof of the building, pointing toward the gates. Spinning around, she took an involuntary step backward as she saw broken and bent black spears flying toward her – the remnants of the gates. They clattered into her shield and fell to the ground.

When I say so, go to the Arena. I will hold them while you take its power . . . wait . . . She glanced at him to see his eyes narrowed with concentration.

—The Ichani are weakening, Akkarin sent.

Sonea looked at the Ichani. Kariko stood straight and smiling. The rest of the Ichani looked no less confident, but the strikes against her shield had weakened.

Akkarin took a step forward, then another. Kariko's face

darkened. Sonea followed as Akkarin began to walk toward them. She sent her own strikes at the Ichani and felt a surge of satisfaction as they backed away.

Then, as she felt soft dirt under her feet, something slammed against her mind. She pushed it away, but it returned to hound her again.

—*Mindstrike. Shut it out.*

—*How?*

—*Like*—

Something sliced up the side of her calf. Sonea stumbled and heard Akkarin gasp. Looking down, she saw the leg of her robe flutter open to reveal a long cut. Akkarin grasped her arm.

But instead of supporting her, he let his full weight drag her to the ground. She landed on her knees, turned to looked at him and her heart froze.

He crouched beside her, his face was white and twisted with pain. Bright red drew her eyes to his hand, which was wrapped around the glittering handle of a Sachakan knife.

The knife was buried deep in his chest.

'Akkarin!'

He dropped to his side, then rolled onto his back. She leaned over him, her hands fluttering over the knife as she tried to decide what to do. *I must Heal him*, she thought. *But where do I start?*

She tried to prise his fingers from around the knife's handle. He let go and grabbed her wrists.

'Not yet,' he gasped.

His eyes were full of pain. She tried to pull out of his grasp, but his grip was strong.

Then laughter, cruel and humourless, cut through the silence.

'So *that's* where I left my knife,' Kariko crowed. 'How good of you to find it for me.'

Sonea suddenly understood how it had happened. Kariko had dropped the blade into the disturbed earth. As their shield passed over it, he had sent the knife upward. A trap. A trick. Not unlike what she had done to get into the shield of the murderess.

It had worked.

'Sonea,' Akkarin gasped. His eyes shifted beyond her, and she saw the University reflected in them.

From somewhere above, she heard shouts. Flashes of magic lit Akkarin's face, but she could not bring herself to look away.

'I'll Heal you,' she told him, struggling to twist out of his hands.

'No.' Akkarin's grip tightened. 'If you do, we may lose. Fight them first. Then Heal me. I can hold on like this for now.'

She went cold. 'But what if—'

'We will die anyway.' Akkarin's voice was firm. 'I will send you my power. You must fight. Look up, Sonea.'

She glanced up and felt her heart stop. Kariko stood less than ten paces away. He was staring up at the University, from which strikes were raining down. Looking up, she saw two familiar faces next to Balkan's.

'You're not even shielding, Sonea,' Akkarin whispered.

She felt a chill run down her spine. If Rothen and Dorrien hadn't attacked, she and Akkarin would both be—

—Take my power. Strike while he's distracted. Don't let everything we have done and suffered for come to nothing.

She nodded. As the strikes from the University lessened, she drew in a deep breath. There was no time for fancy tactics. Something direct, then. She closed her eyes and drew on all her power and all her anger at Kariko for what he had done to Akkarin and Imardin. She felt Akkarin send his strength to join hers.

Then, opening her eyes, she focussed everything at Kariko and his allies.

The Ichani leader staggered backward. For a moment his shield held, then his mouth opened in a silent scream as heatstrike burned through his body. The next man backed away, but managed only a few steps before her magic shattered his shield and burned through him. She felt a surge of triumph. The last Ichani stood his ground. She felt her strength slipping away. He began to advance and she felt a rush of fear. A last trickle of power came to her, and she sent it forth. The Ichani's eyes widened as his shield wavered. Then, as the last of her magic flowed out, it fell. Heatstrike tore through him, and he crumpled to the ground.

All was silent. Sonea stared at the three bodies lying before the University. A wave of exhaustion washed over her. She felt no triumph. No pleasure. Just emptiness. She turned to Akkarin.

A smile curled the edge of his lips. His eyes were open, but fixed somewhere beyond her. As she moved, the hands about her wrists loosened and fell away.

'No,' she whispered. 'Akkarin.' Grabbing his hands, she sent her mind inward. Nothing. Not even the slightest spark of life.

He had given her too much power.

He had given her everything.

With shaking hands, Sonea ran her fingers over his face, then bent forward and kissed his lifeless mouth.

Then she curled herself around him and began to cry.

CHAPTER 39

A NEW POSITION

Rothen reached the end of the corridor and looked up. After the devastation of the city, the undamaged majesty of the Great Hall was both heartening and somehow shameful. The Ichani Invasion, as the five days of death and destruction were now referred to, had been a battle between magicians. It seemed wrong that nothing within the Guild grounds had been damaged when much of the Inner Circle was in ruins.

It could have been far worse for ordinary Imardians, Rothen reminded himself. There had been few non-magician deaths. The Guild, however, was nearly half its former size. There had been rumours that the Higher Magicians were considering recruiting from wealthy merchant families outside the Houses.

He crossed to the Guildhall, and slipped between the doors. During the week since the Invasion, the meetings of the Higher Magicians had taken place in one of the small preparation rooms at the front of the hall. Until a new Administrator was elected, it was considered inappropriate to use Lorlen's office.

Reaching the preparation room door, Rothen knocked. It swung open. As he stepped inside, he noted the magicians present, knowing that he was glimpsing the faces of the Guild's future hierarchy of power.

Lord Balkan paced the room. It was obvious from the way the others had automatically turned to him for leadership that he was a strong candidate for High Lord. Lord Osen watched Balkan calmly. Though clearly still deeply upset by Lorlen's death, he had gained a quiet purposefulness since being given the task of organising the city's recovery. Lorlen had been grooming Osen as his replacement for the last few years, so it would surprise no-one if the young man was elected Administrator.

So many Warriors had died that only a few candidates remained for Head of Warriors. Lord Garrel had been present in the last few meetings, which Rothen felt didn't bode well for the future. Balkan had also been managing the lesser Head of Warrior Studies role, but Rothen had heard the man suggest that the position would be filled by another at a future date, so perhaps Garrel's sly, narrow-minded ways would be counter-balanced by a Warrior of more sensible character.

Lady Vinara would remain Head of Healers. Director Jerrik had made no indication he wanted to change his position, and no-one had suggested it. Lord Telano would probably remain Head of Healing Studies. No mention had been made of choosing someone for the role of Expatriate Administrator so far.

Lord Peakin would probably replace Lord Sarrin. One of the older teachers would be given the Head of Alchemic Studies position, Rothen guessed. He could not help wondering, now and then, who his direct superior would be, but most of the time he was concerned with more important matters. Like Sonea.

And she was clearly the reason the Higher Magicians

had summoned him today. As Balkan noticed Rothen's entrance, he stopped pacing.

'How is she?'

Rothen sighed and shook his head. 'No better. It will take time.'

'We don't have time,' Balkan muttered.

'I know.' Rothen looked away. 'But I fear what will happen if we push her.'

Vinara frowned. 'What do you mean?'

'I'm not sure she wants to recover.'

The room's occupants exchanged worried glances. Vinara did not look surprised.

'Then you must convince her otherwise,' Balkan said. 'We need her. If eight outcasts can do this much damage, what might an army do? Even if the Sachakan King doesn't take advantage of our weakness, it would only take one more of these Ichani to ruin us. We need a black magician. We need her – or for her to teach one of us.'

It was true, but unfair on Sonea. It had only been a week since Akkarin's death. Her grief was natural. Understandable. She had been through too much. Why couldn't they leave her alone for a while?

'What about Akkarin's books?' he asked.

Balkan shook his head. 'Sarrin was unable to learn from them. I have fared no better—'

'Then *you* must talk to her,' Vinara said to the Warrior, 'and when you do, you must be able to tell her exactly where she stands with us. We can't ask her to live for our sakes when her future is uncertain.'

Balkan nodded and let out a heavy sigh. 'You're right, of course.' He looked around at the other magicians. 'Very well, we must hold a Meet to discuss the position and its restrictions.'

'We already have discussed it, when Sarrin was chosen,' Peakin pointed out.

'The restrictions ought to be refined,' Garrel said. 'At the moment the only requirements are that she remain within the Guild grounds, cannot hold a position of authority, and cannot teach. It should be spelt out that she must not use her powers unless requested by us all.'

Rothen resisted a smile. *Us* all? Garrel was certainly confident of gaining Balkan's position.

'Well, we'd have to change that rule against teaching, for a start,' Jerrik added.

Vinara looked at Rothen. 'What do you suggest, Rothen?'

He paused, knowing they would not like what he had to say.

'I don't think she'll agree to any restriction that keeps her within the Guild grounds.'

Balkan frowned. 'Why not?'

'She has always wanted to use her powers to help the poor. It was part of the reason she decided to join us and it has given her something to hold onto,' he glanced sideways at Garrel, 'in difficult times. If you want her to live, don't take that from her.'

Vinara smiled thinly. 'And I suppose if we proposed she undertake some kind of charitable work in the city, it would give her reason to stay with us.'

Rothen nodded.

Balkan crossed his arms. His fingers drummed against his sleeve. 'That would also help us regain the favour of the people. We didn't prove to be particularly effective defenders. I've heard that some even blame us for the invasion.'

'Surely not!' Garrel exclaimed.

'It's true,' Osen said quietly.

Garrel scowled. 'Ungrateful dwells.'

'Actually, it was certain members of the Houses who expressed that opinion on their return to the city.' Osen added. 'Including members of House Paren, if I recall correctly.'

Garrel blinked in surprise, then flushed.

'Should we extend the area of confinement to the city, then?' Telano suggested.

'The idea of confinement was to ensure our black magician didn't have access to large numbers of victims, should he or she grow hungry for power,' Peakin said. 'What is the point of having an area of confinement, when it includes the highest density of population in the country?'

Rothen chuckled. 'And you'd have to persuade the King to redefine what is considered part of the city. I don't think Sonea intended to restrict her help to those within the Outer Wall.'

'Confinement is clearly unworkable,' Vinara said. 'I suggest an escort.'

All eyes turned to her. Balkan nodded approvingly.

'And if the help she wants to give is Healing, she still has many years of training to complete.' Vinara looked at Rothen.

He nodded. 'I'm sure she's aware of that. My son has expressed a wish to teach her. He thought it might revive her, but perhaps, if he is to assist her in this work, it could be a more official arrangement.'

She pursed her lips. 'It would not be appropriate for

her to return to classes. It is not wise for a Healer to have only one teacher, however. I will assist as well.'

Rothen nodded, suddenly too overwhelmed by gratitude to speak. He listened as the others continued the debate.

'So will we still call her the "Black Magician"?' Peakin asked.

'Yes,' Balkan replied.

'And what colour robes will she wear?'

There was a short silence.

'Black,' Osen said quietly.

'But the High Lord's are black,' Telano pointed out.

Osen nodded. 'Perhaps it is time to change the High Lord's robes. Black will always remind people of black magic, which, despite everything, we do not want to encourage people to think of as wholly good and desirable. We need something fresh and clean.'

'White,' Vinara said.

Osen nodded. 'Yes.'

As the others voiced their agreement, Balkan made a strangled noise.

'White!' he exclaimed. 'You can't be serious. It's impractical, and impossible to keep clean.'

Vinara smiled. 'Now what would a High Lord be involved in that might stain his white robes?'

'A little excess wine consumption, maybe?' Jerrik murmured.

The others chuckled.

'White it is, then,' Osen said.

'Wait,' Balkan looked from face to face, then shook his head. 'Why do I find myself thinking you've made your minds up, and I won't win any argument about it?'

'It's a good sign,' Vinara said. 'One that suggests we have chosen a strong set of people to be our Higher Magicians.' She looked around the group, then smiled as her eyes met Rothen's. 'You still haven't guessed, have you Lord Rothen?'

He stared at her, puzzled by her sudden question. 'Guessed what?'

'Of course, it still has to be put to the vote, but I don't expect anyone will protest.'

'About what?'

Her smile widened. 'Congratulations, Rothen. You're to be our new Head of Alchemic Studies.'

From the top of the two-storey house, it was possible to see that the rubble formed a perfect circle. It was a sobering sight.

Yet another to add to my list, Cery thought. *Along with the ruins of the city walls, the long lines of bodies that the Guild had laid out across the lawn in front of the University, and the look Sonea had in her eyes as Rothen finally persuaded her to leave Akkarin's body.*

He shivered and made himself look down again. Hundreds of workers were sorting through the rubble. A few people had been found alive, buried near the edges of the destruction. It was impossible to know how many had been hiding in the houses when they were blasted to ruins. Most were probably dead.

All because of him. He should have paid more attention to Savara's warnings about what would happen when an Ichani died. But he had been too concerned with finding a way to kill a magician to think about how his people might survive the consequences.

'Back here again?'

Arms wound about his waist. A familiar spicy aroma filled his senses. His heart lightened for a moment, then began to hurt again.

'Must you go?' he whispered.

'Yes,' Savara replied.

'We could use your help.'

'No. You don't need me. Certainly not as a Sachakan magician. And you have plenty of volunteers to do non-magical work.'

'I need you.'

She sighed. 'No, Cery. You need someone you can trust, completely and unconditionally. I will never be that person.'

He nodded. She was right.

But it didn't make parting easier.

Her arms tightened. 'I'll miss you,' she added quietly. 'If . . . if I'm welcome, I'll drop in whenever my duties take me this way.'

He turned to face her, and lifted one eyebrow as if considering.

'I might have a few bottles of Anuren dark left.'

She smiled broadly and he could not help feeling better, even if it was just for a moment. Ever since the final battle, he had felt a terrible fear of loss, and he had tried to keep her from leaving. But Savara didn't belong in Kyralia. Not now. And he was letting his heart's demands overtake commonsense. That was something a Thief should never do.

Hooking a finger under her chin, he lifted her head and kissed her, slowly and firmly. Then he stepped back.

'Go on, then. Go home. I don't like long goodbyes.'

She smiled, then turned away. He watched her saunter to the hatch in the roof, then descend through the ceiling below. When she was gone, he turned to regard the workers again.

Much had changed. He must be ready for the consequences. Snippets of information had come his way, and he was probably not the only one to realise what they might lead to. If the King did truly intend to end the yearly Purge, there would be one less reason for the Thieves to work together. And then there were the rumours of certain deals already being made between the other underworld leaders.

He smiled and straightened his shoulders. He had prepared for the day when Akkarin's support ended. Deals had been made with useful and powerful people. Wealth had been stowed, and information gathered. His position was strong.

Soon he would find out if it was strong enough.

The carriage rocked gently on its springs. Outside, endless fields and the occasional farmhouse slowly passed by. Inside, Dannyl and Tayend raised wineglasses to each other.

'A drink to Lord Osen, who decided that you would best serve the Guild as Ambassador in Elyne,' Tayend said. 'And for letting us travel overland.'

'To Osen,' Dannyl replied. He took a sip of the wine. 'You know I would have stayed, if he'd asked me to.'

Tayend smiled. 'Yes, and I would have stayed with you though I'm glad I didn't need to. Kyralians are so suffocatingly *conservative*.' He brought his glass to his lips, then looked away and his expression grew sober. 'He's smart to send you back, though. A lot of people will question the

Guild's authority now. It proved to be a bit ill-prepared for war.'

Dannyl chuckled. 'Just a bit.'

'More people will be inclined to think like Dem Marane,' Tayend continued. 'You'll need to convince those people that the Guild is still in charge, when it comes to magic.'

'I know.'

'Then there's this issue of black magic. You'll have to assure people that the Guild really has no choice but to learn it again. Ah, it could get a bit intense in the next few months.'

'I know.'

'It might take years, even.' Tayend smiled. 'But, of course, there's no reason you couldn't stay in Elyne, once your time as Ambassador is over, is there?'

'No.' Dannyl smiled. 'Osen granted the position to me indefinitely.'

Tayend's eyes widened, then he grinned. 'He did? That's wonderful!'

'He said something about Elyne suiting me better than Kyralia. And that I should not let concerns about rumours stop me cherishing and enjoying our friendship.'

The scholar's eyebrows rose. 'Did he really? Do you think he knows about us?'

'I wonder. He didn't seem at all disapproving. But I could be reading more into his comments than he meant to say. He has just lost a good friend and mentor.' Dannyl hesitated. 'Though it does make me wonder how much it would really change things, if people knew.'

Tayend frowned. 'Now don't you get any stupid ideas about that. If you told the Guild, and they got all scandalised and sent you away, I'd still follow you. And when I found you, I'd give you a good kick for being such an idiot.' He paused, then grinned. 'I love you, but I also love that you're an important Guild magician.'

Dannyl chuckled. 'That's just as well. I could change the important part, and even the Guild part, but the magician part doesn't come as an option.'

Tayend smiled. 'Oh, I doubt I'll ever change my mind about you. I think you'll have to put up with me for a very long time.'

EPILOGUE

The black-robed magician stepped out of the newly repaired Northern Gates. As always, people stopped to stare and children yelled her name and began to follow.

Rothen watched Sonea closely. Though he was acting as Escort today, that duty was not the reason for his concern. She hadn't looked this pale since she had first locked herself away in his rooms. Sensing his gaze, she glanced at him and smiled. He relaxed a little. As he had predicted, she had gained much from the work she had begun in the slums. A little life had returned to her eyes and some purpose to her step.

The hospital by the gates had been built in a few short months. He had expected it to take some time for the dwells to overcome their hatred and distrust of magicians, but a crowd of them had appeared the day it had opened, and every day since.

Sonea was the reason. They loved her. She had come from among them, had saved the city, and had returned to the slums to help them.

Dorrien had been by her side from the start. His greater knowledge of Healing was essential, and his experience at earning the trust of farmers and foresters also helped him gain the dwells' confidence. Other Healers had joined them. It seemed Sonea was not the only magician who believed Healing should not be a service offered only to the rich Houses.

As she reached the hospital and moved inside, Lord Darlen stepped forward to greet her.

'How was the night shift?' she asked.

'Busy.' He smiled ruefully. 'When isn't it? Oh, I found another potential recruit. A girl of about fifteen, named Kalia. She'll return later with her father, if he agrees to let her join us.'

Sonea nodded. 'How are our supplies?'

'Low, as always,' Darlen replied. 'I'll talk to Lady Vinara when I get back.'

'Thank you, Lord Darlen,' Sonea said.

Darlen nodded, then headed to the door. Sonea paused to look around the room. Following her gaze, Rothen took in the crowd of waiting patients, the handful of guards who had been employed to manage them, and the curies who had been hired for their knowledge of medicine to help with minor cases. Sonea suddenly drew in a sharp breath, then turned to a guard standing nearby.

'That woman over there with the child wrapped in a green blanket. Bring her to me in my room.'

'Yes, my lady.'

Rothen started to look for the woman, but Sonea was already walking away. He followed her into a small room furnished with a table, a bed and several chairs. She sat down and drummed her fingers on the table. Rothen pulled up a chair beside her.

'You know this woman?'

She glanced at him. 'Yes. It's—' She paused at a knock on the door. 'Come in.'

He recognised the woman instantly. Sonea's aunt smiled and took the seat on the other side of the table.

'Sonea. I was hoping it would be you.'

'Jonna,' Sonea replied, smiling fondly – but tiredly, Rothen noted. 'I wanted to come see you, but I've been so busy. How is Ranel? How are my cousins?'

Jonna looked down at the baby. 'Hania has a terrible fever. I've tried everything . . .'

Sonea placed a hand gently on the baby's head. She frowned. 'Yes. She's got the beginning of bluespot disease. I can give her a little boost.' She was quiet for a moment. 'There. You will have to wait it out, I'm afraid. Give her liquids. A little marin juice mixed in will help, too.' Sonea looked up at her aunt. 'Jonna, would you . . . would you come live with me?'

The woman's eyes went round. 'I'm sorry, Sonea. I just couldn't.'

Sonea looked down. 'I know you don't feel comfortable being around magicians, but . . . please consider it. I'd . . .' She glanced at Rothen. 'I guess it's time you knew too, Rothen.' She looked at Jonna again. 'I'd like to have someone familiar and ordinary around.' She nodded at the child. 'I'd exchange all the Healers in the Guild just for your practical advice.'

Jonna stared at Sonea, her expression reflecting Rothen's confusion. Sonea grimaced, then placed a hand on her stomach. Jonna's eyes widened.

'Oh.'

'Yes.' Sonea nodded. 'I'm scared, Jonna. I didn't plan for this. The Healers will look after me, but they can't cure my fear. I think maybe you could.'

Jonna frowned. 'You told me magicians had their own ways of taking care of things.'

To Rothen's amazement Sonea blushed a furious scarlet.

'It seems that it's better if women do . . . that sort of

care-taking. Apparently men aren't taught the skill unless they request it,' she said. 'Girl novices are taken aside as soon as the Healers feel they're likely to be showing an interest in boys, but I was so unpopular that nobody thought of teaching me. Akkarin,' Sonea paused and swallowed, 'must have assumed they had. And I assumed *he* was taking care of things.'

As understanding dawned, Rothen stared at Sonea. He found himself counting the months since her exile. Three-and-a-half, maybe four. The robes would hide it well . . .

She looked at him and then grimaced apologetically. 'I'm sorry, Rothen. I was going to tell you, at a better moment, but when I saw Jonna I just had to take advantage of—'

They both jumped as Jonna burst into laughter. She was pointing at Rothen. 'I haven't seen that look since I told Ranel I was expecting our first! I think, perhaps, these magicians aren't as smart as they make themselves out to be.' She grinned at Sonea. 'So. You're to have a baby, then. I can't imagine the child growing up with his or her head on right surrounded by magicians.'

Sonea smiled crookedly. 'Nor I. So, will you reconsider?'

Jonna hesitated, then nodded once. 'Yes. We'll stay a while.'

LORD DANNYL'S GUIDE TO SLUM SLANG

blood money – payment for assassination

boot – refuse/refusal (don't boot us)

capper – man who frequents brothels

clicked – occurred

client – person who has an obligation or agreement with a Thief

counter – whore

done – murdered

dull – persuade to keep silent

dunghead – fool

dwells – term used to describe slum dwellers

eye – keep watch

fired – angry (got fired about it)

fish – propose/ask/look for (also someone fleeing the Guard)

gauntlet – guard who is bribeable or in the control of a Thief

goldmine – man who prefers boys

good go – a reasonable try

got – caught

grandmother – pimp

gutter – dealer in stolen goods

hai – a call for attention or expression of surprise or inquiry

heavies – important people

kin – a Thief's closest and most trusted

knife – assassin/hired killer

messenger – thug who delivers or carries out a threat

mind – hide (minds his business/I'll mind that for you)

mug – mouth (as in vessel for bol)

out for – looking for

pick – recognise/understand

punt – smuggler

right-sided – trustworthy/heart in the right place

rope – freedom

rub – trouble (got into some rub over it)

shine – attraction (got a shine for him)

show – introduce

space – allowances/permission

squimp – someone who double-crosses the Thieves

style – manner of performing business

tag – recognise (also means a spy, usually undercover)

thief – leader of a criminal group

watcher – posted to observe something or someone

wild – difficult

visitor – burglar

GLOSSARY

ANIMALS

aga moths – pests that eat clothing

anyi – sea mammals with short spines

ceryni – small rodent

enka – horned domestic animal, bred for meat

eyoma – sea leeches

faren – general term for arachnids

gorin – large domestic animal used for food and to haul boats and wagons

harrel – small domestic animal bred for meat

inava – insect believed to bestow good luck

limek – wild predatory dog

mullook – wild nocturnal bird

rassook – domestic bird used for meat and feathers

ravi – rodent, larger than ceryni

reber – domestic animal, bred for wool and meat

sapfly – woodland insect

sevli – poisonous lizard

squimp – squirrel-like creature that steals food

yeel – small domesticated breed of limek used for tracking

zill – small, intelligent mammal sometimes kept as a pet

PLANTS/FOOD

anivope vines – plant sensitive to mental projection

bol – (also means 'river scum') strong liquor made from tugors

brasi – green leafy vegetable with small buds

chebol sauce – rich meat sauce made from bol

crots – large, purple beans

curem – smooth, nutty spice

curren – course grain with robust flavour

dall – long fruit with tart orange, seedy flesh

gan-gan – flowering bush from Lan

iker – stimulating drug, reputed to have aphrodisiac properties

jerras – long yellow beans

kreppa – foul-smelling medicinal herb

marin – red citrus fruit

monyo – bulb

myk – mind-affecting drug

nalar – pungent root

nemmin – sleep-inducing drug

pachi – crisp, sweet fruit

papea – pepper-like spice

piorres – small, bell-shaped fruit

raka/suka – stimulating drink made from roasted beans, originally from Sachaka

shem – edible reed-like plant

sumi – bitter drink

telk – seed from which an oil is extracted

tenn – grain that can be cooked as is, broken into small pieces, or ground to make a flour

tiro – edible nuts

tugor – parsnip-like root

vare – berries from which most wine is produced

CLOTHING AND WEAPONRY

incal – square symbol, not unlike a family shield, sewn onto sleeve or cuff

kebin – iron bar with hook for catching attacker's knife, carried by guards

longcoat – ankle-length coat

PUBLIC HOUSES

bathhouse – establishment selling bathing facilities and other grooming services

bolhouse – establishment selling bol and short term accommodation

brewhouse – bol manufacturer

hole – building constructed from scavenged materials

stayhouse – rented building, a family to a room

PEOPLES OF THE ALLIED LANDS

Elyne – closest to Kyralia in

position and culture,
enjoys a milder climate

Kyralia – home of the Guild

Lan – a mountainous land
peopled by warrior
tribes

Lonmar – a desert land home
to the strict Mahga religion

Vin – an island nation
known for their seamanship

OTHER TERMS

cap – coins threaded on a
stick to the value of the
next highest denomination

dawnfeast – breakfast

midbreak – lunch

simbà mats – mats woven
from reeds

ABOUT THE AUTHOR

Trudi Canavan published her first story in 1999 and it received an Aurealis Award for Best Fantasy Short Story. Her debut series, the Black Magician trilogy, made her an international success, and all three volumes of the Age of the Five trilogy were *Sunday Times* bestsellers. Trudi Canavan lives with her partner in Melbourne, Australia, and spends her time knitting, painting and writing bestselling fantasy novels. For more information about Trudi and her writing go to www.trudicanavan.com

Find out more about Trudi Canavan and other Orbit authors by registering for the free monthly newsletter at www.orbitbooks.net